A TRUE ROMANCE

'There is a satisfactory sweep and range to Jacky Gillott's A TRUE ROMANCE . . . the quality of this book lies in the seriousness of its perceptions . . . Miss Gillott's feeling for the countryside is marvellous, even amid the encircling gloom of the times' *Sunday Times*

'A quiet, modest book . . . Miss Gillott records with loving honesty' *New Statesman*

'The idea is excellent . . . She writes well – beautifully about the countryside, tartly and enjoyably about personal relations and social absurdities . . . A good read'
Nina Bawden, *Daily Telegraph*

'A novelist who can bring the English countryside and country ways so vividly before us' *Scotsman*

'Interesting and ambitious, and also entertaining' Robert Nyo, *Guardian*

A True Romance

Jacky Gillott

CORONET BOOKS
Hodder and Stoughton

Copyright © 1975 by Jacky Gillott

First published in Great Britain 1975 by
Hodder and Stoughton Limited

Coronet Edition 1976

---

*The characters and situations in this book are
entirely imaginary and bear no relation to any real
person or actual happening*

This book is sold subject to the condition that
it shall not, by way of trade or otherwise, be
lent, re-sold, hired out or otherwise circulated
without the publisher's prior consent in any
form of binding or cover other than that in
which this is published and without a similar
condition including this condition being
imposed on the subsequent purchaser.

Printed and bound in Great Britain for
Coronet Books, Hodder and Stoughton, London
by Richard Clay (The Chaucer Press) Ltd.,
Bungay, Suffolk

ISBN 0 340 21006 0

For the children

Suppose ye that I am come to give peace on earth? I tell you, Nay; but rather division; From henceforth there shall be five in one house divided, three against two and two against three. The father shall be divided against the son, and the son against the father; the mother against the daughter, and the daughter against the mother ...

THE GOSPEL ACCORDING TO ST. LUKE

Part One

Of all the emotions which Human beings feel, Love is the most divine. It is the vital spark which makes Life, it is the expression of the soul.

ELINOR GLYN

Though I speak with the tongues of men and of angels, and have not charity, I am become as sounding brass or a tinkling cymbal. And though I have the gift of prophecy, and understand all mysteries, and all knowledge; and though I have all faith, so that I could remove mountains, and have not charity, I am nothing. And though I bestow all my goods to feed the poor, and though I give my body to be burned and have not charity, it profiteth me nothing.

I CORINTHIANS, 13

I

OLIVIA BENNETT HURRIED HOME AFTER THE FUNERAL. The other mourners watched her go, driving at an unceremonial speed, the gravel spurting violently beneath the Bentley's wheels.

Her husband Leo, with a grave sidelong sweep of apology, turned to those nearest to him as if to explain, silently, that the occasion had been too much for her and they, sympathetically, inclined their heads in understanding. Corin, his son, touched his arm briefly, as a signal that he should come with him and the two girls on the short drive back from Charlton Cloud.

She abandoned the car in front of the house and sped indoors, flying past Mrs. Baldwin at a pace that forced the other woman to step unsteadily backwards under the weight of the tray she was carrying towards the drawing room. (The mourners were expected shortly.) Shaking her head sorrowfully, Mrs. Baldwin gazed upstairs at the whirlwind course of her employer.

A door on the first landing slammed.

With a sigh, Mrs. Baldwin continued her way into the drawing room where sun shone through the long windows on polished rosewood and silver and great luminous boughs of white blossom. A large black retriever rose guiltily from the hearth and padded across the creamy Chinese carpet into the hall where he, too, paused and gazed upwards at the landing before trotting through the open front door and slumping on the stone steps outside. Twice, he whined piteously, then lay his head watchfully on the top of the front step.

Upstairs in her room, Olivia stood with her back to the closed door. Everything had been ruthlessly tidied up, her papers slipped into files, the typewriter placed on the green leather pasture of the desk in such a way it was impossible to use without moving it nearer to the chair. A small bowl of freesias replaced the muddle. She stared beyond the desk through the window to the sweep of garden below. The lawn, pleasantly striped by the mower, reached almost to the great rust wall paled by its smothering of ice-pink clematis. A light breeze made the candles of the chestnut tree dip softly amidst the rich green leaves and the pale fronds of the willow lifted like a young widow's yellow hair.

She closed her eyes and breathed in tightly and felt the silky movement of a cat against her legs, its low and sudden release of purring climbing upward through her so intimately, deliciously, that for an instant she couldn't be sure the sound of sensual contentment wasn't coming from her. The impropriety of it opened her eyes.

"Pollux!" she murmured and bent to pick up the pure white cat, cradling him against her cheek and moving closer to the window so that the small magnolia tree nearest the house appeared in the frame. The purring was sumptuous, rude. No hint of lament gleamed in the golden eyes he slid open for a second. "Oh, *Pollux* . . ." she whispered reprovingly.

She pulled out the chair and sat down at her desk, the cat on her lap. Immediately he began to paddle and claw a nice nest for himself in the soft black material of her dress. She ignored him, ignored the shedding of white hairs, just letting her hand roll lightly over the undulations of his spine and tail as she looked out on the still, walled garden and the blueness of the wooded hills beyond.

So, she was truly dead then. Buried. The earth had been cast in damp crumbs and the words intoned. Like a winter plantation they had grouped around the grave, the breeze lifting webs of black veil and the snowy garments of the priest. As in a dream.

But it was done. Dead. Done. Grief lifted her heart on a small wave, then sank again, smoothly running on. Busily, to halt the sensation, she pushed her typewriter further away and pulled pen and paper from the drawer. Dangerous tools. Her hands rested either side of the paper, inert, afraid to begin. Then she uncapped the pen, straightened the paper and began to write with sharp haste. *In Memoriam*.

She had covered a page with lashing black strokes before the sound of people arriving downstairs halted her. Pen poised, she listened to the murmur, a respectful hum broken by masculine instruction—where to go, where to leave coats, how to make a phone call to Town. Leo would look after things. They would forgive her. Resuming her writing, her eye caught the photograph of her mother and herself on the small table by the bookshelves. They sat together on a sofa, a bowl of lilies beside them, hands devotedly linked. The old lady stared fiercely at the camera. She, Olivia, smiled in admiration of her. (Even now, she could recall the profile as she and not the camera had seen it— small, neat-featured with the sharp dignity of a monarch on a new coin. Loss. The tearing was like that of a plant torn from its host.)

Her eyes slipped past the photograph to the books which lined the room from floor to ceiling. There, in noting her name beneath the titles, lay a little satisfaction. *The Consuming Fire* by Olivia Bennett. *A Rose In Glass* by Olivia Bennett, *Union of Souls, The Valley Prince, A Voice From The Deep, Autumn Moon, The Song of Love, The Posy Bowl, Celandine in Love, Celandine At Home, The Unreasoning Heart* . . . they stretched across their while shelves, nearly fifty spines bearing her name. And the trophies. And the framed, illuminated scrolls—seven of them in all—declaring her duly elected Romantic Novelist of The Year, the first dated 1951. And beside them, the two pages from Ursula Castlemaine's book *The Art of Romance* she'd had mounted and framed, pages which she knew almost by heart because it was a ritual to read them before starting each new book.

Her eyes returned to the true source of it all. To the photograph. That frail, determined face. The hand that held hers was small and bony, like the feel of a bird, but strong. She stared and waited for the words that would describe her loss but they hung, uncoloured, in her mind as her body breathed and the cat slithered more deeply in her lap.

For twenty-five years, from the moment her mother had come to live at Clouds, her life had determined Olivia's own. A breakfast tray was carried upstairs each morning. Her clothes were chosen and laid out on the chair. Olivia read to her, listened to memories of the difficult earlier years when the pair of them, abandoned by a man in search of a fortune (who, having made it, lost it), had struggled in circumstances that seemed almost to belong to a different century. She had helped her to paint, administered her medicines, included her in nearly every newspaper's photograph ever taken, telephoned her every day when away from home and just as frequently, taken her too. She had taken her to Nice, to Positano, to Innsbruck, Venice, Basle, Cairo, San Francisco—taken her to the Palace, taken her racing, taken her to great abbeys, across oceans, deep into caves where bison still blushed dimly on the wall. Had her *always*, it seemed, in her mind or by her side. Without ever saying anything very much she had become quite celebrated in her own right as the mother of Olivia Bennett. All this, and now absence.

When the earth had scattered on the pale wood of the coffin she had known it was all over, sealed off by a descending weight like the closing descent of a safety curtain when the clapping stops. She knew with a certainty that surprised her that there would be no voice calling to her through a dark drift of petals, no sudden sense of invisible presence. Her mother's presence had been entirely earthly and just as it had been total in life, so her absence would be total in death. It was odd, how definitely she felt that.

No, if her presence were to be somehow continued it could only be done by writing about her now and hotly, as if to conquer the feeling that each new day passing without Mrs. Bennett's physical imprint upon it, would blot out a further piece of her.

Again, she began writing, using her pen swiftly, like an artist might sketch—getting down the lineaments of a fading apparition.

Downstairs, friends, neighbours and relatives moved in subdued talk. Without Olivia actually there, the need for their carefully miserable pitch of conversation was hardly necessary, but she was above. They were not anxious for her to catch an animated sound. Teaspoons tinkled nervously against the china.

With the exception of Chloe, a tall, golden-haired girl, who wore a long white dress sprigged with flowers and who ate her sandwiches hungrily, it was a sombre gathering. Leo, resisting the temptation to comment on his daughter's dress, drew her aside and asked, softly, whether she would go and find her mother; persuade her to join them.

"She may not want to," replied Chloe, eating.

"Ask her," pleaded Leo. "Would you?"

But Chloe didn't go. She couldn't see why Olivia should be troubled. Presumably she'd gone upstairs for a howl and the last thing her mother would want would be to appear publicly with a stained and swollen face. "Give her time," she shrugged, moving towards Corin and winking at him solemnly. "A *gleam* of a tear, a *hint* of swallowed pain . . . ah, now *that* would be acceptable," she said.

"Cow," responded Corin genially. "Stop eating and circulate."

"Such a wonderful woman!" commented Biddy Hall, Olivia's agent, desperately seizing upon Chloe's nearness.

"Who?"

"Why, your grandmother of course . . . Your mother will be . . ." She searched for a wounded phrase in the waters of her teacup.

"Free?" asked Chloe.

Biddy Hall was shocked. "Oh, really!" she cried.

"Well, it's true. I don't mean it nastily. She might even write some decent books now . . ."

Biddy gaped. She popped, uncertain where to alight. "Olivia writes *wonderful* books!" she cried defensively.

"They *sell* wonderfully well." Chloe's expression was entirely good-natured.

"She gives pleasure to thousands, which is more than I can say for some of my . . . well more, shall we say, highbrow authors?" She laughed awkwardly, "No disrespect to them at all, but there's a very real place for someone of Olivia's gifts . . . someone who consciously tries to please the reader, bring a little happiness. I know it's unfashionable to make one's readers happy. Few contemporary writers attempt it."

"No reason why they should," Chloe sighed, "they're the only people who write the truth and the truth is terrifying. That's why nobody reads books any more. Too near the bone."

"There's a place for both kinds," insisted Biddy, wishing not to pursue this theme. She reached out a hand to Madge Waring, Olivia's secretary. "Miss Waring!" she exclaimed, "I wanted to thank you . . ."

Anxiously Leo glanced towards the door every time it opened. But it was either Mrs. Baldwin with fresh supplies of tea or the dog coming in. Mince, the black retriever was delighted to have company. He wagged his tail laboriously and carefully sniffed up the women's skirts receiving the gently smacking hands with only mild concern.

"It must be a dreadful day for her," murmured Colonel Doggart sympathetically. He wanted at some time to ask for a bag of compost, but checked himself for the moment. "The old lady will be missed."

"Indeed," said Leo. There was a small silence between them.

"Do you know," remarked the Colonel, straightening himself and gazing at the moulded freize, "I was astonished to hear your mother-in-law referred to as *Plumb*. I had no idea . . ."

"Plumb?" echoed Leo. "Oh yes . . ."

"You mean she was not *Bennett*?"

"Bennett, no, that is my wife's nom-de-plume."

"Yes, yes I understand but . . ."

"She called her mother Mrs. Bennett as—well, as a joke really to begin with, but it stuck. You know how these things do?"

"Oh, most certainly," mused the Colonel, "I do indeed. Plumb eh?"

"My wife maintains that no self-respecting romantic novelist can write under the name of Plumb." Leo smiled. The Colonel laughed generously, and then hummed a little. "I say, Mathison, you couldn't spare a bag of your splendid compost could you? While I think of it, that is, not immediately of course. But perhaps, when I go . . . ?"

Corin talked politely to people he hardly knew, responding carefully to condolence, excusing his mother's absence with a lightness people found charming. (So much easier to deal with than his sister.) The planned course of his life—his schooling, his start in the City—offered simple correspondence to their own experience. And for those with farming interests too, he had ample conversation. They discussed the problems of mild winters and the urea content of cattle cake. "It's a pity your father gave it up," said Gerald Causely. "It's a hard life, but I don't think he's ever been quite the . . . oh, who am I to say? Who'd wish farming on any man these days? A pity though, that you couldn't have carried on . . ."

"Well until these last two years, we frankly earned more letting the keep—thirty-five, forty pounds an acre we were getting, you know . . . Since then . . . well, I hardly need tell *you* . . ."

The two men shook their heads. Anyone who could be described as a landowner, rather than a productive farmer in his own right, had lost control of his land, or what use it was put to. Now, in traditionally dairy land, the fields that had once belonged to Clouds were ploughed up for arable cultivation.

"Still," mused Gerald, "it's hard to see what else . . ."

"Oh, I know. If I *had* kept it going, we'd never have stayed in cattle."

"I've sown a little barley and oats myself this year," Gerald laughed. "It's like the old days isn't it? Eh, I don't know what's to happen . . . What's a young man like you make of it all?"

"Me? Oh, I treat it as it comes," smiled Corin. "You should ask Chloe about that."

"Ah, Chloe!" laughed Gerald affectionately. "Her head's full of fancies."

"Is she sleeping all right?" Bart Foster, who was both family friend and family doctor pressed Leo about his wife.

"Well she's taking those . . . whatever it was you prescribed."

"I don't like them, but she must have something to ease the tension. She's like a fiddle string. Won't relax. Won't grieve." He drew in breath thoughtfully, then said, "I expect she'll break quite badly, quite suddenly." He looked warmly at the other man whose face showed its own strain, a distractedness that darted in and out of his normally courteous attention. "Just let it come. Just carry on quite normally until you're needed."

"I wondered whether to stay at home . . ."

"I shouldn't worry."

"I do, though." Leo grinned, self-deprecatingly.

"I shall keep an eye on her. No, the sooner a normal routine starts, the better. For her, anyway. Once she feels the routine is steady, she may let herself give way. She's a very strong-willed creature, it won't be easy for her."

"It's a damnable time altogether."

"It is," smiled Bart and he reached out an arm to draw Amy, the youngest daughter, towards them. "Now, child," he said, "you mustn't hide your face. Not even when it's wet with tears." And he brought her head gently to his shoulder.

As the conversation slid away from mourning matters and turned with greater appetite to life, people began to realise it was time they should leave and yet were reluctant to go without taking Olivia's hand or leaving a single kiss upon her cheek. And so they lingered, toying with their plates, burying their faces in the blossom to catch its fresh, sweet scent.

Leo knocked at the door and receiving no answer, quickly let himself in. "Are you all right?"

Olivia looked up, startled. "Oh, I didn't hear you!"

"You're not crying?"

She raised a hand to her cheek and gave a slightly shamefaced smile. "No . . . no," she murmured, "I'm writing." As Leo looked puzzled, she added, "About mother, I feel there's no time to be lost."

He sat down in an armchair, drawing it near enough the desk to take Olivia's hand. He looked at her tenderly, "Is that the best thing to do?" Silently, she looked down at the cat in her lap. "Aren't you protecting yourself that way?"

"Protecting myself? From what?"

He gestured vaguely. "From . . . grief? From the situation?"

"I don't know." She turned her head away, looking at the hand-written pages.

"You're still determined she should fill your life?"

Olivia said nothing.

"It's my turn now," he said gently.

She stared at him, horrified.

"Oh, now . . ." he held her hand more firmly, to contradict any sense of reproach, "I mean you have . . . the *time*."

"*Time!*" She echoed faintly. There were things he couldn't understand.

Things she didn't understand herself. Time was her enemy. Her fear, her greatest fear was to drift in an unstructured, unjustified shapeless swathe of time. Her mother had given it form.

From the moment she'd come to live at Clouds (two years after Olivia's marriage) her presence had been like a hidden energy driving her daughter into this room, peopling it with abandoned beauties, villains, squires, people brought by inexorable moral ruling to a just consequence of their actions. Together, they'd created a world where justice was unequivocal, law unchallenged, rewards properly allotted. And the fuel of this perfection was love. Love triumphant. Together, they'd slipped into a time sleek with order. It wasn't entirely fanciful. Its hopes and ambitions were exactly those of the outside world, only less imperfectly expressed.

"Time!" she repeated, reaching both hands out to Leo, and leaning her body towards him, not touching.

Her mother had made welcome demands on her time. Twice

a week between the sinking hours of five and seven, Olivia spent time reading aloud what she'd written, both of them absorbed by the tissue of chivalry.

"Oh lovely, yes, that's nice," her mother would sigh. And if she showed signs of not quite liking a certain passage, if there were minor improprieties or good was not quite in the ascendant, then Olivia would mend and alter until her mother's face once more relapsed into a satisfied trance, secure that dreams were truths.

"Time to relax," said Leo. "Time to think."

But worst of all, was this fear that because her mother had, in some undefined fashion, been the motive force of all she wrote, the energy, she was now in danger of being deserted by its profitable flow. And this presented not merely a problem of time, but something else she sensed only dimly. As though the baroque halls erected over the cellars of her unconscious would prove to be impermanent, cardboard things.

"Time to do what *you* want to do."

After twenty-seven years he still didn't understand this deep difference between them. That leisure, for someone of his background required no apology while for her, it provoked guilt. The first two graceful, idle years of marriage, the time before her son was born had been a mixed delight. She couldn't accustom herself to an absence of demands. It had been a relief to have her mother to care for; existence was better justified.

He looked at her slenderness, her perfection. She was, at forty-eight, a handsome woman. "I'll try to spend more time at home," he said.

She smiled at him then, but distantly. "You mustn't worry about me," she said.

"But I . . ." He longed somehow to say they had the chance now of drawing closer together, but didn't, for fear of sounding as though the death had come as a form of release. He didn't feel that exactly. Old Mrs. Bennett had never *intruded*. A rather quiet, withdrawing woman, she couldn't in all conscience, be accused of that. All the same, he thought, all the same . . .

"The guests . . ." Olivia was murmuring anxiously.

"Yes, of course." He got to his feet, a big man, tall and broad with a fine head of dark hair, the curling texture only tipped with grey, he seemed large in this small room. "I'll go and look after them. Won't you come?"

"Forgive me . . ."

"Very well."

Quietly, he left and the cat stirred in her lap. She leaned forward over the desk and slid up the window a little to let in a breath of the scented May air. There was a faint, warm smell of cut grass. The sea of white flowers glared in the sheltered beds.

One or two people had fetched their coats and stood about chattering purposelessly. Leo made whispered explanations. "She's rather distressed. She needs to be alone. I'm sure you'll understand." Of course they did. They admired Olivia. They expected her to behave like a heroine. Not heroically, but tragically.

"Can't you get Peggy out?" breezed Chloe.

"Shh!" mouthed Leo. "Leave her, would you?"

"*Peggy?*" repeated Colonel Doggart, following Chloe into the hall and looking baffled, "Peggy?"

"She means Olivia . . . let me come with you and arrange for the compost to be loaded into your car."

"Peggy?" insisted Colonel Doggart looking to Chloe for enlightenment.

"Peggy," she said. "*Mum*. Olivia Bennett is only twenty-five you know." And holding an apple between her teeth she helped him on with his coat.

"Ah!" said the Colonel comfortably. "That's most awfully good of you, Mathison . . . since I've been reduced to one horse, can't get enough of the stuff." And he lumbered out after Leo.

"I don't like leaving without a word," fussed Biddy Hall, drawing on black suede gloves, "but I do understand. Give your mother my fondest love. I'll write I think, yes, that might be best. Don't let her spend too much time on her own. It isn't good for her."

"We'll take good care," soothed Corin.

"I'm sure you will. Tell her I've sold the Japanese rights to *The Splendid Sword*, that should cheer her up."

"It will."

When Leo returned, Bart Foster made his farewells. "You must both come round for dinner — the moment I can get my hands on something worth eating," he added with a grimace.

"In the meantime . . ." And he let his guardianship be known by a look.

The others kept their leavetaking hushed for fear of sending disturbance trembling through the house.

"Amy's crying again," said Chloe. "I'll go and cheer her up. Perhaps she'd like to go out for a ride."

He stood alone in the hall for a moment, half aware of Mrs. Baldwin gingerly clearing cups and plates from the drawing room. When she came into the hall she hesitated, then asked if it would be all right to clear Mrs. Bennett's room now. "Mrs. Mathison wasn't very happy about it before. I thought, *now* . . ."

"Please," said Leo. "If you would."

It seemed very final. More so than the funeral. He found himself wanting things to be 'tidied up', and was mildly shocked by his own eagerness. Perhaps he had minded the old lady's presence more than he'd realised, but he didn't explore the thought. He was an accepting and kindly man (except in his business which he regarded as a separate part of his being altogether, or had done until recently when certain worries had begun to prey on him). The only deep distress he felt about the death was on his wife's behalf; for her, he grieved.

But there was no question, the house felt younger, airier. He couldn't help being aware of it. Perhaps, he suggested to himself a little guiltily, it was because all three children were back together in the house at the same time. He went to find Amy to comfort her before the time came to drive her back to school.

Lurching down the pitted track home in his Land Rover, Colonel Doggart chuckled to himself. "Plumb!" he cried, "Peggy!" And he laughed out loud. "Well, well, Peggy Plumb! There's a damn good music-hall name." And bubbling to himself he drove on, barely able to wait to tell his housekeeper this amusing piece of gossip.

2

THE FUNERAL HAD GONE FROM OLIVIA'S MIND.

She was back, deeply engrossed, in the times she recalled most easily, the times she talked of most frequently to the young, tired men and women who came in search of the same lethargic interview year after year. The faces changed, the questions resembled one another; the answers were identical.

They were not the *earliest* years she remembered best, not the very earliest, not the ones that are said to be crucial — Olivia couldn't recall those any better than anybody else. Those she'd always skipped over, saying very little about her father for the good and simple reason there was little to say. After he'd finally left them, her mother had barely mentioned him again. Olivia had been five, or maybe just six at the time, certainly not old enough to have a critical attitude towards the man. Her sole recollection of him was so bathetically theatrical, she couldn't be sure she hadn't imagined it for herself in an effort to fill a cut-out shape on the page. Just one frame, one shot of a man flinging open the door of the cottage and standing there, arms outstretched. A man too tall to enter without ducking slightly. A man who put a bag or rucksack down on the floor. It had dubious echoes of a Victorian mezzotint she seemed to remember on someone else's wall.

No, her memory of William was chiefly as the object of her mother's blame. The small clutch of facts she *did* possess had seemed exciting to her as a little girl, but now they were nothing. He'd been five years younger than her mother, a little wild by all accounts. Restless anyway. Seized by the twin notions of making a fortune and travelling, neither ambition easily open to an assistant forester on the Wickford estate.

But he'd gone all the same. To the Cape. Her mother, the more practical of the two, refused to go, said it was wiser to secure the tenancy of their cottage till his return by making herself invaluable to the Eastholmes. Principally, she had done the household's mending, but her skill was such, that if a special dress was needed for one of the girls, or an embroidered chair back needed careful restoration, the work seemed to fall more and more frequently into her hands.

William had returned after two years (in 1929 probably, Olivia was hazy) boasting of his fortune by which he had meant, she supposed now, looking back, his modest savings from working on the railways. It can't have been more than modest, since it was spent in three months and in four he'd gone again, working his passage to Australia they heard. Wool dealing, they heard. And though a silence fell at that point, somehow, through the inexplicable osmosis of communication Olivia had known ever since she was six or thereabouts, that he had bigamously remarried in his new land and that somewhere, at the opposite end of the world, there were brothers and sisters she would never see.

Surprisingly, she hadn't dwelt on this extension of her family, not even furtively. The shame of it all had been too great. Her mother had sat beside the window catching the last of the natural light, sewing as if her fingers were mechanised, her lips pursed. And though she never mentioned the man willingly again, he lurked behind all her beliefs, her instructions and most of all, behind her provisions for her daughter. The need for security. The need to escape the smear of poverty. She found no dignity in poverty though she contrived to create an impression of it, chiefly perhaps, by separating herself from the other poor, but in a routine daily sense, by insisting on cleanliness, a correctness of manner and a clarity of speech for which Olivia remained undyingly grateful. It was a syllabus that had helped ease her out of a narrowness of life more painlessly than is possible for most people who make the crossing of class frontiers. (Or *was* possible she reflected.)

"For all the difficulties she faced," she wrote, "she tried to bring me up according to her idea of a young lady." And she remembered how keenly she'd been made to listen to the wireless, not for the information to be had—for the beauty of the speakers' articulation.

"We were allowed to remain in our cottage (the Eastholmes

were landowners of a truly benevolent kind). This met our basic problem of shelter. Clothing, my mother made, though she cared nothing for her own appearance beyond neatness. For me, she went to endless trouble, working miracles with odd fragments of fabric, altering the occasional garment that was given by the family, smocking it or changing either collar or sleeves so that it was no longer recognisable as somebody else's but wholly, proudly, my own.

"Food was not always easy. We grew vegetables in our tiny garden and kept a few chickens but there was never any surfeit even when the different crops came into season for there was always a sense of winter. We stored like squirrels, salting beans, pickling cabbage, bottling tomatoes and beetroot, even drying any mushrooms we found in the early autumn fields. Every apple from our one tree was inspected for bruises and, if free of them, carefully wrapped in newspaper and stored in a dry shed outside. Potatoes were put into sacks and carrots stored in boxes of earth. Prudent as we were, there were times when cruel weather or the limits of our small garden meant that we lived off potatoes or swedes for three or four days at a time.

"But somehow my mother managed to rear me healthily. It can't have been easy on a diet so very short of protein. Our main source was eggs and the milk that I collected every day from the home farm. Meat we ate once a week only, on Sundays. And during those periods of the year when the hens went off lay, my mother would go on looking in the nesting boxes day after day, vowing out loud that one of them would get its neck wrung, in the hope the hens would hear and be terrorised into laying. Occasionally, the method worked. A few eggs we were able to keep in isinglass which was effective but gave the eggs an unpleasant taste. With the result that, to this day, I will choose almost anything else in preference to an egg, although there's no question that because of them, I grew strong and healthy."

She paused, trying to recall other evidence of want. The truth was, that as a child she'd lacked the perspective of experience to realise what they had gone without. Certainly, there was the continual contrast of the Eastholmes' own style of living, but not until she was in her teens did she think of comparing herself with them. The contrast with the other employees' way of life was not so very disparate.

Gazing out now on the sumptuous garden, she had the honesty to realise that her burning sense of deprivation had increased with her own, later comfort. But that didn't, she reflected, invalidate it in any way.

There had been no bath, no indoor lavatory, no electricity, no outings, no excursions beyond the long daily walk to school and back, a weekly visit to the dancing teacher and two journeys every Sunday to the small family chapel where the estate workers knelt facing the altar and the profiles of the Eastholme family who blossomed above their high, closed-in pews, a part of the pattern of saints and angels.

No parties, she thought. No friends.

No friends . . . that struck her suddenly, as odd. Friendship was not one of the things poverty took away from people. But her mother had been proud and intensely shy. She had worn her abandonment with the air of one publicly disgraced but defensively impenitent and it was that, Olivia supposed, making a slow box of dots on her blotter, which had made her withdraw. Though to be fair, the lack of a husband to worry over, sigh for, or even, cheerfully, to criticise, robbed her of a whole area of communal gossip. Had she been a widower, it would have been different, she thought. And her mind turned to the two women who had defied her mother's hurt diffidence and persisted in calling from time to time on some small, transparent pretext or other. The parish priest's wife whose name she couldn't recall, a hot-faced woman with a whine in her great, cloth chest when she breathed and a handful of pamphlets always. And Mary, Mary Harrison, who must have been, Olivia thought, closer to her own age than her mother's, a little anyway. A young woman who had married a widower with two grown adolescent children and seemed unable to have her own. Nobody had told her this, but she absorbed it from their whisperings. It was a female difference which had placed her in a category she could share with her mother, Olivia supposed. They felt themselves regarded as incomplete by others, and sometimes, when the crenellations of self-esteem were damaged, felt it themselves.

To still the weakening spasm of pity, she wrote on, the words almost illegible with haste.

She wrote until it was nearly time for dinner (which Mrs. Baldwin had kindly stayed on to prepare) and then slipped out to enjoy a little of the still bright evening.

The house stood in its own small valley, the stream, which had once been used for milling, running close by. The wheel itself, rescued from general decay had been ornamentally replaced at the side of the house, above a pond rather too small for its proportions, but pretty enough. A pair of ruddy shelduck slid across its small dark surface, breasting a drowned scatter of fallen petals.

Behind the outbuildings and stable yard (to the rear and to the right of the house) hilly pastures rose, folding into one another all the way to the horizon where the steeply wooded rise of Corford camp showed violet through a gap in the hills.

To the front of the house, flanking the beech-lined drive was the only pasture which remained solely in the family's possession, two smaller paddocks on the right, as she walked towards them and on the left, a flat five-acre meadow. It was here that she walked, the dense growth of bluebells and cow parsley alongside the post and rail fence brushing softly against her legs.

She had come to look at the brood mares and foals who grazed, knee deep, among the long clover grasses starred with dandelions, buttercups and daisies, eating as much as they could before it was time to be brought in. She walked slowly across the field so as not to disturb them though they knew her well and one mare, the handsome old grey, Cecilia, now raised her head and whinnied softly before dipping her muzzle again into the cool green grass. Her baby stood alert for a second, ears pricked, tiny tail raised, then slithered its lithe neck beneath its mother's belly.

She stood watching their steady movement across the meadow. Their tails switched lazily, not yet seriously troubled by flies She noted how Rosie, the brown mare, now three weeks overdue, had separated herself from the others and stood with resigned patience beneath the oak tree which now, so late into leaf this year, was dressed in golden green. The large copper beech too, had a good red flush to it at last.

The peace of it was kind. The rich quiet growth of life after this late spring helped soften the image of a lowering coffin that remained silently before her eyes. She felt the earth sigh luxuriously as if it were offering up its breast to the animals feeding upon it.

Southwards, from lower down the valley where it broadened to contain the village of Charlton Cloud, she heard the bell ringers begin their Thursday night practice at the church. The bells, which earlier in the day had struck their single, doleful note, now sang gladly. She turned, thankful that she and Leo would not be dining alone—the two of them had seemed to reinforce the space that lay between them at table during the four days that had passed since Mrs. Bennett died. It had been difficult to eat. Difficult to speak. Now she felt a wholesome hunger as though the act of writing had been a muscular effort. As if it had physically moved her out of the numb shock that follows death. She quickened her step back towards the house, its lovely brick warmed by the low, western sun. Eager to meet and talk to her children properly, she hurried and noticed the first swallows of the year circling around the rooftop. Summer had begun.

They looked up as she came in the dining room, silently exploring her face for tears. Whatever it was they found there, it differed from the expectation of each one of them. Leo thought his wife looked elated as if she had been drinking, Chloe, that her mother was making one of her brave efforts, Corin, that she showed signs of strain. Amy felt a bitter rage that her mother's face was not streaked with the same sorrow as her own.

They greeted her mutteringly and Corin rose to draw out her chair at the table.

"Well?" enquired Leo reaching for his soup spoon and holding it poised in his hand until she answered.

"It is a most beautiful evening," she said. (Was it only this afternoon that her mother had been buried? How time pulled away from events.) "Amy, how long can we have you to ourselves before you must go?"

"I said she could stay tonight," Leo intervened, "I've rung Miss Culpeper."

"Oh good, thank you, dear. Amy darling . . . ?"

Amy stared into her soup bowl and then with a fierce gesture, tucked her long tawny hair behind one ear.

"Amy darling, Granny Bennett is happy now. We must be happy for her."

Chloe groaned quietly.

"How can she be happy under the ground?" demanded Amy scornfully, without looking up.

"Her soul is free now," insisted Olivia gently.

"Oh really . . . !" Chloe began, then with a sudden onrush of tact, coughed falsely and passed the bread to her mother. "Sorry," she said. "Bread?"

"Poor Amy," soothed Leo and ran his hand over his youngest daughter's hair. "You loved Granny Bennett didn't you?"

The child sobbed.

"Oh, Leo . . ." Olivia was reproving. She rose and went round to Amy's side of the table, kneeling beside her. "Look, darling, we all have to die. I know it's hard to imagine but we reach an age when we're *glad* to die. We get tired, weary with things . . ." She paused, pleadingly.

It was very hard to say all this. And it sounded false. But anxious herself to believe what she was murmuring into the iron ear of her daughter, she went on. "Old life continually makes way for new life . . . when it's someone we know and love, it's difficult to see the pattern, but it's there, darling . . . it's . . ." She bit her lip and rallied herself. "Why look, Amy," she persisted, shaking the child's arm gently, "there's Jean Abbott in the village expecting a new baby and Mary Drummond too. And . . ." She cast about. "And Rosie, I've just been to see her. She's strayed away from the others so it could be tonight. We'll bring her in, shall we? Tonight, just think!" Seeing no response, she went on in a duller tone, "And the swallows have come . . . and the leaves have opened . . ."

"How *can* it all go on!" Amy's voice rose at the cruelty of it. Olivia half-shared her fury, but she pushed angrily at her persuasion for both their sakes. "Birth and death," she said, "are life itself, the mutual celebrations of it. Death . . ." she paused, "*death* . . ." But she said no more, holding Amy awkwardly to her and thinking how frail the maturity of fifteen was. She felt the hotness of Amy's tears.

The others softly continued with their dipping and sipping, one eye on Olivia. These protestations of Amy's they had expected to come from Olivia herself but here she was, apparently convinced by what she was murmuring, unexpectedly serene.

Leo, in particular, watched with cautious astonishment, hearing sentences the unbereaved like to mouth in helpless comfort of their friends. After four days of existing in a dull stupor, refusing to deal with the facts of death, she was more steady and seemingly *refreshed* than any of them. He distrusted the change.

Slowly, Amy's cries subsided, sliding evenly into her mother's shoulder. She was exhausted. She hung there on the bony, black shoulder, a brooch digging sharply into her, longing to sleep a dark, dark sleep that would exclude all these unruffled people. She let her mother raise her and help her upstairs. Together they stumbled down the corridor to her bedroom and she felt herself eased gently down on to the cool, silky quilt.

Olivia drew the curtains to block out the high radiant light that still flooded into the greenish ceiling of the sky and then went to slip off Amy's uncomfortable new shoes. She covered her over without undressing her—the child was so near to sleep it seemed unkind to disturb her.

Kneeling down beside the bed, she kissed the damp face. "It will heal," she whispered, fighting a terrible fear in herself. Then, vehemently, "I promise you."

Amy was silent. Sleep was overcoming her, rolling irresistibly down over a thin fire of hatred for her mother. She heard the composed voice whisper "Good night", heard the soft movement of shoes over the carpet, the click of her door and then a brisk step down the landing, a lighter running down the stairs. The hate flared up in a single yellow flame before being totally extinguished.

Their conversation stopped when Olivia returned to the dining room.

"All right now?" asked Leo.

"Asleep, poor lamb." Olivia sat down and pushed her cold soup away.

"Perhaps she should stay at home a little longer."

"No. No, I don't think so." She rolled the stem of her wine glass between thumb and forefinger, "No, it's best she should go back to school, away from the . . . away from the atmosphere. The clearing that has to be done." Olivia thought with dread of the papers and clothes that awaited her attention.

"If you say so," said Leo, uncertain and he rose to carve the small joint of cold lamb.

"I intend to go in the morning . . . Unless of course, you need me." Corin glanced at his mother. She smiled. "No, darling, no we can cope."

Sometimes she had to curb herself against a disappointment in Corin. His charm, his manners, his conventionally good looks, were impeccable without being in any way striking. He lacked vivacity.

The girlfriends he occasionally brought home were mutedly pretty, tinkling and dull. She wondered, dutifully, whether she should not find him something to do here at home, whether he might not feel more useful if involved, but the truth was, she ached to get on with her writing undisturbed. Even now, the urgency of it tightened her bones.

"You adore your children don't you?" demanded Chloe suddenly after taking a healthy gulp at her wine.

"Of course, darling." Olivia looked up surprised.

"You'd do anything for them wouldn't you?"

"Of course," affirmed Leo.

"Well then," Chloe went on smiling wickedly, "I have a request to make."

Corin laughed.

"Oh, Chloe!" Olivia gripped her daughter's hand warily. (Her lovely, bold and difficult daughter with whom she felt she had so little in common.) "Come along then!"

"Sheep Cottages . . ." began Chloe.

"Ye-e-es." Leo handed her a plate and looked cautious.

"They're still empty?"

"Ye-e-e-s." More doubtfully still.

"Well I hate to see them wasted," said Chloe, "so I suggested to my friends that you'd probably be grateful to have them restored and lived in. We could adapt the outbuildings quite easily —one of them's an architect and good with his hands . . . and there's a carpenter . . . And the bit of land that goes with them, well what is it—one and a half acres?—if we could be allowed a little more, the four-acre field below it, for instance, that nobody else seems to want, it would give us a good start—and it includes that hazel coppice, which would be useful. And the spring, of course, means there's water already to hand. Anyway, I thought it would be a good idea and a couple of them are coming down tomorrow to have a look." She stopped. And grinned.

Leo threw back his head and laughed. He couldn't help himself. "I was thinking of running a few ewes up there," he said.

"It would be nice to have me at home, wouldn't it?" Chloe turned to her mother. "You could keep an eye on me."

A grimly disapproving sound escaped from her mother, who abruptly pushed her glass towards her husband. "Pour me some wine, Leo, would you?"

"Not another commune?" groaned Corin.

"What do you mean . . . not another?"

"Oh Christ," he sighed. "Do you need to ask?"

Covert looks were exchanged around the table. The countryside was thickening with groups of people, the new refugees, drifting into unsuitable buildings. They'd come seeking safety and found confronting a new enemy, the families whose homes were already long established in the valleys, families whose own store against the future was small. It had begun with weekenders, then families who had tried to establish new lives altogether but found themselves faced with practical difficulties they'd never dreamed of; many had lost heart. But now, so it was rumoured from other districts, the trickle was a steady flow. There were squatters, people who came with nothing and refused to go. Hitherto their own valley had remained free of the intrusion because of its remoteness from any one of the bigger towns, but a kind of watchfulness prevailed everywhere.

"Oh come on!" urged Chloe, gazing round at the wary expressions. "It's the sort of thing you should approve of." She appealed to her mother. "Founded on love."

"There's love and *love*." Olivia was not to be drawn.

"Are you serious?" Leo resumed carving, one alert eye on his daughter.

"But of course I am!"

"What sort of friends?" Guardedly, Olivia began helping herself to salad.

"Oh, hippies, drop-outs, drug-addicts, unmarried mothers, that sort of thing."

"No, seriously."

"Seriously."

"Chloe!" Olivia sounded a warning.

"O.K., O.K., we'll draw the line at junkies. You'll like them, I promise you."

"What's the point of it all?" Corin sounded weary. "You're just avoiding things."

"What about your Finals next week? What about your career? Whatever *that's* going to be," added Olivia contemptuously.

"Oh, don't worry about *that* . . ."

"If you're really serious, Chloe, it'll be done on a business-like basis." Leo now sat down.

"Leo!"

"Money." Corin put in.

"Precisely," said Leo with a grateful look at his eldest son. "Rent."

"We'd buy the cottages off you."

"No you wouldn't. You'll pay me a fair rent for a year and then, if it's still together, if it's viable, I'll turn that into a deposit for a mortgage."

"*Leo!*"

"Oh, Daddy!" Chloe dropped her knife and fork with a

clatter and ran round the table to hug her father. "You're a honey!"

"You're a fool, Leo."

"I retain the option to approve my tenants, mind."

"But Leo darling, you haven't gone into any of the details. How can you . . . how do you know. . . ?"

"I trust Chloe."

"Well, yes of course, so do I. Naturally. But it's not just Chloe is it? And what *about* her career?"

"My darling mama, you've always loathed the idea of my having a career. Anyway, nobody wants graduates any more, education's a liability."

"You *must* do your Finals, Chloe, I insist."

"I shall. But then I shall do something *useful* with my life."

"It's too much!" Abruptly, Olivia brought a slender white hand to her forehead.

"Well what else do you suggest? Everything's breaking up. It's done for, the kind of world you're still — God knows how desperately — hanging on to. What can my degree do for me, assuming I get it?"

"You can help, *do* something."

"Do something!" cried Chloe scornfully. "Everybody's saying they must do something, and look where it's got them, into the next best thing to a police state. Hanging on. Grabbing hold. *Doing* something, I suppose, is voting for a restoration of capital punishment." She rounded harshly on her mother, referring to her position on the referendum earlier that year.

"Well—?"

"Oh . . ." She slumped in disgust.

"Got your windmill ready?" enquired Corin. "Got your milking stool?"

Chloe dealt him a malevolent look.

"What makes *me* angry . . ." Olivia launched herself in a manner that threatened to be familiar. Instantly, the exasperation between brother and sister met, melted and flowed mutually out towards their mother.

". . . *Is*. . . ?" said Chloe.

"This refusal to fight for what's good, worth having. Hard-won, for heaven's sake. I *know* . . ."

And the eyebrows of her children rose together.

"I *know*," Olivia repeated, "what poverty is. I *know* the struggles people had. I *know* how women watched their babies die because they hadn't the money or there wasn't the medicine to help them. I *know* what it is to go hungry."

"Nobody's denying all that," said Chloe a trifle unsympathetically, "but those were the days when *some* people had money and others just hadn't. That was the injustice. It's not the same now. For a while everybody had money, or more money. Now everybody's got to go without. It's a different situation."

"So Chloe's going to put it all right with a weaving loom and exchange of beads," Corin explained to his mother.

Leo smiled to himself. The thought uppermost in his mind was that he wanted Chloe here to keep an eye on Olivia. It was the perfect solution.

"It's fatuous," said Olivia sharply.

"Corin makes it sound fatuous. Look," and Chloe tried to screw herself up to explain. "Look, I can't *do* things in the sense you'd like. I can do a few practical things, the most practical thing being food. We can provide our own food and actually," she looked a little nervously at her parents, "hope to widen that a bit, in the village, involve other . . ."

"I knew it!" Corin threw up his arms. "A co-operative!"

"Oh, what's the point?" She gave up. "You make everything sound so silly."

"It's hard to know," sighed Corin with extravagant ruefulness, "just who's the *more* romantic of you two. You must admit" (turning to his mother), "your daughter takes after you."

Olivia, accustomed to gibes of this kind from her children took no notice but stared at Chloe, awaiting a further naïveté.

"What's most needed," valiantly, Chloe tried once more, "isn't really windmills or anything like that, they're just the tools—tools appropriate to a particular attitude, a particular outlook. And in exactly the same way," she looked anxiously at her father, as though for a second she felt that whatever it was she was trying to say might affect his readiness to have her and the others as tenants, "in much the same way, it's not . . . well, what's gone *wrong* isn't so much oil, or inflation or pollution, or any of the other things. . . . Not in themselves, they're symptoms. It's the attitude of mind that permitted such things to happen. It's the way of thinking that's got to change."

"And how, my darling, are you going to change the world's mind living up on the hill in a derelict cottage?" Olivia pulled her napkin out of its ring and flourished it angrily.

"You can't *impose* things like that."

31

"Well, don't sound so dismissive, *tell* us."

"Not if you're going to be so turdish."

"Promise," smiled Corin delicately.

"Well," again she looked for support to Leo and he gave her a mild and encouraging nod, "Well, the real problem is that the ... the system that grew up out of all the old, *wrong*—not wrong so much, arrogant, unrealistic attitudes ..."

"Such as?" Corin wasn't going to let her flannel.

"Such as, for example, a belief in man's incomparable excellence, in the supremacy of rationality—a grossly unrealistic view for an irrational species to take—oh, and the belief that wealth can create justice all by itself, *all* that sort of thing."

"You're getting fuzzy at the edges," Corin gave an acid smile.

"You're making me lose my thread, you pig."

"Sorry."

"Well then," she took a deep breath, "the system that grew out of all *that sort of thing*," she emphasised the words rudely for her brother's benefit, "has changed people so much, actually altered their personalities so much, that they're virtually robbed of the very things that will help them survive reasonably well. And I don't mean," she went on forcefully, refusing to succumb to another intervention from her brother who was now rolling his bread into small grey pellets, "I don't just mean the stupidity of destroying the physical world in order to sustain the artificial world, though heaven knows, that's serious enough, I mean changes in the head. In the heart perhaps. I mean ..." And she shook her hands from the wrists in frustration. "Oh, hell, I mean ..."

"I should get on with your meal," urged Leo.

"There are several questions going begging already," observed Olivia who restrained herself remarkably so far, but Chloe had started and she was going to finish. She'd gone quite pink in the face.

"Look, the splitting up of society, that partly, but much more, the way wealth's helped all those so-called philosophies of individual freedom. It's bred loyalty and loving and dependence and sacrifice right out of people, wiped things like that out, almost as successfully as it's wiped out tuberculosis or something like that." She ignored at least two contemptuous snorts, "But it's true!" she asserted. "That freedom—it doesn't matter which kind, economic, sexual, even in a way, artistic freedom—it has another side, the freedom to reject people. Anyway, it's a contradiction in terms, the freedom to be yourself, you *can* only be yourself in relation to other people, anything else isn't freedom, it's isolation. It's lovelessness, that's what's got to be relearned. Loving. Loving in a group. Most groups aren't bound together by anything other than hatred for another group these days, that's why I don't want to join them. That's why I want to try here. Make a start at least..." She faltered, sensing a blank reception, and cut clumsily into her meat.

"Well," remarked Olivia, after a pause, reaching for the pepper grinder, "of course, *love*. That's what I, in my small way..."

"I don't mean that sort." Chloe spoke more sharply than she meant. "I mean the hard kind, the day-in, day-out kind, the giving kind. The kind that puts self last."

"I'm sure your mother understands you perfectly."

"Yes, of course. I'm sorry."

There was an assiduous sound of cutlery.

"I suggest we stick to practical details for the moment."

"I'll tell you my view of human nature," volunteered Corin, ignoring his father's suggestion. "That it's incapable of living in communes. Schemes like yours break up in no time."

Olivia began to cry. Instinctively she pressed her fists to her cheeks to stop the tears' disfigurement.

"Come." Leo went to her and brought her into his arms, against his body. He felt a great relief, as if the weeping had come like rain after a drought. He led his wife into the small sitting room that adjoined the dining room and reaching out one arm to light a lamp, took her more closely, sank down beside her on the sofa and cradled her until the weeping had run its course.

Eventually, when Mince came and laid his placid head on her knee, she stopped. She fondled the dog's head gently.

"That's better," said Leo, lifting a strand of her dark red hair away from her face. "A difficult day."

Chloe came in with some coffee for them. "Better now?" she asked, and went to let in one of the cats who was scratching at the window. She thought her mother looked old, suddenly.

The cat, a fine, long-haired tortoiseshell, bounded into Olivia's lap ignoring the dog and hungrily rasped the salt off her face. "Oh, Pax, you idiot," sighed Olivia.

At least my animals love me, she thought, resentful that Chloe should have damaged this day, distracted its attention from death. She seemed to have created noise and change. All her family, with the exception of Amy, seemed big and harsh, uncrumpled by event. Already now, as she stroked the cat, she could hear them talking more about their future plans—conversions, a firm of brokers, the price of barley meal and a cricket match Corin had to arrange. So matter-of-fact, so insensitive. Her left hand, pressed down by the weight of Leo's, was going dead. With effort, she withdrew it. He hardly noticed, just turning to smile unconsciously, in mid-sentence, and turning away again.

Without bothering to excuse herself, she got to her feet and climbed wearily upstairs to her mother's room, pausing outside for a moment before daring to go in. Still clutching Pax beneath her arm, she summoned up the strength and pushing the door open, reached inside for the light before crossing over the threshold.

The bed. Smoothly made. The desk, cleared and shut. The dressing table, empty save for a silver-backed hairbrush and hand mirror neatly placed side by side.

It could have been empty for weeks. So quickly, then. Death packed away like an old suitcase in a store cupboard. The room, delightfully pink and cream in the sunshine, now looked, beneath the single, overhead light, as hollow as an hotel room out of season. There were no slippers. No scraps of cotton wool. A faint astringent smell obliterated the warm odours of human occupation.

She went to pull open the wardrobe door and with one hand noisily rattled through the empty clothes. Smooth, black rags, the very things she had daily picked out with such care and pleasure for her mother to put on, useless now. Their uselessness enveloped her. Touching them was slightly repellent, as though they'd taken on some of the slippery chill of death. Stepping back she pressed her cheek to the vibrant silky body of the cat, feeling the pleasure that trembled in it.

Her eye settled on the desk where all the letters and documents of many years were locked. These she knew she would have to read carefully to help her with the book, but the idea was repugnant for the moment. Another time.

She went over to the window, suddenly anxious to unseal it and have a little of the night breeze stir inside the room but her attention was caught by the jewel box on the window sill which ought to have been locked. She checked it. It was not. Lifting the ornate silver lid, she ran her fingers through the precious things she had bought to please her mother. A fine, five-strand collar of pearls, lovely opalescent things, an emerald pendant. Many pairs of ear rings, which she had rather come to like wearing—gold, pearl, sapphire and diamond ("As long as it's something *small*"). A Georgian cameo ring of carved coral, a diamond spray brooch, a thin silver chain and locket decorated with tiny amethysts which sprang open accidentally. Inside, coiled a lock of golden hair. Her own. The same corn colour as Chloe's. She put it away, quickly closing the box and forgetting to open the window. As she made to leave the room, she caught sight of herself in the oval pier-glass . . . red-haired, white-faced and clasping a multi-coloured cat to herself as if expecting someone to seize it from her.

The reflection frightened her because she saw fright in it.

The nakedness of its display was shocking. Like discovering one seeping blood from a wound that was deep but too fresh to be at its most painful. She could read it accurately as fear for a life that had been so scrupulously maintained, so totally, in her writing, her style of being, dressing and behaving, so totally bound up with her mother's existence, it stood in peril of losing its motive force. As though the engine had cut out.

Fragment by fragment, through childhood and beyond, her mother had prepared her for this life and she had lived it out within her mother's gaze. Like actor and audience the performance and the pleasure of it was dependent on their mutual presence. To Leo, the performance was barely noticeable. To her children, it was nothing. She stared at her haggard face and felt the emptiness of the room swell and expand until the walls themselves seemed to pull away from her.

The cat leapt out of her arms and fled the room as if pursued. Swiftly, she hurried after it.

As she passed through the kitchen, pulling a coat over her shoulders, she met Corin.

"Going out?"

"Yes, darling, going to check on Rosie. Are you washing up? How sweet . . . you could have left it for Mrs. B."

And without stopping, she let herself out into the cold, clear night. There was no need for a torch. The moon, almost full, gave everything a still, pale clarity.

Rosie waited by the gate and whinnied thankfully when she came, happy to be led simply by a hand on her mane. Once inside the lighted box Olivia could see the sweat staining her neck and belly and noticed a thin, fine spray of milk leak from the mare's udder when she moved, It would not be long.

There was no point staying here, waiting. The mare wouldn't foal with somebody watching.

Olivia returned to the house and found the others making tea in the kitchen.

"You mustn't stay up for Rosie," protested Leo. "You're worn out. Anyway, she'll cope better on her own, she's an old hand. You go up and I'll bring you some tea."

They were talking about Sheep Cottages, she guessed. And wanted to go on discussing it without her. Too tired to object, she gave in and kissed her two children lightly on the cheek.

"Sleep well," said Chloe kindly.

But sleep wouldn't come. Leo arrived with the tea, drank half his own, yawned, slumped into bed and slept instantly. The simplicity and heaviness of his sleeping prevented her own. As his breathing became more careless and deep, she grew stiffer and stiffer. Painfully, she tried to go over the details of the service which had flowed indistinctly round her that afternoon. The words of the service which she'd heard—and loved—on other occasions, at other funerals, had escaped her entirely, caught emptily, like seed pods, on the air.

But her mind wouldn't admit the formal closing words on life even now. It tightened wilfully, keeping her both from rest and recollection.

At two, she rose and putting on Leo's thick winter dressing gown and a pair of his socks she went downstairs and out into the yard.

A few feet away from Rosie's box she stopped. She could hear the mare's soft straining sounds. Steady, regular grunts. Then a slithering rush, and a few seconds later, small, subdued whinnies of delight.

Olivia put the light on and saw Rosie licking the dark wet foal at her feet, its eyes full of attentive shock.

"*Clever* girl," she whispered and creeping in, stood back quietly against the wall waiting for the foal to rise.

It was difficult. It was still attached by its cord to the afterbirth.

She didn't want to touch the baby in case her scent made Rosie reject it so she waited anxiously for its own first movements to make the rupture.

The mare gave deep trills of encouragement, pushing at the foal with her muzzle. It struggled half-way, front legs unfolding first, then tumbled over. Again and again it tried, but unbalanced by the extra weight holding it back, crashed helplessly, first on one side, then on its head. Worried, she remained still.

The foal was visibly tiring, the effort to overcome the weight of the afterbirth too much for it. After a short rest it tried again, its stick-like legs slithering in all directions, somehow knotting themselves in the cord which tightened at every fresh attempt to stand.

With as little movement as possible Olivia slipped out to the tack room, sterilised a pair of scissors in the boiler and brought them back to the box with thread, iodine and cotton wool. So much time had passed already there was no point in ringing the vet; she would have to cope on her own.

The small creature lay stretched out, its ribs heaving up and down, the thick white cord entangled around its legs which gave spasmodic twitches. Bending down carefully to avoid a kick from one of the small sharp hooves, she tied the twine tightly round the cord, then levering her arms beneath the foal, dragged it bodily as close as she could beneath the mare's udder. The extra fight it put up succeeded in breaking the cord at the ligature. Swiftly she smothered the navel in iodine.

It rose. Uncertainly, it wavered, its legs going a grasshopper shape. She tried to guide it to the milk but as it stretched out a questing muzzle, the mare squealed and swung away, her ears back.

"Come on now, my love, come on. Let the little one feed."

But Rosie was unwilling. Her infant smelt strange. Again the foal collapsed on the straw. Olivia was frightened the mare might trample on her baby or even turn on *her*, she looked so evil.

She dared not leave them to go for help. Keeping up low words of encouragement she let the foal rest its weight on her as again, exhausted, it clambered to its feet.

The critical time was seeping away. Unless the colostrum could be got into the foal, it would die. Life was slipping out of it already.

As she approached the mare, pushing the foal, shuffling it, against her own thighs, Rosie struck out with a hind leg, narrowly missing the baby who fell against Olivia, catching her off balance. Together they fell into the bloodstained straw.

"Come on, little one," she urged. "Be brave." But it couldn't get up. It raised its head then let it fall heavily back.

"All right, Rosie; steady, mare, easy now." She crawled to her feet and stepped cautiously towards the mare who gave an angry squeal as she felt her udder touched. Trying to keep one eye on the mare's head, talking still, Olivia drew gently on the udder and the action seemed to soothe the mare. She relaxed and let Olivia milk her. With as much of the yellow liquid as she could cup in the palm of her hand, she carried it to the foal and bending close to it, she lifted its head and let it suck the milk down.

Four times she drew off the milk and poured it carefully into the baby. A quiver of life returned to it. The urge for food drove it more steadily to its feet. Towards its mother. This time, after a mild protest, Rosie allowed it to suckle and stood patiently, head down, eyes half closed while the infant greedily explored and took a stronger hold.

It was all right. Wearily, Olivia leaned against the wall and watched strength flow into the foal. Then, when she was sure Rosie wouldn't rebel, she went to mix a warm feed for her.

When she returned and saw mother and child well settled with one another, helpless tears of relief flowed down her face. "You clever, clever creature," she whispered, scratching the mare's withers. "You love."

And turning off the light she left them, stumbling back to bed without disturbing Leo at all.

This time, there was no difficulty. Heavy with weariness she slept immediately and deeply—so deeply, that although Leo came with tea in the morning to tell her he was about to drive Amy to school, she stirred without hearing and slept on long after her unhappy daughter had left.

3

IT WAS HALF PAST TEN BEFORE MADGE WARING DISTURBED OLIVIA.
"Miss Bennett?" she mewed, her head extending nervously round the doorway. "May I?"

Olivia sat up in bed wearing a cream satin robe that matched both coverlet and quilted headboard. The whole room was cream and gold and lemon. It smelt of mimosa.

"Of course," she said, putting the silver coffee pot down on her tray. "Have you had coffee, dear?"

"Yes. Yes thank you," Madge Waring glanced uncertainly at her employer, expecting signs of strain. The face, already immaculately, though not heavily, made-up, bore only the palest stain beneath the eyes; a mere smudge of lilac. "Are you sure you want to do your correspondence this morning?"

"Life," said Olivia, "*must* go on." (She made it sound like show business.) "Routine's a wonderful guarantee of that, Madge, I must try and stick to my routine. Not the outside appointments, by the way, those I want left for a while, but *our* routine, Madge. *Here.* Anyway," she added gaily, smoothing the sheet, "my readers still expect to have their letters answered, don't they? Have you seen the foal?"

"Not yet, but I heard . . . you are *wonderful*!" Madge Waring sat down on a cream Adam chair towards the foot of the bed and radiated admiration.

"You see?" sighed Olivia. "New life . . ." *New life* . . . her heart echoed.

"Now, what demands are being made of us today?"

There were twenty-five signed photographs to be despatched. "How *are* we for photos, Madge dear? Getting low I imagine. Perhaps you could order another five hundred prints?"

"Would you like some new ones taken?"

"Whatever for? All that fuss, heavens. Don't you like the old one?"

"Oh, very much. I just . . ." Madge stared down at the soft, inspired portrait of Olivia before handing it over to be signed. It reminded her, well, it was hard to pinpoint really—of something from a film annual of the forties. But then Miss Bennett was not unlike Vivien Leigh, so . . .

Efficiently the two women worked through publisher's queries, dates for speaking engagements later in the year and well into next, the annual general meetings of the National Trust, the RSPCA, a specimen cover for *Beloved Orchid* ("a touch lascivious, don't you think?") and requests for money.

"Ten pounds for the Famine Relief, ten for Help the Aged, ten for the Retired Donkeys' Home, and five apiece for Beauty Without Cruelty, the Battered Wives Association and York Minster . . . what does that amount to this week?"

"One hundred and eighty-five pounds." Madge Waring made a quick account. "What," she added hesitantly, "about the Anti-Blood Sports League? They're trying again."

Olivia sighed. She pondered a moment, stroking her throat. "I can't," she concluded. "Try a tactful letter."

"They're very persistent."

"Oh very well, Madge dear, let's be done with it. A fiver."

"There's an invitation from Brownhills University asking you to speak on the motion, 'This House believes in an oppressed sex'."

"What do you suppose that means?"

Madge Waring read through the ill-spelt letter more carefully. "The oppression of women."

"Yes, but does it mean women should be or *are* oppressed?" said Olivia impatiently. "Really, the level of today's education is appalling. Find out what they mean, Madge, without implying they're illiterate."

A note was made. "I've cancelled your Meals on Wheels turn today," said the secretary, plucking at her good tweed skirt, "I didn't feel you would be . . ."

"Oh dear, well—I hope they'll forgive me."

"Of course they will." Madge Waring's eyes glowed behind her glasses, "You're in a state of shock."

Olivia gave her a brief, stabbing look. "You may be right,"

she murmured, toying with the sugar tongs, "I fear you may . . . I'm not quite myself."

"Perhaps we'll leave it there then."

"Very well." She felt suddenly languid and leaned back against the silky hillock of pillows.

"Oh, did I tell you about the Parish Council meeting next Monday?"

"Yes, dear, you did. I'd like all arrangements cancelled for a month. I'd like a little time . . ."

Gathering her papers together, Madge Waring stood up and began to retreat backwards.

"Madge dear?"

"Yes, Miss Bennett?" Olivia's head was turned away towards the window.

"Has anyone mentioned this notion of Chloe's. . . ? This . . . the Sheep Cottages scheme?"

"Two young men called just before I came upstairs. They've all gone up there now, I believe."

"Ah . . ." Olivia's copper hair spread in healthy tendrils across the pillow as she turned back again to speak to Madge Waring. "I shouldn't discuss it with anybody, Madge. It's most unlikely to come to anything — one of Chloe's more fanciful — you understand me, dear, don't you — In the village. . . ?"

Madge Waring's loyalty was unimpeachable. "I understand perfectly," she replied in a confidential tone. (The young men *had* looked a little wild.) With a slight stooping motion and inclining of the head, she left.

All the things she wanted to do, the things she *should* do failed to draw her away from the heaviness that weighted her down in bed. She could give in, just lie there with the curtains drifting and the birds calling in fright to their fledgelings. So easy, just to stay. Last Friday (only a *week* ago?), last Friday at this time, she was bringing her mother back from Communion and pointing out to her the sudden rush of wild flowers in the hedgerows — all spring and summer curiously mixed by a flood of warmth after weeks of cold, rainless weather. Last Friday. Saturday. Sunday.

On Monday morning, carrying the tray of tea, she found her, horribly still. Not lovely in death. A pink hairnet, her mouth open, cheeks fallen in, as if caught in mid-breath. About to cry out from a dream. One hand clutched the sheet, not violently, but firmly enough to need the fingers prised a little.

Beneath the pillow protruded a copy of *The Enchanted Lake*, face downwards and open.

She had screamed then, and dropped the tray.

Olivia pulled against the lead that filled her arms and legs, rose, dressed and checked her face. She had, what her admirers called, 'wonderful bones' and a skin that had stayed unusually fine, though not without expense and care. Slowly, she brushed her hair and saw, in the mirror, Leo come in.

"The foal's fine," he said, pleased to see her up.

"And Rosie?"

"Radiant." He gave a short laugh, then pushed his hands in his jacket pockets and shuffled. "I've just delivered Amy."

"Oh! *Amy!*"

"She's fine."

"Yes, school will be best for her." She brushed her hair more sharply, then satisfied, swung round on the stool to face Leo. "Look, darling, this scheme of Chloe's..."

"Ah. Yes."

"Do you think it's wise to encourage her?"

"Why not for goodness' sake? It's something to while away the long vacation."

"You think that's as long as it will last?"

"Probably."

"But they'll all be ... *living* together. I mean ... anyway, she should be deciding on a career, planning ..." She gestured feebly with her brush.

"Let's just see ... And I'll be glad to have the buildings put right. We lose nothing by it." Leo was obstinately cheerful.

Olivia turned back to the mirror, studied her face, and began to tint the cheekbones.

"I wonder what my readers would feel about it?" she said gaily, leaning forward to allow the light more fully on her face.

"Your readers?" echoed Leo blankly. He didn't understand.

"Well, *darling!*"

"No, I'm sorry," he puzzled. "How do your readers—?"

"You couldn't call me one of the more, well, I'm not exactly an advocate of *free* love and so forth." She drew back to study

42

the effect of the blush on her cheek and deciding against it, took a little tuft of cotton wool to remove the robust glow.

"No, I know that."

"Well, can't you see? For them, I represent all the good, solid values." She turned to him, eyes large. "Love, honour, responsibility, those sort of things and if they were to read somewhere —and they will, rest assured about *that*—if they were to read that Olivia Bennett, living in the beautiful home that she's made with *their* help, has some sort of hippy commune full of pot smokers and bastard children, they'd feel dreadfully let down. *Betrayed*, Leo. I do *not* exaggerate."

She did, of course, but he wasn't prepared to argue that. He dug his hands deeper in his pockets and made a gentle, querying hum. The important thing to him was Chloe's presence here and Bart's urging him not to be deceived by Olivia's active, purposeful appearance. As long as he was obliged to spend the greater part of his week away in Town, he could think of no better arrangement. Besides, as he now said to Olivia who stared at him woundedly, "It'll give you an interest. Perhaps you can help them get going. Think of all the advice you could give on livestock, planting, that kind of thing. And why," he threw out, "should they be anything but charming? Why should you assume Chloe's friends will be unprincipled and dirty or whatever it is you imagine they'll be? Have you ever disapproved of her friends before?"

"I've hardly met them." Olivia turned away dismissively. She picked up a little mascara brush and rubbed it vigorously into the black cake ready to apply to the already finely coated lashes. "That, anyway," she remarked, one eye closed as she stroked upwards, "is beside the point. I'm sure they're likeable children, why not? They might even work quite hard, but is that how it will seem to my readers? You *may* say," she went on quickly before Leo could say anything, "that my first duty is to my children, not my readers and that's a perfectly fair point but, really, don't you feel Chloe's reached an age now where she ought to be made to stand on her own two feet? It's not as though she's in trouble, if she were in trouble, well, that's a different matter altogether, but she's not, and I think she should be able to understand how *delicate* this could be for me."

She seemed to be sliding rather rapidly from one point to the next without completing any of them, but Leo was accustomed to this pattern of things. He watched her separating two congealed lashes with a pin then stepped closer and put his hands gently on to her shoulders. "All right, I think she was tactless pressing it on you . . . so *soon*, but you know Chloe. Give them a chance. Talk to them, see if you like them. They're coming to lunch."

"Oh." Olivia sat grimly upright, somehow freeing herself of his light grasp. She began the obsessive massage of her hands, a ritual practised thrice daily, whitening, smoothing until she achieved the texture of alabaster. "I wonder," she said bitterly, "what mother would have made of all this." And she was angry with all of them for not allowing Mrs. Bennett a decent and respectful interval of rest.

"It's all mock," explained Chloe as they stood on the lawn and gazed raptly up at Clouds.

"Go on!" challenged Pete. "It's a period res. Isn't it?" And he stepped backwards into the lower branches of the cedar tree to get a better look.

"Mock seventeenth," said Chloe. "A beautiful job. The only bit of the original left is the old walled garden—I'll take you there and show you what care they took to match up the bricks . . . it's a work of art, really." Her eyes ran over its familiar architecture. "My grandfather did it all in 1926."

"What was *he* then?"

"Oh, a farmer, like Daddy was, once. It was nice then, when we were kids, harvesting and haymaking and so on . . . I don't know really why he stopped. It's terribly hard work though you know." She reflected for a moment, "I sometimes wonder whether he just wanted to get out of the house, away from the noise."

"Noise?" Pete laughed disbelievingly, looking upward at the spaciousness of sky.

"The typewriter. Bash, bash, bash, all day long."

"Oh," he laughed again.

"Anyway, he went. About, what, oh, eleven years ago, when I was . . ." she counted, "nine, I suppose. Went into the office end of the grain business. A broker's. I'm sure he hates it."

"He must be mad. I like it here." Andrew flung himself down on the grass and closed his eyes.

"Perhaps he'll come back now."

"Why? The situation?"

"Well, our situation, here, not *the* situation."

"Why?"

"Now Granny's gone, I mean. He may feel more at home."

"A monster?" Pete slung his denim jacket over his shoulder.

"Oh, heavens, no!" Chloe was horrified by the idea. "No, quite the opposite. Very quiet, timid. Only too easy to ignore until you felt guilty about ignoring her. Oh no, it's just that she was *there*." She couldn't explain it any better than that. She pushed up the long drooping sleeves of her dress to feel the sun on her arms. "And I suppose she got most of Mummy's attention."

They let their eyes travel pleasurably over the white-painted woodwork, the misty blue petals of wisteria that hung in clusters over the front of the house, the handsome, purplish-leaved Burgundian vine that grew up the sides and crept about the first-floor windows. Turtle doves warbled overhead.

"I love it," said Chloe and she hugged herself. "Come on!" she urged the others. "Come round the back way and I'll take you into the enchanted garden."

They followed her past the still, green depth of the pool, grossly overhung with hazel and elder, making a circuit of the house until they came to a small, peeling, white-painted wicket gate almost hidden in the rear wall by swags of evergreen honeysuckle.

"I used to pretend it was magic going in here," said Chloe.

She pushed open the gate and they looked into the peaceful, sunlit garden where Mince lay sleeping beneath the magnolia stellata, his body strewn with its confetti. The beds were luxuriantly planted with white flowering shrubs and plants—lilac, deutzia, viburnum and alyssum. Above them, a tangle of flowers continued up the old walls where the pink of a clematis mingled with the darker pink of a climbing rose already in flower and the untidy, espaliered boughs of crab apple blossom. Beneath the white, spread the cool flat leaves of an untrained fig that grew sideways of its own accord and disappeared behind silvery-leaved foliage plants. A small Glastonbury thorn and a willow made short noonday shadows on the grass.

"I like it," breathed Andrew and tried to catch an orange-tip butterfly that fluttered out of reach. "What's that noise?"

"The typewriter," laughed Chloe. "She's playing our tune."

"I've been longing to meet you!"

Olivia descended the stairs with the grace of an ex-ballerina, arms outstretched.

"I'm so glad you could stay to lunch. You must come and tell *all* your plans!" And she bore the young men off in her embrace.

There was no resisting Olivia's charm. To have tried, would have been like swimming against a warm tide. With an air of intense absorption, she burrowed her way into the backgrounds, hopes and beliefs of the young men, beguiling them hopelessly.

"I do *admire* you so!" she sighed. Which is a remark a woman of forty-eight can safely make.

Peter and Andrew, unable to help themselves, allowed her flattery to draw them on like shingle on to a beach. Andrew, sandy-haired and frailly-built, used his hands feverishly (like little crabs, thought Olivia) to explain the technical details of methane conversion and energy collectors. Olivia, the acolyte, leaned forward, fingers locked in concentration. "You'll have to explain to me what you mean by millicals!" she laughed (a trifle girlishly, Chloe felt). And obligingly, Andrew did so, solemnly telling her the importance of measuring efficiency in terms of energy units rather than profitability or productivity.

"It all sounds very knowledgeable doesn't it?" Olivia appealed to Leo, who nodded, amiably.

Their enthusiasm touched him. He found it naïve, but that too, attracted his sympathy. He wanted to see if they *could* do things that he had known, on any large scale, were impossible. When, eleven years ago, the man from the Min. of Ag. and Fish had called, outlining the intensive, automated improvements necessary if the farm was to prosper—and had performed small, black calculations on his clipboard to demonstrate the need for capital investment around ten and a half thousand—he'd sadly decided that such farming was abusive and he wanted no part of it.

Having made the decision, he'd turned his back on the farm completely. He'd put on a dark suit and taken himself off to a great glass and concrete office in the City (subjecting himself to the very conditions he'd thought unfit for his cattle) where a loathing for what he did gave him the perverse energy to do it moderately well. Or had done, until 1972, when the grain situation went almost totally out of control. The problems that continued to flow from that time grew more unmanageable with each succeeding month. *Anything* was worth a try now, thought Leo to himself watching the ardent concentration of the boys' faces. He couldn't dismiss from his mind the grey, staring face of the girl who'd stopped him in the street last week pleading for money to buy a little food.

"The cottages are easily knocked together!" Peter was talking, excitedly. "A large kitchen-living room downstairs . . . at least, I'm *hoping* the chimney won't pose a problem . . . five bedrooms, six maybe at a pinch, upstairs."

Peter had spent two years in a Planning Department so full of querulous protest at the ruthless improvements discussed (they were never put into any shape, merely discussed; there was no money to spare) they'd thought him politically suspect. He'd been severely censured by the Chief Planning Officer himself.

When he'd shouted that it was people, not politics at the heart of his anger, they'd assured him silkily that people were their chief concern also, and turned away to assess the amount of space required for multi-level housing beside the railway.

". . . the little dairy's already there at the back, and as many outbuildings as we shall need, to get started at least." He went on, ticking items off on his fingers and even Olivia found the electricity of his eagerness lift her heart above its persistent, dragging weight. Her smile never wavered.

"More drinks, Leo," she mouthed silently, so as not to interrupt the welcome flow of future planning.

Corin returned from the village. He'd stayed on at home although his mother had implied there was nothing he could do, because he was curious to see more of Chloe's companions. He took over the pouring of drinks from his father and helped himself generously to whisky. As so often, in harsh periods, drink was obscenely plentiful. He'd already treated Crozier, the kennelman, in the Ploughman's Arms.

Out of an impulse he'd gone to visit the grave, but having been spied there, the morning had inevitably passed in talk . . . to Mrs. Cross, the post lady, old Ash, who was simple and spent his days on the bridge waving to anyone who passed by, whoever they were. Sometimes strangers, when they'd passed in their cars, had told their children to look away. Now there were few cars.

He'd met Mrs. Inchcape whose bees produced the best honey in the district and swarmed everywhere but in her own garden, though nobody minded since they could claim ownership if they felt like it. Everybody kept a skep in case. He hadn't avoided Mrs. Drummond who ran the sweetshop and newsagents and was a relentless authority on world affairs. She was the only one really confronted with the outside world as it stared up at her in all its black wickedness, from her counter. She'd run out with a bar of chocolate for his mother.

Corin listened gravely to their plans to start digging that very afternoon.

"It's a bit late for sowing," he said.

"Not *too* late." Chloe came and sat on the arm of his chair.

"You've got Finals next week."

"Oh, that'll soon be over." She waved the ordeal away.

"What'll you do for money?"

With a flutter of uncertainty, Chloe glanced at her parents. "Oh well," she mused, "I've got my twenty-first cheque still . . ." She paused to assess their reaction. "And everyone else has been earning, *saving*." She stressed the word as if thrift might persuade doubters of their seriousness. "Between us we can put nearly a thousand together."

"How many of you?"

"Six. Well, six to start with."

"Goodness!" cried Olivia, growing uneasy again. "It makes me quite nostalgic!" Her nostalgia was ambivalent. She and her mother had been turned out of their cottage when the land workers had come to Wickford. "Do you remember, Leo, the war effort? Now," she pressed, "tell me who the others are."

"There's Sarah, who's a potter and clever at that sort of thing," Chloe began, "weaving, sewing and such-like and Mab, who teaches what they call home economics." She gave a snort of mirth. "And Joe, who's been running a magazine . . . well, six and a half really. Sarah has a baby. A very *nice* baby . . ."

"Oh yes," said Olivia dangerously. She darted a look towards Andrew and Peter to see if either of them laid claim to it. It was, she supposed, Joe's. "How lovely," she said. "A baby." Questions beat against the walls of her mind like moths, rising above the slab of depression. "I'm sure it must be time for lunch," she said.

She led the way into the dining room where Mrs. Baldwin was lifting a steaming, golden-crusted pie on to the table.

"Mmm," breathed Andrew, the nose of his pale, peaky face leading him on like a hound. *"Meat!"*

The food tasted dry and unpalatable to Olivia who fiddled with it, endeavouring to keep her tone bright. The idea of the baby, fatherless, possibly, had darkened her resolve to be agreeable. She could sense only trouble.

The boys ate hungrily, like children.

"How long do you suppose you'll need to take cover?" enquired Corin after a while, watching them.

"Take cover?" Peter looked up at him questioningly.

"Or do you take the apocalyptic view?"

"I don't get you."

"Is this, I mean, the end of the world as you see it, or will you be packing your bags and moving on after it all blows over?" Corin regarded Peter quizzically.

"Oh, Mrs. Mathison, your little boy's a real trouble maker," said Chloe in a silly voice, to cover her embarrassment.

"It's all right." Peter put his fork down and smiled at Corin. "I don't have any visionary powers," he said, almost apologetically. "But just using plain common sense, I'd say it's neither the end of the world nor a temporary problem."

"Panic," said Corin, "that's all it is. All you need is nerve, ride the storm, eh, Dad?"

"Things do tend to resolve themselves, certainly."

Andrew broke in, as quirky and alert as a bantam. "It's a practical matter," he said. "Not a moral or political one, not primarily, though you *can* look at it that way if you like..."

"Chloe does."

"Oh, I know *Chloe* does. I'm more interested in the practical side and looked at *practically*, there's no chance of a return to the kind of prosperity there was in the sixties. The kind I grew up with. No way."

"Yes, but it *is* political." Peter put the end of his fork into the pale halo of hair to scratch. "It *is*. The old parliamentary democracy was bound up with the old industrialism. It worked pretty peacefully as long as the mills ground on and it's only because people assume things'll come right—they'll get the spanner out of the works as it were—that they put up with the shit-awful system of government we've got now. Assuming things'll come right, they're prepared to. The question is," and he found a specially sweet scratching, "what if it doesn't come right, what do you do with this government then? You're stuck with it."

"Nonsense," asserted Corin. "People aren't such fools as you take them for. Nor such puppets. Your decision may be to run for cover, but there's plenty more putting their ingenuity to good use. You know," he ran his tongue over a thread of meat between his teeth and settled himself more comfortably, "the kind of authoritarianism *I* can't stand," he mused, with oblique reference to the government, "is the kind that wants to limit human genius, limit the brain, say things can't be done. Seems so perverse. No," he raised a hand, "don't throw the nuclear bomb at me, I know not everything we've done has been perfect, but the brain's capable of alteration, correction, capable of mastering new situations..."

"Things do have a way of working themselves out," repeated Leo desperately. He thought of starvation.

"Anyway," Corin continued, "how long, do you suppose?"

"It's not just a matter of knowledge," it was Chloe now, boiling with rage, "but how it's used. With pride? Or with humility? There *are* no perfect schemes, can't you see that? Man *isn't* perfect, that's the most important thing in all the world to know. If you know that, you know you can't impose blanket solutions. Man *is* imperfect... less than God and liable to be wrong..."

Corin laughed out loud. "Well done, Chloe," he cried affectionately. "You've learnt to admit you could be just a teeny, weeny, little tiny bit wrong."

His sister hurled half a loaf of bread at him shouting: "If *we're* wrong, at least we'll do a bloody sight less harm than your lot!"

The loaf missed Corin and landed with stunning accuracy in a trembling, fluted raspberry mousse on the side table behind him. Fragments of pink fluff flew through the air and stuck to the silky, gold wall covering, a gilt mirror and two Dutch flower paintings.

Olivia gave a faint moan, pressed her napkin to her lips and reached out a hand for Leo. "My pictures!" she cried.

"No harm done," soothed Leo, quickly getting to his feet and dabbing at the damage. "Mrs. Baldwin's mousse was always very light."

"*Children!*" exclaimed Olivia.

But Corin was weak with laughter and Chloe was on her feet screaming at him.

"My God, Corin!" she yelled. "What in hell's name has all your marvellous expertise done! Where's it got us?" She gripped the edge of the table as though testing it before vaulting. "Filth! Starvation! That's what it's done for us... destruction... Aberfan! *That*... Oh, stop laughing, you sod, and listen to me!" In frustration she turned to Peter. "He won't listen to me!" she cried, wringing her hands, and then turning again to her brother. "What's so marvellous then about your rational world? The trouble with the *rational*," (she stressed the word contemptuously) "is that it can't take the emotional into its calculations, it can't accommodate the human, it can only make places unfit, in the end, for human habitation. Oh, *Corin*!" And her hair swung like the impatient silk of a horse, "You frighten me!"

"Don't trouble yourself..."

"And the others. So many like you ... believing in magic. Calling it *reason*! It's not reason, it's superstitious faith in yourselves—because you're all you've got left to believe in and you're wrong, wrong, wrong!" She was very close to tears.

"Oh pull yourself together." Corin had ceased laughing. He was simply irritable. "What about this God of yours?" he said rudely, "He's a pretty dab hand at disaster. Fairly hot on destruction and disease. Nothing He likes better than a good, old-fashioned tidal wave or two. Don't talk to *me* about wonderland, darling."

She was white with anger. She walked round the table and this time, to be sure of her target, stood in front of him and brought her hand crashing down on his face.

There was a crack like an iceberg being struck. Then a long silence.

It was Olivia who moved first, but Corin who spoke. "Living in peace and harmony, eh?" he sneered. "I give your commune one month." And swiftly he rose, and left the room.

"Go after him, Chloe."

Leo was too late. She had already gone.

"Well!" Olivia released the knuckles of her right hand from her cheek and poured herself a glass of water. She raised it and smiled tightly round at the others. "A rather difficult few days, I'm sure you'll understand. Poor Chloe."

She had been taken aback by Corin's venom. At the same time, she'd found herself in sympathy with him. It made her angry to hear human effort, human aspiration so wilfully dismissed. It reflected on her. As though her whole way of life were under attack.

How dare they, if they considered comfort (that had been worked for) was somehow immoral, how *dare* they come here begging for things, eating her food, drinking her drink. To say it was built (as one of them had, earlier, before Corin arrived), to say it was built on totally false foundations was insufferably insolent.

"Please pour the boys another glass of wine," she urged Leo, "I'm sure they need it."

She smiled at them over the rim of her own glass. "Families!" she lamented lightly. "Still . . ." She bent her profile towards them as a sudden pain burnt through her. Not a bodily pain.

There were murmurings, the touch of glass on glass.

"My mother was buried yesterday," she said tautly, not looking at them. "Perhaps you know."

She heard their ugly, inelegant mutterings. She heard too, with absolute clarity as though a speaker, having overcome its technical troubles suddenly blared forth, the words of the psalm that had been spoken at the graveside.

"The days of man are but as grass; for he flourisheth as a flower of the field. For as soon as the wind goeth over it, it is gone: and the place thereof shall know it no more . . ."

(It was then she had stepped forward and cast a handful of soil on the coffin.)

The wail of terror which had risen in her and been held in her throat until she feared it would force itself upwards and out of her eyes and skull, rose now, thrust brutally against her temples.

The room darkened. Reddened.

To save herself before it went quite black she heard herself say calmly, "Forgive me, there's some writing I must go and do. Please excuse me."

And she walked (she thought, steadily) from the room.

Chloe sat on the edge of Corin's bed. Her brother lay fully stretched, arms folded behind his head, eyes screwed up against the smoke that spiralled from a cigarette held precariously between his lips. One side of his face bore the scarlet print of her hand.

Abjectly, she pleated and re-pleated the snowy folds of her dress. "*Horrible* of me . . ." she muttered and gazed up out of the high dormer window at the translucent bough of beech leaves that dipped into sight and out again.

"Forget it."

"But it's the sort of thing . . ."

"*Forget* it!"

"The sort of thing that's against everything . . ."

"You believe?"

"Yes."

Corin gave a cold laugh. "You're human," he said.

"That's what I mean." Chloe tucked up her feet on the edge of the bed and buried her head in her knees. "I should never have told you," she said in a muffled voice.

"Oh don't *fuss*."

She meant about God. Chloe was newly returned to God, so surprised and bewildered by herself she'd told nobody. Except Corin, yesterday. The words of the service, which had seemed to her so freshly true, so reaching out in their relevance from the old mysteries, they had prompted her to tell him. It made her all the more ashamed of her anger now. It was precisely the kind of anger she saw spreading in silvery, mercurial threads throughout the world. A poisoned fury.

"I'm sure He'll forgive you," said Corin ironically, and she restrained a further burst of indignation.

"I don't see Him in a personal sort of way," she said quietly.

"The vicar wouldn't like that."

"I know. I once heard him say you can't pray to electricity," she laughed more cheerfully, "and yet, I suppose that's what I do."

She found praying difficult. It was only one mad step away from speaking to oneself.

How could you pray if you believed that God was not a thing with ears but an energy that created and sustained all living things? An energy whose complexity and steadiness and richness and order could be reproduced in men if they, observing the patterns of natural existence, perceived the principles of modesty and fellowship invested in them and drew those principles into their own moral philosophies. *The days of man are but as grass* . . . Grass. But how did you pray to the energy of grass? Or frost? Or dung?

"I shouldn't have hit you," she said for the third time.

"All *right*."

They remained as they were without speaking for a while, only the soft soughing of the branches disturbing their quietness.

"Why did you go to the grave?"

Corin took the cigarette out of his mouth and stubbed it out in a tin lid. "I don't know. Curiosity."

"Well?"

"It looked very . . . *ordinary*. Wait till they get a headstone though. Just wait."

"Mm."

"The flowers were dying . . ."

(*. . . he flourisheth as a flower of the field . . .*)

"There's a whole heap of rotting flowers behind the church. Compost with labels attached. Always in our Thoughts. In everlasting remembrance of Harry."

"Hopeless."

"Will you miss her?"

"Who, Gran?"

"Yes."

"In a way, yes. Except I don't think when we grew up she was very interested in us. She preferred Amy."

"That's because she could always manipulate us as children to annoy mother. Give us sweets when they weren't allowed. Tell us we could stay up and watch her telly when we were supposed to be in bed."

They laughed.

"You *must* stop mother talking about her hard times. I could see those two looking thoroughly cynical before lunch when she dragged it all up again."

"Andrew and Pete?"

"Ahuh. I must say for you, Chloe, they're an improvement on some of the things you've brought home. Did you see mama's nostrils quivering over their naturally ungroomed appearance?"

"That doesn't mean anything."

"I shouldn't be too sure."

"They're very fine people. They know what they're doing."

"Well hopefully they won't run away from cows or spy out the territory through binoculars to see if there are savage insects about, like your last little friend — Alastair, was it?"

"Poor Alastair, he'd never been anywhere more rural than Regent's Park." She giggled suddenly, "It was a bit unfortunate that Clover kicked him."

"And the doves shat on his glasses."

They both collapsed into giggles, curling up and squeaking helplessly like small children. Chloe nuzzled her head into her brother's shoulder and shook weakly until the laughter subsided. It was better now. She relaxed and lay across his chest looking at the ceiling. "Hey," she said, her mouth still twitching, "I love you really, you bum. It's just that you've got it all wrong."

He hurled her off him on to the floor and wriggled his toes in her ribs starting the watery spiral of laughter off all over again.

From the floor beneath rose the pounding sound of the typewriter.

4

"THE ONLY TIME SHE EVER ACCEPTED WHAT, WITH THE greatest distaste, she called charity, was one deep winter when I, at the age of twelve, had finally worn through my much cobbled shoes.

"Keeping me away from school was torment for her since she placed the very highest value on my education, modest as it was. But there was no alternative. Until Friday afternoon, when a new pile of sewing and payment for the preceding week would arrive together, there was simply no means of providing any adequate protection for my feet.

"But the enormous, chauffeur-driven, maroon and black car drew up at our door on the Thursday. My mother sitting as usual beside the window, leaped, startled from her chair, pulling at her apron and urging me to go and brush my hair yet again that morning. Obedient, and puzzled by her agitation, I did as I was told. When she opened the door she pushed me behind her, but peeping, I saw a figure that seemed to me then like a fugitive Russian princess.

"I was enthralled by Lady Eastholme's winter beauty. The glowing pink and white skin of her face was framed by glossy furs. She stood there for a moment, outlined in the doorway against a landscape of snowy larches. I heard her explaining that because of a severe outbreak of influenza on the estate a number of people were having trouble collecting their milk and firewood and she had come to check for herself. I saw her eyes travel to my stockinged feet, felt my mother tug at me, understood, with the curious instinct children have that she'd known I was absent from school and that she'd come to satisfy herself as to the reasons for it. To this day, I don't know quite how the matter of my shoes was raised. All I recall is the burning and trembling of my mother beside me, and, later in the day, the arrival, in a biscuit-coloured box, of a shiny black pair of button-over shoes, wrapped and stuffed with tissue paper, completely unworn. They were the most prized and beautiful shoes I had ever had, utterly impractical for the mile and a half tramp to school, but *beautiful* . . ."

After the first desperate spasm of writing, Olivia's fingers began to move more erratically over the keys. A brief account of school life, an affectionate summary of her mother's educational ambitions for her and then a slowing of effort as the muscles of her memory resisted the pressure she was forcing on them. Impatiently, she got up from her desk and walked, with short unrhythmic steps from one object to another, a hand fiercely pressed to her forehead, as though she were trying to squeeze events out of it.

Stopping in front of the photograph, she stared at her mother's face, willing something out of the arrestingly dignified expression.

She had been caught leaning a little forward, an alertness about the eyes and brows as though she were about to speak, about to address a question or comment to the photographer himself, but had been prevented by swift action of the shutter. It had never struck Olivia before, this sense of speech being suddenly blocked. She'd always found the photograph an unusually vivid pose. In spite of the formally seated arrangement of the two women, it was precisely that sense of movement towards the camera that had freed it of a stuffy self-consciousness. But *now*, all she could see was the unspeaking moment. She turned away, her eye catching Ursula Castlemaine's familiar sentences, which seemed by contrast, loudly over-confident.

". . . The first task in my opinion, is the selection of one's Heroine, most particularly, the selection of a Name (ideally, it should conclude with an 'a', there being no more feminine ending in all Language).

"Without first securing a Name, it is quite impossible to establish Character. The one flows quite simply from the other though I am aware that this is not a respectable literary view to hold.

"Character is not a fixed quality, but a tender, growing plant which flourishes according to the climate of Circumstance. No Enemy of either Accident or Coincidence—both of which are more common to Life than Rational Persons care to believe, and are therefore perfectly proper to the Plot—the Circumstance I consider generally appropriate to the development of the Romantic heroine is one in which Adversity is triumphantly overcome..."

It still made her smile. With a sigh, she settled back to her desk, scratching out a previous sentence and starting it again.

"She had wanted me to stay at school until I was sixteen, completing my Matriculation, although I realised that each further year I spent at school cost her dearly in terms of comfort. Nevertheless it was her passionate wish that I should set out in the world with some kind of qualification. 'In the end it helps both of us,' she insisted whenever I tried to protest.

"And protest I did. For these were the war years. I was fourteen when war was declared. And although we lived, unlike so many wretched people in the major cities, without much visible sign of the battle itself, *all* our futures seemed to hang in question. All of us longed to do something of direct help and usefulness. There was talk at one time of Wickford being used as a girl's boarding school, then as a convalescent home, though ultimately (as I shall have reason to write later) a large country house some eight miles away, near the country town of Anstead was chosen as a home for wounded flying and naval officers. But talk of it crystallised my own ambitions. I wanted to nurse and begged my mother to let me leave school. It was the only time in our lives I believe we came close to squabbling. But she was quite indomitable. I was to remain at school until my exams were over.

"In the end, because my desire to help the war effort by nursing conflicted with my equally strong desire to start earning a decent salary as soon as possible and relieve my mother of her long burden, I took a short secretarial course..."

Again, she ceased typing. The close-packed events of the time ran together in a sudden blur, dissolving and re-emerging in disordered fashion. She had touched upon a point of time when (as now) confusion grew on a dull bed of anguish.

Through the window, beyond the old walled garden, she could see a group of people walking up the sandy track that led between the hills and over the ridge to Sheep Cottages. Chloe's flowing white dress distinguished the group for her She watched them until they disappeared between the high tangle of flowering hedgerow, then turned back to her typewriter.

"Our situation was exacerbated by having to move from the cottage at Wickford. In 1942, the Eastholmes' land was taken over by the War Ag. (the County War Agricultural Executive Committee as its full title was) and all the grassland in the park was ploughed up. It broke my heart to see so many of the fine old oaks cut down, but at least we were able to think of it as a tragedy that had to be borne if our country were to be saved. Far harder to bear from both an emotional and a practical point of view, was the loss of our home. A group of conscientious objectors, working on the land, was to be billeted there. With what tears..."

Even now she found her heart shrink small and black. She saw the fixed, suffering lines of her mother's face as she folded and packed, emptying drawer after drawer. She could feel now, the December iciness of that small fireless room, visualise the small trails of vapour that came from breath expended in effort, not speech. Silently, heavy with foreboding, they'd unhooked pictures and curtains, wrapped newspaper around pieces of crockery, put small scraps of food in greaseproof paper, rolled the ticking-covered mattresses and tied them with string. Never speaking, never daring to. Her mother refusing to look at her, simply dismantling their old life as speedily as she could.

The old van which they used for carrying hay bales and odd bits of machinery went, bumping arthritically, up the sandy track over the hill, a cloud of black smoke tethered behind it.

Olivia found that she was trembling.

"Well!" said Mrs. Drummond (who was related by marriage to Colonel Doggart's housekeeper). "Well I never!" she repeated, leaning over the newspapers on the counter. "Peggy Plumb, eh? Just fancy!"

The foal's head was thrust thirstily under the mare's belly.

He sucked, then turned to look at her, bright and suspicious. His mother nuzzled him reassuringly and Olivia took a step forward, arms cradled outwards.

When she closed her arms around his chest and rump, he erupted backwards in alarm, but she kept a firm hold and pressed herself slightly against his quarters to prevent his falling over backwards. The first move having failed, he tried two plunges forward, squealing excitedly. But again he was held. He could feel the calm encirclement. He could feel the steady heave and fall of his mother's flank. Shuffling a little closer to the milky smell of the mare, he allowed himself to go still.

Olivia felt the tension ebb and after a few seconds let him go with her left arm, reaching her hand slowly up to his withers and scratching him gently. His tiny neck arched with pleasure, then feeling himself free, he scuttered round the front of the mare to the far side, away from the stranger.

"He's a good little colt foal," observed Barber, who'd been watching from the door. "A real good 'un, with a nice pair of hocks on him."

"Yes."

"You did well," he said. "We might've lost 'un."

It was praise indeed. Olivia nodded gratefully. "We'll put him out tomorrow."

"If 'tis fine, yes," said Barber looking up at the high cirrhus-strewn blue.

She felt better. "About ten then tomorrow," she said. "When the dew's dried off," and whistling to Mince, she set off along the track towards Sheep Cottages.

After it left the course of the stream, it was a steep climb uphill. She stopped half-way and looked back at the house. From here, you could see the foamy white blossom of the walled garden, one corner of it blue where the shadow of the house fell across it. A mile southwards, between lower folds in the hills, rose the tall fifteenth-century tower of the church.

Her breathing easier, she resumed the climb between deepening banks as the old road sank into the hill. The air was thick with the crushed scent of wild garlic which spread lusciously up the bank, almost concealing the entrances to the badger set. Overhead, the may, now in full white flower, met and dimmed the sunlight. Just over the top of the hill, the track divided, one fork running north, to the cottages, the other descending the hill and curving south through another narrow valley until it joined up with the road that ran past the front of Clouds. She walked northward, the track no more than a broad ledge above the valley, Mince running on ahead. Below her, on either side of the hills, were ancient ridges, the outlines of Celtic fields. Here and there bright green fronds of bracken burst through the old brown growth. Rooks dipped and flew below her, then rose again to the row of elms on the far hillside.

Mince heard the others before she did and bounded off out of sight around a curve of the hill. When she arrived, she was surprised to see two blue and orange tents erected in the field. They had a purposeful air, she thought. Walking past them she made her way into the yard and heard voices coming from within the cottages. They looked impossibly dilapidated. Windows and doors were broken or hanging from their frames, the roof had collapsed at one end, but the local stone – a warm, honey-coloured stone, of which the cottages were built – looked strong and good.

"Hi!" A head poked out from an upper floor window. It was Andrew's wispy, sandy head.

"Are you coming up?" he said.

"Is it safe?"

"Just about. I'll give you a hand." And he disappeared.

She pushed inside and was overcome by the dank smell of old animal habitation and damp plaster. Yellowed newspapers littered the stone-flagged floor and a torrent of soot had poured down the chimney into the wide hearth. She realised there was a bread oven within the chimney which she'd never noticed before.

"It's O.K., isn't it?" cried Andrew eagerly as he stepped gingerly over a few missing stairs.

"It rather depends what you're looking for," she answered non-committally, "I don't think I'll venture upstairs, thank you."

"Oh come on, it's all right. I'll hold your hand!"

"Thank you, but no." She shook her head courteously, and looked around again. "It looks as though sheep really have been living here."

"Yes," said Andrew, a little dampened.

Chloe's head appeared at the top of the stairs. "Can you *see* the possibilities?" she called.

"I can see possibilities costing several thousand pounds," she replied. The idea of Andrew holding her hand annoyed her.

"You won't put us off," said Chloe and disappeared from view.

Some banging upstairs brought a fine spray of plaster dust down. Olivia choked.

"I'll make you a cup of tea if you like," said Andrew hopefully and, taking her arm, he drew her outside. "I'll be back in a minute." He raced off towards the field where the tents were.

She explored the yard which had become a dumping ground for any severed or disused piece of machinery in the area, and tripping over a chain harrow, peered into the outbuildings on the side opposite the cottages. There was room to milk four cows, a loose box with a loft overhead, though there was no connecting ladder any longer, and a small barn with a great deal of daylight visible through the rafters, In here was the broken tub of an old cider press, rusted scythes and billhooks, another harrow of a different, diamond pattern and a complete but cracked and mouldering set of harness. In the dry corner someone had stacked bags of fertiliser. Astonishingly, they'd not been stolen.

On the far side, behind the barn, the stream bordered (and then ran through) a small orchard full of old unpruned apple trees, a few dead, but most of them still yielding a surprising amount of blossom. Their twisted trunks were drowning in cow parsley, dock and nettle.

On the other side of the house, the side you approached first, was another overgrown patch, once a vegetable garden. A few bean poles remained standing, and a sturdy crop of rhubarb added its great leaves to the general growth. But mostly it was overcome with couch grass and tendrils of bindweed.

The field in which the tents poked such jaunty orange cones above the long grasses, was in slightly better shape. She could see Andrew there, just the top of his head. He must be kneeling down among the white and purple clover. Walking towards him, a dab of yellow caught her eye and bending down she found one, then several, yellow cowslips. "They're getting quite rare now," she called delightedly to Andrew and waded closer to him.

"That's nice," he said, smiling up at her, pleased to see her there. "Kettle's boiling."

"This was grazed the year before last." She glanced round at the field. "But you can see where the ragwort's taken hold. And the docks are bad."

He nodded, smiling still. He was such a small, frail creature, curiously elfin with those fleeing curls.

"Isn't the view marvellous!" he said, making her look out across the dip of the valley. Beyond the lowest slope of the hills to the north she could see the great Vale of Whitmore spread out in the sunlight, its wide, shallow bowl melting at the furthest edge into another range of hills. The vale itself was dotted by the strange magical hummocks, tufted with trees, that once—so it was said—raised temples above water. "Yes," she said, "I'd forgotten it was so high up here."

"Don't you come up here then?" He poured steaming water into a large red, enamel pot.

"Not often. You can see nearly forty miles on a clear day."

"It's got everything we need." Sitting back on his heels he drew in his breath pleasurably. "Everything."

She felt resentful. The lowering sun fell warmly on the golden stone of the buildings. They were protected from the north by the remaining rise of the hill, well clad with hazel and, further up, Scots pine. (People would talk, attempt to wound.)

"Tea?" He stretched out a mug towards her. It was chipped and grubby. "You can sit down," he said, talking to her as though she were a child, patting a rug he had put on the grass.

Chloe and Peter came running towards them, whooping. "Great!" they chorused together. "Tea!"

"We'll start digging after. Want to help?"

Olivia looked at her daughter with gently exaggerated scorn. "Really, darling!" she said.

"Corin brought all the tools up in the van—*he's* going to help. He's gone for a walk."

"*Whose* tools?"

"Well, yours— you don't need them at the moment. You, *personally*, don't need them at all, let's face it. I asked Barber . . . he didn't mind. Any biscuits or anything?"

Olivia wished irritably, that Chloe would stop making it sound as though she, Olivia, were the only one with any objections. She did not feel *mistress* of the situation. Everything about herself felt awkward—the way she sat now, on the rug, legs neither stretched out nor bent. Fidgeting. The way her hair blew across her eyes, cutting her off from a clear view of things. The way it caught on her glossy lipsticked mouth. The sting of gnats on her scalp. The tickling of grasses. This was not how she liked things. She liked to be in control.

The tea was heavily sugared. She sipped it gingerly and looked at Andrew's little white hands taking a biscuit. (In Barber's thick fingers, or Leo's even, a biscuit looked delicate and difficult to handle.) She knew they wouldn't be able to cope and longed cruelly, to tell them so.

"I can't think why Leo didn't do it up and sell it as a holiday home," she remarked. "That sort of thing was fetching the most tremendous price four years ago."

"Good thing for us he didn't." Chloe tossed back her gleaming hair and brushed crumbs from her mouth with the back of her hand.

"Anyway, the bottom has fallen out of the market," said Peter.

"Nonsense."

"Nobody's got the money any more. They can't get mortgages."

"Oh, it'll pass," Olivia said, "it's bound to." Chloe gave her a quizzical look. "You all *enjoy* being so gloomy!"

They ignored her and gulped their tea down, anxious to get back to work.

She wandered after them, Mince trailing along behind pretending to look for rabbits, but he was too ponderous to catch any.

As they thrust their forks into the recalcitrant earth, they heaved and gasped, pulling hard to release the prongs from the deep bed of couch grass. Again and again, they thrust and pulled, making small impression on the securely rooted weeds.

"Hey look!" Peter brought up a lone potato plant and bent down to scrabble the small brown tubers free of the soil. He held them out in the palm of his hand, four pale brown things like pebbles. "That's encouraging," he grinned.

Corin wandered up the hill and laconically joined in the work, more interested in examining odd fragments of glass and pot he found in the turned soil. "This is two weeks' hard labour," he complained.

Chloe gave up, her freckled face scarlet and glistening with effort. "Phew!" she heaved, leaning against the wall beside Olivia.

"What you need is a rotavator."

"No thanks. Absolutely not."

"Why ever not? This digging's absurd."

"Technology."

"What do you mean?"

Chloe shrugged sulkily.

"That's a bit purist of you, darling. You haven't the time to be purist—seeds should have gone in long ago. With Finals next week—shouldn't you be doing *that* sort of work by the way?— it'll be June before you get anything in. You *need* a rotavator."

"What sort of things do you suggest we plant?"

"Oh heavens, I don't know. Ask Barber."

"Yes you do know," argued Chloe, passing a grubby arm across her forehead to keep the hair from her face. "You may not have actually dug and hoed for years, but you do know."

"Oh, there are all *sorts* of different varieties nowadays. Truly, I'm not up to date. Anyway, you need a rotavator."

"I've *told* you . . ."

"Well, it's just silly, darling, not all technology's harmful. You'll be telling me nobody should use the Pill next because it's techno-whatever." She didn't know why she'd said that. She didn't want to know. Didn't want to hear.

"I don't..."

"That's all right, darling, I wasn't questioning your..." She thought of spongy internal organs, blood and tubes. She didn't want to know about her daughter's insides. Sucking noises. Warm smells.

"I'm only telling you."

"All *right*. Thank you, darling. It's none of my business, I know. Look..." She swerved. "There are some bedding plants in the greenhouse still, lettuces, beans and things, why don't you have a look in there?"

"*Great* idea! Good, yes!" Chloe started forward eagerly from the wall.

"I still maintain you'd help yourself enormously by using a rotavator," Olivia called after her daughter who had bounded towards the others.

But they just smiled at her politely, taking no notice.

A few minutes later, she pleaded sweetly with Corin to drive her home in the truck.

Later, at bed time, Olivia sat before her mirror, rubbing garlic cream into her face. Her hair was coiled into metal clips.

"Nice to get right through a meal without incident tonight," commented Leo, pulling his tie free of its knot. "Did you get those boys the blankets they needed?"

"Yes." She smoothed Vaseline on her thin brows. "Delilah was in the airing cupboard with a new batch of kittens, I wondered where she'd got to." She massaged her forehead in small circles with her finger tips. "How many more things will those children be demanding, do you suppose?"

"Oh they need quite a bit to get going. We can provide most of it though." Deliberately, he kept his voice casual, sitting down to pull off his socks and keeping a wary eye on her reflection. She creamed away.

"Four kittens," she said. "Delilah's *such* a beauty... my best beloved." She moved her attention to the fine skin around her eyes. "Are they planning to stay next week when Chloe goes back?"

"I imagine so, well . . . yes, that's what I gather."

"Mm."

"Why don't you want them?"

She opened one eye. "I've told you. And Corin said Mrs. Drummond already knows they're there. Once *she* gets going . . ."

"Oh, it'll pass." He turned his back to her to put on his pyjama trousers.

"And I worry about Chloe . . . what's going on? I mean, presumably one of them's her boy friend, though I can't tell *which* one . . . perhaps it's both . . . perhaps it's this other one, Joe, was it . . . Joe, perhaps it's him and he's already the father of a baby belonging to some other girl that's coming. I mean, it's all so untidy and horrible. Chloe could get hurt."

"Why don't you ask her which one's hers? I must say it didn't occur to me that either of them were. They just seem very friendly together."

"How *can* you ask? They think all that sort of thing is so prying and old-fashioned and anyway, if I did ask she'd treat me to a lecture or something. Of *course* I can't ask!" She sat back and looked at her face, gleaming and bald. It sat in the neck of her maribou-edged negligée like a vulture's. Satisfied, she rose and padded over to her bed as Leo slumped into his.

"And quite apart from anything else," she went on with true concern, "it's just a fatuous exercise. I mean, there they are with a crumbling ruin, an overgrown jungle to deal with—fondly imagining they can turn it into a self-supporting paradise within weeks—I never heard anything so half-baked."

She did a few circling exercises with her neck.

"It's as useful an undertaking as anything else," Leo said firmly. "They'll learn something."

"At whose expense?"

"Oh come now, Olivia, that's not like you." For she was, in her way, generous.

She sat on the edge of the bed, swung her slender pearly legs neatly beneath the gold sheets and lay back in silence awhile.

Leo picked up a book. "I mended the fencing in the nursery paddock this afternoon," he said.

"Why? Why didn't you let Barber do it—that's what he's paid for."

He looked at her profile gleaming in the lamplight. "I like to do it. Anyway, Barber said you wanted to put the foal out there tomorrow." He flattened the pages. "I like doing it," he repeated.

It gave him the energy he needed to face the City, doing things with his hands, out of doors. He needed to do things like that, to feel himself strong still. Skilled. Barber's equal. He could have built a house once, if he'd had to.

"Thank you, darling," she smiled meekly.

He continued to stare downward at the open page, flicking its edge faintly with his thumbnail. "They're staying," he said, "I've told them they can stay. I'd like them to achieve something."

Olivia gazed at him without speaking. It was rare for Leo to oppose her. "I see," she said.

All right, if he wants it. If *he* wants it, *I* want it.

Just like the time he'd decided to work in the City though it meant being away from home all week. He'd made no apologies, voiced no doubts, just said, quite brusquely what he'd decided to do and she'd found she wanted it too.

He could have stayed here, fiddled with things, trimmed hedges, cleared the mill pond, but she didn't want him (any more than he himself wanted) to live on her earnings.

It was nothing to do with money.

"Very well, Leo, darling . . . It's your decision."

She didn't sound as though she'd surrendered, but he knew her. For all her dominance, a lithe and steely quality she had, she also possessed a curious loyalty to him that she welcomed the opportunity to satisfy now and then. He had to give her the opportunity. Because he disliked division he didn't press this aspect of himself often enough, he knew that. He chose rather to spoil her because he loved and admired her and because even now he saw uncertainties in her that moved him.

When he'd switched off the lamp, he leaned back and thought of her as she once was in the early years. Eager to be told and taught. Even when they'd first met and he was the patient convalescing, the one who needed help and guidance, she'd hung back, waiting to catch the colour of his command or longing.

In her severe clothes, she'd had an air of timidity, as if afraid of herself. She'd drawn herself in to her very essence, keeping her movements, her voice small. Her eyes down. Like somebody who feared what effect their contact with the world might have.

She had worn her hair, thick and yellow, like Chloe's, in plaits bound round her head.

As she once was, he thought wistfully. As she still is somewhere, sometimes.

Saturday was squally. Violent bursts of grey weather raced across the sky, replaced only seconds later by blue and burning intervals. One hillside would be caught in a running swathe of sunlight while its neighbour drooped low in a shroud of rain. And then, erratically, the order was reversed.

Olivia was busy. She'd pottered round the greenhouse selecting seedlings in wooden boxes, then gone upstairs to consult her books, make a few notes and several phone calls.

She'd been up long before Chloe, who finally tumbled out of the house wearing somebody else's enormous blue anorak, and went toiling, thick with sleep, up the hill towards Sheep Cottages.

"Darling!" Olivia called from her open window, leaning out as far as she dare above the blowing lilac. "Chloe!"

Her daughter turned and blearily searched out the voice, then waved. Olivia ran downstairs with her lists. "Here you are," she cried, bumping into Chloe in the kitchen. She pushed aside all the congealing breakfast things (Mrs. Baldwin didn't come in at the weekend) and made Chloe sit down with her. "I've noted a few things down," she said. "Cabbages, lettuces, potatoes, artichokes—for the pigs, if you're planning on pigs—sweet corn . . . it's a bit late, but you might be lucky . . . Onion sets I've laid out for you; beans; runner, French, broad—you'll find some plastic cloche things in the workshop—you don't object to plastic do you?" She looked anxious. "Fruit's a bit late, but you'll get some apples off those old trees . . . Strawberry plants, alpines, you can get in, and actually, I noticed some old raspberry canes amongst that jungle yesterday afternoon. They might bear. Now . . . hens. You must have hens. I can spare three of ours and I'm borrowing a cockerel for our broodies. I've asked Gerald Causely to ring his friend Adams about goose eggs—geese will be useful to you keeping the grass down. As for that—"

"I say, Pegs," said Chloe admiringly, "I do believe you're joining the commune!"

"I can't imagine anything more ghastly," her mother replied. "But I can't bear to see you all messing about. Now, what about goats?"

"Yes, we thought about goats. But I'd like a house cow."

"No, darling, a cow would produce far too much milk for you. And eat too much into the bargain. Anyway, goats will tidy things up nicely—I've rung the man at the wood yard about that—he keeps goats."

"Steady," cried Chloe, her eyes beginning to open with amusement. "Leave something for *us* to do!"

"There are bound to be rats. You can have two of Delilah's kittens in a few weeks, *darling* Delilah!"

Chloe stood up, gathering the bits of paper together. "Let me show them all this to start with," she grinned. "Thanks Mum!" And she kissed her lightly on the head.

Olivia watched her go filled with torrential excitement. For a second, she enjoyed the idea of being 'modern', and forward looking. Busily, her imagination had re-shaped the community of young people into something austerely dedicated, curiously platonic. She saw the place whitewashed, plain, noble. Certain elements, which didn't quite conform, she laid aside for the moment, concentrating only on the more admirable aspects.

The clouds flew away to the east and sunshine stalked rapidly in their wake, splashing the kitchen with brilliance. Gaily, she pulled on an old mac and went out looking for Barber to give her a hand with the foal.

" 'Tis a bit uncertain," he said looking up at the sky.

"Just for a moment. Just to give him a little air. We'll take them straight back after a bite of grass!"

"If he gets this wind under his tail . . ." he warned, good naturedly.

Together, they ventured out, Barber leading Rosie with a careful eye over his shoulder to see how Olivia coped with the foal. It nosed at the air with astonishment, standing rock still.

She pushed its quarters forward with her right arm, letting it go into her cradling left arm which she held around its small chest. Rosie, suddenly seeing the gap between herself and her baby widen, neighed wildly and demanded all Barber's attention for a moment, But wavering, the foal came closer and all together, in a halting bunch, they edged through the gate into the paddock. After a moment's crooning and scratching, Olivia let the foal go.

He stayed immobile on his tent pole legs for a second, drawing in the sweetness of breeze and herbs, then leapt towards the sky, Finding he touched earth safely, he tried again. And again. Higher and higher. Then he discovered something new. Speed.

His mother swung back and forth in agitation as he tore round her head stretched out, ears flattened. Then he tumbled over and they laughed.

He was up and off again, flying through the buttercups. Rosie, one distraught eye on him, succumbed to a snatch of the cool and luscious grass and ground it between wary pauses.

As they stood watching, a small red truck appeared up the drive. Olivia stepped away from the horses so as not to alarm them and waved, pointing onward up the track to Sheep Cottages. The driver signalled his thanks and accelerated.

She stood looking after the truck, admiring the sparkling new rotavator, bound to its back.

5

MRS. CROSS HAD SPOKEN TO HER UNCLE, BEN PALMER, who had delivered the post before she took over his duties and he, it was true, *did* recall letters addressed to a Miss or Mrs. Plumb, but had always presumed it was one of those nannies or mother's helps or suchlike that had been around the place at the time. It had never troubled him, he said, not being a nosey parker.

This was being discussed now in the churchyard by a group standing near the new grave.

"It's bound to say on the headstone," pointed out Mrs. Cross. "So everyone'll know then."

The women tittered, looking sideways at one another beneath their brown and navy straw hats.

"I don't know what you're going on about," shrugged Josie Adams, who was the youngest of the group and sick of the lot of them. She wrinkled up her big plain face and remarked, sensibly, "It's only a name after all. The way you're going on, you'd think you'd found out a guilty secret."

But they still sniggered behind their gloved hands, "*What* a name!" exclaimed Bessie Penruddock who ran the haberdashery, her face pink with excitement. "It makes you laugh, you must admit!"

"Doesn't make me laugh," said Josie, chewing something. "If you think about it, Bessie Penruddock's a pretty funny name."

"It's all my own though!"

"It's *her* own."

"Not as she admits to." And all the women whose shops and interests had profited from Olivia Bennett gave little murmurs of conspiratorial agreement.

"Here they come!" hissed Olive Palmer. "Always got enough petrol, seemingly." And they turned self-consciously away from the grave as the Mathison family drew up in their Bentley at the church gates.

Leo led the way, Olivia in pearls and black, on his arm. She kept her head down, giving only small smiles to friends and neighbours, dreading the moment she would have to walk past the pyramid of wilting flowers. Her hand gripped tightly into Leo's flesh.

The bells began their single, striking note to hurry them into church and people loosed themselves from gossip to follow behind the Mathisons.

There was a shuffling readiness within the church, a sense of knees being eased, gloves withdrawn. Feet clipped quietly over the old sienna tiles, their heraldic devices almost smoothed away by years of tiptoe.

Gaspingly, Mr. Broderick leaned against the organ. (His need for two pairs of glasses led to strange complications at the keyboard.) He felt a little vicious because the Mathisons had hired another organist for the funeral.

The Mathisons dropped to their knees, all that is, but Olivia who didn't trust her stockings on the hassocks and simply bowed her head. (Stockings were so hard to come by.) Her crushed black velvet hat looked like a sinister rose.

She prayed for her mother's soul. Leo prayed that everything would be all right. Chloe prayed for the gift of prayer and Corin didn't pray at all.

The choir processed down the church, a choir of kindly, ruddy men, of boys whose voices increased the uncertainty of pitch, and small, pretty children with elastic bands and very old pieces of bubble gum hidden in their pockets. Together, on this, the first Sunday after Ascension, they rose and sang, varying their pace considerably to keep up with Mr. Broderick.

The church had been built (at many differing periods) of the same warm stone as the cottages. Its oaken roof was vaulted on the wings of angels. Less conspicuously carved, concealed within the panels by the craftsman who had known people would allow the time to look up and gaze on his work were tiny emblems ... a corn sheaf, a cider barrel, a mouse, a flute and other secret things. Chloe hadn't yet, after years of looking, discovered them all.

To her, it was perfect. Just the smell, of old wood and fumigants and lilies, was enough to make her feel faint. These days she allowed the swooning sense to take hold. She no longer thought it a nonsense or illusion. In fact, although the vocabulary was extravagant, she believed it was nothing less than the transcendental power which Henry Claremont, in his great rich voice, now pleaded should cleanse the thoughts of their hearts. The inspiration of the Holy Spirit.

Her lips chanted the words, each one a new testimony of love ... "We praise thee, we bless thee, we worship thee, we glorify thee, we give thanks to thee for thy great glory, O Lord God, heavenly King, God the Father Almighty ..."

For such a long time she'd fought against this seizing of her spirit, thinking it emotional and false. Unable, in the middle of an academic training when proofs and evidences were demanded of her, to determine any sound cause for this sense of God that filled her as plainly as her own bones.

Then suddenly, she'd let all the rational quibbles go, responding simply to a conviction too clear to be called mystical, and having freed her mind, had seen that the rational objections were booby traps separating her from firm ground. Finding her way through the obstructions had been at first difficult, until she discovered her guide in the *person* of Christ, not in doctrines, not in His teaching specifically, not in any dependence on historicity—it barely mattered whether the documentation were exact—but in His person and life and example.

That moment had come during the Passion at Easter when she, with all the others of the congregation had been forced to say in the words of the printed sheet, "Crucify Him! Crucify Him! Crucify Him!" And she knew then for sure that those words were the lifelong denial she and others so righteously practised. They were all part of the crowd in Jerusalem.

Mr. Thomas creaked respectfully up the aisle to read the lesson, his neck lividly bursting out of a starched white collar. Carefully, he climbed. Carefully he took his glasses out of his top pocket and settled them on his nose, checking to see that the Bible was open at the correct page. Coughed.

"I am the vine, ye are the branches; He that abideth in me, and I in him, the same bringeth forth much fruit; for without me ye can do nothing."

Chloe listened, hungrily.

"This is my commandment, That ye love one another, as I have loved you. Greater love hath no man than this, that a man lay down his life for his friends."

Mr. Thomas bent his head. "Here endeth the first lesson."

Christ on the Cross. So simple. So complex. All things come together in that single loving image the rational called morbid.

As a child it had frightened her, this thorn-crowned, bleeding body suspended over the church like a curse. She'd lacked the experience to understand it. Even now, she lacked it. But once the distortion of educated scorn had been peeled from her eye, she saw the beauty. The true, hard beauty of love in suffering, of sacrifice, austerity, and perhaps, most difficult of all, the beauty of forgiveness.

"And now, our prayers . . ."

The children stirred and settled resignedly.

". . . hear us as we remember those who have died in faith, and grant us with them a share in thy eternal kingdom . . ."

Olivia pressed her knuckles together. The image of her mother, sitting in a corner of the drawing room staring into space, came and went like a blown kite.

She struggled to remember days, moments, situations. Clawed for a moving, speaking image. None came. Only this billowing, fading outline of a woman who was silent, whose eyes reflected clouds. As if the old lady refused to talk.

This then, was death was it? Silence? Death, like a dust sheet being slowly drawn over the furniture of the mind.

"Dear God, *please* . . ." she beseeched, silently. But the waxwork sat in the drawing room chair.

This can't be what most people feel, she thought in panic. This *nothing*. Desperately she tried to imagine into herself the emotions she had imagined for other, imaginary characters. She'd made them fling themselves across graves, seize their hair, made loss tear at them like wolves . . . She plumbed these ersatz emotions into her system, but it was fruitless. Real death was death.

Attempting another course, she plunged back to her infant years, the ones that came up at her most sweetly and this was easier, like slipping through water. The perspectives stood ready waiting for her.

She knelt as she had knelt then, in the little chapel, stealing a look at the profiles. The church smaller, the figures larger. The thickness of her mother's black coat beside her, the pile turning brown with age.

In the pews, at right angles to them, the family group—so positioned it seemed to be they who were worshipped, in their thickly textured fur and velvet. All six children clustered together, the smallest girls close to their mother. At this end, more clearly visible, Piers and Harry, the sons. Harry Eastholme who turned his lowered eyes to look at her over the carved acanthus, and winked slowly.

A stiffness through her mother's arm, the confusion. The hotness of her cheeks.

"Seeing we have a great high priest who has passed into the heavens, Jesus, the Son of God, let us draw near with a true heart, in full assurance of faith, and make our confession to our heavenly Father."

The words, different from those used in her childhood, brought her back into the heart of the service.

Chloe who had sneered at confirmation when she was fourteen, moved her thighs to one side to let the others pass and longingly, watched them gather at the altar rail. Jealously, almost, she followed the movements of dully-shaped, felted figures entitled to feed on Christ and doing so in a routine fashion. She searched their faces as they turned and came quietly back to their faces, hunting for signs of transfiguration, but found none.

Her own face was sheeted with silent tears.

Her parents returned to the pew, Olivia deathly white and drawn. Glancing at her daughter's face, Olivia saw the runnels of weeping and mistaking joy for grief, was more than ever frightened by her own, arid bereavement. She touched Chloe's knee comfortingly as she sank down.

Tomorrow, she reflected, she would be left alone with her sapless sorrow.

Tomorrow, thought Corin. Tomorrow. Back to normal. Commodities. The market, he thought, with a wholesome apprehension of these things. Even the fruity taste of wine in his mouth was appetising, a prelude to more. To good talk. He began to feel amiable.

"Please God," prayed Chloe hopelessly to herself, as Mr. Broderick offered the communicants a reckless musical accompaniment back to their places, "Please God . . ." And it sounded so foolish.

Then she saw that foolishness was an important part of it. One had to be prepared to be taken for a fool. Prayer was a constant renewal of commitment to the original 'foolish' act of faith. And now that she knew faith was no sloppy, unintellectual thing but on the contrary, perhaps the most difficult mental affirmation ever made, she understood that the act of praying was also meant to be difficult. Like standing up before the crowd at Jerusalem. It *had* to be difficult.

"Please God," she tried again, "help me love my mother more. Teach me to be tolerant. Teach me *how* to love. This, thy servant..." Her mind trailed away and then came back again quite specifically. "Please stop me being angry about the rotavator — and angry with Andrew and Peter for being pleased with it. Oh, help me reach my mother."

The murmuring of the priest had ended. The last of the communicants crept back to his place. The music sputtered to an end.

"Together let us say the prayer of dedication."

And fervently, Chloe, still terrified she spoke into silence because she lacked either the gift or goodness to be heard, joined with all the others of the congregation in offering their souls and bodies to be a living sacrifice.

"Please," mouthed Olivia between her soft gloves, "please help me reach my mother."

A new tumult from the organ freed them.

"Come along," said Leo.

Many people came towards them, bringing their condolence and pity like awkwardly shaped packages.

"She was a wonderful old lady," murmured Bessie Penruddock who'd barely spoken to Mrs. Bennett — seeing her chiefly, sucked up into a corner of the big car while someone else came in to buy whatever she needed by way of tape or silks.

(Early judgement had been that Mrs. Bennett was a snob, but they came to see shyness and if it was difficult to like someone who had the greatest difficulty speaking, then, so the general judgement had gone, she deserved warmth and admiration on the basis of her handicraft alone. She won her classes every year at the Flower Show. They were proud to have so skilful a needle in the village.)

"Buried on Ascension Day itself..." breathed Lily Crozier, overcome by the wonder of it. (It had not occurred to Olivia.)

The yews stirred in the churchyard as Henry Claremont came towards them, white robes billowing. He was full of kindness.

"Don't hesitate to call on me for anything," he urged, as they parted. "And good luck with your exams, Chloe, I'll be praying for you!"

As they lingered at the graveside on their way out, Josie Adams tugged at Olivia's arm. "Pardon me," she said. "Those goose eggs you wanted . . . Dad said he'd bring they over this afternoon if that's all right."

"That would be most kind."

"I'll come and collect them on my bike if you'd rather," offered Chloe.

Josie looked at her long dress briefly. " 'Tis all right," she grinned. "I want to come and see what you're doing over the hill there."

Chloe laughed and Olivia threw a long, grim look at Leo.

"About three then?"

"Fine. Yes, three-ish."

Josie left. As she walked down the long sloping path she showed a great deal of strong leg beneath her short skirt.

"Naturally, they're curious . . ." said Leo quickly and good-humouredly. "It's very acceptable that they should be. Very pleasant. As I said, natural." And taking his wife's arm, he reached into his pocket with his right hand, felt about for the car keys and threw them to Corin. "Here!" he called. "You drive!"

6

SHE HAD BEEN RIGHT TO FEAR THEIR GOING.

She stood outside in the chilly early morning sun (it had a neurotic brilliance that promised rain later) and waved goodbye. It was an effort not to gather up the satin robe and stumble after them on her wrecking mules.

She held up her hand, long after they'd gone out of sight; quite still. There were two more hours to be negotiated before either Madge or Mrs. Baldwin arrived. Two hours, more, alone.

The meadows beamed with dew.

The emptiness of the house bellied out at her. No pale blue petals floated to the ground.

Inside it was very still. The flowers stood like florists' victims in their vases. The grandfather clock had stopped again. Walking through the hall and into the drawing room she carefully lowered herself on to the sofa, moving a full, stale ashtray as she did so. She stared at the empty chair opposite.

Without deliberately avoiding it, nobody had sat in Mrs. Bennett's chair since her death. The blue, ruched satin cushion was propped stiffly in the angle of the seat. Within easy reach of the chair, stood the inlaid rosewood sewing table, its many cunning flaps and drawers enigmatically closed. Olivia picked up two empty glasses from the floor and let them dangle slightly in her loose grip, clinking.

She tried to force an image in the chair.

Closing her eyes, she tried again. There was a brief, illusory flash, a dab of flesh tone, but it vanished the moment she opened her eyes. She hadn't dreamed of her mother once in the past week.

The sun held coldly steady in the east, lending the pale blue upholstery a chill and slippery air; she disliked this room in the mornings. Glancing at her watch, Olivia saw that it was a quarter to seven, the time she would normally have risen and prepared tea for her mother. Together they would have heard most of the seven o'clock bulletin, lightly discussed the plans for that day, flickered through the papers, decided what clothes to wear and then—at about eight o'clock—Olivia returned to her own bed with the post so that she could be quite ready for Madge when she arrived at nine. While Madge got on with her part in the correspondence, Olivia dressed. That way, not a tremor of time was wasted.

Time hung on her like webs.

Her eye caught a rose sealed in a glass bubble on the mantelshelf; a gift from an admirer. She gave the glasses in her own hand a reassuring chink and chided herself silently. This would not do. Perhaps Madge was right. Shock. Perhaps shock had this odd effect. Or maybe it was the sleeping pills. She wasn't used to them. They made sleep so thick and heavy that waking was like struggling out of mud. Whatever the cause, this simply wouldn't do.

She tried to think briskly. Quite suddenly, and not without a sense of impertinence, it struck her that she could write rather differently. Her heroines could possess vices. They might steal, murder, seduce. The idea was liberating until she remembered her readers. Well, the change could be *gradual* . . .

And then a further, more dreadful thought pressed forward— that she need not write at all.

No, she responded quickly, her gaze shifting from the chair to the rigid blue drapes of the curtained window, nonsense. She wrote to please a larger public than her mother alone. *Enjoyed* the attention of a larger public.

But the realisation remained that she was free now to write a different kind of book altogether. The knowledge did not come with any clear sense of gladness. Rather, as a challenge that she didn't altogether welcome. For one thing, she wasn't sure she *could* write any 'better' (and that was definitely part of the challenge that presented itself . . . to write within more respectable literary bounds).

She had, she knew, a competence. She was able to meet the relatively modest targets she set herself without strain, but she was also aware, however fiercely she defended her chosen form in public, that her application was without any of the so-called torment that 'artists' allegedly suffered. For a moment she peered out at the gaping prospect art presented and then retreated from the idea. It was absurd even to consider it. She was perfectly well satisfied with what she had, however limited others thought it. Anyway, the only people who actually sneered or teased were her own children (who didn't matter). Serious critics had long ago given up treating her as a joke, perhaps because she was scrupulously careful, unlike others in her trade, to avoid being associated with elixirs of life, or crafty undergarments or creams based on minced pigs' testicles. And being careful about her image, she now considered (reluctantly) that any excursions into the wilder landscapes of art, were not for her.

No, she decided, her gaze returning more boldly to the chair. She would complete the book about her mother, give more of her time to Leo and the children . . . *children!* Hardly children any longer. She would . . . plans, her darting rescuers, flocked into her mind. She would (she got to her feet, braver now, hardly conscious of the desolate sound of her mules flapping on the polished boards) redecorate, plant, shop . . .

Fetching the radio from the kitchen, she carried it upstairs to her bedroom only half-hearing news of further rationing proposals for Europe and the announcement of a provisional Palestinian government as she swiftly dressed, creamed, exercised and composed a letter to Amy in her mind. *Poor* Amy! She could tell her about the kittens and the foal and the baby geese they hoped to have. She would promise a new dress.

Mince padded behind, following Olivia's flurried course with difficulty. Up two stairs, then down. Into this room. Into that. The dog sensed more plainly than she herself, a precarious elation, an unleashing, a trembling that was as much excitement as fear. Things had changed.

Mince, his moist black nose alertly lifted towards his mistress, could trace a new chemical on the air.

"What do you make of that?" Heseltine threw the tapes down on Leo's desk.

He read the news and ran a hand through his hair. "Ye gods!" he muttered. "The whole of the Middle East! The Government's got to do something now hasn't it?"

"What *can* it do?"

Neither man answered. There was no answer.

"It's up to the States," volunteered Heseltine at length. "And Christ knows what they'll try and do. Bloody chaos, eh?"

Leo felt himself sweat. It had always been difficult coming in here on Monday mornings, but once he'd done it with a certain cheerful resignation. Nowadays, Monday mornings were like stepping out of a quiet garden and finding it was on the cliff edge. Below, and all around, the sea boiled.

"You all right, Mathison?"

He forced a sportive laugh, made a light, wiping gesture of face. "As all right as anybody can be!" he cried, hoping his superior would go. "Had a particularly difficult journey this morning."

"Your bloody fault. Shouldn't live so far out."

"My wife's mother died . . ." It was a curiously irrelevant remark. Heseltine puzzled it for a moment, trying to fit it into the preceding pattern of their conversation. "Hm," he said. "Sorry." Privately, he thought Mathison was losing his grip. "You won't forget the Bartlett meeting later today will you?" he reminded him, lifting himself off the edge of Leo's desk.

"Oh, Good Lord, of course not, no. I must check the figures through before then." Leo made some anxious, shuffling movement of the papers in front of him and Heseltine took his cue. "World reserves down to three days," he called over his shoulder, having already looked at the figures.

The phone rang in the outer office, where Leo's secretary sat, a girl with long legs, long hair, long nails and no understanding whatever, thought Leo, of the importance of grasses. When she came in with his papers he longed to explain to her about grass, but her smooth face was as blank and beautiful as a pebble. It would be quite useless.

"The Bartlett figures," she said. "Lovely day."

It was a horrible day. He was sweating because the mild outdoor sunshine, processed through the glass acres of his office window, had reached the temperature at which an egg would fry. Outside and miles below, the traffic growled peevishly.

"Terrible journey," he said.

"Oh dear!" cried the girl solicitously, "I *am* sorry . . ." and she smiled at him without asking what had made it so terrible.

"I'd like you to get a message to my daughter at the Examination Halls . . . get her to ring me here as soon as her paper's over. I'm worried whether she ever got there or not."

"Of course." Again her interest remained wholly unaroused.

He turned over the sheets of paper. Heseltine was right. The world stockpile of wheat was right down. The knot of anxiety tightened by a further twist in his stomach—he was deeply worried that the price he'd stated to Bartlett's (a pet food firm), would turn out to be far below the actual level. (And he'd thought he'd overestimated for safety as it was.) Although he acted only as adviser to this and other companies and the consequences of his advice were not therefore borne directly by him, the mood of the market was such that mistakes of any kind were not ignored. The heads of middle management in particular, were much prized, but soon there would be a shortage even of those, for lopping.

An ambulance tried to terrorise the traffic, screeching and whining at it to get out of the way. Leo took two capsules from his drawer and gulped them down without water.

Unreasonably, he felt angry at finding himself in this situation. Angry that it should have happened—that no rain, no strong new strain of rice or wheat, no large hole in the ground—should have appeared in the right place at the right moment and prevented this mess. And he was angry to find that he was among those considered by many, to be in some way responsible. He didn't feel responsible. He'd done his best (and been well paid for it), but the human race had continued doggedly to expand while the heavens had persistently emptied storm and sunshine on to the earth, against all expectations of the calendar. He felt responsible for neither of these eventualities. The capsules, dissolving slowly in his chest, sent nauseous fumes up the back of his throat and he had to put a hand to his mouth for a moment.

He knew it wasn't market forces. He was a farmer. He knew the importance of proper husbandry. And all right, yes, he knew that the kind of operation he'd cheerfully practised from within this office, was the very thing (in another form) that he'd refused to practise on his own land. It had seemed *right* here. As long as people continued to have food in their mouths, as long as he couldn't run the soil through his own fingers, feeling its injury, the machinery hadn't seemed to matter.

His etiolated secretary advanced over the beige pasture with a number of queries she wanted settled.

"Look," he said to her, nodding across at the maps on the far wall. "You know what those are don't you?"

"Maps of course," she cried prettily.

"Yes, but what sort? What do they show, tell?"

She thought about it, flicking her long hair over one shoulder.

"They're distribution maps," said Leo. "Do you see the yellow bits?"

"Ye-es," she murmured, going closer and studying them with a blind seriousness. "India, Africa and ... ?" She jabbed a finger questioningly at another yellow area.

"Indonesia," sighed Leo.

"Oh, of course. Indonesia."

"They show a proportionate reduction in cereal imports fo the past year. Or, if you prefer to look at it that way, an increased incapacity to pay the price."

"Yes, but they're getting help aren't they," she said comfortably.

He stared at her. *Grasses*, he thought wistfully.

"Do you ever wonder," he asked her eventually, "about us?"

Her normally impassive expression was so jumbled by his question he had to re-phrase it. "About *this* country?" he said.

"Oh yes," she responded eagerly.

"Well?"

"Well I'm on a diet actually at the moment, so it's not too bad."

"No."

"But, obviously, I mean, not everybody's ..."

"On a diet?"

"Well, you know what I mean. No." She had the grace to blush a little. "No, I think we'll be all right in the end."

"I'm sure you're right," he said. And he *was* sure. But the price that would have to be paid—the cost to the conscience—was abominable. This country, the others, clustered together like smiling members of the winning school team ... they'd get by.

His eye slid across the hot space of his office, past the tropical fish tank, the bored assortment of exotic plants, the supple pieces of leather and aluminium furniture and wondered how, politically, the decision to let the yellow areas of the map pale to white, would be expressed.

First would come the blame. The blaming of other countries whose unscrupulous behaviour had brought it about. Then the blaming of things that God was meant to organise. (It would be tasteless to chastise God Himself for the weather and the creation of new life.) And last, the need in times of crisis to look after our own.

"Can we settle these letters now, Mr. Mathison?"

He very nearly asked her what the point was. He could so

easily have walked out then and there. For a long time he looked at her, unconscious of his silence. Food, unlike belief or money, bred few philosophies. It was just the pap that differentiated life from death. Animal pap. Swill.

"All right," he said heavily. No point in walking out. No point in gestures.

"Sit down," he said. Gestures were food for the intellect, not the stomach. There was no moral stand. A single law governed human welfare and it made a comedy of morals ... the merciless ruling of supply and demand; now at its most naked.

"Did you make the call?" he asked.

"The call?"

"To the University Examination Halls?"

"Oh yes. Oh I did that *right* away!" She was pleased with her efficiency, unworried by her ignorance of grasses.

His first duty, Leo thought thickly to himself, *did* lie with his own family. As Heseltine would say, "Charity begins at home."

Corin looked at his watch. "Time for aperitifs," he declared.

Hugh Millar looked at his own watch. "Before half past ten?" he queried. "Besides, you've only just arrived."

"Exactly. Terrible bloody journey. I need a stiff drink."

Hugh laughed, his blond countenance easing. "Well ..." he wavered.

Corin tore a tape out of the machine and, scanning the latest figures, saw no reason to stay in the office. "Come on," he said.

"Shouldn't you be on the floor?"

"Business is hardly brisk." Corin threw the screwed-up piece of paper away. "Come on, old chap, the firm's not going to go bust in your absence."

"I saw your father arrive half an hour ago," Hugh accused, getting to his feet.

"He must have sprinted a shade quicker from the station then." Corin stuck his head into the next door office and yelled something about an urgent appointment to a girl bent over a filing cabinet. "Whatever the crisis," he observed, withdrawing his head again, "I don't think girls should give up shaving their legs. Now, a double brandy, Millar?" And he steered him out of the building taking care to go to a pub some distance away.

"I must say something of the old excitement has crept back into travel," he declared as they entered the Three Tuns and earned a resentful look from the barman who was sitting at a table with a copy of *Fur and Feather*.

"Two double brandies please! Yes, we got here in the end. Got to a station where, thank God, the Amalgamated Bloody-Minded were allowing ten minutes extra for tea break so we were able to cling to their train. And I mean *cling*. Trouble is we seem to have lost my sister."

"I'm afraid you'll have to begin at the beginning," said Hugh mildly. "Do you mean the lovely Chloe?"

"Chloe? Lovely? Funny isn't it? I think of her as a girl who grew too large for gymkhana classes. She's a big girl, my sister."

"Gorgeous."

"Addled, though."

"*Addled?* What do you mean, you lost her?"

The brandies arrived and painstakingly Corin took Hugh over the details of their journey . . . "And when we got back to the car with our pint of juice, she'd disappeared. Like two lemons we hung about for half an hour before we realised she'd left a message scrawled on the boot. 'Course, any girl who'd got her brains together would leave a message in a more convenient place."

"Mightn't we be needed in the shop shortly?" Again Hugh nervously consulted his watch.

"My dear Hugh, there's no point in minding an empty till. Besides you owe a round now."

"You're right, I suppose."

"There's one last opportunity for a killing on the futures market. After that, I'm going to pack it in." Corin signalled to the barman. "Then . . . Canada perhaps?"

"Are you serious?"

"My dear Hugh!" Corin gave a look of wide-eyed astonishment at such a doubt. "I'm a survivor."

"In that case," said Hugh, not believing him, "I'd welcome another opportunity to meet your sister before you go." He found the barman was awaiting some instruction from him. Another customer came furtively in.

"If she turns up somewhere . . . But no," added Corin on second thoughts, "she's gone too silly for you now. She's just ripped the old man off to the tune of six acres and then tells us all to lead a humbler kind of life. She's gone religious."

"Oh Lord," said Hugh gravely.

"There's a lot of it about. That's what we ought to be into really."

"Religion?"

"Not the *word*, the accoutrements, prayer mats . . . meditation pictures, that sort of thing."

Hugh's eyes narrowed, trying to judge his companion's gravity. "You *could* be right," he whistled.

"We could certainly treat ourselves to a business lunch later to help discuss the thing properly."

"Good thinking!" cried Hugh and began to giggle.

The switchboard operator who took the message asking that Miss Chloe Mathison should ring her father when she came out, laughed. "I doubt if Miss Mathison will get in," he mused, looking out of the window.

The crowd swayed and ribboned comfortably enough below. "It's when the pattern breaks up you know there's trouble," observed the experienced operator. "Look, like that!" And there, a small rosette sprang to life, a bursting open of people.

"Daft, I say," said the part-time, married woman. "If they don't want to take exams, they shouldn't come to University. Stands to reason."

"My view exactly. The police have got quite enough to do as it is."

The double-glazing hid the roar.

When the car had run out of petrol earlier that morning and the two men had walked off in opposite directions to try and find some (having driven past three stations with Closed signs outside) Chloe had not at first thought of hitching a lift. Knowing there was to be a boycott staged outside the Halls, she knew also there was no hurry to get there in time to begin her paper at nine. What she hadn't known when she'd left home that morning was which side of the barrier she would stay.

Like the others, she thought exams irrelevant. Like the others, she believed that of all the subjects to be examined the most irrelevant was Anglo-Saxon. Like the others, she had claimed that thirty per cent of one's study time devoted to a dead language was no way to prepare an individual usefully for the community.

But she hadn't, at seven-thirty that morning, when a lorry obligingly slowed, finally made up her mind whether to protest and then go in or to remain outside. All she had agreed to do, was to march with the Women in University lobby, whose survey on the effects of menstruation on examination performance, showed that any test conducted during menstruation was a most unreliable measure of ability and pointed out, in addition, that stress disrupted the normal monthly flow so profoundly, the incidence of menstruation amongst female examinees was thirty-four per cent higher than in any normal group.

But Chloe was not menstruating.

She forced her way to the front of the crowd, ignorant of her own reasons for pressing. Pressing even against the arms of her friends . . . There was Maggie and there, Kathy Rumboldt, her face stripped by disbelief, caught in fragments, like quarters of the moon as the crowd tossed back and forth. "Let me through!" she cried. "Let me through!"

It became plain to the confused young policemen that this was a student genuinely wishing to get into the building — it was obvious from the abuse being hurled at her by the others. They let her through and she burst beyond the barrier, stumbling to her knees then picking herself up to turn, mesmerised, for one last look. She didn't know why she had done it. She saw a head pulled back by its hair at a horrid angle to the spine. Anger that had passed beyond the human. Faces tangled like molecules in furious dance. Jerusalem, she thought fleetingly, and numbly passed inside.

She looked at Bede's account of Caedmon and it seemed primitive and awkward, a pebbly stretch of diphthongs and consonants. All she could manage was a stilted guesswork. Why on earth had she bothered? She looked round at the handful of earnest students, at the invigilator trying to ignore the insect buzz below and thought grimly how much better it would have been to stay outside and claim, like them, that this was a foolish use of time. But even as she gazed at the stony words she suddenly remembered that 'ytemestan' came from 'utera' — outer, last, and her excitement was pierced by the unlocking of language. She picked up her pen and noticed a gleam of spittle on her arm.

When the bell rang for lunch, Amy was the first out of the classroom. Ignoring the sharp voice ordering her to come and put her books away, she ran down the corridor, her hair flying like a bronze pennant.

Densely brown, boiled smells of gravy and custard trailed towards her but she swerved away from them, racing through the sports shed, between long lines of racquets, hockey sticks and cricket bats ... out into the sunlight.

A babble of voices, feet and jostling flesh animated the main building behind her. Quickly she walked across the playing fields heading for the far fringe of the elms. The grass was smoothly shaved of daisies. It had a crunchy spring to it. Purposefully, Amy walked across the centre of the sacred pitch feeling the weight, deep in one pocket of her bottle green skirt, of Shelley's *Selected Poems* and the *Women Only Calorie Calculator*.

Once across the field, she plunged into the trees and down a sudden slope full of difficult bracken and bramble which tore at her hideous clothes. She half-ran, half-slid down the damp, sandy bank, her progress jerked by ground elder and ivy. High above, birds chortled and whooped at the intruder, their wings sounding huge among the leaves.

She found the place she wanted, a winding stream almost hidden by overhanging hazel and thick banks of bluebells. One loop of the stream was wide and still and deep, as though its movement came to a cool pause here. Tall, thin poles of sunlight pierced the leaves, scattering on the water's surface. Clearing a space, she sat down and leaning back against the smooth trunk of a birch, worked out how many calories she managed to avoid by missing lunch.

At least a thousand. At breakfast she'd managed to mess up her cornflakes to make it look as though she'd tried. The tea was thirty calories ... that meant, say, sixty altogether so far, which left her an allowance for the rest of the day of six hundred and forty if she were to stay within her limit. Terrific! That allowed for a doughnut at tea-time which she very badly wanted although there *was* something indefinably vulgar about doughnuts ...

She took out her calculator to see if it mentioned doughnuts. The nearest thing was Bun (sweet). Three hundred and seventy-five. Which left ... two hundred and sixty-five – quite enough for her to get by on at supper time without someone fussing.

Amy wanted the part of Ophelia in the school play this term.

The choice of *Hamlet* had been determined by the emergence of two extremely good fencers in the Sixth Form. Their acting was less distinguished than their fencing which left the field wide open to several ambitious classmates, most of whom were disqualified by being taller than Hamlet and Laertes. A search had started lower down the school. Amy's main rival was Esther MacNally. Esther was catarrhal but much thinner than Amy. At least, it was this that she convinced herself merited the assault on her own body. It was nice to have a reason when so much in her life remained hateful and vague.

She stretched her legs out in front of her, dangling them from the knee over the bank. Her thighs looked squashy, like boiled marrows. They disgusted her. Roughly, she pulled her skirt down and felt in her pocket for Shelley's poems.

So much of the time she wanted to cry. She had wanted to cry before Granny Bennett had died. Now it was worse. Or better, because there was a weak, engulfing cause for crying. She looked for things that would bring it on . . . Small flowers. Buds. The mercury streak of a raindrop across glass. The spitefully softening outline of her own body. She opened her book at 'Alastor'.

"Hither the Poet came. His eyes beheld
   Their own wan light through the reflected lines
   Of his thin hair, distinct in the dark depth
   Of that still fountain; as the human heart,
   Gazing in dreams over the gloomy grave,
   Sees its own treacherous likeness there . . ."

She closed her eyes, imagining her own pale, ethereal self, the self that inhabited an unkind green uniform. She wanted inner and outer self to come together in some form of resemblance instead of parading themselves in this vile comedy of beauty and bottle green. She saw the loathsome reflection in others too . . . in the heat and odours of the games field. In the downy alterations of the changing room. In the inward sourness of breath.

In the collision of adult and adolescent so many possible images offered themselves for imitation, but all seemed opposed. There was no pure element. Only the intolerable bewilderments of Ophelia. The world offered nothing but calamity yet lacked a place for her own calamitous nature. Nothing fitted. And Granny, who'd believed in her, had gone.

"It is a woe 'too deep for tears' when all
  Is reft at once, when some surpassing Spirit,
  Whose light adorned the world around it, leaves
  Those who remain behind, not sobs or groans,
  The passionate tumult of a clinging hope;
  But pale despair and cold tranquillity,
  Nature's vast frame, the web of human things,
  Birth and the grave, that are not as they were".

She closed her book and wept.

Amy wept for her grandmother, for her own frightened sense of desertion, for her late, puffy little breasts, for the world's great canopy of sadness, for games this afternoon, for her inability to feel anything but wrong wherever she was, whatever she wore, whatever she said.

She thought of the doughnut and made herself swear not to touch it.

She wished to die.

7

"How often, when life appears at its very darkest, joy is close at hand! I have found it to be so again and again.

"The move to Anstead lowered us both. The two small rooms that we had found to live in above a shop in the High Street, were both noisy and isolated at one and the same time. We missed our country peace, and our little garden so much that it took some time to recognise the advantages of our new situation — the fact that for the first time we had indoor facilities (although shared), constant hot water from a gas heater and shops (literally) on our doorstep.

"But more important than these minor luxuries, was the course events were to take. Within a year I had secured myself a secretarial job at the hospital and there, on my very first day, I saw the man I was to marry. *Saw* is scarcely the word! Leo Mathison was swathed in bandages, only his eyes and mouth visible. It could hardly be love at first sight!

"Those of us employed in secretarial work used to take patients for walks in our lunch hour or sometimes at the end of the day. It seemed to fall more and more frequently to my lot to escort Leo Mathison, first in a wheelchair, then on crutches, then with a stick alone. Finally one day, when I called to take him out, he stood up without any aid, stepped towards me and smiling, said, 'Now *I* may escort *you*.'

"I was radiantly happy for him. And, I must confess, happy on my own account. Although I'd been most careful not to show a particular warmth of feeling to any one patient, I could not avoid sensing a mutual attraction between us . . ."

The sound of the typewriter was like artillery.

Olivia crashed across the keys putting silence to an end. The morning, so purposefully begun, had gone wrong. Full of contained tension she hit the keys as if they were a mechanical means for re-weaving the holes that appeared in the net.

"He talked chiefly of his home and boyhood, of the countryside he missed so much. He yearned for the hilly landscapes and their racing variety of light and shade. The flatness of the fields around Anstead made him so deeply homesick it was perfectly natural for me to invite him to my home.

"The day came . . ."

His frame had filled the room so hugely, his physical presence had added to the social clumsiness they'd all felt. Every time he'd turned, a piece of furniture rocked as though to declare itself cheap and ill-made. In his hands he had clutched a small bunch of marigolds picked from the hospital garden and since neither Olivia nor her mother had known for which of them they were intended, neither had offered to relieve him of the wilting flowers. Etiquette — their ignorance of it — overwhelmed them. Never had they been so helplessly conscious of social difference. The threat of emotion confusing what had until now been exact mannerisms and attitudes paralysed all three. They'd smiled past one another for an infinitely long time.

". . . It was my mother who took hold of the situation. Having scraped together enough of our rations to bake scones and a seed cake and having produced from her treasured hoard a remaining jar of home-made gooseberry preserve, she insisted we sit down and eat these good things.

"She was full of nothing but kindness and yet her encouragements to Leo that he should swiftly get well and resume the life so cruelly interrupted for him, seemed to me on that afternoon, to underline the impossibility of our relationship. We were separated by so many things. By age — there were twelve years between us — by . . ."

The agony of it remained alive still. The unjust feeling she'd had that Leo was quietly but firmly being pushed back into the world from which he'd come. The fear that he would read the message and worse, heed it. But most terrible of all, the lurking feeling in herself that this was, indeed, the proper thing for him to do.

"For the first time that afternoon I heard him speak of the joys of flying—of the enthralling solitude that, above all other form of battle, gave a man the sense of conducting his war alone and to his utmost. When he spoke like that I knew it was wicked and selfish of me to wish he might never be allowed to face that challenge again. But I knew I *had* to face the possibility of losing him. My mother, I think, understood that more keenly than I at the time. She knew it was a prospect I must come to terms with.

"What I didn't understand was that the dilemma was as painful for Leo as it was for myself. When, only a week later, he left for retraining, he treated the event as a matter of course. He said neither that he loved me, nor that he would miss me. Merely that he would try and keep 'in touch'.

"The hurt that I suffered would have been unendurable had it not been for my mother's wisely pointing out that he had two battles he must fight and these must be met and overcome first. if he were able to regard himself at all worthily as a man. Worthy of me. She explained to me that he had two battles to fight; one, the battle we all fought against our common enemy, but secondly, and just as important, the battle he had to wage against the enemy within . . . the fear that his flying skill might now be inadequate. Until these conflicts were settled, she said, I must put him out of my mind.

"She regarded Leo . . ."

Olivia paused, her fingers claw-like over the keys.

Since this morning's discoveries, she wasn't sure she dared write with such conviction about her mother's thoughts. Oh, the discoveries were small in themselves, trivial almost—like turning a familiar corner and finding the view . . . not *altered*, nothing so dramatic. But not quite as expected. The steady forward flow of her confidence was gently dammed.

After dressing, she'd come to the decision that she *must* open her mother's desk and sort out the documents that would help her with the biography. It was cowardice preventing her from doing it. A superstitious fear of disturbing the personal belongings of the dead.

But she'd waited until Madge had arrived, the small key held tightly in her palm. She'd wanted Madge's company. She'd wanted a witness. It was less impertinent, less prying to have two people. One was an intruder, two were simply doing a job.

Reassuringly, Madge had regarded it in exactly that way. "Of course," she'd said, reaching automatically for a notebook and pencil. A ritual part of bereavement.

They'd gone to the end of the landing and opened the door, Madge squashing sneezes down in her nose and murmuring something about the hay fever season.

She had turned the key and gently lowered the desk lid.

It was, apart from a few scattered paper clips and a faint silvery glitter that must have dropped off Christmas cards, entirely empty.

"Try the drawers," Madge had said.

Making an effort to seem calm, she'd unlocked and pulled out each of the four drawers in turn. Two were empty. One contained neatly tied bundles of letters which she had swiftly untied and checked. They were letters from Corin, Chloe and Amy to their grandmother, punctilious letters from school. In the bottom drawer which smelt oddly of peppermint, there were just three letters in a brown envelope. The envelope itself was quite new, though the letters (obvious from an immediate glance) were old.

Olivia, kneeling on the floor had sat back on her heels, puzzled.

"It's probably with the solicitor," Madge had said.

Blankly, Olivia had turned her head.

"The will. With Mr. Butterworth probably. I'll call him shall I?"

"Ah . . . oh, yes," she had murmured distractedly, not attempting to explain her confusion.

Madge had gone to the phone, her step encouragingly exact.

Alone, Olivia had risen, holding the new brown envelope in her hand and feeling inside it, had withdrawn the thin, mottled sheets. Checking the dates, she had unfolded and flattened them in order on the desk lid.

Jan. 18th 1929   Jo'burg

My dear Doris,

Well, I am her after all. I did not fall off the edg of the world but you wud not like it I dont think. I am leaving her to go upcountry after I have got the necessarys and will write you again when I get ther. It is very hot. Take this muny I am enclosing to the Post Office I now it is not much but it will be better that I can solumnly promise you. Well, I am not much of a riter as you well now but try not to feel bad about it becaus it will be for the good of us all in the end. Try to have faith in me as a wif must you will see in the end it was rite for me to go. You wud not have liked the ship at all my dear. That is all for now, it is funny to think ther may be snow in

England, I hope littel Peggy is well I am well. Your sinseer husband, William.

March 23rd 1931

Doris,

I am leeving now as I am no good to you or the littel girl as you have said offen. You are rite. You will find ten pounds under the water glass in the larder it will see you rite awile and you have my permisshun to sell my cloths such as ther is. It is a pity but for the best as I am not a marrying man and shud have been a salor I think like my farther I like the see. The littel girl will be all rite with you I now you are a good clean woman. Dont worry about me I will not bother you. Goodbye, William.

October 1st 1942.   Wickford House,
                                                    Wickford,
                                                    Suffolk.

My dear Mrs. Plumb,

I am writing to you personally although you will be receiving an official letter from the War Agricultural Committee informing you of their need to billet land workers on the estate as from the beginning of next year and their requirement therefore to take over all available dwellings.

Your position, as you will understand, is very delicate and I have pressed your case most forcefully, but I am deeply sorry to say it is the official view that as you are not a full-time member of the estate staff, you will be requested, in a time of national need, to surrender your tenancy. I am arranging for a substantial form of compensation to be forwarded to you immediately.

I cannot emphasise enough how distressing this is to me in view of the suffering you have already endured, the courage with which you have brought up your daughter alone and, not least, in view of the wonderful and skilful work you have done for me.

This is a time of suffering for all the nation but so often, it seems to me, the principal burden is borne quietly, undramatically, by the womenfolk. For you, who have endured the problem of supporting yourself by your own efforts so long, this extra blow must seem especially cruel. If I can, in any way, help you by finding a means of employment or supplying references, this I will most certainly do.

In the meantime, allow me to express my deep appreciation of your courage and of the long and excellent service you have given us. May God be with you and your daughter in the years to come.

Sincerely yours,
             Evelyn Eastholme

Madge Waring had returned looking faintly rushed, her spectacles two loyal circles of bewilderment. "There *is* no will, Mr. Butterworth says. Your mother declined to make one . . ." She had hesitated, troubled by this flouting of the orthodox.

"It wasn't the will exactly, Madge dear . . ." Her voice had hovered over the inexplicable. "No . . ." she'd murmured. "No, I shouldn't think she'd want the worry of such a thing, poor darling. No, it's . . ." And she'd gathered together the three faded letters with a sigh that was almost aggressive.

Madge hadn't understood, though she'd noted the emptiness of the drawers. "Perhaps she had a clear-out. Perhaps she destroyed everything."

"*Destroyed* everything?"

"Perhaps she thought everything she had was yours." Madge had still not accounted for the lack of a will. Yes, perhaps that was it. It seemed both touching and likely. "The jewellery and everything," she'd added, still casting about for illuminating possibilities.

She'd been halted by a sharp frown on Olivia's face which made her feel she'd said something offensive. Under rapidly lowered lids, she'd caught another, wilder look not meant for her. An outwardly directionless look that swept blindly across space; a jagged black beam.

"All my letters!" Olivia had cried. "Photographs! Everything, postcards, reports, all that!" And then she had turned almost accusingly to Madge. "Where's it all gone, Madge? All the things that were here?" She had run her fingertips down the side of her face, as if seeking reassurance from its outline.

The two women had stared into their own deserts unable to help one another while the sun, slipping around the side of the house, had withdrawn from the room.

"I can't imagine . . ." Olivia had begun, then reached out

against the wall for support as a sense of gale seizing flowerheads from their stalk had torn through her. A terrifying feeling that her mother had, in some way, attempted to take a part of *her*, Olivia, beyond the darkness of the grave.

"I think," she'd said, after a pause, as lightly as she was able, "I think I'd better get down to some work."

"Mother regarded Leo with some awe, perhaps even with a perfectly justifiable feeling that he was *too* good for me. Certainly she was anxious to prevent my suffering any hurt and tried very hard after his departure to pretend that everything would go on as before . . ."

It was no good. The truth remained elusive.

It was partly the fault of a worn memory she told herself, though the feeling was rather of a memory that had gone into spasm. And partly her sheer inexperience. She had never attempted to write the truth before and felt badly the lack of a professional, objective eye.

She gazed out at the chestnut tree which had grown far too large for the walled garden and needed to be felled (as long as the roots hadn't nestled under the house foundations) and tried to confront the absurd notion that the lack of documents in her mother's desk was in some way *deliberate*. Perhaps she'd suspected a book might be written about her and hadn't wanted it. But she wasn't to know she would die, surely? Or did you, at eighty, dwell on the likelihood more than you allowed anyone to guess? And what of the few things she *had* left? The very saving of them seemed ridiculously significant — ridiculous, because the attempt to burden things with significance, however tempting, could lead to wrong and foolish conclusions. Olivia possessed sufficient professionalism to be aware of that, and yet . . . Her mind tangled with curiosities.

A creamy-breasted song thrush loosed its melody at her beyond the glass. Noting the cloud, she leant forward to push the window a little further open.

What pricked most sharply (worse than pricked . . . worse than a thorn. A lodged barb of steel), what *hurt* most was the disappearance of her own letters. They could be somewhere else. With the solicitor of course . . . and then again, she realised he would surely have mentioned it before now if that were the case.

There would have to be a more thorough search.

Pushing her typewriter impatiently to one side, she opened the three notes again and laid them out next to one another.

Her father's handwriting was small and awkward. It used the page like a children's playground darting up and down, visiting corners. The ink, once black, had faded to a brownish grey. His letters reduced him in her mind. Not just as a spirit (no hero, this) but physically. The image of a man too tall to enter the cottage door, went. A smaller man, sly, weak, sidelong, stumbled in. Reading his inadequate notes again, she experienced a pale sense of the bitterness her mother must have known and never voiced. She glimpsed the sealed lips, an almost silvery seam of pain. Behind the closed face lay an inviolate depth of pain that could never be known, never be entered.

As she recalled it, she realised with a sense of shock that the silence of suffering had actually frightened her as a child. (I hadn't known that till now, she thought. I didn't *know* I was frightened.)

And she saw that the life on which she'd turned her poor focus was smeared with ambiguities, like small, delicate lichens which had appeared until now to be a part of the bark on which they grew. Microscopic species, difficult to classify.

Sharply, she pulled the paper out of her typewriter and before crumpling it, read through the last paragraph again. "Certainly she was anxious to prevent my suffering any hurt..."

She hesitated. How many motives had she missed by gazing simply through her own point of focus? A biographer had to creep round his subject bending to one spyglass after another, as though making quite sure of his victim. The technique was oddly repugnant.

But without willing it, her mind had already begun a circular prowl. Perhaps her mother's own experience of marriage made her not just cautious—more than that, maybe genuinely opposed. Maybe... jealous?

She shuddered at her own unpleasantness. This stealthy pursuit of motive was the thing she most hated in modern plays and novels, this fastidious searching after the worst, a glad seizing upon bile stains and excrement. It was abhorrent. Life was not a grotesque underbelly of grubs and spite gnawed through to its sleek surface.

Suffused with guilt, she shuffled the letters in front of her and read them again with a surge of compassion. Poor darling, she thought, seeing rejection in each one. Poor love.

Each letter mentioned money. A buying off sum. And more

than ever, stinging with indignation on her mother's behalf, she was glad that she'd repaid each wretched year of her mother's life with one of pleasure. Or nearly, anyway. The debt had not quite been balanced out.

Outside, the weather, as she had known it would, began to change. A sharp, thin veil of rain cut across the garden whipping the blossom before it. The cleft in the hills where Corford camp had stood was now filled with blankly angry cloud.

Madge came back with a light knock. "Coffee," she said, "and bills."

"Bills? Already?" Olivia took the coffee (she never lunched when the family were away). On the first Monday of each month they went through the previous month's accounts. "June, then," she said.

"Would you rather leave them till later?" Madge was nervous of any further distress.

"They won't go away, will they? No, let's get it over with."

Although the ritual was performed for Madge's satisfaction largely, Olivia was glad of the distraction. Submissively she uncapped her pen as the papers were placed like a meal on the tweed lap. Only Madge ever really looked at the figures. Only Madge could have assessed what Olivia was worth, what the household extravagances were. "Nice, isn't it . . ." she said with real relish (as she always did). "Nice to get them paid off!" Her glasses sparkled over the neatening activity. Debts to Madge, were imperilling things.

Olivia was reminded of the letters. Of their compensation. Each one a seal of redundancy.

"The Fortnum's account is unusually large . . ." Madge perched over it, blinking.

"Oh, well . . . *food.*"

"*Unusually* large. . . ." (Olivia wished Madge wouldn't tap her large, purplish teeth with a pencil.)

"Amy's tuckbox I expect."

"Shall I look into it?"

"Oh heavens, Madge, what a depressing idea . . . I can't bear to think what food costs these days . . . Let me have it."

Rain hissed against the window. She filled in a cheque for the right amount. It *was* large. She thought of the ten pounds left under the water glass and blenched inwardly at the disparity of the sums. "We must economise," she murmured, becoming aware of an apprehension in Madge who sat, taut, her mouth now firmly propped open with her pencil. Her knees were pinned together, her legs splayed, so that her feet turned inwards.

"All right, dear?"

"I was just thinking, Miss Bennett. It's very awkward ... I'm very reluctant, truly, but since ..."

"Dear me, Madge. A *problem*?"

Olivia picked up her cup, sipped and replaced it in the saucer without removing her eyes from the brownish hunched figure of her secretary.

"Since you mention it ... since you mention the cost of *food* that is. It *is* getting rather *difficult*, Miss Bennett." The last sentence was delivered like a burst of indigestion. Madge put her hand to her mouth in apology.

For a second, Olivia stared. "Oh," she said. "*Ah.*" (Madge lived with an older sister whose arthritis had crept from her spine down her arms twisting her hands like scrap.) "You should have said," cried Olivia. "How much more will you need?"

"Oh, Miss Bennett, you are so extremely good. I realise I'm handsomely reimbursed as it is ..."

"Now, Madge ..."

"A pound a week?" Madge Waring tried not to sound imploring and reduced her real need by two thirds.

"Let's say one pound fifty dear. It's more than deserved."

"You're too kind." She took off her spectacles and cleaned them feverishly.

"Shall we press on?"

"Of course." Madge was recovered. She picked up the quarterly bill from the electricity board. "In view of the strike," she said, "I can't think how they've got it to this total but I took the liberty of ringing them and they explained that to use less power required more power. I'm not sure about that."

She glanced at her employer for instruction, but Olivia wasn't listening.

"It's no use," she spoke firmly. "I need to look round Mother's room again. I'm not satisfied."

"Shall we finish the bills first? Get them out of the way?"

Unwillingly, Olivia allowed herself to be persuaded and signed away a further three hundred and sixty pounds unheedingly. Then she strode along the landing with the athleticism of an adolescent, pursued at the run by Madge Waring and a white cat.

She had forgotten the drawers built into the base of the bed and concealed by the sprigged pink and white quilt. To these she went instantly. Falling on her knees she tugged energetically — and fruitlessly — at the first.

"It's jammed, that's all."

"Let me help." Madge, too, crouched on the carpet and held one brass handle while Olivia gave all her strength to the other.

"Ready? *Pull!*"

The drawer lurched out knocking both women backwards. Out of it leapt and tumbled a collection of tins.

Tinned beans, tinned tomatoes, tinned bamboo shoots, tinned creamed rice, tinned grapefruit segments — sweet corn, soup (celery, chicken, oxtail, mushroom and cock-a-leekie), tinned peaches, tinned custard, tinned pilchards, tinned ox tongue, plums and sardines. The variety was dazzling.

Olivia, slightly sprawled but still elegant, stared in disbelief. Then, "Come on!" she cried and made for the next drawer.

It was easier. The contents were less heavy. It was packed with walnuts, raisins, glacé cherries, brown sugar, angelica, cornflour, rice, almonds, endless herbs in cardboard drums, loose nutmegs, packets of Instant Whip and yeast and aspic.

There was a slightly musty smell, as though even the herbs had been stored a long time.

"*Well. . . !*"

Olivia wasted no time but half crawled, half hopped round the other side of the bed, signalling Madge to follow.

The other two drawers were similarly stuffed. One, only half full, had nothing but bags of salt in it.

"I don't understand it."

Madge Waring, who had, for the past ten years been of the view that Mrs. Bennett's mind was progressively weakening, felt no surprise. It was the sort of thing old ladies did. But somehow she felt she had to suggest some other possibility. "Perhaps she liked an occasional snack," she offered helpfully. Gazing at the quantity of clearly uneaten food, she realised it was a silly thing to say. She began to tidy the packets and tins away.

"We can't leave them there," said Olivia somewhat sharply. And then, similarly feeling the need to explain out loud something she couldn't begin to grasp, she remarked without looking at

Madge, "Of course she had a frightfully difficult time as a young housewife. Perhaps the habit of . . ." But she couldn't say *hoarding*. "Perhaps she never quite lost that fear of being without."

It was embarrassing to be surrounded by all this hidden food in the current situation. There were penalties for this kind of thing.

"I can't think where she got it all. Every time she went out, she must have bought something."

But Madge Waring, whose own circumstances gave her a more certain insight into Mrs. Bennett than Olivia would permit herself to have, thought privately that the old woman must have been systematically stealing for years. She rubbed her aching knees quietly and said nothing.

8

CHLOE HAD TO PEDAL HARD ALONG THE LANES. HER BIKE was old, without any gears. It demanded effort.

The white bridal display of wayside flowers was now spotted with pink campion and blue, low-growing periwinkle. The banks grew so profusely with cow parsley it brushed her legs as she cycled by. At one point she had to swerve to avoid the half-concealed body of a dead badger. The size of these creatures never failed to surprise her. This one had claws the size of primitive harpoons.

Henry Claremont had invited her to call after evensong.

"Yes," he'd said, "there's to be a confirmation in six weeks or so. I see no reason why you shouldn't be 'done'." And he'd laughed uncomfortably seeing that his ironic use of the popular expression had made her wince.

She pressed eagerly forward on her pedals leaning low over the handlebars to help herself up the slope leading towards the church and nearby vicarage. Four or five white marbled butterflies rose from the hedge as she panted past. Early, this year, she thought, and stood up out of her saddle to get herself to the top of the rise.

Henry Claremont, still wearing his cassock, stood by his gate staring upwards into a huge pear tree the shape of a lettuce that's bolted.

"Ugly object, isn't it?" He smiled at her as she pushed her bike towards him, panting. "But I thought if I pruned it the blackbirds might not make use of it any more. It seems to be their music tree." They both looked upwards at a female blackbird singing an urgent ballad of famine as her mate flew back triumphant, two worms wriggling in his yellow beak.

"Barber told me how to prune an apple tree today," said Chloe, watching the ritual overhead. "So that a bird, flying from any angle, can pass straight through the branches. Isn't that lovely?"

"Isn't it," agreed Henry Claremont looking ruefully at his cylindrical pear tree.

"Come along in, Chloe. Or shall we stay outside? It's a most beautiful evening."

"I don't mind." She was suddenly awkward, faced with the prospect of speaking intimately to someone she had known long but not well—not well enough to speak to about the most private mysteries. Of these she spoke only to Joe. And not always even to him. Mostly, the dialogues were exchanged in her own head. She wasn't sure how well they'd emerge in talk. She bent down and pulled her trouser legs out of her socks.

"You look well," remarked Henry, turning to find he was speaking to Chloe's backside. He glanced upward again at the evening sky, a thin, clear arc of blue. At this hour, the sun lay low, throwing its beams only along the tops of the hills, making the valleys deep and violet. In the distance, a curving line of Scots pines pushed their viridian foliage within the sun's ray, their slender branchless trunks disappearing into darkness.

"Exams go well?"

"Fair." (That seemed noncommittal. She tried harder.) "I wasn't ever, you see, worried about them. Once I'd realised they prepared, qualified me for nothing . . ." (Now she sounded irresponsible).

"Always a useful thing to have behind one," murmured Henry gently.

He led the way to a group of white painted chairs and a table close by an arbour of evergreen honeysuckle to one side of his ragged garden. He caught her gaze. "I leave the nettles for the butterflies—or so I tell myself," he added. "To be quite truthful, I like it overgrown. It becomes the house better."

"I know what you mean." She smiled, relaxing a little. The house, built two hundred years ago of lovely, honey stone, was the countryman's version of a town house—small but regular and absurdly porticoed. It would have looked pompous in a formal garden.

They sat down.

"*Now* . . ."

"Yes?"

They settled like pigeons. Awkward. On the alert.

"Yes, as I said, I have a handful of children being 'done'—I'm sorry . . ." He gave a sidelong smile. "Being *instructed*, prepared. Formally, so should *you* be of course, but if you'd like to drop along to their last few classes? Any other problems, points, you can come to me to discuss . . . I see no reason why that shouldn't be adequate."

"I see." She felt disappointed.

It was not that she wished to be closed in lengthy sessions with Henry Claremont (why had he never married? she wondered). She wished for nothing of the kind. After a long, private journey of her own, she wished simply to come to the gates and enter in. Not stand about outside chatting. But the moment of entry, that mattered. The *decision* mattered. The decision mattered most of all. It was of such consuming importance that it felt diminished by this almost off-hand arrangement. She might just as well be asking if there was room for one more on the annual coach trip to the coast.

Already, the occasional bat had begun to fly in swift scissor movements round the cypress trees.

"You have to produce a certificate of baptism and, er, godparents must be informed."

"Yes." She put her hands together between her knees. There was a pause, silent save for the soft flip of the bats.

"Is there anything you'd like to talk to me about now?"

It was like a sex talk. She felt a rush of heat to her face. Beneath her hair, her ears were tingling.

"I don't think so," she mumbled, useless.

(Why had he never married? There was some obstruction in him.)

Inwardly, Henry Claremont sighed. One voice—the rusty voice of God—bade him rejoice at increasing his flock by one (though goodness knows how many had deserted). The other, a mean, androgynous voice, simply cried, Women! and tumbled away down a melancholic iron pipe.

Henry Claremont, with his handsome actor's face (boldly creased, extravagantly mouthed) and his handsome actor's voice, knew, after many years of honest examination, that he was a sound pastoral man and a poor spiritual man. He found solitary worship difficult and it was so rare for him to meet the truly, joyfully religious person that after wondering whether it was something in him that prevented their approach, had decided they were a breed half eaten by extinction. The Devil had tricked the best people. So often, he sighed nervously, the believers were either vicious or temporary. Chloe was a clear case of the temporary. Still, what right had he to grudge her confirmation — recruits were so few all must be welcome. He looked at Chloe who was trapping one plimsolled foot under the other — true that she was a little older than the standard temporary case. But not much.

He leaned back, crossed his legs in the pose of a man easy with the soul and thought how much simpler it was to deal with the diocesan committee or the cricket club.

"Why do you want to be confirmed?" he asked.

She looked up quickly, the rich gold of late sunlight burning the edges of her hair. He couldn't see her features distinctly, only the rim of white-gold. For one, disturbing moment, he saw her as a medieval angel, and then, in the difficult light, his eyes involuntarily dropped to her tennis shoes.

"Because He said so." She sounded surprised.

"He?"

"Do this, He said . . . Do this in remembrance of Me. And I haven't been doing it."

He was forcibly struck by the simplicity of her reply. He sat thoughtfully, one hand unconsciously raised against the gnats. Overhead, the blackbirds began the assertive 'Pip, pip' of their roosting song.

"And I want to," added Chloe eventually. She thought his silence meant he expected a fuller explanation from her. She struggled, trying to pull meaning out of her mind, dragging something instinctual through a computer which spat printed messages. "I feel . . . it's a way, through Christ, of reaching into the heart of the world. It's everything . . . it's the essence of things. It's life and death. Joy and suffering. Male and female. Toil and pleasure . . ." She wavered.

"Go on," urged Henry, interested, "please."

"A symbol of, I mean. It symbolises all things, the duality, the coming together. I *think* that's what I mean . . . the synthesis that *is* meaning . . . it's difficult . . ."

"But in the first instance," pressed Henry, fearing the customary, youthful proclivity for magic, "*fundamentally*, the eucharist is . . ."

"Oh, fundamentally, yes, the body and the blood of Christ. And the taking of it in fellowship — that too, that matters to me.

Terribly." She looked over the starred hedge of hypericum to the blue rim of hills beyond, then went on: "And the act of eating and drinking itself. That *is* life, isn't it?" She turned to him, eagerly.

"The sacrament is all those things," he acknowledged. "It's endless. But it's rooted in reality for all its symbolism. Rooted in historicity." He insisted on this to prevent her travelling too far from him into a mysticism he distrusted. Or was it paganism?

Chloe sensed his reservations and didn't attempt to express a feeling she had that in surrendering herself to the infinite, incomprehensible imagery of the eucharist she would, in some way, be absorbed into the fabric of existence itself. Into both the visible and invisible world.

Close by, the church clock began to strike eight. Each stroke of the bell travelled from strength to irridescent wavering and vanished without any sense of sinking.

"But that's it," she said. "When the reality of the ritual remains as powerful as the symbolism. That's it." She bit her lip and sucked in air, trying to express herself more clearly.

"Yes?"

She really tried. "I mean, eating, drinking, that's what stands between life and death. And that's all really. Food *is* reality. When people don't have to think about it continually—grow it, hunt for it, that sort of thing—when they don't have to gather it and prepare it properly, then they're freed from the need to face reality. Do you see what I mean? People lose any true sense of their dependent, animal nature. They can fantasise."

"I'm not *sure* . . ." Henry began, taking out his pipe as the prospect of a rather longer conversation than he'd envisaged, opened up before him, "I'm not certain that it's . . ."

But Chloe wanted him to be quite clear what case he was expected to argue. "Money," she said. "Money's become the modern, the substitute source of dependence. All that was once harvest, storing, exchange has become reward, gain, profit, savings, do you see?" She pressed him. "And I believe—though I know I don't put it very well—that it's a false and dangerous dependency. That it's," she gestured desperately, "that because money is itself a symbol, but treated as a reality, that it allows people to live out dreams. It offers an escape from truth, from the world of *need* to which we properly belong." She drew breath and went on. "Because money's infinite, people can't accept the idea of limitations without a sense of grievance, injustice . . ."

"I *think* I understand you." Slowly, Henry Claremont lit his pipe. "But I'm afraid," he laughed, "I'm probably a long way from fully understanding what it all has to do with confirmation."

Chloe slumped forward on her knees, exasperated by her own poor efforts, her fingers thrust through the thick wheat of her hair. She turned her head and watched the first fragrant wreaths of smoke rise from Henry's pipe.

"Because," she re-asserted quietly, "because I believe that the truth, the reality that Christ asks me to accept is the only one. It's full of pain *and* purpose . . . just as His death was. And that—and the one aspect's inseparable from the other. He tried to show us something incredibly difficult to understand, that in poverty there is wealth, in discrimination there's privilege, in limitation, there is abundance and there it all is—in the bread and the wine. So simple. So beyond simple understanding." Her head drooped again as she sought to clear the jumble in it.

Henry Claremont was moved by her and being moved, was suspicious of himself. He feared romantic religion. Other people's emotions he regarded with alarm, being unable to judge whether they were fully in control of them or not—he was inclined to think of 'emotional' as synonymous with 'uncontrolled'.

"I think you'll manage splendidly," he said. "Come along to my classes on Thursdays at six-thirty for a rather more down-to-earth look at the implications." Immediately, he knew he sounded reproving and wished he had not.

Chloe rose to her feet as if dismissed.

"Oh, don't rush off. A cup of tea? Coffee?"

"I haven't got a lamp on my bicycle."

"It won't be dark for a while yet." Now he could hear his own sense of apology expressing itself in oblique ways. He fussed. "I shall go and make one."

When he returned, the western sky was ribboned with pink and lilac streamers.

"How is your mother coping?" He returned to more general topics with a guilty thankfulness.

"She seems frantically busy. It's displacement activity really."

"Displacement?" He set the tray down.

"Taking her mind off things. She's held up very well. Too well."

"I must call on her. Is she writing?"

"Oh yes . . . about Granny. She says she can't remember things though. Not that," and Chloe laughed fondly, "her memory has ever been amazingly accurate."

"She must be glad to have you there. And . . . and all your friends of course. Immensely comforting." (Sometimes he could hear himself, the perfect parody of a clergyman, saying the lines faultlessly. 'Immensely comforting', he thought. Really!)

Chloe smiled, drank of a mouthful of what she had thought was tea but discovered was very watery coffee, and promised, "Oh, she *will* be. At the moment we're just an embarrassment really. Freaks."

"Oh no, you do yourselves a disservice!"

"Young people have a shocking reputation — you must have heard."

Henry Claremont *had* heard. He raised cup and saucer together to his mouth to avoid spilling drops on his cassock and made some disbelieving noise in his coffee.

"Mummy, of course," continued Chloe, "is a classic case of the money-disorientated."

"Mm?"

"I mean, she tried to buy herself a whole new personality. Understandably, it was the thing to do at the time . . . the post-war young, you know . . ."

Henry Claremont attempted an understanding nod — his face giving a perfect impression of complicity, his spirit lagging somewhat.

"The nicest thing about her is that she's never really managed it." (Chloe told herself this. It was part of her strategy for rediscovering her mother in a more affectionate light.) ". . . in many ways, she's a very basic person really . . ." She grinned. "Wherever she is, you know, there's an animal never very far behind . . . like the little lamb. *They* recognise her all right."

Chloe liked this conception. It recommended her mother to her strongly. She struck out at the hysterical cloud of gnats. "I think she'll come round to us."

"I'm sure she's *more* than delighted to have you there. So many of the young leave home altogether."

Chloe finished her cooling coffee but didn't move. Henry, noting this, enquired how the work was coming along.

She explained that only Andrew and Peter had been there for the past week, said they'd performed miracles, considering. She didn't mention how much the rotavator had helped. "The big assault begins tomorrow," she said, "after Joe's arrived."

"Joe?"

"Oh, Joe, he's . . . well . . . he's the inspirational force." She meant it had all been his idea in the first place.

"And a good worker too, I hope!" Henry allowed his rich chuckle loose.

Chloe, about to reply, hesitated, "To tell you the truth," she mused, "I don't know. We've mainly talked, really." She laughed, "I must go," she determined, "or P.C. Jenkins will have me."

"Oh dear me, yes . . . the *fuzz*," responded Henry, trying out the word. It seemed grossly inappropriate. P.C. Jenkins was a large, red-faced man with a gift for growing onions.

"Thank you for the tea—the coffee, I mean . . . And everything."

"Oh, most interesting, delighted to have you back . . ." He hesitated, not knowing whether he quite meant in the village or in the flock, but thought better of clarifying himself and followed Chloe to the gate.

She pulled her socks over her trouser legs and stood astride her bicycle.

"It's a big step to take when you're older," Henry conceded. "I'm glad . . ."

They smiled at one another through the gilt and purple light, then looked away.

"Another fine day tomorrow."

"It's been too dry. Nothing's growing . . ."

"Yes, the farmers have been saying . . ."

They gazed at the fading glory of the sky and read trouble in it.

"Oh well, goodbye!" And Chloe lifting herself on to her saddle, began to freewheel down the hill.

Between the hedges it was quite dark and drenched with the damp scent of wild garlic. On the level, where the road opened up a little, she pedalled fast catching the thick, agreeable smell of the first summer silage from nearby farms; a rich erupting smell of fomentation.

She closed her mouth so as not to swallow flies.

Tomorrow, Joe.

9

"THERE'S A *'PERSON'* FOR YOU IN THE HALL."

Olivia came into the greenhouse where her daughter was selecting some more bedding plants. "You ought to wear gloves, darling—you're going to ruin your hands."

"Joe?"

"I believe that was the name, yes." Olivia's gaze flew upwards to the vine, now healthily reaching across its wires. "It might fruit this year," she remarked, but Chloe had pushed past her and gone. Olivia brushed a few crumbs of soil from her black and white silk dress.

"Great!"

"Hi!"

Joe slipped his rucksack from his shoulders and embraced her. "You made it."

"You see." He spread his hands. "Yes."

He was smaller than Chloe—not just in height, his frame was altogether lighter. His long dark hair was drawn back from a neat-featured face and secured by a rubber band. The yellowish tone of his skin, the thin moustache and dark eyes gave him a Mediterranean air. Or, as Olivia reflected, returning to the hall, the air of a gipsy.

"Hello again," he said solemnly.

Why do the young so rarely *smile*, thought Olivia, offering to make coffee.

"You have *coffee*?"

"Oh yes . . . we're very fortunate here."

She had a feeling about this boy. He was Chloe's boy, of that she was sure. Ushering him into the little sitting room, she let her attention ripple over him. She discovered particles of dirt . . . a thin film of grease. She thought, for some reason, of a neglected beach.

"Some pad," observed Joe after she left the room to attend to the coffee. His gaze travelled over pictures, furniture, flowers with a slow gravity. "Your natural scene, uh?"

"It's odd seeing you here."

"It's odd being here. I feel odd."

Olivia came back and embarrassed her daughter.

"What do you *do*?" she asked, arranging herself judicially in an armchair.

"I do a lot of thinking mostly."

"That's useful," observed Olivia drily. "What do you think about?"

"He's a poet." Chloe sprang to.

"Life, shall we say, in all its forms."

His manner was perfectly courteous but Olivia suspected him. Her charm acquired a cold, metallic quality. "So few of us have the time," she said, "I envy you."

Her use of this glittering blade was practised. Turning it fractionally, but persistently she scooped forth much that she wanted. Joe, she discovered used the dole with integrity (he actually called it the dole). He fell back on it during the weeks his small magazine had nothing to pay with. That way, he explained, the magazines were indirectly Government subsidised. He made it sound immensely reasonable.

He was twenty-five. He had travelled across Europe to Asia Minor and India— His family were working class and prejudiced. ("About what?" . . . "Everything.") They came from Whitechapel but had moved on retirement to a houseboat permanently moored off Hayling Island. He never saw them. He was not university educated but had stopped off at a couple of technical colleges, preparatory to launching himself as a photographer. Then, "pissed off by it all", had given up the idea. He aimed to be a more complete human being than the present system allowed for, he said. "We're breaking out of the single-vision era," he declared as though quietly announcing an event of major importance. He drank his coffee black.

Olivia, aware of a softly hissing impatience from Chloe, scanned his wrists for abscesses and needle marks, but finding none, pressed mercilessly deeper with her own fine instrument of enquiry. "I hope you can survive on what you find here," she remarked lightly.

"We must."

"Must?"

"That's the aim we've set ourselves."

"We'll have to give you a little help to start with. I hope *that's* not against the rules." She gave Chloe an arch look and adjusted her gold wrist watch. "Sharing, after all, is clearly part of your aim."

"It depends how oppressively it's done."

Olivia rode this, unperturbed, reminding herself how she had divided the hoard of tins and other provisions between Mrs. Baldwin and Madge Waring. Joe was saying:

"If you give, then you have to give freely, with a sense of gladness. Not as a piece of trade exchange, labour exchange. Not trying to establish a sense of obligation."

This last remark, again seemingly without intended rudeness, struck the weak edge of Olivia's metal. She allowed the precision blade to slip, "I speak — and give — as a parent," she replied, sitting very straight. "Children owe their parents nothing."

The phone ringing in the hall provided her with a natural reason for rising. As she excused herself and began to walk with calculated poise towards the door, she heard Joe, for the first time, laugh. She stiffened.

"Parents," he said, "can behave like superpowers. *Worse*. We agreed to treat aid from parents with extreme caution. Chloe must have explained."

"Chloe," said Olivia turning with an unsweetened smile, "feels no need to explain such things to me. *Delighted* to have met you." And with a minimum of movement, she left the room.

"A real gas!" said Joe admiringly to Chloe.

She carried the plastic bag he'd filled with soiled underwear and jerseys while he laboured uphill under the weight of his rucksack. Chloe stopped to draw breath. "Phew! I'm going to have to ask her if I can have one of the horses — it's impossible even to get a bike up here." She slung the bag over her other shoulder and resumed climbing.

"*Horses!*" Joe whistled softly. Horses to him were a piece of heraldry, a clear badge of wealth and privilege. (As, presumably, cars had once seemed to horse owners.) "Shit!" he breathed.

He kept stopping to look backwards, his black eyes darting in assessment over the view like till buttons. "How much of it's yours?" he asked. And he kept checking. "That field? That bit? What about the wood?"

It seemed huge and empty to Joe. For all his theories about man's relationship to land, the Fresians and Aberdeen Angus crosses he could see grazing placidly below, never mind the gaps between them, looked offensively luxurious. As for the fields that lay wholly empty they were quite unpardonable.

"You could feed half Whitechapel off them,' he remarked.

"They're being left for hay."

"What do you mean?"

She looked at him. She'd always thought of Joe as knowing everything.

"It'll be cut in a couple of weeks—for winter feed. If," she added doubtfully, "there's a bit of rain to make it grow."

They toiled uphill again.

"What's that?" He put a hand over his eyes to discern a shape dissolving into the burning blue.

"A hawk of some kind," she said, swivelling on her heels to follow its flight.

"Hey! It's the buzzard! There's a pair fly over here sometimes." She stood watching its lofty flight, excited.

"*Buzzard?* Hey! Wow!" Joe repeated thoughtfully.

They entered the cooler, more heavily overgrown part of the lane where flowering hawthorn shielded them from the sunlight. Little birds hopped through the thorny branches trying not to be heard. A slow-worm lay thick and oozing across the path. Joe kicked at it with the toe of his sneakers.

"It isn't *perfect* . . ." Chloe ventured nervously in advance of their arrival.

"Oh," he shrugged beneath the weight of his rucksack. "Perfection doesn't exist *here*." He meant in the visible world. "All I ask is that the total-related environment, the activity, that'll help us reach inner . . ." His head was down. He was sweating. The words sounded mechanistic in the lane.

They went on in silence until they reached the top of the hill and branched left for Sheep Cottages. All the brightness at this point lay on the far side of the valley. On theirs, it was cool. In the sunshine the sheep clung to their hillside in unshorn discomfort. It was new pasture for them and they cropped urgently rather than find a gorse or thorn for shade.

Chloe and Joe rounded the bend of the hill and walked into the noonday brilliance that held Sheep Cottages in its hot, still grip. Nothing moved. Not even the long grasses which were beginning to flower. Their silvery tips simply pointed where the breeze had last blown them. As they walked nearer Chloe could hear the bees busy among the clover.

She shouted.

The soil of the vegetable patch, newly broken and partly planted, was already drying in the sun. Its surface looked crusty. A fork was stuck in the earth.

She shouted into the house. No reply.

"Dump your stuff," she said and hearing the subdued running of the brook went over to the orchard to see if they were there.

They lay below her on the slope stretched out like gingerbread men. Fast asleep and stark naked. The stream tumbled quietly beside them prevented by a buoyant fringe of bracken and nettle from spraying the vulnerably white areas of their bodies.

Chloe shrieked with laughter. Joe ran down and sprang at them, whooping, leapt the stream and then, cupping his hands, threw slings of icy water at them.

In all the screaming and angry howling that burst out, the two goats, tethered at the bottom of the orchard, started a wild bleating and ran against their chains, trying to break them but succeeded only in catapulting over at the sudden limits.

The three men embraced, ignoring the fracas. Entwined, talking, they began to walk uphill towards the house. "Whatever happened to the workers?" called Chloe from the gate. "Layabouts!"

But they just laughed. They'd been trying to dry themselves off without towels. Midday was the ideal time for bathing.

There was much to see. Much to talk over. After Andy and Peter had each pulled on a pair of jeans all four clambered over the promising rubble of the main buildings, scraping a place for Joe's sleeping bag and pointing out the view from each window, as if incredulous that it could be repeated more than once.

Peter outlined the work and repairs to be done, speaking quickly and technically as he pointed out rot, damp problems, the difficulty of knocking down any wall since all appeared to be structural. They were all two feet thick. The biggest job, he explained, and the one he wanted them to work on as soon as they could, was the roof which needed to be totally altered on its south-facing side if he was to achieve the right angle for his solar energy collectors. "We must have a tank for rain water collection, over and above what we can divert from the stream. They say the spring's never run dry . . . isn't that so?"

"True," said Chloe, trying to force a window open.

Peter buried both hands in his hair to scratch his scalp. Falling plaster had made all of them itch. His main problems for present, he said, were with waste recycling. "I need a lot of help with the plumbing," he declared looking hopefully at Joe. "How good *are* you? . . . The outside bog's fine for the moment but it'll freeze your bollocks off in mid-winter. Same goes for a bath . . . the stream's beautiful right now, really beautiful. Chloe goes home for a bath, the scab."

"I get too dirty for cold water," she grinned defensively and looked at the hands her mother had warned her to protect. Already the nails were broken and the fine lines and whorls of identity clearly marked in black. She turned them over with pride. The skin was beginning to blister at the base of her fingers. "You should see what they've done outside," she said. "All of us. Come and look."

They climbed down the ladder which now, since Peter had stepped right through a stair, provided the only connection between upper and lower floor.

"*Calor* gas. . . ?" queried Joe, spying a small stove.

"A gift from Mrs. Mathison. It's bloody useful, quicker than the camping thing." Andrew brushed wisps of hair off his face, "I can convert it later," he asserted. "I've got the big oil drums I need."

Every movement made dust rise and glisten like insects in the sunshine that now slipped through the kitchen window. Soon they would be able to whitewash the walls and rescue a little light and height in here. For the moment, Chloe had done what she could to brighten the atmosphere by putting four pots of scented pink geraniums on the window sill. Their sweetness, released by the sunshine stealing over their leaves, disguised the plainer smells of plaster and mouse droppings.

Joe followed them outside, silently noting everything down with his eyes. He saw grass growing through the barn roof, hens scratching in the yard—their movements watched by a pair of collared doves who swooped languidly each time a hen made her squawk of discovery. He saw a stack of window frames, complete with glass leaning against the cowshed, a concrete mixer, at least six metal pails with brushes or sticks protruding from them in readiness. He noted the absence of a gate to the yard though the gatepost and hinges remained, was aware of the dancing of butterflies (or moths... when they were either creamy or brown as these were, he couldn't be sure), and thought to himself he had never smelt air so clean.

The others were proudly standing by the large, dark oblong of earth they'd prepared for vegetables.

"I did the bean poles," said Andrew with satisfaction, looking at the wigwam of stripped hazel.

"We put potatoes in right away. Maincrop," explained Peter, adding, a little self-consciously, "Majestics and Pentland Crown."

Joe nodded. "What are the other things?" He pointed to the rows of tiny limp foliage and other rows simply marked off with string and neat white stickers. He could see small gleaming movements in the soil; spiders and ants.

"Cabbages, cauliflowers and lettuce."

"Beetroot, carrots, turnips and ... artichokes."

"Sweet corn," added Chloe, "I did that."

They ached with tiredness and pleasure at what they had done. Joe bent down, picked up a handful of friable soil and let it run through his fingers. It felt pleasantly warm. Beneath the paler, crusting surface, it was dark, almost black.

"It was surprisingly full of humus," said Chloe.

He smiled up at her. "Good," he said, seeing her happiness.

He wanted them to go and talk, to lie on the long grasses of the field.

"No, it's to be kept for hay," Peter said. "Mrs. Mathison suggested we took our tents off it."

They carried their lunch of cheese, home-made bread and goat's milk (which Joe privately thought disgusting) under the last blossoms of the apple trees and there spread it on one of the paper fertiliser sacks that were so plentifully abandoned round the buildings.

"Any hassles getting here?" Andrew broke off a piece of the heavy, flat brown loaf.

"Not too bad. It's better to travel alone."

"Right. *We* travelled together ... They're suspicious of you. We must have done half the journey on foot." Andrew balanced a lump of crumbly cheese on his bread and made a bold bite.

"Funny isn't it ... ?" reflected Joe, gazing through the lace of low branches to the sheep-studded hillside beyond.

"Funny?"

"The peacefulness of it all." He gestured in a general way, waving his blue enamel mug at the tumble of water, the quiet cropping of goats whose white backs shimmered between the buttercups and the stillness of the elm, ash and beech trees that blended their greens below them. He rolled over on his stomach and looked in the other direction, up the hill they lay on. Sun fell through the ivy-covered apple trees. Somewhere, out of sight, he could hear the single, liquid cry of a bird. "You'd never think there was anything wrong," he said and rolled back again. "It's weird." He threw the remainder of his milk away.

They didn't pursue the reflection but lay or leaned back, in a guiltily contented quiet.

It was true, thought Peter to himself. I've been too busy to think. Too exhausted by hard physical labour to philosophise at nightfall. The change, now he thought about it, surprised him. The same change he realised, must have overtaken Andrew as well. Neither of them had sought out or gnawed upon the world's worries with their usual relish. Seeing nothing to say, he picked a blade of grass and chewed it.

Andrew was more disconcerted by the same response. *Were* they escaping? He scraped at some moss with his thumb nail and pondered the possibility. It did feel a bit like it.

No, he thought, the first thing is to feed yourself without taking away from anyone else. Take yourself off the world's meal table. Then . . . And he wasn't sure. India, perhaps, he thought idly.

He lay back, arms beneath his head. All he *could* say with any sense of conviction was that in some curious way, the digging and plastering and hammering that had occupied him for the past ten days felt like the only wholly honest acts of his life. There was in them a commitment, so ungrudging. so clear, each act—blunting the edge of a nail to make it cleave to the wood better, shutting the hens up at night against foxes, cutting down the hazel branches to make his bean poles, carrying the early morning water in each day—each thing had become a separate act of love. Worship, even.

But he didn't say any of this because he wasn't sure Joe would understand. If anybody *should* understand, mind, it was Joe. That was the funny thing. But it wasn't the same as when they'd just talked about it. In a week or two, Andrew mused, then he'd understand better.

Chloe poured more milk from the earthenware jug for those

who wanted it and shooed a bee away from the lip. "You'll get used to it." She smiled at Joe.

"Used to it?"

"The milk."

"Oh."

He got to his feet and walked down the orchard to study the goats more closely. They knew he was strange and stood very still, their tails lifted, hair ridged along their spines assessing his approach with their ears, not their eyes. The eyes, in the profile they presented to him, were blank as agate.

When he touched the unhorned head of the nearest one, she urinated in defence of her territory, then walked uncertainly a yard or so away, waiting for him to go before she dare lower her head to eat.

Joe was glad he had his back to the others. He had a strong and (he knew) paranoic feeling that the bloody goat was reacting to him rather as the others had. They were settled. In possession. And yet it had all been his idea to come.

Half-heartedly, he made a wheedling noise at the goat who ignored him. "What's his name?" he called over his shoulder to the others who lay, propped up on their elbows, watching.

"Amaryllis!" Chloe collapsed with laughter.

Amaryllis shed a cascade of firm brown pellets and put her head down to eat. This redoubled the laughter behind him. "You've offended her now!"

Defiantly, Joe took another step towards her and this time she turned, lowering her head as if to butt. With difficulty, he held his ground. "Bitch!" he breathed, and after winning a battle of eyeballs with her, looked beyond to the luscious rise and fall of the valley.

He'd seen other, larger expanses of open countryside than this . . . the bleak and barren heights of Turkey for instance, which gave no promise of supportable life at all. They'd been far more alien. But he'd been travelling *through* that landscape, simply looking, moving on. Here he would have to stay. His sense of difference heightened with this conclusion. He was at a loss, without maps. Stay for a while, anyway, he thought, until I understand.

Chloe's arm was slipped through his. "Tonight, I'll show you how to milk her," she said. "It's not very difficult. It just makes your fingers ache that's all." They walked uphill, arms loosely locked.

"You know what it is?" he said suddenly, looking into her face with a fierceness that made her laugh again.

"What?"

"You're all so beautiful!"

She threw her head back with mirth.

"It's true. Look at you. And *them* . . . !"

But she knew what he meant. Within so short a space of time the boys' bodies had become tanned, their muscles cleanly defined. The pallor they had brought with them, the dust in their eyes, had gone.

"I suppose they *have* changed. It's just being outside."

"Maybe."

Joe could now identify at least one cause for his feeling apart. His body was physically apart. Not just in size—he had come to terms with his smallness, years ago at school and since then had felt no need to defend it. Not just strength either, though that came into it. (When neither your status nor being is linked to your bodily strength, he reflected, it's not a thing you think about much.) No, he had the skin, the texture of a different creature altogether. From a different place. It was his plumage, belonging to other shapes, shadows and colours, that marked him out as an intruder. Unlike them. They melted into trees and sunshine. They could lie unseen in the grass.

He asked what job he should do that afternoon with an ill grace.

In the evening Chloe called him to the goats and made him sit down in the soiled straw to reach under one of them for its udder. The animal warmth dismayed him.

"Like this," she said and showed him how to trap the top of the teat between thumb and forefinger, using the other fingers to flush the milk down. It hissed into the bucket sweet and generous.

"Now you."

But he couldn't get the knack. Nothing came out. Using two hands together was impossibly uncomfortable.

"She's holding up on you. Come on, you! Give!" And she massaged the bag more vigorously than he would have dared. "Now," she said. "Try."

This time he got a squirt before the goat bunched her quarters up.

"Give it time," said Chloe. "There's plenty of time."

He looked at her, absorbed in her milking, her wrists loosely rhythmic. The quick, soft hiss. And he knew Chloe was queen. The power had crept out of him, into her. He, the man, would always wish falsely to be the master. But he was not.

There were no masters.

10

"I DON'T THINK SHE'LL COME," SAID MADGE FIRMLY OVER the phone.

"She simply must!" Biddy Hall's voice betrayed desperation. She adjusted her tone adding, "It's simply not good for her to be walled up like this. She'd got to *make* herself... Got to come to terms."

The real purpose of her call was to ask Olivia to come up to Town for a meeting with a couple of foreign publishing executives and a producer who wanted to develop a serial out of one of her books for American television. (One of the few consumer goods that continued to sell healthily was the romance.) "Look, get her to ring me back, Madge, would you... just for a gossip?" She allowed herself to sound pleading.

"I don't think she'll come," repeated Madge doggedly. "She's very involved in this book." She was in fact refusing all engagements, even invitations from close friends like Bart Foster. It wasn't *quite* right thought Madge. But she didn't interfere.

"How's it coming along?" Biddy asked grudgingly. She regarded the biography as a nuisance, as an *obstacle* to Olivia's writing. Also, as a waste of time since she couldn't see a market for it.

"It's hard to tell as she's typing it herself. I haven't read it at all but I have the *impression* she's finding it slower work than usual."

"Oh dear, well look Madge, between us we must get her out ... Tell her I rang. Work on her would you?"

Madge, who resented Biddy Hall's conspiratorial manner,

returned to her correspondence. It was mostly, to use Olivia's own phrase, "gracious refusals". She seemed to be taking her mourning very heavily. And there was, Madge sighed to herself, as she dabbed with an eraser, the book. She dismissed from her mind the observation that however obsessive the book, her employer appeared to be doing far *less* work than usual. Miss Bennett, as she told her sister, seemed "restless". And no wonder, the atmosphere had become thoroughly unsettled with all these young people streaming in and out. Their company seemed, to Madge, to be endless. Even *she* felt fidgety.

She opened another letter and finding it was the complete statement of accounts she'd requested from Fortnum's (on her own initiative) looked through it with careful interest.

The over-all amount had certainly been pushed up by price rises alone. Inflation, on Madge's calculation, accounted for at least two per cent increase on the previous month, but there'd also been a special purchase of two five-pound boxes of hand-made chocolates (for the British Legion raffle), Amy's hamper, of course and another hamper — three times the cost — ordered about the same time with additional delivery charges (£3.00) to an address in Hounslow. *That* explained it. Madge, with a prick of guilt at querying the bill (though you couldn't be too careful) folded it up quickly and moved to a demand from the publisher that the latest set of proofs be returned, corrected, forthwith. He pointed to the need to publish as swiftly as possible before stricter paper allocations came into force.

Madge sighed and lit the first of the three Gauloise cigarettes she allowed herself each day. She smoked awkwardly, holding the cigarette between her knuckles and pressing her lips against her fingers when she brought the filter tip to the very centre of her mouth. Within minutes she was encircled by smoke.

It would mean nagging, she thought glumly. Getting the proofs read. She flicked vaguely in the direction of the grey metal wastepaper basket and noticed Corin's distant figure walking downhill from Sheep Cottages . . . why Corin had come home in the middle of the week she failed to understand. It wasn't usual. Anyway, she thought, a five day week was a five day week. This was no time to be taking days off just when you felt like it.

She let her glance linger. Such a nice little boy, he used to be. But nowadays (she picked up another letter), he could be . . . unpredictable. Edgy.

It was a poison pen letter. Well, no, that was too strong an expression. An unpleasant, unsigned letter. It sneered. It's all right for you, rich bitch, it said.

A letter like this was so rare, it shocked Madge. Miss Bennett had her critics, but they didn't write personal letters. There were even, on occasion, insane and suggestive letters which she dealt with, keeping them from her employer. But this was neatly typed, grammatical, correctly spelt and if anything (Madge searched her mind for the word) *political*. It accused Miss Bennett of using fantasy comparable in its evil to propaganda, of perpetrating oppressive views and abusing her "power for communication with women".

This last phrase made her assume it came from one of the more vicious feminist organisations. The number of girls involved these days in street fighting and bomb incidents made Madge shudder. It was unnatural.

She couldn't bring herself to read it a second time. She applied her lighter to a corner of the letter and let it curl, then flame in her fingers before dropping it in the wastepaper basket.

In the next room along the landing, Olivia sat watching Corin's approach.

He was carrying a gun, though she couldn't think why. It was an absurd time of day to go and shoot anything. She couldn't for that matter, explain what he was doing here at all. He'd simply (rather rudely) said he was "bloody fed up with the office" when he'd turned up this morning and gone upstairs to change.

Vaguely, she wondered whether he'd been sacked. But it seemed improbable. Unemployment didn't appear to reach in that direction. He'd looked so surly when he emerged from his room, she wouldn't have dared to ask.

All this *upheaval*, she thought with a mixture of irritability and fearfulness. Even Leo. Suggesting, at the weekend, suggesting that he should retire early. "By the end of the year?" he'd said doubtfully. It would mean, he'd added, living largely off her income. How would she feel about it?

"Well of course we can," she'd said, astonished by him. She thought he'd always abhorred the idea.

And immediately he'd started urging a holiday on her saying she needed a rest. But she had no desire to leave Clouds at the moment. There was too much to be done.

Corin disappeared from view between the house and the stable yard. Guiltily aware that she had let her thoughts wander, she returned to her work. It was laborious. When Leo had read through what she'd written so far, he'd laughed several times to her annoyance. "I don't remember it quite like that," he'd remarked. And then, putting down the sheets after he'd finished reading, he'd pondered quietly for a few moments before venturing: "You won't like my saying this, but if you *want* me to perform a critical role...?" (He'd lifted a heavy eyebrow at her and she'd nodded.) "Well then, I'd say there was more about you than her. Nothing wrong with that, it's a question of balance that's all, and what you have in mind." He had looked at her in gentle judgement and she'd had to acknowledge he was right. "Go back to the beginning," he'd advised. "Fill it out. You're in too much of a hurry."

It exasperated her going back over the same ground. It *looked* barren a second time around. In the end, she spent more of her day thinking than writing with the horrifying result that she was getting down only three or four pages by tea-time. The average was making her despair. Normally she wrote straight off with barely a correction, aiming for a minimum of 6,000 words a day. Now she was fortunate if she could produce 2,000. And the effort exhausted her quite beyond anything she'd ever attempted before.

Of course, she told herself hotly, she *had* been subject to an abnormal amount of interruption.

Even as she thought it, the doorbell rang. She imagined it was Corin being annoying.

Corin had seen the figures of the two girls coming up the drive. They walked slowly beneath the swaying beeches, each holding a handle of the carry-cot and leaning their weight away from it.

"Christ Almighty!" he thought. "More of them," and swollen with anger, he turned on his heel going all the way round the back of the house to go into the gun room. There, so placed that he could hear whatever conversation went on in the hall, he took a rag from the shelf and began cleaning his .22.

"Come in, will you?" Madge answered the door since Mrs. Baldwin didn't come in the afternoons. "Miss Bennett can't be disturbed for another hour. Not until tea-time." She looked at her watch. "Well, three quarters of an hour say. Will you wait?"

They'd asked for Chloe but Madge felt they should be presented to Miss Bennett first for a preliminary examination. Covertly, she regarded them through her whirlpool lenses, finding it very hard to distinguish clear differences. Both had long hair and long dresses. "Perhaps you'd like some tea now," she said ungraciously.

"We could look around," offered the mousier of the two. (She appeared also to be the mother since it was she who bent to pick up the baby. It showed signs of temper.)

"Thank you, please."

The other girl, rounder, shorter, had smooth dark brown hair, very brown eyes and a rosy countenance. "That would be nice. We can look round after. Will Chloe be long?"

"I couldn't say," answered Madge, determined that the two young women should not be left to wander about the place unwatched. She didn't approve of the freedom that appeared to operate.

The baby, large but somehow still furrowed and furious looking like a very young infant, began hitting its mother's head.

"I'll put the kettle on," murmured Madge, retreating.

"I can always feed the baby," smiled its mother at Madge's vanishing figure. "Bring his nappies would you, Mab, we'll go and sit in there."

They turned towards the drawing room. Madge had neglected to show them beyond the hall where the only chairs were two upright Jacobean chairs of carved oak, painfully uncomfortable and chiefly reserved for careless hats and coats.

As they moved, a door which appeared to be part of the panelling, opened and Corin stepped out still holding his gun.

"I'll drive you up there later," he said and strode away in the same direction Madge had taken.

The girls giggled and continued on their way into the drawing room. It smelt sharply of lilac and floor polish.

When Madge returned she was appalled to find the mousy girl had unbuttoned her dress and was busily feeding her gluttonous baby. She seemed hypnotised by the act, not looking up once as tray and tea things rattled grumpily together. "Can I leave you to look after yourselves?" Madge spoke in a throttled voice. "I have things to attend to."

Half an hour later when (extravagantly) she took fresh tea to Olivia, her lips were still stapled balefully together.

"My dear Madge! You should have told me they'd arrived! Did you send Barber up to fetch Chloe?"

"I thought you should see them first," breathed Madge darkly.

The girls had wandered down the drive to gaze at the mares and foals who nosed their way through the poppies and ox-eye daisies which had now added their brightness to the meadow.

As Olivia approached, two of the mares raised their heads and whinnied, shrilly echoed by the bony, alert little foal she had helped to deliver. His coat was pale and fluffy now like a toy animal's. Absorbing the smell of strangers, he did no more than reach his small muzzle in Olivia's direction, keeping his tail end pushed firmly against his mother. His legs were arranged like guy-ropes.

"You must be Mab and Sarah . . . am I right?"

Shyly, the girls confirmed this, looking at one another lengthways.

"And the baby. What's baby's name? Isn't he gorgeous!"

"Biff. Well hardly, I mean, he's beautiful to *me*," Sarah tried to turn the head of her child towards Olivia, but he was more interested in the horses. "He does look as though he received a blow at birth, that's why he's called Biff." She grinned cheerfully and Olivia was forced to smile back. "I'm sure he'll straighten out," she said reassuringly.

"Let's hope so for his sake." Sarah hitched her infant on to her hip and began following Olivia back to the house.

"She's terribly rude about him," commented Mab unnecessarily. "I'm afraid we've left some dirty nappies in your lounge."

"Now then let me see, which of you is the potter?"

"She is." Mab indicated Sarah.

"How wonderful. I've always longed to try potting myself."

"I'll teach you," offered Sarah.

"That *would* be exciting!"

Olivia hurried on.

Corin, driving round the corner of the house, drew up in the van. "I'll take them," he called. "Hop in!"

"Darling, I've hardly had a chance to speak to them yet!"

"You'll have plenty of opportunity," he replied dryly not

looking at her but instead watching Mab clamber in the back. Sarah sat beside him clasping the grunting Biff.

"Where's your luggage?"

"At the station."

"I'll get it later." He switched on the ignition, and reversed a few feet.

"Oh! The carry-cot! The nappies!" squeaked Sarah. And then, to Olivia, "Would you mind?"

And Olivia found herself walking into the drawing room, picking smeary, redolent nappies off the floor and hauling a carry-cot out to the van. She was furious with Corin.

"See you soon, darlings!" she cried, waving to them all, and returning indoors, poured herself an early sherry.

Without telling anybody where he was going, or why, Joe had been out for hours exploring.

He was just a little shamefaced about the three small books on fishes, birds and wild flowers he'd stuck lumpily in his pockets and had slipped away, while the others removed tiles, to match things to the pictures wherever he could.

Climbing to the very top of the hill behind the house, he'd looked out northward to the strange Vale of Whitmore around which, Chloe had told him, so many legends had grown. Grown and tangled with one another, with legends of other places like marvellous, flowering briars.

Rising over the Vale, on the western rim of its scoop, stood the vertical slopes of Corford camp, so deeply wooded no stranger would know the foliage concealed three deep ramparts until he began the steep climb for himself and grew puzzled by a formation that couldn't be natural however beguilingly and anciently clothed with oak and thorn.

He had made for it, climbing down through the fields, finding lanes and bridle paths hidden by their high-growing hedges, whose course, though arbitrary to him, had once, perhaps a thousand years before, been the highways of farming men. They had led him, disruptedly, to the lower slopes of the earthworks where a small farm nestled. He'd seen nobody there, but heard clanking preparations for milking coming from the yard. A black and white dog had barked once then disappeared, grinning.

Alone on the great green plate of land at the top, overlooking, so it seemed, not just half England, but an untailored swaddling of time in which armies flowed through the clefts of the valley, came and went, besieged and were massacred (here, Chloe had said, the Romans killed every Celtic man, woman and child as an example, their bones remained still, higgledy-piggledy). Here, where men lit warning fires, farmed, slaughtered cattle and stored their grain in pits, here he had felt the ceaseless inevitability of event. As though the land, like a patient beast, stood ready for the weight of casualty to be placed upon its back.

Alone below, concealed by trees and bramble, he had bent to his books trying to record the shape and movement of birds in his eye while turning feverishly to the right page to identify them. Something tiny and reddish had scuttled up an elm trunk into the leaves before he could be certain of it.

Mostly, he'd seen only birds he knew perfectly well like blackbirds, thrushes and crows (or rooks, perhaps). Magpies were easy too, but he'd been quite unprepared for their abundance. "One for sorrow, two for joy", he knew, but he must have seen fifteen of the showy birds in all and what the significance of that figure was, went unwritten.

Smoothing down the pages of the book he discovered he had spotted rosy-breasted bullfinches and goldfinches (though their company had risen from the hedge so swiftly, he couldn't be sure . . . perhaps, he'd thought, looking at the mediocre colour plates, they'd been female bullfinches).

Flowers were easier. He'd collected them as he went, settling down on a broken, mossy wall above the river to spread out his drying treasures, carefully counting their petals and noting the shapes of their leaves. (On the wall itself speedwell grew, but he hadn't seen it until he rose to leave.)

The varieties were bewildering. And having no idea of what kind of soil he was on his guessing had not been usefully narrowed down. Looking about him, he'd eliminated chalk, but after that bold stroke, had been rather stuck.

Painstakingly, using his fingers as though he were handling surgical instruments, he'd sifted through his finds and discovered that in the higher fields, (so steep the cows had formed a natural terrace of steps for themselves), he'd plucked campion, a small pink, and bird's-foot trefoil, its yellow pea-like flowers tipped with tawny orange.

He thought he'd found this flower again, lower down among the lanes but peering closer, realised it was different. With great pride, he'd classified it as vetchling. But the discovery which had delighted him most of all was a minute red flower he might easily have walked over without noticing. Yet its name was as well known to him as the dandelion's. It was the concealed, exquisite scarlet pimpernel.

Eventually, he'd clambered down to the river (into which their own stream flowed) and followed its curve around the hillside to the bottom of their own valley. Here he lay now on the far bank, flat on his stomach, head propped up on folded arms, studying the book on fishes. It was cool and quiet. Even the coarse-leaved comfrey and forget-me-nots were coolly coloured.

The river was shallow, fast-running and brown except where sunlight perforated the canopy of alder and broke the water into golden fragments.

Joe was happy. He was getting to grips with the place. Soon the names would signify familiarity rather than botany. Soon he would cease to be an onlooker and start to form his own relationships with these things — look to them for food or signs of weather and season.

He let his hand trail in the cold, fast-flowing water and immediately there was a shadowy movement among the stones. He cursed himself for not watching carefully enough.

According to the book, this should be a perfect place for trout, but he would need a different book to find out how to tickle them which is what he most wanted to know. Dampness stole through his jersey and soldered his aching joints together. He remained motionless, staring down. The water rushed softly under the trees. All else was still.

He jumped at the crashing sound in the undergrowth on the bank above. Then he stiffened. The sound repeated itself, twice . . . like an animal moving then pausing to scent. A fairly large animal, thought Joe, not daring to roll over in case he attracted it.

In the brief silence that followed, he realised with some foolishness, that there was no animal in all England that was going to attack him. His instinct, though correct, was inappropriate to his century. Smiling to himself, he turned over, tucking two of his books back into his hip pockets and peered upwards through the leaves.

More crackling. Now he saw a pair of legs in baggy trousers, trousers that were tucked into green gum boots almost buried in the bracken. Although the rest of the figure was obscured by branches, he recognised Corin. He had stared very hard at Corin earlier that afternoon when he'd leant against the wall of the Cottages delivering a sour commentary on the work that was going on. It was partly because of Corin that Joe had walked out. He found him a deeply negative influence.

The legs descended further into view. The trousers, though roomy in the leg wouldn't meet around the waist and were held up with baler twine.

Corin, noticed Joe, was carrying his gun. For the second time he stiffened. His instinct had been right after all.

"Thought you were there!" Corin shouldered the .22 and stared down.

How could he possibly have known, Joe wondered. He'd been lying perfectly still watching for trout.

"Hi!" he called. "I thought you were a deer of some kind." And he rose painfully to his feet.

Corin stared at him coldly. Absently, rather. "Mm. Well, I wasn't." He turned away and pointed at a loose slip of earth on the bank between the trees. "There *are* deer . . . that's one of their runs. D'you see?"

He did now. He wouldn't have done.

He clambered towards Corin, determined to seem friendly. They were, it struck him, the same age near enough . . . worlds apart, though. *Worlds*. No, he was trespassing in Corin's world. The gun then seemed natural.

"What've you got there?" Corin tried to seize the handbook on fishes.

"I was watching for trout."

"Better later in the day. Evening. Still, there are a good few about. Look!" And he pointed into a calmer, gilded pool some ten feet below where they stood. It was protected by toothy rocks from the general race of water.

Joe looked and could see nothing.

"Seven, eight, oh at least eight." Corin's voice was low.

Still Joe looked and saw only the illusory dapple of light.

"Come on," said Corin. "We'll wade over further down stream," and he led the way crashing ferociously. A jay rose screaming through the trees. Joe guessed it was a jay.

After Corin had found the crossing place he was looking for and splashed through to the Sheep Cottages side of the river, he stood waiting for Joe to catch up. Joe, who was without boots, was soaked.

"Here!" said Corin suddenly unslinging the gun from his shoulder and reaching it out towards Joe. "You have it. I'd like you to take it."

Joe drew back. "No thanks," he said cautiously. "I don't go for violence." He stared at the gun.

"Oh, you twit!"

Joe retreated a further step.

"*Take* it!" Corin insisted, stepping forward and pushing it against Joe's body. "Thank you, no." He broke away and began to climb through a barbed wire fence into the lower field.

Corin puffed after him. (He was beginning to carry too much weight.) "You'll need it," he called.

"What for? Self defence?" asked Joe sarcastically, pausing to wait for him.

"No, you clown, well, maybe. No, for hunting of course."

"I'm vegetarian."

"Chloe isn't."

"Well . . ." Joe shrugged and started walking again, shoulders hunched.

"Of course you'll have to hunt."

"Is that what you've been doing all afternoon?"

"Me? Oh, I was just . . . loafing, wandering about," Corin took a grey handkerchief from his pocket and ran it over his face. "Chiefly, I was looking for you to tell you the girls have arrived."

"The girls? Oh great!" Joe's face lightened. He lengthened his stride feeling the unaccustomed pull on his calf muscles.

"Anyway," persisted Corin hurrying behind him, "you *will* have to hunt. Good God, I caught you trying to lift trout, what's that if it's not hunting?"

"I don't like weapons," asserted Joe doggedly.

The jeering voice behind him went on. "Call yourself survivors? You don't *begin* to know what it's about!" And then, a few yards further, "Man would be extinct by now if it weren't for weapons, you idiot."

"And now he's able to make himself extinct. With weapons." Joe halted again.

Corin came up clumsily, half stumbling. Above them, the goats began to bleat.

"Oh, stop arguing and take the bloody thing!" Corin thrust it against Joe's ribs.

"*Take* it!"

Something in Corin's voice (a pleading, hysterical note) made

Joe capitulate. He told himself that he was being negative too . . . that this was Corin's awkward way of reaching out.

"O.K.," he said slowly, "since you insist. Thanks. But . . ." He didn't add anything. It felt funny, standing there holding a gun. It was heavy. He felt powerful.

"Here you are." Corin emptied his pockets of ammunition and handed the bullets to Joe. "No damn good without these," he laughed cheerfully. He was triumphant, having accomplished his purpose. Relieved.

The goats stopped.

"Well!" Corin slapped his thighs and straightened up. "I said I'd collect the new inmates' luggage. I'll come up with you."

They completed their climb in silence, Corin now ahead, Joe struggling under his load. Both hands were full of ammunition since his pockets were already bulging with handbooks. He had difficulty crawling through a hole the goats had driven in the hedge and Corin made no attempt to help him but bounded ahead, newly agile.

By the time Joe reached the yard Corin had vanished in a blue cloud of exhaust as the van bucked down the rough track.

Everyone else was clustered in the yard. Sarah was amusing Biff by throwing the remains of a bread pudding to the hens who ran shrieking from one tossed lump to another.

When they spied Joe, armed, they laughed and shouted.

"Hey!"

"Viva Ché!"

But he went to greet the girls, too overjoyed to heed the whooping chorus.

They were complete now. He hugged them singly and together. Then he took Biff in his arms and tenderly kissed his scowling son.

Midsummer

"Then we can chalk it all up to love?"
"I suppose so."
"It's an amazing business, this love."

Set Fair by JOAN BUTLER

Midsummer

AT THE END OF JUNE, THE NUPTIAL GARMENTS OF THE countryside were put away until the following year and the landscape settled down into a heavy, more uniform maturity of green.

The farmers watched the sky from day to day waiting for the grasses to reach a perfect moment between flowering and seeding. A few, fearful that the mild and steady sunshine could not hold and that the rain, when it came would come ceaselessly, cut early and made silage of what growth there was. It was little enough following the dry spring.

But the weather didn't break. Each successive day for three weeks, the sun rose to a clear, high mark in the sky. The strawberries sweetened. In the fields, the beasts grew a fine bloom on their coats, fully recovered from a skeletal winter. Between hard, clay banks, the brooks ran low.

By early July the fields and valleys buzzed with the slow, fat sound of tractors. Behind them, unfolded long, pale, twisting stripes of cut grass. It was turned once, twice, then gathered into sweet green bales and left out to dry on the new neat tablecloth of pasture. Hares suddenly appeared, bounding across the cleared expanse. The colour of the land turned to pale gold.

The rain came without warning. Without any of the preliminary, staring heat that transfixes flower heads before a storm.

Andrew, Joe, Peter and a number of other friends who came and went in easy tides had been helping Gerald Causely haul bales in return for his cutting their own small stretch of grass. They stood idly by in his barn watching the weather hurtle past. For two days they waited, hoping a fresh interval of sunshine would dry the bales out. On the third day they returned to their own labour inside the cottages.

There was no need to go as far as the stream for water. Rain rolled off the eaves into the great rain butt providing them with all the water they needed for a week.

Mrs. Cross, the post lady, told them that the river, where it flowed through the village, had risen to near flooding point and they went down to hang over the bridge and see for themselves, their boots thick and heavy with mud from the dissolved track to Sheep Cottages.

"What you lose with one hand, you gain with the other," Gerald Causely remarked as he peered out at the leaden skies from beneath his greasy cap. "Bad for the hay and good for the barley."

And he wondered fatalistically as he watched his bales turn black in the sullen outpouring of rain, just what this winter would mean.

The rain helped keep Olivia at her desk. She gazed through the runnelled glass at the sodden garden below. The shrubs were resisting the weather fairly well but her long-stemmed fragrant lilies, the tobacco plants and carnations, drooped with abuse.

The rain drove her imagination inwards.

With great effort and difficulty she followed Leo's suggestion that she fill her mind with detail of the rooms, the clothes, all the small surrounding objects of the cottage. "It should help bring it back," he promised. "Just try."

She tried.

In her mind, she moved across the mantelshelf above the black, leaded iron hood of the grate, placing there, very gingerly, three brass monkeys. See No Evil, Hear No Evil, Speak No Evil. Then, a small hand-painted jug, just big enough for primroses or violets. It was cream with a brown rim and brown lettering — 'It's a long lane that has no turning'. A Coronation mug. No, a souvenir mug made on the accession of Edward, Prince of Wales. No, it had not been there . . . it had disappeared.

With amusement, she realised it must have been replaced by the plaster shepherd boy. Perhaps it had been broken. Perhaps the abdication . . .

She moved on. A picture. A child with rabbits and daisies above a verse of 'All Things Bright and Beautiful'. Another. A photograph of her grandmother, brown and Victorian, a lace over her hair, her face empty of everything save concentration.

Down to the sideboard, dark oak and ugly. A brass bell. A brass and copper ashtray, never used, but still dulled despite all her cleaning, by the sooty blows of her father's pipe. A pair of brass nutcrackers in the shape of a dragonfly. A silver paper knife. A silver toast rack. *None* of these things ever used but cleaned and put back at precisely the same angles to one another like ceremonial treasures.

The walnut tea trolley with its dented biscuit tins tidily placed on the lower shelf. One with a picture of King George V and Queen Mary on its lid, the other bearing tartans, thistles and small misty views of Edinburgh in symmetrical lozenges.

On all these things, on the trolley and sideboard as well as on the occasional table and the backs of assorted brown chairs, were stiff, creamy linen cloths embroidered by her mother. They were to protect the objects beneath them from ever being dirtied or marked. But they were not to be dirtied either. She saw them in her mind's eye, clean, starched, part of the general stillness. Journeying among these things brought little sense of home. More like visiting one of those dioramas in which you feel the owner (if he's not a stuffed and smiling dummy) lies dead upstairs.

The rain brought the young people into the house more often. Olivia was irritated by the way they dropped in for a bath or slumped into a chair watching television in the afternoon, if it was too wet to get on with the roof. Sometimes they brought other strangers with them. People who were lending a hand with the building or to do with Joe's magazine. Often they were not introduced, or introduced so vaguely, no conceivable conversation could flow from the encounter.

Olivia noted that visitors had started to call on Sheep Cottages approaching from the other end of the track, the end that joined up with the main road, thus saving themselves from going through Clouds. Perversely, this annoyed her too. She felt as though the whole venture had acquired a momentum of its own, passing out of her province. One day she rebuked Sarah sharply for letting Biff maul one of Delilah's kittens.

The weather brought out everybody's gloom. As though the clouds which hung over so much shocking city debris had drifted their way. It was there—the gloom—all the time of course, sleeping like a cobra in the soul, but without any deliberate conspiracy of silence, nobody ever referred to the situation. The situation simply was. You had to get on despite it. Get used to it. And anyway, they were better off here than some folk; what was the point of complaining. Only two remarks in the village ever signified any awareness of the way the world creaked. "What's it all coming to I wonder?". and "I just don't know, I don't, really."

But they watched the weather more anxiously than they'd watched it for over a quarter of a century. No matter what else happened, as long as sun, rain and frost came at kindly moments, they would get by.

As the baled hay darkened in the field more cattle were silently marked down for slaughter. In the cottage gardens, the proudly netted rows of soft fruit, the vivid overlapping leaves of beans and lettuce all seemed, momentarily to halt in their growth. The peas were without sweetness.

But the weeks of malefic rain ended. As the school holidays drew near the children were indulgently let out for longer and longer intervals to play in the neighbouring fields. Their faces grew brown again, brushed with sun. Their arms were full of the new month's purplish flowering—scabious, knapweed and vetch all bunched together with umbelliferous sprays of Queen Anne's lace.

Though the birdsong was fading as fledgelings learnt their own way round the world, the children's cries were clearly heard through open windows by their mothers. The women looked up from their stoves as they filled their houses with a glorious storing smell of warm fruit and hot sugar. Next the wine would be made, the beans salted, the potatoes lifted and stored, the onions hung and the cabbage pickled. Before one knew it, the nuts would be ready to be beaten and the apples racked.

The bees resumed working on their winter provision. So did the young people at Sheep Cottages. The bio-bog, as it was called, provided less power than Andrew had hoped for. "Quite enough to keep a greenhouse going," he'd asserted defensively, and promptly built one. Small, but quite enough for tomatoes and seedling plants.

To everyone's surprise, the huge, carefully measured sheets of plastic that were to be fixed to the southerly slope of the roof, arrived, and with all the extra helpers who called, work began in furious earnest. The steadiest worker was Bill Adams, Josie's father, a small farmer whose troubles the previous winter had finally forced him to sell out to Gerald Causely for whom he now worked, happier, he claimed than he had ever been. " 'Twas the worry of it," he claimed again and again speaking through a mouthful of nails or stretching his stocky power to its utmost behind a mallet. It was Bill's goose who'd provided the eggs their hens had failed to hatch. "They hens am'nt silly," he said. "They know a goose egg when they see 'un. If they sit on 'un their legs won't reach the floor. You got to tease they along a little bit."

Always gentle, always amused, he watched their efforts, putting them right only when they asked his help. The top of his bald head above the line of his cap was quite white. When he pushed his cap back to scratch thoughtfully, his skull looked like the neatly peeled top of a brown egg.

Every evening he was to be found in the Ploughman's Arms nursing a stout and defending his title as skittles champion against all comers. Some wives these days, wouldn't let their husbands go to the pub more than two nights a week but as Bill said, they drank more on those two nights "than I do drink on a se'ennight".

Every Thursday during the six weeks that made up midsummer, Chloe joined the children in the village school and together with them, pondered over the meaning of the Creed, the nature of evil, the nature of pain, the person of Christ, the meaning of God and the mystery of the afterlife. Sitting there, on a chair far too small for her, at a desk that grazed her knees, solemn discussion of these topics set her spinning in the timeless gyres of time. In any age but the present, except that it was the present. The topics were as wholesome as ever they were, unsolved by any epoch but continually attempted like rampart upon rampart. It didn't matter, she thought, what form one's query took—it could be Sarah's astrological approach, Joe's blend of Zen and other things or even pagan mythologies—it didn't matter. For her, in the school hall where the walls were bright with square, painted cows and potato prints and underwater scenes, it was the image of Christ that beckoned, but it didn't matter. What mattered, was perceiving that the soul existed, as real, as demanding of exercise as one's legs or bowels.

The children listened meekly for the most part to the patient flow of Henry Claremont's voice, neither believing nor disbelieving, just hearing what they assumed was the truth, coming from such a person.

"Who then is the head of the Church?" questioned Henry one evening of a small girl in a clean, pink, hand-knitted twinset. "You sir," she answered simply.

It helped, to approach in this plain manner. It gave an authentic ordinariness to the more glamorous of Chloe's passions. The discovery that it was possible, at different levels, to share the same belief with the children, rooted her faith more steadily and brought a sense of fellowship that had been absent from her solitary explorations. Approaching Christ in the vernacular, her love for Him became less and less of a public embarrassment.

It was a small and ordinary thing that helped Olivia in her searching through the deserted cottage. She came upon it after prolonged exploration of the dead places.

It was a bag of buttons. A round, raffia basket with coloured strands of blue, green and red woven through it. Stitched to the raffia was a circular piece of fabric (a fragment of an old, floral curtain) drawn together at the top by a silk cord, part of a dressing gown cord. And inside, all jumbled together, her mother's collection of buttons. Carved wooden buttons with dancers painted on them, elaborately beaded buttons, silvery buttons crinkled like tinfoil, buttons covered in pony hair or sequins, buttons like pennies, buttons like jewels. She had played happily for hours with these, saving them up for wet days when the cottage was darkened by the dripping pines outside. The button bag had been a treat. And she somehow knew, that watching her play, her mother had shared the absorbed pleasure. She watched mother and child herself from her different niche of time and tasted their pleasure. For the first time, with any clarity, she was able to see and hear and feel a living image.

Part Two

She lifted her eyes to that glad summer sky, and thought how the sunlight and summer of her life had passed away for ever.

"I have tried to be fortunate as well as happy—tried to have all good things," she reflected, "and in trying for too much, have lost all."

Taken at the Flood by MARY ELIZABETH BRADDON

Charity suffereth long, and is kind; charity envieth not; charity vaunteth not itself, is not puffed up. Doth not behave itself unseemly, seeketh not her own, is not easily provoked, thinketh no evil; Rejoiceth not in iniquity, but rejoiceth in the truth; Beareth all things, believeth all things, hopeth all things, endureth all things. Charity never faileth; but whether there be prophecies, they shall fail; whether there be tongues, they shall cease; whether there be knowledge it shall vanish away. For we know in part and we prophesy in part. But when that which is perfect is come, then that which is in part shall be done away.

I CORINTHIANS, 13

11

THE SUPPER WAS FIXED FOR THE EVENING OF AUGUST 10TH, the day Amy was due home. The day of Chloe's confirmation.

Olivia went to the station, five miles away at Combe Cloud where trains still occasionally, if unpredictably, stopped. It was fully two months since she'd set eyes on her younger daughter. (Amy had gone straight from school to spend a fortnight with friends in Wales.)

Amy was the only person to alight from the train, but the conductor climbed down to help her with her luggage so there was a slight delay watched by mild, abstracted faces at the windows. Nobody worked on the station itself any longer. It was simply a platform well seeded with hogweed and rose bay willow herb.

"Darling!" Olivia crushed her daughter to her, then held her away in some surprise, her eyes scaling the newly tall and slender figure. "How elegant you look!" Her eyes roamed.

"I'll take that." Amy seized a large blue suitcase, avoiding her mother's gaze. She'd just torn up and stuffed into the blocked lavatory bowl, a letter from Emma's mother. Addressed to Olivia, Amy had read Mrs. Anstruther's worried letter to her mother with rage.

"Did they send my other stuff from school?"

"Yes, darling—I haven't touched it all yet. In fact it's still downstairs in the hall, nothing seems to get done these days. Now come on." She took Amy's sharp elbow, "I've got a surprise for you. Come and look before it disappears!"

Hauling Amy after her, she rushed out to the station approach and sure enough Amy's old black pony Cygnet, under cover of noise from the train, was striding purposefully homewards pulling a small, red-painted cart behind him. Mince sat up in the back, his tongue lolling cheerfully.

"Hey!"

When he saw them, Mince leapt down and wagged his whole body with shame.

"Whoa, Cyggy!" yelled Olivia breaking into a run.

"Who said you could use my pony?" shouted Amy puffing alongside.

Her mother, bent on retrieving the animal, ignored this remark. "Try and head him off, darling!" she bawled. "I'll jump on behind."

She managed it. Taking a flying leap, remarkable even in someone half her age, she seized the reins and, slowing the pony, eventually turned him round to go back for the luggage littered all over the ground.

"There we are! Oh what fun!" cried Olivia. "Do cheer up, darling. Anything wrong?" And she halted the pony while Amy bent to load the cases. "I hope you enjoyed your stay with the Things, you look awfully well I must say."

"Anstruthers."

"What, darling? Steady."

"Anstruthers. Not the Things."

"Yes, I know that, sweetheart. Lovely tan. Did you go out in the boat? Buck up, there's a good girl, this creature's aching to be off."

Slowly and silently, Amy lifted her cases and bags on to the back of the cart. Every time she bent down she felt sick.

"Are you cross about something?" Olivia glanced back over her shoulder, pleased to see all that blurring puppy fat gone from Amy's face. The child had good bones after all. She looked much less like Leo, now.

"Of course not." Wearily, Amy climbed on to the back of the cart. Since the only seat was the driving seat, she sat on the flat bottom of the cart, one arm looped over the luggage, the other round Mince who licked her face ravenously.

Olivia flapped the reins and they strained off down the empty lane. "Do you like it?" she called over her shoulder. "Isn't it jolly? Peter and Andrew helped put it together from all sorts of bits and pieces old man Adams had. Oh, you've never met the boys of course. Are you comfortable back there, darling? I should have put some cushions in, how silly of me . . ."

She bubbled on. Amy closed her eyes trying to think of an excuse for not going to the confirmation party. By waiting two hours on Cardiff station, she'd managed to avoid coming home till after lunch. That was one problem solved.

". . . I'm so glad Chloe decided, it's tidier, somehow . . ."

The Anstruthers had seemed to accept her story that she was eating less out of concern for the Third World. Or so she'd thought, until she'd read the letter to make sure. Caroline Anstruther had written down the name and address of a good psychiatrist, hoping the suggestion caused no offence.

It had offended Amy who knew perfectly well there was nothing whatever wrong with her. She was rather glad that Mrs. Anstruther, receiving no reply from Olivia, would have to conclude her advice had been misplaced.

They jogged through the village, rocked by Cygnet's short stride. People came out of shops and doorways to smile at them. As they passed over the bridge the pony's clattering hooves doubled their sound and Olivia waved to old Ash who, seeing a horse-drawn vehicle pass in front of his gaze again, found his eyes marred by weeping.

John Crozier, hearing the hooves, came out of the kennel yard to investigate. "Only another month till cubbing begins!" he called out, seeing who it was.

"There goes Peggy Plumb!" cried Bessie Penruddock to her sister from behind the cards of bias binding and elastic.

Small green apples clustered on the orchard trees they passed. In the fields, the barley added to this ripening yellow month, coloured by tansy and ragwort and banks of lady's bedstraw. A few farmers had grown maize as a silage crop this year and it pressed up against the field boundaries, sunburnt, close-packed and foreign looking.

"*Look!*" called Olivia, her tone marvelling. And obediently, Amy looked up to see swallows circling together already in rehearsal for their long journeying southward. With the harvest not yet done they had sensed some urgent need to practise their flight from winter's quiet creeping approach.

"So early!" cried Olivia, and then: "Nearly there!"

She admired the shapely curve of her gloved wrists handling the reins and wished Amy would snap out of this *thing* . . . brightly, she chattered on hoping to distract her daughter, and succeeded in concealing Amy's silence from herself.

There seemed, to Amy, to be an awful lot of people about, most of whom she did not know. The place looked like a holiday camp, she thought. They leaned against the post-and-rail fencing, sat in the meadow, lay under the beeches and squatted on the doorstep.

"Who are they all?" she whispered to her mother as they unloaded at the front door.

"Frankly, darling, I don't altogether know. Friends of Joe's, to do with the magazine or something. I think they're here for the day."

Amy was astonished by her mother's apparent calm. Even she could tell that the three sitting on the doorstep were sharing a joint.

"They seem mostly quite pleasant," hissed Olivia.

The luggage was dumped in the hall beside Amy's school trunk in the hope that either Corin or Leo would deal with it later. Barber appeared and led Cygnet away.

"Come and see the foal, Amy darling. The one I wrote to you about? I've waited all this time for you to choose a name . . . do come along." Olivia seized Amy's stony hand and dragged her down the drive. They bent under the fence, smiling at a knot of people which included Sarah and Biff. At least, Olivia smiled, Amy stared unflinchingly.

"If you like him, he can be yours!"

She called Rosie and stood, awaiting her approach holding tightly on to Amy's hand. The old brown mare came slowly out of her restful shade, the colt trotting beside her. His baby fluff had fallen away now revealing a rich, bay coat. Ears pricked, he bounded ahead of his mother, searching the voice out more accurately.

She called again and he gave a piping whinny of recognition. With a sudden squeal, he bucked delightedly then flew across the field at a gallop. "Mind out!"

There was a chorus of screams, a flurry of movement.

In the corner of her eye, Olivia saw one of Delilah's kittens hop through the grass in front of her pursued, at a swift crawl, by Biff. They were directly in the path of the colt's heedless gallop. She flung herself forward, bent down and hurled herself to one side clasping the kitten.

The colt neatly bounded over the baby, skidded to a halt, wheeled and came whickering, towards her.

"Oh, my God!" Sarah, white-faced, fell on Biff and clutching him to her, glared in horror at Olivia. "Oh, Christ!" she muttered, burying her face in the soft, unperturbed body of her baby.

"All right?" called Olivia lightly, then seeing Sarah's expression, hesitated a little before saying, "I knew he wouldn't hurt the baby. He could *see* the baby."

It was true. Her instinct had been quite right, but feeling her remark strike ice, she faltered. The girls gathered round Sarah.

The colt pushed at the kitten in her arms and it boxed his muzzle with two swift, sheathed paws.

"Well, Amy?" Olivia spoke a little shrilly to her daughter who formed part of the consoling group round Sarah, "Do you like him?"

Amy lifted her head and gave her mother so undisguised a look of contempt, Olivia felt quite faint. Something unpleasant lifted against her scalp and drained the sunlight from the afternoon.

It was nasty, but short-lived.

"What do you think? Florizel? Or Boswell perhaps. . . ? His sire was called Wishing Well," she explained weakly. "Think about it, darling."

She turned on her heel, still holding the kitten. "I'm going to fetch a sweet or something for Biff."

In less than two minutes she was back brandishing a box of costly, smooth-coated Chocolate Olivers. The group had not moved. It seemed absorbed in mutual stroking. Happily, Biff pulled at his mother's hair.

"I found all *these*!" stated Olivia accusingly. She looked straight at Amy whose own gaze slid sideways. Her mother had been looking in the tuck box.

"There's a rotten apple in there and a cake with mould on it."

There was no response. Angrily, Olivia bent down, tearing the wrapper off the expensive biscuits and offering one to Biff, crooned: "There you are, my darling. You *mustn't* go frightening your mother like that!" And she pecked at his warm, musky skin.

Then she left and Biff tried to bury his two teeth into the bitter chocolate. Finding it hard and sugarless, he spat it merrily into the lap of the nearest girl.

The church was full to its very limits.

An air of festival danced above the sombre organ. An excitement, a whispering that the music couldn't quite conceal.

Flowers Olivia had cut early that morning from the walled

garden, massed with those of other gardens from the village. They tumbled in white and yellow sprays beside the altar steps. They leapt from unexpected niches in the honey walls, wove patterns amongst the carved figures on the dark oak screen and filled the tawny, speckled air with a wedding fragrance.

Chloe stood with the children in the front pews.

All the girls had been dressed, with old-fashioned insistence by their mothers, in white. There were only two boys, their hair crushed to their heads, their ears scarlet with scrubbing. All were terrified. The young ones by the occasion and the crowd and a fear of forgetting their lines. Chloe, by the gravity of what she was doing. She couldn't look in front of her at the ritually prepared altar table, but kept her eyes down among the prayer books and hassocks.

They came in steady procession.

The choir, white-surpliced, the giggling frightened out of them. Henry Claremont. And then the Bishop. His mitre, the height it gave him, his gold and purple cloths made sure nobody entered into this ceremony lightly. When he turned to face the congregation, a silence reached out from him, striking every man, woman and child in the body of the church like a moonbeam.

Chloe felt herself tremble.

She closed her eyes. Thought of the long, plain table. Thought of the thirteen men gathered round it in a circlet of love and fellowship and fear which she now shared. She thought of the treachery powerful out of all proportion to its mean presence. That too, she feared in herself. The cowardice of humanity.

Together with the children, she murmured the responses.

". . . And let our cry come unto thee . . ."

Singly, then, they went forward to be blessed, watched by their friends and families.

Chloe went last.

The hands that closed over her hair were surprisingly strong. Almost fierce.

"Defend O Lord, this Thy servant with Thy heavenly grace that she may continue Thine for ever; and daily increase in Thy Holy Spirit more and more until she come into Thy everlasting kingdom. Amen."

"Amen," echoed Chloe.

It was done then. That bit. Now the truly awesome part.

". . . Take, eat, this is my Body which is given for you. Do this in remembrance of me . . ."

". . . Drink ye all of this, for this is my Blood of the New Testament which is shed for you and for many for the remission of sins; Do this as oft as ye shall drink it, in remembrance of me . . ."

The wafer was a dull, sticky symbol. A piece of mass production. The wine, vulgarly rich.

It was all right then. There was no magic. Only truth.

She felt utterly steady and sang with a clear voice.

There was much kissing.

As the small crowd gathered under the low-ceilinged rooms of Sheep Cottages, each guest embraced Chloe. "Welcome," said some. And "Greetings."

"Not much room to sit down," observed Olivia drily.

"It looks nice," said Leo. "They've done well."

Oil lamps and candles smoked lightly against the freshly white walls. Wherever there was space, on shelves and on window sills, there stood jam jars full of wild flowers.

Olivia was surprised to see so many people from the village. "Mrs. Drummond! How nice to see you! It's all a bit primitive I'm afraid!"

"'Tis very pleasant. Very pleasant indeed." Hilda Drummond looked round approvingly. Through the archway to the kitchen, she spied her bottles of elderflower wine gracing a table spread with food. A smell of warm yeast still lingered in the rooms. "A real treat in these times," she said.

"There's little enough to celebrate," Olivia agreed, raising her voice above the general hubbub and turning with new smiles to Mrs. Inchcape who had just arrived and stood, blinking, a large plate of fresh, oozing honeycomb in her hands.

"Let me help you!" called Olivia over the heads, but Mab was there first with thanks and welcome. "Mrs. Baldwin!" Olivia cried, "and Barber!"

Amy sat in a corner on the floor unnoticed. Not that most of the people there would have felt any compulsion to force her up and drag her forward had they seen her. They would have assumed she was doing exactly what she wished to do: not that she was hiding. Or, that if she *were* hiding, that, then, was what she wished to do. She stared through the legs or looked, occasionally, upwards and saw her brother drinking his own whisky. Through the backs and shoulders and ripples of hair, Bart Foster smiled at her once, raising his glass but the figures shifted across him. Her mother appeared to be nailed to the wall though her hands and mouth made social movements. The light fell waywardly. Greedily, Amy chewed at the skin down one side of her thumbnail.

It looked lovely, thought Chloe happily. And when they were gathered round the long pine table, ready to eat, she spread her hands out to her neighbours as a sign that they too, should do the same, and smiled round at her friends with affection before saying a brief grace.

Olivia, caught awkwardly by the blessing and half-seated already, sank quickly on to her stool. There were no formal place setting and clearly, all were expected to get up and help themselves to food as they wished, but for the moment she found herself seated between Joe and Bill Adams. She could smell the sour musk of goat.

"How hard everybody's worked!" She brought her long white fingers together in a temple of approval.

"Everybody's brought something," said Joe.

"What a good idea! And what did you bring, Mr. Adams?"

"A summer pudd'n and a beystyns pudd'n," said Bill shyly. "I've got a cow just calved and it seemed a right shame to waste the first milk." He pointed to a bright yellow pudding, so rich it looked like custard.

"Wine?" Andrew was pouring. Paper cups, toothmugs, anything, was offered up. The laughter and gaiety increased.

Leo, gazing at the table, was moved by the effort that had gone into creating it. There were bowls of radishes, raw onion, carrot, baby turnip and cucumber. A small piece of home-baked ham, savoury egg pies, a huge onion tart, like a catherine wheel, cream and cheeses and fruit tarts, a summer pudding streaming with royal juices, a close-textured sponge cake, wedges of honeycomb and several different kinds of bread. His glass was filled. For a moment he was too overcome to do anything but sip quietly at a wine a degree too sweet for sophistication, but one that was, for all that, the wine of his boyhood, the wine of his own lanes and woodland.

Through something close to sorrow, he caught sight of his daughter Amy busily helping other people to food and he smiled at her, pleased to see her open up.

The plates were passed, filled, emptied, passed again. Corin chased his wine with whisky and thought his mother grossly over-dressed in diamonds.

"Of course," Olivia was saying to Joe, her social manner spread over her dislike for him like a clear varnish, "of course, it's a temporary problem."

"It doesn't help you to think that. Not in the end."

"But it's *true*, my dear. A sickness, that's all. It's bound to get better."

"It's over."

"Oh goodness, such defeatist talk!" Olivia turned to Bill Adams for support, but he was concentrating on a crumbly piece of cheese.

"It *was* sick." Joe looked straight at her. (With, she thought, amusement.) "And now it's dead."

"Anyone would think you were delighted."

"I am in a way."

"Oh really!" She reached impatiently for her glass, but it was empty. She redirected her hand into a small, encouraging wave at Amy who looked away.

"It had to die," said Joe, "there weren't the means to keep it alive, that way of life. It deserved to die, you *could* say." He stroked his growing beard affectionately with a scratched and dirty hand.

"Those were the good times."

"Good?" He smiled.

"Oh, you young!" she said aggressively. She hated his complacency. He had the odour of moral complacency, the worst kind of all. "You just don't know," she said. "The thirties. The years when I grew up. You just can't imagine the sort of things that happened in my lifetime, things my mother had to endure, the dreadful life of women. Children, barefoot . . ."

Joe swung round on his seat and poked out an unshod foot, wriggling the toes at her mockingly. For a moment she stared, lost. Then: "Yes, but you don't *have* to," she said.

"No," he answered, "but I don't care if I do have to. It's no shame to me."

Her glass was half-filled by a stretched and wobbling arm. "Thank you, darling," she cried and turned again to Joe but he intercepted her. "It's all right," he said softly. "You mustn't be frightened."

"Frightened?"

"Better times *will* come . . ."

"Exactly what I was saying," she declared triumphantly. "*Exactly* what I said!"

"Ah, but you meant it would be like it was before. Just the same. Just as *comfortable*. It won't."

"My dear Joe! You do rather talk as though you had exclusive rights to a crystal ball." She pulled a small face to remove any sting. "Anyway," she resumed more lightly than she felt (a dull, red anger was rising in her). "Anyway, you can't say that people like my mother didn't deserve the kind of comfort she was able to enjoy at the end of her life."

"Because you became rich."

"Not just that at all. Because of . . . because of . . ." she searched for something that would find a response in him, "well, an ending of class differences, a widening of opportunities. I don't mind in the least admitting that my marriage wouldn't have been socially 'on' a hundred years ago. You mustn't assume it was all *money*."

"Oodles and boodles of money," he said, "to be decently spent. It always has to be justified, gross expenditure . . . there are always good reasons to be thought up, found." He looked at her enigmatically. "Improved means to unimproved ends," he said.

"I beg your pardon?"

"Thoreau. I think, anyway. Nothing's good unless it's both intended to be good *and* well arrived at."

Olivia indulged herself in a withering glance. Gnomic sentences do not impress me, it read. She reached for a plate of potato scones and offered it to Bill Adams who accepted one courteously. It was he, not Joe, who smelt of goat.

"This wine," Joe picked up his chipped cup, "is good. It was made without profit and it's not being drunk because any alcohol would do. It's not being drunk in order to get drunk. It's made with love and drunk with love." And as if trying to prove his point he drained his cup without taking his amused eyes off her face for one second. She found him childish.

"Well? What about all this then?" Unable to restrain herself, she gestured around her. "What about this place, this scheme." She felt exploited by him. "Why come here? Why do this?"

"Why not?" He raised his eyebrows. "It was freely offered."

"Why aren't you *out there* . . .?"

"Out there?"

"Involved in something useful. *Involved*."

"We *are* involved. We *were* involved. In a magazine, but they closed it down."

"Who did?"

"The authorities."

"How?"

"Oh . . ." he sighed, thought better of enlarging. "It's a long story. Anyway, what's gone wrong isn't remedied by doing, well, the kind of things you think."

"No?"

"No, what's gone wrong is between people. The space between people. It's not money or police or bombs or anything like that. They're symptoms. It's here . . ." And he moved his hand between his face and hers, lightly running roughened finger down the side of her jaw. She drew back involuntarily.

"There," he laughed. "Like that."

"Oh, Good Lord . . ." she fussed. Looked for a handkerchief. Nodded again at Bill Adams.

"That's got to come right first. Before the other things. Well, there's one other thing. Food. That's all we need . . . food and love. Love and food." Again he raised his fingers and this time reached for her hair. "No!" he protested as she recoiled, "Don't be frightened."

"Don't be so absurd," she snapped and stood up scraping her stool back with an ugly sound (lost beneath the amiable babble). "Forgive me," she bent stiffly towards Bill Adams, "I must fetch my bag."

But Joe caught her hand firmly. "Going back to the beginning again," he was saying. She let the surge of general sound come between them. "Learning the habit of loving . . . all over again . . . Things do not change; we change."

"I'm sorry?" She tried not to appear to be pulling away.

"Thoreau. I think, anyway." He laughed and let her go.

Sarah settled beside Leo. "You're not eating," she said. "You must." And putting her baby down on the floor to explore the woodland of legs, she cut a generous slice of curd tart and placed it before him.

He thanked her. "It's a long time since I tasted this," he said.

"Enjoy it," she urged. She watched him bite into it and laughed. "What does it remind you of?"

He thought slowly. "Of summer," he said, "and . . . kitchens . . . and cornfields." He laughed with her, at himself.

"Go on then, have some more!"

"I will . . . I am." He took another mouthful, swallowed and asked courteously, how the roof was coming on.

"Oh fine, fine." Her thin face was curiously alight. "Everybody's helped. And when we've finished ours we're going to do one for the Barbers."

"Barber's old parents? In Brick Cottage?"

"Mm." She took a crumb of curd tart for herself, stuck on the tip of a forefinger.

"That's nice of you."

"Well that's the idea," she stressed, meaning, he supposed, part of their philosophy.

"And then Peter's going to build me a kiln."

"Yes?"

"And then . . . well, we see how it goes."

"The money?"

"The bread, right."

"How are you managing?"

"O.K. So far. We do jobs." She shrugged. "The magazine should help us a bit through the winter. If not well . . ." And she peered beneath the table to see how her son was getting on. "What about you," she enquired disarmingly, looking up again, "You O.K.?"

Her bluntness, her innocence, charmed him. "O.K.," he responded. "Well, not too good, but then it's general."

"I suppose, yes."

There was a pause between them filled by the pleasant gossip of the table.

"And all of you . . ." he ventured at last out of curiosity, "do you . . . get *on* together all right? No great quarrels?"

Sarah laughed outright. "Sure we quarrel. There's been one or two heavy scenes, not much to be honest. Nothing like the last place I lived in. Or the one before that. Nobody spoke to one another at all there."

"You *have* been around."

"Right," she gave a rueful grin. "No," she said, "we're rather orderly here." She sounded surprised herself by it. "The other places, they were kind of sloppy, you know, we sat around being beautiful. That sort of scene. Here . . ." She thought for a moment.

"I think you *are* being beautiful. Together, I mean," he added, embarrassed.

"I'm glad." Biff hauled himself to his feet and tried to struggle into her lap. She lifted him and stroked his thin, silky hair.

Somebody asked for salt and Leo passed it across the table.

"Here . . ." she was still reflecting on it, "we're rather regimental really. No, that's not fair . . . disciplined though. We all work pretty hard. Order, that's the thing. I used to be into unstructured levels of existence but Joe says order exists in all natural forms, so why not here, amongst us."

"Why not."

"I used to think chaos was the natural state you see, but it's not. Not at all."

"Yes, I do see." He picked at the last crumbs.

"Order from within though, that's the great difference. Coming from within, voluntarily. Nobody *imposes* anything. That kind of order, Joe says, just has to break down, and he's right."

"So he thinks the present government will break down."

"Oh sure," she said airily. "He just says — well, we all say — give it time. No need for coups or that kind of thing. It's just into something so impossible it can't last."

"I see what you mean," he said gently.

"The theory is, that to kind of break free from the old system, there's got to be this present stage. A sort of brutal stage before the final convulsion, it's the last clinging on. A last attempt to hang on to what I suppose you think is the *normal* way of life."

She made it sound so simple. As though the uniforms, the tanks, the thick silence of the streets would, one meek dawn, simply melt away. She lowered her head to burble at Biff and the skimpy, curling twists of her light hair fell forward in a curtain.

"What if they conscript?"

"But we already *are* working on the land."

"In a sense, yes."

"Oh, but we are! Milk, Biffy?"

"I envy you," said Leo.

"Envy? Why? You have all you need. More than you need."

"Ah, you don't have the pain of separation."

"Separation?"

"From old conceptions."

"Oh."

"People have to believe, as they get older, that what they've done's been worth while. To be told it was false is very hard. Like being found guilty of a crime. It's hard to let go."

Why, though, he thought wistfully? Why so hard when everything I've done has turned out to be a failure? One thing after another . . . the farm, the business, the Air Force, ultimately turned down for active service . . . not my fault any of it, but failure.

155

He looked back at the pitiless repetitions of his life. Such modest failures, all of them.

"Yes," she murmured, a little blankly.

She couldn't enter into the long passage of his experience. It was Babylon to her. A lost Empire; history. Indistinct tales ... not desperation, pride, faith, bitterly born achievement.

She felt the dampening seat of Biff's pyjamas.

"Try to understand," murmured Leo, in apology for himself, "that it's in the nature of the elderly to try and restore what they found best. We all pass through a heyday, an era that we think of as our very own, inimitable. A period, no more then ten years perhaps. The rest of the time, we spend resuscitating it!" He laughed self-deprecatingly.

"You're not old!" She was quite indignant. "Anyway," she said, "that's what we're trying to do too ... making a journey back to ourselves, trying to recreate the garden in which we grew best, if you like," she caught his eye and placed her cheek to Biff's head.

"Oh, now," protested Leo mildly, "I'm a practical man, not a philosopher."

"Look!" Freeing one hand from her embrace of the baby, she gestured round the table, a spread of agreeable debris now. "Here's practical philosophy," she declared. "It's here, don't you see. It works." She shook her hair back from her eyes and grinned. She had very pearly even teeth, like a child's. "The place where food came off shelves and conversation out of the air, never was a *practical* proposition. You mistook it, that's all. You mistook the glasshouse for the garden."

He allowed himself to be rebuked by her. He had no desire to argue, to destroy her confidence in what she did. Whatever outcome cynicism led him to predict, he preferred that the world might, if it could, fall into these hands and not the cruel grip of officers.

Whatever the future, it was beyond his handling now. Winter. He was beyond dealing with it. Winter would come. He felt like an old man—he felt it was his turn to be cared for while the winds blew. It was up to others to be bold now. He would go into that winter one of its victims.

He felt inexpressibly weary.

"This magazine," queried Corin leaning against the kitchen

door and watching Chloe trying to wash up in the crush. "What's it about? What's it called?"

She rinsed a mug and looked at him carefully. *"Orbits,"* she said shortly, "that's what it's called." Its name had been changed.

"Mm." He swirled the Scotch in his glass. "Underground I take it." He swallowed at his drink.

"You could say."

"Bit dangerous isn't it?"

"Why should it be dangerous?" she enquired evenly.

"Operating on the premises."

She treated him to an expression of unconcern and lowered a pile of plates into the water.

"You want to be careful what you keep about the place."

"We're not political."

Corin snorted. "That's a judgement *others* make about you," he said wryly. "These days you need to think carefully before putting a rhyming couplet together."

Chloe made no reply.

"I thought you'd like to know," Corin went on, lowering his tone to a more confidential note, "that I'm joining the Army."

A plate slipped with a splash into the water."

"What do you mean? The ULF?"

"Good God no!" Corin was amused by the idea. "The Urban Land Force is full of middle-aged women. No, you fool, the *Army*."

"Whatever for?"

"I thought I'd join before they *hauled* me in. More chance of a commission if I go now of my own free will. And the drink's very cheap." He grinned at her. "Come on!" he urged, "don't stand there gawping. We all feel the need to *do* something."

"Oh, Corry, why *that*?"

"Well there's nothing doing in the City . . . just a lot of cocktail time, and it seemed marginally more sensible than setting up house in the country. Anyway," he took a last gulp and dropped his glass in the scummy water, "it's either that or Canada, I've decided."

"Oh, *Corry*. . . !"

"For God's sake!"

"It's the sort of thing you'll have to do."

"Yes, I know it's trying having to line up five hundred innocent citizens a day and shooting them as an example to others. Oh come on, Chloe!" He reached out and squeezed her shoulder,

·157·

"I'll spend most of my time polishing boots and helping old ladies over the road. A superior sort of policeman that's all."

"It's a meal ticket," she said scornfully. Tight-lipped, she began scrubbing a pan. But she was also frightened. Ever since the government had exploited the IRA situation—even, it was strongly rumoured, causing some of the nastier incidents themselves to help inflame public feeling—since then, they'd held powers they were no longer diffident in using. She scrubbed far harder than was strictly necessary.

"Well, I can't stay here can I?"

"Why ever not? There are things you could do."

"I'd rather defend my family than live with my family," he grinned. "On the whole, it's easier."

The day had been dirtied. Chloe turned her back on him.

Amy refused to drive home down the track with her parents.

"It doesn't save any petrol for *you* to walk," observed Olivia, whose reluctance to spoil her shoes had been responsible for their using the car in the first place.

"I prefer to walk," said Amy stubbornly. So they left her to pick her way downhill in the pale bloom of moonlight.

Across the valley two tawny owls shrieked and keened at one another. A cow, whose calf must have been weaned away that day, kept up a regular distant moan. Closer by she could hear the night swish, like sea on gravel, of cows eating and had a powerful sense of small, nocturnal creatures slinking away through the undergrowth.

Although she'd told her parents she wanted to be alone, she was not alone. Nor was she frightened. The company pleased her.

12

"THE FIRST MUSHROOMS!"

Olivia came into the kitchen, her arms full of gleaming white fungi gathered early from the horse meadows.

"We'll have them for breakfast," she said blithely. "What a perfect morning!" She put the mushrooms down on the draining board and tore off her headscarf before first kissing Leo who was unscrewing the coffee machine and then lightly bending over Amy, as though dealing with an animal it was best to be wary of. Amy was reading a book at the table, head down, fists pushed against her ears.

"Morning, darling! Won't that be delicious? Look what I've got!" She hung over her daughter anxiously awaiting some response then, looking at Leo, shrugged and crossed the tiled floor to select a frying pan from the bright collection on the wall.

"Brrr!" she continued gaily, giving a mock shiver. "There's quite a mist on the fields." She picked over her collection. She'd found shaggy parasols and blewitts as well as field mushrooms. The harvest was sudden and heavy. "I also found a few blackberries ripening already," she went on, to nobody in particular. "Must tell Chloe. Goodness, winter's starting early." Beyond the window, it was golden.

With a contrived air of bustle, she darted about, washing the mushrooms, melting fat in the pan, diving for a colander from a cupboard beneath the sink. Leo finally succeeded in separating the two halves of the coffee machine. "Ha!" he cried in triumph and looked round at the others his gaze slowing painfully over his daughter. "Well!" he announced, with agonized cheerfulness. "Spare a thought for Corin today." Today Corin started his basic training in Aldershot.

"I know, poor love . . ." Olivia, dropping mushrooms into the spitting fat, turned her head. "Still," she said, voicing the nation's most commonly and despairingly used phrase, "at least he's *doing* something."

They babbled, the adults, quietly attempting to heal over the silence infecting the atmosphere. Amy's attenuating silence.

"Ah well, I could wish it hadn't all been so *sudden*, but, there we are . . ." Olivia shook the pan. "At least we don't have the worry that he'll be sent abroad." Even that was equivocal. "Well, I . . ." she began, but let the matter fade.

The dark, dying summer fragrance of the mushrooms filled the kitchen, making the appetite's wheedling juice flow.

(Just *one*, thought Amy, without raising her head. Just one . . .)

"I shall have to get the hunters up soon." Olivia fiddled with the pan, tipping it from one side to the other. She found herself continually searching for remarks that might strike a spark of interest in her daughter without having the effrontery to speak to her directly. Nothing. She tried again, addressing herself more openly to Amy . . . "You could help me get them fit and going again. It's nearly the end of the month and I haven't done a thing yet." Frantically, she exchanged looks with Leo. "You might even get some cubbing in before you go back to school, darling . . . you'd enjoy that."

A shapeless grunt emanated from Amy. Releasing her head from the press of her knuckles she looked up, but not *at* anyone.

"I don't know how you *can*," she growled.

"Can what? Hunt? . . . But you love hunting, whatever do you mean?"

"*Oh* . . ." Amy gave up and let her head sink back over the book.

"No, come on, I want to know what you *mean* . . ."

Leo gave his wife an uneasy look and raucously, began collecting knives and forks.

"At the *moment* . . ." Amy leaned back in her chair, hands in pockets, her oddly elongated legs stretching beyond the far side of the table. "It's so ghastly . . ."

"Oh Lord, don't tell me you've joined the unbearable!" It was a family joke. She meant those who called hunting the unspeakable in pursuit of the uneatable. She put only two slices of bread under the grill, knowing Amy would refuse toast. "I won't believe it," she said firmly.

Amy hadn't the energy for an argument. She kicked at the rungs of the chair opposite.

"You *know* they don't begin to understand." Against all her better judgement, Olivia was beginning to sound impatient.

"It's so *heartless*."

"Heartless? *Cruel* you mean? Oh, Amy, really, you know better than that. *You* know that if you want to be cruel you go around shooting at them. Poisoning them. As for killing them at *all* . . ." Gingerly, she turned the toast. "Well, once the unbearable admit they leave rats and mice running freely round their town houses, O.K. The only problem is, foxes are much prettier." She banged three plates down on the table.

"I mean heartless *generally*, with things, people as they are."

"I don't understand you. You've grown up with it, grown up with . . . known hunting people all your life. You know they're not heartless. In fact they have a damn sight better knowledge, love for animals and the countryside than anyone. Townies just have a completely distorted view of the thing. It's the concrete mind."

"That's not what I meant at all," Amy burst out, exasperated.

"Well, you might make yourself plain."

"I'll see to that," said Leo, seizing the pan.

Pleasure began to seep out of the morning. The mushrooms lay shrivelled and black on the plates. Amy, taking hers, pushed most of the food to one side and carefully cut a single mushroom into six pieces which she slowly picked at one by one.

To break the cloudy silence, Leo spoke. "Well, *whatever* your views, Amy, at least you can help your mother exercise."

"I don't feel like it," sighed Amy.

Every issue they raised, they used to beat her with. On and on. Why couldn't they leave her alone?

Relieved to see her daughter eat something however fragmentary and mean, Olivia allowed the silence to settle like a windblown sheet. Over the past three weeks, she'd come to dread the way every word she uttered was met like a blade that had to be opposed. She was weary with fighting, weary with the efforts to tempt Amy's appetite, weary with the argument about the Third World, wearied by the disturbing and continual flow of visitors and dispirited by her failure to make any progress in her own work. She was even tired of Leo's loping presence in the house wishing occasionally that she *had* agreed to go with him to Sweden or Turkey or Nassau, Moscow even, any of the places he'd suggested rather than have him spend his holiday fiddling with things round the house.

After she'd complained about his 'tinkering', he'd gone off to help the group at Sheep Cottages and that annoyed her even more. When they met at mealtimes she was alternately enraged by his enthusiastic chatter about progress up there and Amy's limp abandonment of her food.

Although she and Leo had agreed to ignore Amy's refusal to eat properly as far as they could, supposing it was a phase that must pass, if only for reasons of sheer hunger, it had now gone on so long that her frustration was barbed with real fear.

Mechanically, the kitchen clock pushed time aside as the family hobbled through breakfast.

Madge Waring, cycling up the drive an hour later, saw her employer wandering out towards the mares across the meadow.

Her heart sank. Another morning typing out refusals. The flow of work dwindled daily. So common now were the intervals of idleness, she'd taken it on herself to correct the proofs of *Beloved Orchid*—a task Miss Bennett would normally have attended to most anxiously herself. Madge's interference was partly prompted by the tone of the publisher's last letter.

She called out "Good Morning."

Without turning back towards the house, Olivia raised an arm in greeting.

Miss Bennett, as Madge told her sister gravely, was taking a very long time to get over her mother's death. The two women shook their heads over the situation night after night as they sipped their sugarless tea and stared into an empty grate they avoided filling with wood or coal until winter weather forced extravagance on them.

The dew lay longer upon the grass these mornings. Although the leaves were full upon the trees and neither hips nor elderberries were much more than green yet, autumn threatened to come early. The signs were there for those who knew them.

At this hour, the mares had not yet retreated from flies into the shade of the oaks and beech but grazed hungrily at the sparkling grass. It had been cropped too close. They should have been moved on to different pasture a month ago, but what was to spare had been kept in the hope of a second hay crop. The earlier cutting had proved very poor. Many of the bales had burnt in the stack and were now mouldy.

For now though, the animals looked well. Olivia watched them, their peace creeping into her. Later, when the sun grew hot she would bring those there was room for, into the loose boxes and enjoy the sight of the foals stretched out carelessly asleep in their deep nests of straw.

She loved them.

The fine intelligent heads of the mares. The high, nervous anticipation which never lay far beneath the surface even when they grazed in safety. A sudden gesture, a strange noise or shape and it sprang through them like a rush of flame, giving their movements a wild brilliance.

The eagerness of the foals touched her, their confidence within the perimeter of their mother's scent, the ecstatic races they had, one against the other, even the loser exultant with speed. All this released a warmth in her that she sometimes found complicated by the ambiguity of human responses. This was where she came when her own kind overwhelmed her, when she needed to restore the open simplicity of feeling that only the infant human is allowed.

She hadn't heard Leo's approach. He startled her.

He slipped his arm through hers and they stood awhile, leaning lightly on one another enjoying the animals and the clear sunlight.

He kissed her cheek. "We must talk about them," he murmured. "What's to be done about them."

She stiffened. He felt her bones freeze. She knew what he meant. "I can afford to keep them through the winter," she asserted roughly. "*We* can, at least. We managed last winter and we'll manage this."

Leo said nothing. The mares, in a ragged line, fanned slowly towards them, eating.

"I'll write another book. I'll . . . it would be the *last* thing, Leo—" her voice slipped upward slightly and she checked herself, "the *last* thing I would let go. Everything else, the cars, clothes, furniture, *anything* else first."

Rosie, the old brown mare, her age shadowed in the sockets over her eye, grazed in moving snatches, drawing closer to them all the time, her baby following.

"I know," said Leo, "I know."

He searched for the kindest phrases and found only hard things to say. They had to be said. "Whatever you do," he sighed, "it makes no difference." He linked his arm more closely with hers. "I'm not a registered farmer any longer so I just don't get the feed allocation. Money doesn't help. And even if I *did*," he went on, cutting across her schemes and possibilities, "even then, the brood mares don't, on paper, appear as economic stock any longer. The market's fallen through. It's gone. They've become *pets*." He uttered this last word with hurt and hate. He knew she was going to suffer.

Olivia was silent.

"It's not that we can't afford the feed," he repeated, desperately. "We just can't get it. Animals like these are a classified luxury. And the land they stand on is needed for planting." He let this remark settle for a moment. Then again: "They want to plant here. I had a letter last week."

As Rosie reached them, she made a soft mumbling sound of affection and pushed persistently against Olivia's arm until she stroked her.

"What's to be done then?" Olivia's gaze fixed on some sightless distance.

The mare blew pleasurably. "We can't sell them."

"No . . ." He sounded doubtful.

"Well then?"

He unlocked his arm from hers and slipped it round her waist. "We *could* sell them . . ."

"For meat."

He nodded and glanced away.

Olivia continued rubbing Rosie's forehead and gently pulling at the mare's ears without taking her eyes off the unseen horizon. "I see," she said and then, after a pause. "I won't do that, Leo."

He turned towards her, began to speak, but she cut him short, her voice hard with unloosed weeping. "You must shoot them Leo. You. When the time comes."

He walked back with her to the house in silence.

At the door, they stopped and he kissed her finely skinned forehead, noticing with a small sense of shock, that the copper was growing out of her hair. A thin frost of white attacked the roots. He held her hands tightly, scanning his mind for something to say. But with a last forlorn pressure of his hands on hers he merely remarked that he would see her later.

He left for Sheep Cottages.

In the contrasting darkness of the hall she blinked and screwed up her eyes to adjust the shrunken apertures. A youngish man in gold-rimmed glasses, his thin, colourless hair brushed hopefully across a visible scalp, was hunched against the wall, cradling the telephone to his ear. He smiled with an air of embarrassment, put his hand over the mouthpiece and mouthed, "O.K. if I use the phone?"

She shrugged and walked past him upstairs.

She climbed slowly, taking the time to linger over every familar object her eye drew towards her like old past friends needing reintroduction. At the pieces of well-placed china, at the dark, undistinguished family portraits on the wall — of no great value in the saleroom, but part of the house, part of existence. She wandered along the landing, dimly aware of the young man's quiet voice below, looking at, touching each thing she passed. The carved oak chest, almost black now, once said to have been used for vestments, now full of spare blankets and sleeping bags and placed in an alcove with a fine eighteenth-century blue and white Chinese vase on it.

Above, on the wall, the single valuable picture in the house, a Tillemans, a study of Lord Berkeley about to hunt. And then the collection of flint and pottery fragments, arrowheads, hand axes, the lip of a Samian ware beaker, all found at different times (years ago) on Corford Camp and which now, irrationally, had pride of place in a narrow, glass-fronted cabinet. On the lower shelves, less easily seen were two small iridescent Roman glass bottles, a Pictish runic fragment, an early carved Egyptian scarab in some greenish stone and bone needles of the Magdalenian period that had been found in the Dordogne by Leo's grandfather. It was a cupboard full of scraps and shards that had fascinated each of the children in turn when they'd been small. Each one had been influenced, to a greater or lesser degree by the extended sense of time and relationship carried within these small, cracked pieces of waste. They held no special interest for the collector who hunted out better preserved or more indicative pieces of evidence than these — they were little more than souvenirs.

There was a small mirror, the silvering badly worn, surrounded by a stump-work frame depicting the companionable people and animals of Leo's great-grandmother. Beneath it, on a small ledge, a shell, pinkish-white and complicated, that Chloe, aged six, had brought back as a present from her school trip to Lyme Regis (the fossils had not begun to interest her at that age), a set of careful water colours—mountain and moorland birds—the merlin, the ptarmigan, the dotterel, the curlew and the golden eagle, a gilt, oval-framed cluster of embroidered flowers worked by her own mother.

She came to her study door and opening it, went in. The air was stale as though Madge had been in here smoking one of her pungent cigarettes some hours before.

After a moment's hesitation, Olivia crossed to the phone to ring Bart Foster's surgery, but she remembered the young man downstairs was still on the line. She picked up the receiver and let it crash back, just to remind him that he was exceeding his privileges.

When, finally, she screamed out loud, she frightened Leo to his feet.

"Stop that! Stop it!" he snapped helplessly at Olivia who, half-standing, half-crouching over Amy's chair, had grabbed her daughter by the neck and was forcing the girl's face down as close as she could to the sticky yellow omelette on the plate.

"Eat it!" she screamed. "You've ... got ... to ... *eat* it!" Each word, separately emphasised was accompanied by a fierce, downward pushing movement on Amy's neck. The girl tried to turn her face aside, dragging the tawny tendrils of hair through glutinous, smearing yellow.

"Get off, you bitch!" she yelled, smothered, her head banging among the cutlery. "Fuck OFF!"

"Amy! Olivia! *Amy!*" Leo didn't know which one to seize first. Throwing his napkin aside, he ran round the table, stumbled against an empty chair and grabbed for Olivia.

Mrs. Baldwin's head appeared through the hatch and rapidly withdrew.

"Control yourself!" He grappled with Olivia who was astonishingly strong (no wonder she'd got the better of Amy.) Still she would not let go of her daughter's hair. All three of them tore at one another, shouting foul and unheard orders.

"She's *got* to eat! She's got to!"

"Let go of me, you cow! Cow!"

Amy's face was twisted with pain as Olivia, pulled away by Leo, tore at her hair.

"You wicked girl! You wicked, dreadful, *cruel* girl! You'll die! Do you understand, you fool . . . *Die!*"

Her fingers were being prised apart by Leo. He feared he might break the bones her grip was so insane. She was oblivious to him. "We're trying to help you! . . . Trying to do all we can for you!" She howled and swayed.

"Let go of her, Olivia, you're hurting her. *Please!*"

Amy, with an appallingly brave and desperate twist (it seemed, in a single movement) pulled herself free, kicked over her chair and struck her mother a clumsy blow across the face.

"Oh, my God!"

All three stood as they were for a minute, Leo staring down at Olivia's hands which, held wildly by his own, grasped two thin sheaves of hair.

"Oh look!" Olivia's voice paled and trembled. "Oh, dear God, look what you've done!"

Amy picked up her plate, the streaming omelette now congealed and crushed upon it, and hurled it at the floor stamping on it with a venom that ran like poison in the features of her face. Her mouth was quite crooked and white.

"No, no! Don't do it!" moaned Olivia, slipping backwards into the firm shield of Leo's chest, letting herself be supported by him.

But Amy couldn't stop. The plate became a powder, then, pounded with the egg, a paste that spread over the deep, precious crimson of the Persian carpet.

Leo, clasping his wailing wife to him, watched, mesmerised, knowing somehow that his daughter must go on to the end.

When the destruction was done Amy turned breathlessly to her parents, her face glistening with a pale, oily sweat, then, lifting the irises of her eyes curiously upward and over, she fainted, sliding into a weak heap at their feet.

All afternoon, Olivia spent locked in her study writing furiously. Abandoning the typewriter as too lumpy a tool, her hand shook as it raced across the page though the action of writing itself, the need firmly to grip a pen between thumb and forefinger, helped progressively to steady her nerves.

Something violent and hateful that had been prodded awake in her, demanded to be soothed. She wrote against it, madly, like a man bricking in a breached wall before the full force of water flowed through taking all that remained standing, with it.

She had begun a new chapter, indifferent to the fact that the previous chapter was unfinished. But her mind had snatched up certain events and she yielded to it, afraid of delay.

Purposefully, she had begun writing about the year 1951, the most important year in many ways; the easiest to remember.

Her mother had then been living at Clouds for two years and Olivia had begun writing with unpredicted energy and success. The first book she hadn't thought to publish. It was a nothing. A pastime, a hobby. By the time the second was finished, she'd begun to regard her hobby differently. The third converted her to suspicion of a talent in herself—a remarkable talent for industry and application if nothing else.

Using an assumed name she had sent all three to a publisher of the kind she noted dealt successfully in sub-literature. All three were published simultaneously in 1950. The following year witnessed five further printings. By October, the month of the general election when Churchill was restored to power, she had been elected Romantic Novelist of the Year, the first of seven occasions on which she was to be so honoured.

A freedom, a sense of being someone in her own right—which had begun with her marriage and the economic easing that was a part of it—had broken into fuller flower. It was a vital year.

As she wrote she became conscious, for the first time, that the changes in her personal life at that period, were (in a way that she might be guilty of tailoring slightly) a reflection of the general change in atmosphere. It came back to her with that selective vividness the mind is capable of producing; an emblematic sharpness.

It was a year that had opened damply and depressingly. Rain sheeted ceaselessly across the country. The news from North Korea threatened to involve the country in a further war before it was healed from the wounds of the last. The lingering exigencies of war gave peacetime a sparse and leaden character that seemed unready to be shaken off. And yet it *had* been a turning point. Peace *was* finally wedded to prosperity.

She smiled to herself as she recalled the Festival of Britain, that much ridiculed and (as it had seemed at the beginning of the year) wholly inappropriate folly. And yet it had worked.

Like thousands of others straining to mark the beginning of a new era in a way that would become it, she and Leo had travelled up to London, gazed enchanted at the lights along the Embankment, watched the dancers spin beside the sparkling, velvet swathes of the river. They had picnicked in the Pleasure Gardens, joined the crowds swelling the Dome of Discovery, submitted to an excitement so unaccustomed it had felt illicit.

"It was a good time. The pall seemed to lift at long last. All of us felt able to look forward once again (in the way our Victorian forbears must have done) to a future that was to be glorious and the tangible fruit of our own joint endeavour. Everybody was anxious to work towards it. To be a part of it. The atmosphere was comradely, which may seem a queer word to use in view of its political overtones, but everywhere there was a sense of something more challenging than friendship, more noble than mere wealth . . ."

She paused, wondering if she were right. Yes, there had been something admirable in the mood of the time. It wasn't simply a defiant abandonment of austerity.

Hurriedly, she wrote on, describing her election, the award-winning luncheon, the new outfits she and her mother wore, the famous people they sat beside, and the theme of the short speech she had given, a theme of gratitude for her own good fortune in particular and the country's fortunes in general. (She experienced a minor doubt that she *had* made quite such deliberate reference to the times, but there was enough in the Press clippings to justify her claiming that she had.)

The words came in easy torrents.

. . . The prize-money that was spent, as it was intended it should be, on foreign travel — on her mother's first journey abroad, sick, but resolute on board ship ("creatures designed to live on land can't *expect* to feel comfortable bobbing about like this") . . . her stoicism as they drove southwards through France on the wrong side of the road . . . her excitements, guardedly expressed.

". . . It was the little towns we stayed in overnight that enchanted her. Reared in the belief that garlic, herbs and sauces were only ever used to disguise something unpleasant, mealtimes were something of an ordeal for her, though she faced up to the ordeal with spirit, but the atmosphere of these places and the architecture. in all its changing forms between Normandy and the Riviera, enthralled her utterly.

"She liked to dine either very early or very late so that she could walk and look as long as possible. I think she wouldn't have eaten at all had it not been for me! As it was, she would watch me impatiently or quite often, would rise two hours earlier than I, returning to urge me through my *petit dejeuner* with news of the wonders she had found."

It was the churches that had impressed her most.

The obsession had quite irritated Olivia who was anxious to speed southwards in search of more leisurely Mediterranean pleasures. ". . . My mother's curiosity meant that we arrived in Nice two days later than intended and I shall always be grateful to her for that . . ."

She stopped, looked at the page and went right through it, crossing out the 'my' that preceded every mention of 'mother'. Paradoxically, without the possessive pronoun, the relationship sounded closer.

"Until I pursued mother into the great dim spaces of Rouen, Chartres, Orleans (and many other wonderful church buildings, some quite small and humble) I hadn't realised what wicked desecration our own churches . . ."

She heard the doorbell ring, heard the door being opened downstairs by whoever had rung (no footsteps went to the door). Clearly somebody who felt no need of formality, somebody from Sheep Cottages come to use the phone again. Or to watch television. They seemed to enjoy the children's programmes that were shown at this hour. There were no other programmes worth watching, they claimed.

As she sat, stiff with resentments, waiting for some giveaway sound among the general stirrings of the house, her concentration began to wander.

The cathedrals, which she couldn't recall in any great detail, simply as caverns stained dark blue and crimson by the high, sun-pressed glass, had actually filled her with a drowning sense of oppression. She had known that was wrong. That her response had been wrong. She had blamed herself for that feeling, attributing it to some lack of feeling or sensitivity in herself . . .

Idly, one ear still alerted to the signals below (whoever it was seemed to have gone into the kitchen, or the little sitting room perhaps) she wondered why buildings, whose beauties she credulously read about, in guidebooks, beauties, she could, with one passionless part of herself recognise, should have weighed her down so.

She saw Mince shift from the last triangle of sunlight in the garden and come towards the terrace below, wagging his solid body in welcome. The caller, presumably, had stepped from the little sitting room, out through the french windows on to the terrace and sat there, in the still warm but late afternoon shadow. She could hear no murmuring thread of conversation.

It was, she supposed flatly, returning to her self-inflicted query, something... something to do with her God, her image of God. Well, not the God of her *choosing* exactly, the one that had been provided for her. Like a school uniform or a council house. General issue. A stern and punishing presence that furnished one corner of her life.

One might as sensibly have asked Olivia whether she believed in the chair she sat on as whether she believed in her brass-faced God. The question couldn't arise because of its implicit absurdity. He was. And the larger His temples, the more colossal His proportions... the better His eyesight, the more cruel His penance.

The only way to prevent such a person ruining one's life completely was to be a little blind to one's faults. To know them was to be destroyed—not by sin, but by a sense of sin. And though Olivia didn't recognise this mechanism in herself in any intellectual fashion, she was sufficiently aware of the difficulties of coping with her God, sufficiently impressed by His awfulness to be mildly surprised that anyone whose life was free of His presence, should choose, deliberately, to invite Him in. She didn't understand Chloe.

And yet she knew, as she let these thoughts flicker insubstantially through her half-attending mind, that Chloe wouldn't be ... *depressed* ... by the cathedrals at Chartres or Orleans, any more than her own mother had been. Equally, she sensed that whatever feeling it was, these sacred places had inspired in the older woman, it was not at all the same feeling that Chloe would experience.

No, she thought, pressing her pen to her lips and tasting the pleasant school flavour of ink, no, the *feeling* my mother had—not the feeling, the view she took of It, Him, was more like mine. But she liked it like that. And I don't.

She'd never before objectified this feeling that had just hung, web-like on the ceiling of her mind. She felt as if she'd retreated from something without retreating in the sense of escaping; rather, to observe better.

It was strange. For a moment she had a quite unexpected sensation of coolness, strength... and then, before she could either wonder at it, or be overcome by the impertinence of her focus, she was distracted by the sight of Leo below on the lawn.

He was signalling up at her, raising both arms from the elbow like a mechanic bringing a plane in safely to land. He brought her back into the day. He signalled that she should join him in its little tragedies and horrors.

Reluctantly, she rose and leaning over the desk pushed up the window.

"Bart's here!" called Leo. "Bart's come. He wants to talk to you, darling."

Darling Bart. Bart, who claimed the only reason he'd gone into the medical profession was his name. He delighted in the title Dr. Foster. Said it made the illest people laugh when he was announced.

He rose from his chair on the terrace, bending courteously but warmly as she joined them. She took both his hands and kissed his dry, creased brown cheek.

"It does me good just to see you," she said looking at the crisply silvered slate-grey hair, at the perpetual comedy of his face.

"Then why have you avoided me?"

She skirted his smiling reprimand. "Oh, life . . . you know. You've come to see Amy?"

"I've seen Amy. I want to see you."

"Let me find out if there's anything left to drink." Leo got up, unbalanced, scraping his iron chair across the stone.

"See *me*? Amy, where was she?" She realised now it had been Bart at the front door—surely he hadn't been here long enough to examine Amy properly? *Cross*-examine her?

"Don't worry about Amy—she's up with her sister at . . ." He gestured, meaning Sheep Cottages, but the name escaped him.

"But of course I worry about her. It makes me . . ." She fell silent and looked away towards the hills that distantly rose above the pink brick wall. Gnats stung her scalp.

"This thing, anorexia nervosa, that she has—girls' disease, girls who don't want to grow up generally. Ah, I'm not voicing that as a *criticism*." Bart raised an admonishing hand lest she should think he was offering himself as an ally in exasperation. "As a *fact*. It's the motives behind the fact that are interesting, but never mind that for now. *Treatment's* all you're interested in at the moment.

Well," he rested his chin on a cupped hand and gazed down at frayed and ancient turn-ups. He always looked more like a head waiter than a doctor in his old pinstripe trousers and black jacket. "Well now," he went on, "we can force feed her in hospital, we can lock her up—yes, literally. In a mental home. Feed her on a reward system. We can perform a lobotomy . . . it's all right, my dear," as Olivia drew breath, "I've no intention of doing any of those things. They're dreadfully expensive and largely unnecessary, undertaken for the sake of the parent rather than the child, if you see my meaning. No, much the best and cheapest thing is to leave her alone. She *will* grow into a woman however hard she tries to prevent it. Or she'll die. I don't think she wants to die, not really. She was fearfully upset about not being Ophelia in the school play, were you aware of that? No, really," he continued, not waiting for an answer, "really she wants to look like some image she has of herself, so I took the precaution of bringing with me," he plunged into his untidy black bag, "a camera. On the pretext of taking photographs of developments so far at . . ." Again he gestured feverishly. Again, Olivia knew what he meant." I've taken a few pictures which should help shock her every bit as effectively as ECT treatment, which is another possibility. *Now*," he went on emphatically, "the thing to find out is not so much what's the matter with Amy as what's the matter with you."

"There's nothing at all wrong with me." She sounded a little severe. She ran a hand round the inside of her polo neck and tugged it a little closer to her chin.

"You're under considerable strain."

"We all are."

"True enough." Bart mused for a moment. "Things don't improve—though *here*." And he looked round at the house, the garden, dampening now as the sun retreated beyond the walls. With a slow, ecstatic arching, the white cat rose from beneath a mass of lacecap hydrangeas. "This may be the most peaceful place left in all England, but the strain still seeps through."

She hated him to say that. It made her feel unsafe.

"Anyway," he added, "you have other things . . . your mother. You haven't, you know," and he looked at her quizzically, "you haven't allowed the cleansing of grief, have you? From what I learn." He continued, against her will, to hold her eye. "Until you've been through that you won't let go. You won't be free of it."

"I can't. That's just me, we're all different. Perhaps I don't need that."

"Not so very different you know. Ah, here comes Leo. Well done!" he exclaimed perceiving the dusty bottle of claret.

"Running down stocks," commented Leo setting down bottle, glasses and opener. "It should be very fine."

"And nobody better to appreciate it!" Bart leaned back in his chair, delighted.

"Are you going to prescribe me something soothing?" smiled Olivia knowing Bart's dislike of drugs.

"No, Olivia dear, what I want from you is grief. I can't improve on that. I like the young people," he said suddenly. "Spent the afternoon up there . . . very nice, very *good*." He stressed the word 'good' as if describing the virtue rather than the quality of any particular achievement.

"You'll forgive me," apologised Leo, pouring, "if I attend to a few things. I'll be back to join you in a glass shortly."

"Why so fidgety?" enquired Olivia.

"Splendid," said Bart.

They sipped. Olivia shivered. "It's getting colder," she remarked. "There's a wind blowing up. Rain." They looked towards the west, where the sun still aggressively gold, but small, was threatened by a surly cavalry of cloud.

"It could be bad for the harvest," she murmured.

"Indeed . . . Look!" exclaimed Bart, straightening himself and recrossing his legs.

"This business with Amy."

"She hit me you know."

"Yes I know — nothing very surprising about that."

"She fainted."

"Nothing very surprising about that either. Fainting rarely hurt anybody."

"It's the body's way," Olivia mocked him.

"Well *precisely*. The longer I stay in medicine the less need I realise there is for me. It's the chaps who think they can actually prevent death who get so worked up about their status. All the Meccano merchants. *Amy* . . ." he tried again, "now, why is she doing this? Well," he went on cheerfully, "there are many possibilities and it's most unlikely to be any *single* one. It's a complex thing, but opinion has it that, very generally, it's a disturbance manifested by those who can't face life — or at least, the life that's *expected* of them. That point's very important." He thought about it for a second, then tried to elaborate. "Some drink, some run away, some starve—starving seems to be the female, the adolescent female method, which is not to say there aren't a lot of feminine adolescents amongst men, but it's mostly girls, yes . . . The question one has to ask is *why* should life be so difficult for her to face?"

Olivia laughed ironically.

"Oh I know, it's never been more difficult. There's no apparent future, very awkward thing that, for humans. And it's not really like a war either which humans cope with quite nicely—a definable enemy, a reason for coming together, a hope of victory. No, it's not like that at all I'm afraid. Still, the prospect is always worse for those who don't have the equipment to cope with it. Inwardly, I mean . . . do you see?"

She nodded, her gaze fixed on the engulfing cloud from which a single bright ray courageously burst.

"I'm not certain," Bart thought out loud, "that it's necessarily good for her to be here. In this house. It's too easy to cut herself off from . . ."

Olivia let him continue his ramble, feeling new premonitions of anger in herself. It seemed sometimes, she were in a continual state of anger, full of metal splinters.

"It's so much easier for the religious," Bart was saying. "They have love. Of a particular kind. The irreligious have to depend on human love to keep their strength of purpose and human love is too wily, too equivocal a thing to be able to depend on utterly. Full of motives, failings in a way God's love isn't. Still, it's better than nothing." He beamed amiably at Olivia. She had to smile back.

"You're the most eccentric doctor I've ever known," she laughed. "Doctor of *what*?"

"Oh," he shrugged, "you've got to treat each problem on its merits. They don't all improve for medicine. Makes me laugh, you know," he took a pleasurable draught of wine, "the way all these psychiatrist chaps set about demonstrating love was the critical factor in the stable human personality—something that had to be passed on from generation to generation, like blue eyes only more important than that—heavens, the dullest and ugliest of children can accept himself perfectly happily as long as he's loved. Yes . . ." He buried his hands reflectively in his pockets for a moment. "Anyway, the way these fellows—all so *earnest*—on they go about the way the unloved go out into the world thoroughly deformed, only the deformity doesn't show until it becomes visible in the world these kids, *adults*, for heaven's sake . . . in the world they in turn create. All of us structure a way of living that reflects ourselves of course. Oh Lord!" He shook his head ruefully. "They put it all down in huge textbooks, the more statistics and graphs the better and carry off prizes for demonstrating the self-evident—at least it's always been evident until this century, in this small corner of the world, because everybody's always known that *that* kind of love was perfectly well embodied in God. Makes you spit doesn't it?" He sighed.

"Oh come now, Bart. Not everybody's always believed in a *loving* God."

"I grant you," he nodded generously, "that an unsophisticated notion of God—any old god—incorporates this idea of *placating* . . . of toadying up to a sacred monster. Horrible idea. All *that* produces is guilt. Guilt as the motive force in behaviour. Are you aware," he asked with enthusiasm, "that guilt is almost entirely interchangeable with love as motive force?"

She was bending down to stroke the white cat.

"It's marvellous, you'd hardly notice the difference in anyone's moral behaviour until very real demands are placed on either him or her. Come to that, whole societies can be founded on guilt and get on very decently until put to the challenge. Do you follow me?"

"Not really," she smiled up at him, her hand following the curve of the cat's tail. Bart was a compulsive talker. He always seemed to get through the tangle and end up at the point where he'd begun somehow, but the sound alone of what he said was oddly congenial.

"Oh, it's fascinating. People will go on giving, behaving in an orderly, just and relatively pleasant way out of guilt motivation alone—being nice to their children, helping blacks, subscribing to charities, you know the kind of thing, without any consciousness of what drives them, just as long as their own guilt or self-hatred—the unloved usually basically loathe themselves— can be satisfactorily defused by performing agreeable acts towards others. Happens all the time. But when such a person, or such a *people*— let's say people, because it's true of our nation, I'm sure of it— when such people see reason to hate those to whom they've given more powerfully than they hate themselves, then a *very* dangerous force is released. Love is forgiving. The hate that's bound up with guilt isn't."

She drew her sleeves down over her hands and looked at him, bemused. "Oh, Bart," she said, "*really* . . ."

But he wouldn't be shaken off. He had a point he wished her to attend to. "But look," he insisted, "at the way our so-called classless society polarised again. So quickly. All the vicious feeling that had been held in check, revealed. The very thing guilt tries to hide, *revealed* . . ." He was leaning forward trying to persuade her of his case, but she looked down, shivering and he moved back in his chair. "There aren't many of them, God knows," he said. "But the people who are truly moved by love don't change like that. That's how you can spot them — by their . . . constancy . . . yes, constancy."

"Let's take our drinks indoors," she suggested. He'd strayed so far from the point. A sudden spasm of wind drove the flowers down against the soil.

"Come on," she said amicably. "You can give me your advice about Amy."

"That's what I am doing, you dotty creature!" he cried good-humouredly, standing up and shaking the wrinkles out of his trousers. "You're a rotten listener, Olivia. Still, I do go on. I do *know* . . ." And still talking, he followed her into the little sitting room where Delilah and her kittens seemed to occupy the entire brown velvet sofa. The room was autumn coloured. Warm. Inside it, she instantly felt less shrivelled, less resistant. She felt as though her ears, like every pore in her body had closed with cold. Not that Bart had *really* talked specifically of Amy. He probably thought he had. He was like that. His mind would spring from one lily pad to another without leaving any indication of his direction or intention.

"Amy," he repeated summarising, securing anew a base for his discourse, "Amy will tell you she's trying to lose weight, or she's reduced her appetite to help the Third World. Something of the kind. *And* she'll believe what she's saying. But actually, she's trying to disappear. She finds life difficult and she finds it doubly difficult because she's without the resources needed to cope with it anyway. There. Now you understand that, don't you?"

"I understand you. I don't know that you're right. About Amy. I think she's trying to frighten me."

"She may be. Disappearing is an excellent method of frightening people. Classic if you think of ghosts and such-like. So, she thinks she'll withdraw completely."

"If you say so."

"We all do it, in different ways. Hers is a more literal form of withdrawal, but we all have our own little methods."

"Look at Chloe's friends!" Olivia couldn't keep the derision out of her voice. It quite startled Bart.

"No. Funnily enough, no, I would say that was the last thing they were doing. Having met them." He hesitated a moment then confessed, "I *had* my doubts, but not now ... I think they're trying to do something very important. I think they're trying to work out for themselves the proper scale and nature of interdependence. Well," he spread his hands out, "I *say* that ... we haven't talked a great deal but you can *feel* it ..."

"You sound very sure."

"I think I'm right."

"Oh well," Listlessly she sipped the last of her wine.

"Amy needs you."

Olivia sat up sharply. "My God, Bart!" she cried, "I've tried everything. Everything!" And then her anger plunged suddenly into despair. Tears confused her.

"It's a long process," he warned.

"*Everything!*" she asserted again, her voice rising. "Ask Leo!"

"I have. He told me."

"She just refuses. Nothing works. I can't get food into her." (She bit her lip, controlling her tone without variation.) "She's making me *watch* her starve. It's desperate. I don't know what to do." Her head ached.

"Don't give up," said Bart grimly, "even though she may seem to be abusing you with her body. Don't give up. You may have to change your methods, not just your methods ..." His voice faded away as he saw how hard she found this to bear. He knew there came a point when it was purposeless to be cruel to her.

"Tell me," she persisted, her voice coiling with hysteria again. "Tell me what to *do!*"

"That," he said gently, "would be presumptuous of me. You must find out for yourself. Now," rising as he spoke, "I'm going to find Leo and talk over fruit trees with him. I need a little help too. With *my* young growing things." He smiled and ruffled her hair as though she were a child. "Now dry your eyes so that you can see more clearly what it is you have to do. I'll drop the photographs by when they're ready—at least I can provide you with pictures; they might help. In the meantime worry less about what you should be doing. Concentrate on *being* and you may

178

find it all becomes easier as a result. I'm serious." He bent and kissed her resisting cheek.

When he had closed the door, when his footsteps had taken him beyond the range of his hearing, Olivia began to weep as she had not wept for years. And she wept because her body yearned for it, not because she understood why.

13

ALTHOUGH HE WAS ABLE TO LEAVE THE TAUTLY WIRED tension between Amy and her mother behind him, although he could, for the moment, forget the requisition order locked away in a metal box at the top of the wardrobe, Leo went back to the City the following week with reluctance.

Each mile further from Clouds that he travelled, the problems he left grew smaller, receding to almost homely proportions. His own small responsibilities. Difficulties that were within his power to resolve.

By contrast, the problems lying ahead, seemed as large and ungraspable as the globe itself. The closer he approached the more they lacked all sensible, definable source. The less they possessed a foreseeable outcome. He felt, not that he was going to confront them, but that he was being sucked in by them. Even the car felt as though it were not entirely in his control but being drawn onwards towards the indiscernible eye of the storm by the very force of the thing. At one point, with some forty miles still to go, he was so unsettled by the feeling he made himself stop and get out, just to demonstrate the absurdity of it. And then, it struck him, the childishly superstititious act of getting out was more absurd still. He went behind a hedge and forced himself to urinate, careful to keep the car still within protective sight.

Returning to the wheel and switching on the ignition, he silently rebuked himself. It was simply age. That was all. A younger man would still discover the appetising edge of challenge that no longer ringed anxiety for him.

And then he thought of Corin and doubted it.

On the whole he tried not to think of Corin. When Olivia carelessly applauded his decision to actively involve himself, Leo too, made murmurs of an assenting kind, but the truth was he felt a disappointment in his son that bordered on disgust. A contempt that was capable of shocking him if it stole out of the hold which struggled to contain it.

He knew, and his colleagues knew (he could tell from their conspicuous lack of comment or inquiry) that the boy had not gone out of any patriotic impulse, not in any spirit of sacrifice, but out of unashamed self-interest. Only Thurloe had come anywhere near honesty in remarking that he supposed "it was as good a place as any other to be". That was about it. Leo felt his son's action reflected on *him* in some indecipherable manner; in the eyes of the other men at least. It wasn't paranoid to think so, he told himself. There were definite lowerings, withdrawals, softnesses of tone that would have been appropriate if someone he loved had just died. It was there.

The so-called soup kitchens were still shuttered at the hour he drove past them through the peeling streets, but already people were beginning to hang about. They stood no better chance of getting stuff by coming early. Some probably didn't even need to come. It was just that they had nothing else to do. Some seemed to find a blank interest in simply watching him slide past.

How many of the men, Leo noticed, were unshaven. Soon, he supposed they would be ragged too. They didn't *have* to look wretched; they didn't care. It wasn't poverty or signs of deprivation that he noticed chiefly, but a whipped air of depression. It was the quality he most closely recognised. It was in him too, like a sickness. One had to beware of inward surrender.

With longing he thought of the lanes and fields and hills, already rich with the ripening colours of early autumn, that encircled Clouds.

It was the afternoon.

"Christ!" Heseltine flung himself across the office to close the door after the girl. He hated her being in the room when the crisis really caught at them.

He was frightened. Leo stared at him, distantly surprised by the white folds of tension highlighting Heseltine's face. The man talked rapidly, but coherently. The American harvest had been good. The prices shouldn't have reached this level. He went on and on. Leo saw at first dimly and then with increasing, calm fascination that Heseltine was more alarmed about the company, about its various deals and clients than the larger situation outside it. That didn't seem to occur to him at all. It was as though his mind couldn't expand beyond its local limits without breaking.

"Our experience of the past few years should have led us to expect something of this kind though, we shouldn't be too surprised," murmured Leo and hearing himself, was surprised by his comforting tone. Barlett's would be livid over the hard wheat price, but he'd guessed it was coming. It was almost a relief to have the thing known. "The bluff's been called," he said.

"What in God's name do you mean?" snapped Heseltine.

"The Middle East purchase."

"Bluff? What bluff!"

Dismayed by Heseltine's violent expression, Leo retreated a little. He still felt unnaturally calm. Using nominees, a group of Arab countries had carried out a number of individual purchases, a measure they claimed had been forced on them by the American and European failure to create a substantial grain reserve for the hungry world because of their fears of the effect on prices. Now the Americans were refusing to allow the shipments out. The bluff was called. He spread his hands out silently, unable to express whatever remote and temporary sense of justice it was contributing to the stillness in him.

"You must be crazy, Mathison!"

The two men stared at one another across the deadly pastel office for, it seemed to Leo, an extraordinarily long time. Slowly, as though reading the signals in every lash and line and tremor of Heseltine's features, reading as it were, a judgement upon himself hung publicly upon the man's face, his hallucinatory calm began to disperse. Through every crack that finely slit its surface, the sour vapour of terror began to steal, at first in threads and then combining in coils of mist winding more thickly one into the other until he and Heseltine stared at one another, two men in an identical state of mind.

Olivia looked at the clock. Five-thirty . . . the phase of the day that, more than any other, took on a languor if the house were empty. No evening meal to prepare, no children home from school, chattering, no work to read out aloud to her mother. No mother. She sighed. The weather was too squally for gardening . . . *too* . . . she sighed again and looked at her hands, examining them for blemishes. Finding none, she replaced them carefully in her lap. The windows rattled in their frames as the wind, in wet, ill-tempered bursts, cut round the angle of the house.

She could ride. The two hunters brought back from a neighbour's hillside pasture, where they'd summered, had to be got fit. (Horses hated this sort of weather, putting their heads down, backs irritably hunched, leaning heavily towards home.)

Once, this lively part of the rituals preceding winter, had given her nothing but pleasure. The slow stretching of muscles, the growing anticipation. Now the excitement had been skimmed off leaving only a plain and a practical thing behind. She blamed Amy for spoiling it.

Still, she thought, flexing her shoulders, Amy was not around to criticise. She'd disappeared somewhere taking her sour, spasmodic commentary with her. Olivia rose to go and change and felt her bones complain. Rubbing her aching neck and shoulders with wary discovery of rheumatism, she meekly bent to switch off the small electric fire she'd allowed herself this afternoon. There'd been a fresh reminder about voluntary restrictions today. A warning that phased cuts would be routine throughout the winter months . . . The voice had been distastefully cheerful. There were tips about useful items of clothing that could be made or saved for in preparation; the blandest beginnings of propaganda culminating with the customary fanfare, like stray cats strung together on a line.

Hearing it at all was an accident. Olivia had given up newspapers and the radio. "What's the point?" she had demanded of Mrs. Baldwin, "It's all depressing."

Badger was not pleased to be ridden out. He bent his head well into his chest to avoid the rain and presented his left side to the weather travelling uphill over the slithery stone track like a crab. A heavy, clean-limbed blue roan, he was an animal of forceful will, capable of startling courage when the pace was to his liking and an engaging obstinacy when it was not. He saw it as part of his purpose in life to put human beings in their place. In a ditch or stream, occasionally.

Olivia urged him on, her muscles taxed by his fierce displeasure. But in spite of his disconsolate mood, in spite of the bumping weight on her hip caused by the tomatoes and a marrow she carried slung in a bag across her body, in spite of the cutting, gusty cold, her spirits rose as they always did outside, however unseasonable the weather.

Rain dripped off the hawthorn overhead, heavy now with blood-red berries. The elder, too, was borne down by the weight of dark fruit. In the gaps of the hedge she could see, below her, flattened blonde acres of barley, indented as though a squadron of UFOs had recently landed. But already the valley was irregularly patterned with areas ploughed in defiant promise of the following year.

Occasionally, as she climbed, an angry beam of sunlight, refusing to be overwhelmed, broke through the veil of rain, lighting the tossing wet landscape before being blown out again. By the time she reached the top of the hill, the fitful sun had managed to burn a space for itself and blazed so fiercely that, for a while, it turned the cloud a dark, steel-blue. A rainbow bloomed over the spine of the hill as she turned towards Sheep Cottages and to her astonishment, she saw that a rainbow was not an arc at all, but here, where it leapt the hill and plunged down either side into the narrow bowls of the valleys, was very nearly a perfect circle, a ring of light through which she seemed about to pass. Although it didn't vanish, it appeared to retreat and by the time she reached the Cottages, the shining hoop hung as far from her as ever.

"Hello!"

The kitchen was empty, warm and dry. She called again and stepped inside taking off her mac and shaking it outside before closing the door. In the yard, a few hens wretchedly moulting, clung to the cover of the wall and squawked for relief.

Then Mab came from the little dairy that opened off a passage from the kitchen, a butter press in her hand. "Oh, hello," she said. "Come and get dry. Everybody's about somewhere." She smiled shyly as Olivia went over to the big black stove, rubbing her painful arms with icy hands.

She heard the rhythmic trundle of Sarah's wheel somewhere to the back of the house. A thump and a clatter, that was clearly Biff. Over the constant scent of clay and yeast, something with a winey fragrance bubbled on the stove. She lifted the lid. "Mm! Nice." She sniffed.

"Elderberries mostly," volunteered Mab. "The others are out, picking . . . Peter's milking," She smiled again, wiped a hand on her skirt. "Would you like a warm drink?"

"No, no, you get on with your work. I'll just dry off till they come in. Oh, I've brought something for you by the way." And she nodded at her bag which she'd hung on the hooks beside the door. "I'll get it in a second. You carry on."

Mab disappeared. Olivia heard her working the butter free of its moisture.

A lamp was burning on the dresser, unnecessarily, when the sun forced itself on the roof of the outbuildings across the yard — comfortably, when it was blown off and the window filled once more with restless grey.

Agreeably untidy signs of preparation were strewn everywhere. The huge table was spread with used bowls and jugs, a scattering of flour and the stringy peelings of beans. From a hook above the sink, a muslin bag weighted down with curds, dripped softly at slow intervals.

Something in Olivia eased and lightened. The domestic kindness of the kitchen stole into her memory weakening some of its fortifications. There were correspondences here — the warm, wholesome smells, certain objects, a large brown teapot, the muslin strainer with its yellow beaded corners, a copper jelly mould, a plain white milk jug, the faint spitting of apple wood inside the stove, an aroma of dough rising — things which restored her childhood to her more gently and effectively than all the struggling hours at her desk these past three months had done. There was no sense of narrow time or time's pressure, just a soft, bubbling, stirring continuity easily lowering her memory into other rooms, other cupboards, positioned at only slightly different angles to these. All that time had obtruded between seemed briefly, irrelevant, aberrant.

She saw Peter, draped in oilskins, cross the yard, coming towards the house.

"Hi!" he said, surprised to see her as he came in shaking himself like a dog. "I wondered who the horse belonged to." He lifted the two enamel, one-gallon milk churns on to the table and flexed his fingers. "I'm still not very good at it," he grinned ruefully.

"Milking?"

"Mm. The girls are better for some reason. Their hands I suppose."

"Hey, *you*," Mab re-appeared, mildly aggressive. "Where's my big ladle? You never put *anything* back where you got it from."

"You never look properly." He fetched it from the sink.

"I don't suppose you sterilised it."

"I don't suppose I did," he countered cheerfully.

Any further exchange was interrupted by the noisy arrival of Chloe, Andrew and Amy. They were laden with buckets, bags and baskets which they put down while they peeled or kicked off their boots. "*Foul* out!"

A great sweep of cold air broke through the door, banging it back on its hinges. "Shut it, you clown?"

"Hang on, that's my foot!"

They sorted themselves out, greeted her — all but Amy — and Chloe padded round the table in thick, holey socks, to put the kettle on.

"I should have guessed you were here." Olivia spoke to Amy who passed through the kitchen out of sight.

"She's helping us. We're doing entries for the Flower Show — bit late, but never mind. What're *you* doing? We're doing some jellies and pickles. And entering some of the onions — the ones you gave us actually." Chloe laughed and put the filled kettle on top of the stove.

"I hadn't really thought about it."

"You should."

"Yes, I suppose . . ."

The chattered on neither including nor excluding her. Chloe rubbed her hair dry on a rough, torn piece of towel and it sprang from her head like fire in the lamplight.

"Look how dark it's getting and it's only a quarter to seven."

"Where's Joe?"

"Dunno. Thought he was with you."

"I brought you a marrow."

"Oh thanks, hey, that'll help solve supper."

Amy came back with covered bowls of dough.

"Punch it about, Amy, there's an angel . . . I'm exhausted." Chloe dragged a chair up near the stove, settling herself with her feet up on the rail.

Biff crawled in from the passage followed by Sarah, her arms surrounded with red clay which she went to rinse off at the sink. Andrew made the tea and Amy, with striking obedience, began kneading the dough more vigorously than she was really able. Olivia turned to watch her. She saw what Chloe was doing and felt a sudden, weakening flow of gratitude towards her. Sitting back she relaxed in the companionable atmosphere offering the odd, unforced word of her own here and there.

Taking the second mug of tea that was brought to her by Mab, she sipped and looked secretly over its chipped rim at her eldest daughter, gold and rosy now before the stove.

Was it her imagination or did Chloe glow amongst the company? She looked at her as objectively as she could. Chloe was massaging the damp roots of her hair with her fingers and listening quietly to the easy babble of conversation, adding to it, smiling at someone else's quarrel, encouraging Amy, telling Sarah how many windfalls they'd found already ("Autumn always steals into summer before you've really noticed . . . when the sun stops shining, you notice"), but mostly, she dreamed, the others her background, her face in the shadow, her hair gleaming. Olivia was able to study her without seeming to spy.

They *were* alike, but not much. The same open gaze . . . a boldness of expression that in Chloe, lacked any defensive challenge . . . the same straight nose, though Chloe's features were fuller, they possessed Leo's generosity of outline. One day, perhaps, her bones would emerge more finely—as her own had done. Once, Olivia realised, their similarity would have been far more marked. Their colouring—*her* colouring, at Chloe's age, was like that. Not her skin, which had always been paler, ivoried with tender care, but her hair of course . . . straighter than Chloe's, but wheaty, thick . . . She looked at the girl wistfully.

They were talking about some things they'd picked up at a jumble sale in the village (something she should have gone to). Mab had bought several jumpers and was unpicking them to knit up again. (Her mother had done that . . . One she remembered she had made of the many threads a Fair Isle jumper . . . so *proud*.) Gravely, they wondered whether it would not be better to have two formal fast days each week instead of skimping over the seven days. "It's all right now, with the berries and such. But, winter."

They told her of the giant puffball they'd found two days before and feasted on all weekend. "It was thirty-six inches round and it weighed *four pounds*!" Peter made an enormous and wondering mandala in the air with his hands. "It was just there, in the field. Nothing the night before. Just there, like a pterodactyl's egg." He'd never seen anything like it.

"It tasted like light cheese pancakes."

"Like . . ." And they all tried to think of something else it resembled in flavour.

But in the end it was its own thing. Perfect and strange.

"You're not going to ride that horse home in the dark are you?" Chloe was speaking to her.

The *great* difference, between them—between *us*, she thought—lay in the manner. Chloe was wholly without timidity. Without that mortified sense of her own existence that she had endured. The self-contumely of the poor.

She smiled. "I suppose I ought to go."

"Oh, I didn't mean . . ." Chloe sought to be understood.

"I know. I know, it's dark so soon . . ." But still, as she looked through the window, she saw an angry brassy light surviving the storm. "It's the lamp," she said. "The lamp makes it look darker outside . . . still, I should go . . . Amy?"

"I'll come down later." She thrust a fist into the second batch of dough.

Olivia stood for a moment, her pleasure in the atmosphere increased by the rage of wind outside. Andrew, sitting at the table was threading onions on a string, dangling them like a yo-yo to amuse Biff.

"All right. I'll . . ." She was stiff.

"It was nice of you to come and see us. *Really* . . ." said Chloe. Before she left, she unpacked the marrow and tomatoes.

Badger whinnied when he heard her cross the yard. He wanted to go home.

The evening was wild and marvellous. All the rain had been whipped out of the air leaving a pale, clear gash of lemon in the western sky. Beams radiated from it at so great a height they failed to touch the hilltops and lit only the air itself.

Tightening Badger's girths first, she made a clumsy attempt to mount but the horse swung away from her, startled by the silent appearance of a figure between the outbuildings.

"Mrs. Mathison?"

"Joe?" She was startled herself.

"Hi."

"Heavens, I wondered who it was." She laughed slightly, relieved. It was the black silhouette of a gun barrel above his shoulder that had alarmed her.

"What *have* you been doing?" she cried, lifting herself, at a second attempt, into the saddle. Joe raised his arm so that she could see, as she looked down in the fading light, the two dead rabbits he clasped by the ears.

"Supper," he said sardonically. "We were a bit short," He hesitated, then added in a more apologetic tone, "There are so many around."

"Oh," she answered, gathering her reins. "It's a good idea. It helps keep disease down." She couldn't see his face. Turning the horse, she heard him say, "Maybe. They *are* a bit small . . ."

"Goodbye," she called pushing the horse into a trot.

". . . but I missed the bigger ones," he said.

Although she ran from the kitchen to the hall, the phone stopped ringing when she was a stride away from it.

Leo didn't ring again that evening. He'd tried three times and got no answer.

Instead he went to the hideously fluted drinks cabinet in the corner of his office and poured a large whisky. Everyone else had gone. All the febrile energy gone. One of the four walls was a black glass expanse of sky.

He wasn't to blame for it all. Once again, it wasn't his fault. Distress made him pick over all the random details trying to fit them neatly together just to still the sense of confusion. Once again in his life tides of circumstance had washed over him, treating him with the indifference that takes a child's stray sandal from beach to beach. Bobbing, rotting, useless on its own.

He turned the glass round and round in his fingers slipping a little of the drink on his papers and trying, ineptly to blot the mess with his sleeve.

He had wanted to talk to his wife. She wouldn't have understood. Not the details. But she would have listened quietly; that would have been enough. *Quiet.* All around him the furious exchanges had already started. Each man fixing himself up with a victim—a name, an event, a country, a government, anything would do as long as something of that bewildered fury could be loosed elsewhere out of the dangerously combustible chamber of the self. Talk, talk. He drank thirstily and rubbed the back of his mouth with his hand. He should have liked to talk to Olivia. Quietly.

But she hadn't been there and Leo was left with the time to search for his own victim, for something to impale, left with the fragments to pick over—arranging, re-arranging, making the oddest alignments, marrying items incongruously together— slowly these two restless activities of the mind began an unnatural coupling of their own. All his suspicions, anger and blame merged until he convinced himself that Corin had known something of the scandal. (Scandal was the word he now used to himself, as all the other men had. There were no bluffs called any longer. The vocabulary had undergone consoling change.)

Corin had known. On the futures market, there must have been an inkling. Nobody in futures could have been doing their job properly had they *not* known. His departure became proof of guilt.

Believing this, he couldn't ring Olivia back again. Now he had performed the silent and terrible act of accusation there was nothing comforting to be said between them.

Searching amongst the rubble of the world for causes of collapse it never occurred to him to prosecute his species, most of all, his sex. He had found his son. The magnitude of the problem *demanded* the most dreadful conclusion he was capable of drawing. He had found it. In his son.

14

THE FOOD ON THE ALTAR WAS CEREMONIALLY BLESSED.
The children who, one by one, had carried their harvest gifts to the snowy-clothed table, turned, and blushing, looking sidelong for their parents, they pattered softly across the tiled floor and down the steps.

Chloe, seated between Amy and Joe, held her sister's hand. "The bread looks wonderful," she whispered. "Just see!"

To defy the gloom of the weather which pressed in upon the church, all the choir lamps and great candles had been lit at the eastern end — and there, in the soft pool of light, rested the year's offerings . . . marrows and round tawny pumpkins, cabbages, apples, carrots, bright bunches of dahlias and asters, clear dark jellies and wines that had been displayed at the Flower Show the day before, thick chutneys and jams, and, raised proudly at their head, the glossy brown harvest loaf, that Amy had been persuaded to make, plaited and scattered with seeds.

They sang the child's hymn 'All Things Bright and Beautiful', even Joe, who had come unwillingly. "Being is *giving*, Joe," Chloe had declared, gleefully trumping his existentialist card and delightedly tugging him after her. "Come and see."

So he had. He'd been quite impressed with Henry Claremont: with his realistic refusal to include 'Come ye thankful people come' in the selection of hymns on the grounds that the harvest was *not* safely gathered in, but stood drenched and threatened in deep mud. And he'd been sympathetic to Henry's claim that the situation they now all of them found themselves in, made their thanksgiving the more meaningful, and that men, who had thought themselves quite clever enough to recreate miracles with loaves and fishes, might now discern, in their failure, hidden reasons for humble gratitude as well as reasons for angry resentment.

"*Search*," Henry had urged. "Seek out the beautiful .Its concealment isn't at all the same as its disappearance. It *is* there. For us to resurrect."

And Joe gazing at the flowers that enwreathed the stone, found himself in reluctant agreement. (He knew the flowers by name now.)

"He's O.K.," he conceded to Chloe afterwards. "There's all the *business*, though, all that authority invested in . . . kind of thing."

Chloe, trying to fasten a scarf over her hair in the lashing wind, grinned at him. "It's much closer to you than you think," she said. "It's just prejudice stops you seeing that, honestly!"

"Well," Joe tried to turn his collar up with one hand and shrugged. "I don't know, it's too hierarchical and suchlike for my taste."

"Oh, that's the *Church*!" shouted Choe cheerfully against the wind, heading down the path where her mother stood, an umbrella held grimly over both herself and Henry Claremont. "Not *Christ*! That's just men trying to hang on to a power Christ's told them they don't have, Loony! Oh hurry up, I want to cadge a lift home."

And she plunged her arm through his to speed him through the rain.

Olivia had said yes, of course she would help (as usual) with the distribution, but when she arrived at the church the following morning, Henry wearing a sports jacket and holding an untidy bunch of lists, told her that Chloe and her friends had already set off with a heavy load of gifts. "They're going to get soaked," he said. "They brought a pony and cart!" And he laughed.

Olivia felt the women, packing vegetables and tins into labelled cardboard boxes on the floor of the church, watching her. She showed no sign of surprise.

"Oh well," she smiled, "I'm sure there's still plenty for me to do."

"I've given them the High Street to deal with. If you could cope with the more outlying calls? They wouldn't get so wet perhaps . . . As long as you're all right for petrol, that is," he added anxiously.

"Oh yes, fine."

"We'll load you up then!"

She drove carefully through the rain. Twice, because elm branches had been blown down across the road, she had to take a longer route round to the addresses on her list than she'd intended. She kept a watchful eye on the petrol gauge. Stupid of her to bring the Bentley, but she'd thought it would hold more.

Some of the people she found marooned in their small cottages, she hadn't seen since the previous year. Some, for longer than that. They looked, one or two of them, as if they hadn't moved in the interim. Old Annie Cartwright sat, rugged up beside her caged ferret, her jaw, a toothless rubber hinge, looking as though a faint powdering of dust had fallen on her. "I'm managing all right," she mouthed as Olivia picked up her knitting that had fallen on the floor. "What have you got for me this year, then?"

And Olivia put the things away for her in cupboards that were pitifully bereft.

"Old Mother Hubbard, me!" laughed Annie silently, pointing a finger as curved as a hawk's.

At Tom Griffin's cottage she went out, ankle deep in liquid manure to feed his pig for him. A small, neat man, widowed for five years, he was sitting by the window sewing a button on his shirt. He wouldn't let her do that for him, but his legs were bad, he said sadly, looking out on the puddled yard. The mud and manure had the consistency of wallpaper paste.

"Who's going to hang and cure the pig for you, Tom? It's too heavy for you now."

"It's they children of yours," he said, surprised. "I can get he slaughtered all right, but they said they'd hang and joint he for me. Didn't they say then?"

It wasn't the only occasion on which she was shamed that morning. At one place after another, as she beat her way through long wet grass, crunching fallen apples underfoot, she found that some small job had been done, or that a visit had been made, by one or other of the young people she'd so often charged with idleness or sponging—either to Leo or more commonly, in the privacy of her own courts.

Even now, it was hard to quell an unattractive tremor of irritation.

Leaning against the wall of Brick Cottage, where Barber's old parents lived, she noticed black painted sheets of roofing like the stuff used at Sheep Cottages and an old ungenerous impulse made her wonder how much of it Leo had paid for, how much he knew. But she also knew her own cavilling was ugly. At least she made a considered attempt to restrain it. She wondered *why* the middle-aged were wont to look at the efforts of the young with such hostility—even their good efforts. As if, she thought, pushing open the door of the Barbers' scarlet-creepered house, as if they were made somehow smug or pious by their kindness and one's inimical response fastened greedily on *that* possibility, even if it could find nothing to complain of in the act itself.

The old couple welcomed her and insisted she should have a pot of tea made for her.

"You're wet through, my dear," protested Mrs. Barber, moving her small arthritic body towards the sink with unregarded pain. (She moved for both of them. Since the old man had had his accident and been paralysed down one side, she'd done it all.)

They looked at her with sympathy when she finally settled beside them at the table where they'd been doing a crossword in an old and yellow-spotted newspaper together.

"We *are* sorry about they horses of yours. Jack told us. 'Tis a terribly sad thing." Mrs. Barber's face creased with concern.

Olivia hadn't realised Barber knew. Leo must have told him. Her heart ached to be reminded of it.

"The land's needed for planting," she said tightly.

"So Jack said." They regarded her silently. Outside the trees were tossed about by the wind.

"It's been a poor year all round."

"I don't know what else to do," Olivia said, raising her eyes to stare at the bald progress of the clock.

"Well they've given you a deal of pleasure." Gently, old Mr. Barber sucked his pipe and urged her towards a better view of things. "And they've had a good life, all of them."

He was a man who had dealt with and loved horses all his active life. *His* saying it, he who'd lived so sparsely, he whose body had abandoned him since his spine was crushed by a horse falling on him . . . *his* saying it made Olivia profoundly aware of her own privilege. And deeply ashamed of her self-pity.

"Yes," she sighed. "It's true. It's just . . . that everything seems to be dead . . . Or dying . . ." It was a tactless thing to say. As soon as she'd spoken, she realised her crassness. But the elderly couple didn't react as if they were thinking of themselves at all — their concentration rested solely with her. And as they nodded, musingly, she saw that their unpossessing life, the ordinariness of pain and sacrifice made loss less traumatic for them. They were so accustomed to it they'd become used to seeking out compensations. It was a habit of mind. And the most remarkable thing of all was that they understood the nature and degree of her loss without any corresponding sense of its deservedness or any hint of malicious jubilation. They realised how difficult it was for her and grieved for her. And she saw they were able to do this because they understood human feeling. They didn't imagine what it would be like to possess houses, cars, jewellery and furs, only how it would feel to lose something one loved. It was the love in her they recognised.

She thought of her books — of her heroines, risen from penury to silks and pearls. Dreams . . . she thought ironically . . . dreams.

There were many more calls to make. Many more cups of tea. However short they were, nobody would allow her to go without a drink or a biscuit or a small gift to take away. A sachet of lavender . . . a piece of cake wrapped in tissue paper.

There were cats to be let out, cabbages to be picked, a blocked gutter to be dealt with, a letter to be read out loud. Olivia began to ache with cold and damp.

"Is it true, your real name's Peggy Plumb?" asked Harry White, toasting his slippered feet much too close to the grate, "I knew a family, Plumb, once."

"Is it true, your youngest is terribly poorly?" enquired Elsie Cross who gathered a lot of information through her daughter-in-law, the post lady.

"Is it true, they're to plant conifers all over your land then?" asked Mary Blackford, sister of Colonel Doggart's housekeeper.

Olivia didn't drive straight home. She turned right-handed off the road before the turning to Clouds and went up the alternative lane to Sheep Cottages, the car bouncing and spinning over the track which now had two deep channels of water pouring down it. Although she was exhausted, she didn't want to go back to the empty house just yet. As she steered the car uphill, she half consciously prepared reasons for calling.

She would take Amy home rather than have her soaked a second time. She wanted to see whether Cygnet needed shoeing when the blacksmith next came. She wondered whether they'd like to borrow Mary Blackford's Light Sussex cockerel.

"I'm rather ashamed of myself," she remarked lightly, holding her hands over the welcoming stove. "I've let myself get out of touch with the village this summer. *Summer!*" she echoed grimly with a glance at the heavy, rushing sky outside.

"I bet they haven't lost touch with *you!*" Chloe was chopping an enormous pile of mint on a wooden board.

Olivia smiled. "No, that's true, they haven't. They're very well informed. But then," she added casually, "they've been seeing a lot of you."

"I'm not a *gossip* . . ."

"No." Olivia, noticing the state of Chloe's hands, turned her own automatically, seeking out fine grime and scratches. "No, I believe you. How on earth did Harry White know my maiden name though, I wonder?"

"Peggy?"

"Oh *don't!*" said Olivia quickly.

Chloe looked at her. She thought better of whatever she planned to say. "I should think everyone knows," she remarked with amusement.

"Oh Lord!"

"There's nothing so very terrible about it."

Olivia groaned quietly.

"It might have been Ermyntrude or Nellie or . . ."

"Don't." Olivia forced a brief laugh. "It's just not a name bestsellers were made from . . . Anyway," she straightened herself briskly, "I came to fetch Amy."

"She's gone home."

"Oh?"

"She wanted a bath and we haven't enough water for two baths. We share ours. She didn't want to."

Olivia reserved comment. She turned to warm her back against the stove.

"Chloe?"

"Yes?"

"What *am* I going to do about her?"

Chloe stopped chopping. She looked at her mother thoughtfully. Something quite new suddenly opened between the two women and both were aware of it.

"Look!" She wiped her hands on her jersey and went over to the shelf above the stove, reaching up for an envelope that protruded from behind a jug of bronze and yellow dahlias.

She opened it, took out the photographs and handed them to Olivia. "Bart gave us these this morning."

"Oh yes . . . For Amy." Olivia turned them towards the light.

"For you too. For all of us."

They weren't good photographs. They lacked any composition. The colours were false and harsh, but in the casual activity of the group together, in the sense of . . . *holiday*, almost, they presented together, Amy's drooping shape gave her a curious isolation from the rest. As though she'd been skilfully added to the original picture — and yet not quite skilfully enough since the bloom of her loneliness lent something akin to a tonal difference separating her from the others.

Mostly, they were group pictures, but there was one of the two sisters together, arms round one another's shoulders—Chloe squinting cheerfully into the sun and Amy, wearing a small, lowered smile. Her eyes looked huge and shadowed round the sockets. The temples were smoothly rounded like a baby's before its skull has receded under flesh and feature. Beneath her jumper it was possible to see the shadows of her crustacean collar bones.

"It's a shock isn't it?" Chloe spoke slowly after a long pause. "Looking at her like that. From the outside, even for me." She gazed again at the photos over her mother's shoulder, then went to fetch a two-gallon flagon of vinegar from the cupboard.

It was a little while before Olivia was able to reply. She felt shadows of Bangladesh and Biafra pass through her. Felt both angry and horrified that this was her child. Felt mortified by her failure to look as long and openly as this at her daughter in the daily way of things. When they passed one another in the house or paused to try and speak of something her gaze was fouled by the feelings of resentment and frustration Amy's presence caused.

"Nothing I do works." She bit her lip. "Only food's going to help her recover and I can't . . ." Powerlessness engulfed her.

How ironic it was, thought Chloe . . . how bitter. What had Bart said, ruefully looking at his own pictures? They're not so different, Amy and the newsreel children . . . In a sense, he'd said, their starving stems from much the same thing. She hadn't quite known what he meant then. Now she could guess.

"Don't worry about the eating," she said, spooning her mint into jars. "She can get by on very little . . . I give her bowls to clean out and things to peel and she'll always pick at something. Anyway, she steals quite a lot of things."

"*Steals?*"

"Oh yes. She's probably gone home to do just that . . . she'll get by."

"You mean she *does* eat secretly?"

"A little."

"Then *why?*" She felt an unwilling burst of anger.

"Didn't Bart try to explain?"

"Oh, Chloe, you know Bart . . . he talks in riddles."

"Well, it's complicated."

"I daresay, but . . ." Olivia gave up and sat down at the scrubbed table, abstractedly watching Chloe's movements. Upstairs someone began tuning a guitar. "Where is everyone?" she asked.

"Oh, about. Biff's asleep, that's why it's so quiet. Or *was.*" She levered an eyebrow in the direction of the guitar. "No one will disturb us, it's all right. Joe and Peter will be out till dark building a new hen house and Mab's up there doing the mending."

A silence elapsed. Chloe spoke first.

"Have you any idea how difficult it *is* having a successful mother?"

"Difficult? In what way? I've never forced ambitions on any of you."

"You expected us to do *well* . . ."

"For your own sakes."

Chloe smiled to herself. "And yours, too. You like achievement."

"I just like people to make the most of themselves."

"Within a fixed system of things . . . I mean, your idea of achievement is quite specific isn't it? You're disappointed in me because I didn't attempt to make a career out of anything recognisable."

"I *was,* I suppose." Olivia surprised herself. She picked up a stray leaf of mint and rubbed it between her fingers. "Yes. I thought you were wasting your education."

"And now?"

Olivia shrugged. She didn't know any more.

"Amy feels . . . well, it's hard to explain. She's obsessed with this sense of—well, of *destruction.* I can't think of another word. Distortion, perhaps."

Chloe poured vinegar into each of the jars, secured them and began shaking each in turn.

"I don't understand *that*. Anyway, I haven't even mentioned a career to her, I've learnt my lesson there. All I've done is to try to distract her, amuse her. I've suggested outings and things."

"Hunting?"

"Amongst other things."

"That's just another aspect of it to her."

"But . . ."

"Oh it's no good trying to understand her at any rational level—she's not behaving at a rational level. She's acting out a metaphor, if you like to put it that way. Can you see that? Try and grasp it at a symbolic level, it's a much surer way of understanding emotional behaviour—*all* behaviour for that matter."

(How did Chloe know these things?)

"Everything's based on emotion in the first place. Even," she laughed, "reason. Even moon flights."

It was no good. "Oh God, everything's so psychological these days. It's so exhausting, nothing being as it is. Why can't we just accept people as they are?"

A more melodic strumming began upstairs.

"People as they are just make signs, that's all."

Olivia thought about this briefly, aware of a rhythmic movement of Chloe's arm doing something. "It's less *trouble*," said Chloe, "taking the signs for the real sense, but it's wrong. It gives you the wrong view, I mean."

She sniffed the clean fragrance of mint on her fingers and tried to bring her daughter back to precise things she could discuss. "Well how am I supposed to see this thing she has about hunting for instance . . . it's not a *socialist* objection or anything like that is it?"

Chloe laughed ironically. "Not at the moment, I don't think. Not yet." She scraped the board clean with a knife. "She's too much of a country girl to see it like that yet, though if it suits her mood she might develop that sort of objection. It's just a way of being cross with you. No, it's . . ." And she stood up straight, squeezing her lips and eyes in an engagingly childish way as she tried to think it out. "It's *trapping*," she said finally, "and . . . overwhelming odds, and people assaulting the physical world, and oh . . ." She scratched her head. "All ritual and no meaning. And it's," she relaxed and gave a snort of laughter, "it's all tied up somehow—I'm sorry, I shouldn't laugh, but I don't understand it—with Granny dying. And you . . ."

"Chlo-ee."

"Oh all right, I know it sounds potty, I'm only trying."

Olivia got up and fetched herself a glass of water from the tap. The water was muddy looking.

Peter was hauling a sack of something out of the yard towards the orchard. Even in this grey weather the apples glowed on the trees like lamps.

"Well you *did* ask," said Chloe, behind her.

"Oh I know."

"She's resisting you in every way she knows."

"I know." Bravely and distastefully, she sipped. "Trying to attract attention."

"That's one way of putting it. A harsh way."

Olivia turned sharply but Chloe had her back to her. She'd begun sorting out a mixed bunch of rosemary and thyme and sage into separate piles. The silvery and purple tinted leaves were damply fragrant.

"I also think," Chloe hesitated, trying to unravel something that was vague to her, "that part of the distortion her body recognises—not Amy, not up here," she turned and tapped her head explainingly, "is a distortion of women—no, of the feminine thing . . . as though she wanted her body not to *be* female in a way."

"Oh?"

"Sort of . . . well non-woman. From what she says, not directly, I'm only guessing, she dislikes both the exaggeratedly female, you know, the parody woman all face lift and uplift *and* the aggressively . . . well, the other kind, the militant kind, the career kind. If that's women, she wants to be non-woman, except of course she's got it all the wrong way round, it's the other sort that's non-woman really."

"*Is* it?" Olivia sounded dry.

"Anyway, that's what's happening to her, flat-chested, childish, no periods or anything. A sort of nothing. The living dead."

"You amaze me, Chloe."

Tying her bunches with string, Chloe eyed her mother warily. "It's a fair reflection of the world she sees herself in. Isn't it?" She stood on a chair to hang the herbs from hooks in the ceiling. "The living dead?" She looked down. Then realising she was guilty of all kinds of evasions herself, abandoned these sidelong, analytic attempts and clambering down from the chair, went to her mother and embraced her fiercely, warmly—refusing to be held at bay by the steely pressures she met.

"Poor Mummy," she murmured, tucking a loose tendril of hair behind Olivia's ear.

"It's a muddle . . ." And she held her like a child, swaying her very gently in her arms. "Look," she said, "let me have her. She's welcome here."

And Olivia, trying to fight the tension that kept her obstinately stiff in Chloe's arms, wondered when she, last, had held any of her children like this.

15

"SHE'S A LITTLE BUSY AT THE MOMENT..." MADGE WARING hesitated, holding the phone to her ear with both hands.

"I shan't take more than two minutes. *Promise!*"

Biddy Hall's voice was persistingly gay.

"Well, I could try."

She sounded grudging. She was.

Olivia was getting ready for the opening meet, always an agitated morning. She wouldn't welcome any delay now. On the other hand (Madge silently weighed) the rise in her spirits had been so marked over the past couple of weeks... since Amy had gone to Sheep Cottages really... though the writing seemed to be coming easier and of course, as she mused to her sister, the shock of bereavement was bound to recede... "Well all right, if you don't mind waiting."

"Oh—*before* you go," something alarming was poised on the line. "Madge, tell me..."

"Yes?"

"Has she seen...?"

"The diary item...?"

"How did you know?"

"Oh..."

"Well, has she?"

"No."

She heard a release of breath down the line.

"She doesn't read any papers these days."

"Just as well, eh, Madge?"

Madge narrowed and lengthened at the confidential tone. "I take care," she said coldly.

"I'm sure you *do*," affirmed Biddy Hall. She'd been plagued by people herself, ringing up to query Olivia Bennett's real name. She gave a small, artificial laugh and Madge put the phone down.

At the bedroom door, she stopped and knocked.

"Yes?" A distraught sound.

The gold and white bedroom was scattered with clothes. Olivia sat at the dressing table trying to fasten her stock correctly.

"Every year!" she cried in temper. "Every year it's the same! Oh, Madge, not more letters, I'll never get this thing done properly. And I thought we'd managed everything beautifully!" She turned stiffly, her neck bandaged by the intractable white silk. Her hair was taken off her face and netted in a luxurious swag.

"It's Miss Hall . . . she's tried *several* times. Two minutes she says."

"Hm." Olivia looked at her watch. "Two minutes, Madge?" And she scrambled up, the elegance of her creamy breeches spoilt by an oddly socked pair of feet.

"It's all going well, Biddy. I've done bits here, bits there, in patches. As things came to me, rather. I've just got to join it up now."

She sounded exuberant. She smiled at Madge.

"I'm so glad, darling." Biddy still regarded the biography as an error. The way things were, it might not even be accepted. "Soon get cracking, then . . ."

"It's been extraordinary," Olivia wanted to explain the unlocking effect of Sheep Cottages. The change. The way she could go there without establishing a prior reason for going. Be silent, even.

But Biddy had promised to be brief and she cut in with news that the television producer was returning to this country and was still interested in a serial idea. "He's very pressing dear, what do you say?" (He had at first been touched, then frankly disbelieving about the period of mourning being observed.)

"The end of the month?" It was early November. Olivia calculated out loud . . .

"Fifteen thousand words, say . . . three weeks . . . oh, easily Biddy. All right dear, fix a day and I'll bring my manuscript at the same time!"

"Wonderful!" Biddy sounded dazed. Olivia was clearly over the worst.

The American money would be useful to all of them.

"Perfect morning!" Olivia called out to Barber as she passed him digging out the great pond he and Leo had been working on together. It was Joe's idea . . . trout farming, he'd suggested. She slowed Badger down.

"A good scenting morning after all," he agreed, nose to the wind. "You'll have a good day out. The horse looks well."

Earlier, the mist had lain in pearly wreaths over the countryside making a ruined Gothic landscape out of plain sheds and broken walls. Now it was mild and clear without being sunny. After all the weeks of wet weather the ground had drained fairly well but still had plenty of give in it. They chatted for a few minutes.

"The only pity of it is seeing you go out alone," said Barber resting on his spade. And they silently hovered over the unspoken things, Amy, the labour, the expense.

She hacked on, taking the short cut over the hill passing near to Sheep Cottages and down to the road which wound north and led, some two miles further on, to the village of King's Huish and thence to Peter Doggart's home where hounds were due to meet at eleven.

Glancing again at her watch, showing a little excitement, Olivia lengthened Badger's stride though he needed no urging. He knew exactly what was happening. There were so many greetings, so many people out on foot and bicycles.

Wild clematis foamed on the thinning uncut hedges beside the road. Only papery, rust hazel leaves, blackberry and the small startling yellow motifs of young sycamore leaves were now left. She had never seen the hawthorn berries so dark, purple almost, a far more imperial shade than the translucently crimson hips. The horse began, knowingly, to press into trot that needed checking. He could tell. From the trim, bleached quality of the countryside, its hedges now cut back in neat brown invitation, from the scents preserved in the mild damp air, he guessed.

As soon as the sound of hoofbeats disappeared over the brow of the hill, Barber rammed his spade into the thick clay and went into the house where he rang the Ploughman's Arms and told Leo, who had stayed there overnight, that the coast was clear.

Fifteen minutes later a ramshackle horsebox appeared up the drive. From the other direction Andrew and Bill Adams came walking down the track. The horsebox swung low and wide through the yard and pulled round to the far side of the buildings some twenty yards from the pit where Barber stood. As he waved it closer, he was joined by Andrew and Bill.

"We saw her go," said Andrew. The others were silent. They waited for Leo to clamber down from the driving cab. He came towards them, his features impassive.

"All in, are they?"

"Yes, I brought them in. In case the hunt came this way, I told her, though John Crozier tells me they'll draw well north of here. Up Sawley Hill, he said, since the Vale's too wet still." Barber didn't meet Leo's gaze.

"Yes, I checked it last night." Leo kicked at the earth with his boot. "Thank you for coming. All of you," he muttered.

They continued to stand in silence awhile. A flight of plovers rose off the plough a field away, flapping south.

"Shall we . . ." Andrew began, feeling a lethargy of reluctance settle.

Leo straightened sharply, taking his hands from his pockets. "Damn them. I swore I wouldn't do a thing until those bloody conifers arrived." He made a small, exasperated exclamation. "It's going to be too late to plant the bloody things if they don't get a move on." (They'd been expected for the past month.) "Promised me faithfully, yesterday. Eleven sharp this morning, they said." He looked despairingly down the drive.

"It's not eleven yet," observed Andrew.

"God knows . . ." Leo ran a hand through his thick hair, leaving one strand curving upwards, unknown to him. "I spend a week refusing to have the bloody things, two weeks telling them what farcically stupid things they are to put on good pasture land. Oh, it's all worked out area by area they tell you, and then, when I give in at last, another four weeks it takes them to pull their finger out." Again he turned to look down the drive. "They'll miss the planting period altogether, I'm telling you . . ." He broke off thinking he heard a faint engine noise, but whatever it was, it passed by Clouds.

He visibly pulled himself clear of his irritation. He needed to keep very calm. Methodical.

"It's them advisers," reflected Bill, removing his pipe from his mouth. "As long as they'm advising something, t'int no consequence what."

They looked so beautiful. The people, the horses.

Everything shining. Everything immaculate. Even the old black coats, the same one that was worn by the owner's grandparent as often as not, a little greenish looking, but brushed, carefully taken from a mothproof cupboard. A few pink coats, with buff lapels and brass buttons. Boots gleamed. And the horses, blooming with hard work and health, seized impatiently at their bits, stamping oiled hooves.

Hounds streamed between everyone's legs and everyone moved out of their way. They were the most respectfully regarded of all the creatures present, including the human creatures. Not yet as lean as they would be later in the season, there was little spare flesh to be seen on their brindled, hard-muscled bodies.

It was a small field. Not more than twenty, Olivia calculated on a rough count. It was a weekday of course, but normally, that wouldn't have kept people way. It was chiefly the farmers who were out, since they were the only ones who had the corn to feed their horses. Still, she reflected, her heart rising, despite the decimation of the field, whatever it lacked in mounted followers, was made up for by the men, women and children who came on foot, no matter what the weather or circumstances. They came with their wisdoms and enthusiasm; a keen eye and a knowledge of the country to be covered. There was no deflecting them.

"Morning!"

"Morning! And a fine one too!"

The horses jostled, rump to dangerous rump, hocks quivering under them ready to spring or kick with anticipatory excitement. The farmers rode big coarser shaped animals — the kind of beast that would give them hours of dogged rather than speedy pursuit and might be put away in a field shortly after coming home at the end of the day without ill-effect. Blood horses, veins finely raised, eyes and nostrils alertly open, were hardly to be seen.

"*Olivia!*"

"Good morning."

She greeted her friends one by one, knowing that each of them was sick with shared terror under their affable outward demeanour.

"Once over the first fence . . ." winked Derek Brock, an enormous man with purple jowls, mounted on an animal resembling a medieval war horse.

Once over the first fence, the fear would begin to ebb.

She smiled and accepted a glass of punch from Colonel

Doggart. "Good to see you!" he bawled, sweeping off his silk hat. (Hunting people, Olivia had long ago noted, shouted at the tops of their voices simply because they were used to half a field separating them.) "I say you do wear well. As pretty as ever on a horse!"

He beamed without apparent malice, though 'pretty' was not the word a true horseman would ever have used to describe Olivia in the saddle. She had come to hunting too late ever to be a fluid, component part of her horse. And, Peter Doggart privately thought, had come to it for all the wrong reasons. But she had courage, and for that she'd won back his grudging respect.

His initial pronouncement, when Leo Mathison had brought his young bride hunting for the first time, was "Doubtful origins", though he had not, by that been referring to whatever social class he saw stamped on her—simply, that he could detect nothing in her background that would enable her to understand the sport existed in its own right and not as a showplace for those who thought it a fine thing to be seen there. That it was something done out of love, not vanity. For that kind, he had a personal and abominable rudeness, a slow but systematic terrorist approach in the field. Those who survived it—his habit of taking a jump under their noses, or crushing one of their legs against a gatepost as they bunched through an opening—won his loyal admiration.

He patted Olivia's thigh approvingly. "Guts," he murmured, "you've got guts." And that made up for her awkward bobbing seat and helplessly raised hands, now so familiar a part of his winter scene. "Me," he said, "I'm losing my nerve. Hope you're not. I'll just tuck myself in at the back and enjoy the view." And he passed on, carrying the drinks himself since his housekeeper was terrified of horses. As a child, she'd had one pick her up in its teeth and drop her in a gorse bush.

Impatiently the horses began to whinny at one another, pawing the ground. In the confusion, Olivia slopped her drink and dropped her gloves.

"Hell," she murmured and dismounted to retrieve them.

"Good God!" A ginger-powdered face appeared above her for a moment. It was Helen Bawden, or Helen Watson, depending on which of her last husbands you remembered best. "You're not getting off your horse for that are you? Never get off my horse for anything," she said and swept on.

Bart, who'd drawn alongside, laughed with Olivia. He looked splendid in his silk hat. They gossiped about the only two people in the field who considered themselves (and behaved accordingly) to be aristocratic ... Twin brothers in their forties with oddly feeble, sneering faces who whispered conspiratorially together until a covert was being drawn and then told everybody else to keep their voices down.

They were tolerated only in the confident belief that one or other of them would fall off. Their record was unchallenged.

"Here he comes!" smiled Bart as Gerald Causely arrived looking hurriedly dressed on a fighting grey cob, followed down the road at a canter by his son, equally uncontrollably mounted.

"That's all we've been waiting for," they cried. The late appearance of the Causelys was always the signal to move off.

Hounds were called together. A whip cracked, and the small field, jamming itself behind the pack, stirrups clinking one against the other, moved off down the lane. With some difficulty, they crammed through the muddy opening of a gateway and bounding, bucking their way across the field, made towards the first draw.

"There's nothing gained by waiting," observed Barber, noting a smear of sun beginning to rise as high in the sky as it was able at this time of year.

"But if they don't come?"

"They'll come sooner or later," he said, "and insist you plant them in December as like as not."

"Whether or not," said Leo, trying to weigh the situation up for the thousandth time, "we can't feed the horses ..."

"Best over and done with and no time wasted." Bill Adams knocked his pipe out against his boot, and slipping it back in his breast pocket, straightened himself up for the task.

Andrew felt his bowel dissolve. He began, heartily, to wish he'd stayed behind with the others. Quite apart from anything else, what Leo was planning was illegal. (He couldn't really understand why they hadn't sent the lot of them to the slaughterer's for meat. There *was* talk now of people eating horse-meat. If the French could, why not?)

"You think the pit's big enough?"

"Oh aye."

Leo walked over to the cab and took out the Greener that he'd managed to get hold of. The vet, who was an old friend, had said it was the thing to use if he was seriously planning to do the job himself. He'd looked both doubtful and horrified. "As far as I'm concerned," he'd said firmly, "I know nothing about this business. All right?"

"We'll have to bring each mare and foal out together if they're not to fight and squeal like old Harry," observed Barber. "How much noise does that thing make?"

"It's not quiet." Leo turned the cylinder over in his hands.

"Keep the engine running with the choke out."

"Wasteful."

"They can tell," said Bill. "Never mind the noise, they know."

"I'm just going to call the regional office," said Leo. "Check that the trees are on their way." He kept thinking of Olivia. He could only face telling her if the trees were here.

Barber knew what he was thinking. "We could plough the fields up in strips in readiness," he said. "That would settle it for her."

"I don't know how they want it done . . . Whether they've even finally made their mind up to leave the old trees standing," countered Leo helplessly, then, eagerly almost, "perhaps they can tell me that over the phone."

"Maybe," said Barber. "Ask them."

And Leo disappeared to make a phone call and find a drink.

Hounds found almost right away.

After only five or ten minutes crackling and snapping through the trees they gave voice. The pink of the huntsmen could be seen travelling through spectral green trunks as hounds broke on the far side of the woods and "Gone away!" sounded, as plaintive and eager as the hounds' own tongue.

For a moment, the world lay spread open in its stripped winter beauty as they galloped from the top of Sawley Hill. For a second she saw how this early autumn had given a rare chestnut tint to the woods and ploughland, a colouring that stemmed from the darkly burnt, remaining leaves of oak and elm; a richness that must have come from prolonged wet. Even the air over the paler stubble and drained grasses was pinkened by it. She saw, like a sudden dream, a weasel leaping. And then the speed of the chase brought tears to her eyes and all she could glimpse while she tried to secure her balance as Badger's head sloped away at a steep angle beneath her, was the blur of pumping quarters, the flash of metal hooves and, further down into the valley, the fierce rain of mud divots thrown up by the horses in front.

Hedges loomed up with terrible rapidity; all, on the hillside, with a sickening drop. Out of the corner of her eye, she saw the first of the twins slither up his horse's neck, then over its ears and off, his outstretched hand still grasping the bridle while his horse, free, raced onward.

There was little time to check or balance, or even for the moment care much in which direction they were going. Badger had taken a fierce hold and leapt without any of his customary swerving to left or right wherever the hedge had been smashed a little lower. He rose and flew and she stayed with him.

Soon though, they began to climb again and it was possible to ease up a little, see hounds streaming ahead, up to the furze covered ridge of the next hill.

Until now, she hadn't seen the fox at all. Suddenly, there he was, leanly silhouetted on the ridge, standing still to gaze contemptuously at the pounding field as it tried to close the gap between them. Something in the slow indifference of his turning, in his liquid disappearance over the brow of the hill, made her smile.

"See that?" Bart drew alongside her, his head searchingly raised. "He's upwind of us. I know that dog fox," he claimed. "He's got our measure. Got mine anyway, I'm done in already! How're you managing?"

She was too breathless to speak until they reached the top of the hill and there, she saw, a good half mile away, the pack had checked, breaking up uncertainly. They were close to farm buildings where the scent too easily became confused with others and they puzzled furiously trying to regain their line.

"I do believe he's run along the top of the wall!" exclaimed Gerald, as they caught up with him.

"We can take it easy down here." Bart loosened his reins. "He's probably swung right-handed round the farm."

Below them, somebody on a tractor was shouting and pointing, his voice lost to them.

"Amy wouldn't come then?"

"No. But oh, she's so much better, Bart, you'd never believe . . . though I think she *could* go back to school after half term." She stopped speaking and sat tight, as Badger slithered down the roughly ridged slope.

"It's Chloe's doing really."

"Yes. Oh look! I think they've regained the line!"

An old hound gave cry and began to run, head down, the rest following raggedly at first.

"I should wait a second," Bart warned. He watched carefully, though the rest of the field, more scattered now, were beginning to build up speed on the treacherous slope. Two, more confident than the rest, cut right-handed over a low hedge and ditch thinking they could place themselves at the head of the chase. Fearful they might cut right across the scent, the master glared at them.

"It's the Cogleys, mother and son, of course," smiled Bart. "They never learn—they think it's all a waste of time unless they've got through the day at fifty miles an hour." (The man on the tractor was yelling at them.) "What's he saying? Can you hear?"

They both strained an ear. Dimly, they heard: "*I'll sue you for every fucking hoofmark you make!*"

"Such a *bloodthirsty* couple!" chuckled Bart.

They pushed their horses on a little as the pack settled down to a more determined pursuit in the direction of Piggott's Copse.

"That's what Amy thinks I am."

"What? Bloodthirsty?"

"I think so."

(Bart had been right. Hounds checked again, sterns working frenziedly.)

"Oh," he said, "I can't really think of it like that. That's the..." And he shrugged, watching the pack trying to come to a decision.

He asked her if she'd ever been to Lascaux or Altemira.

"I took mother once, to the Dordogne, but of course, being the French they'd closed the main caves. We saw some. Hey! Look at Derek!"

Without any warning, the massive torso of Derek Brock, as if propelled by a mighty compass needle, swung off his horse and landed, face downwards into a mire of cow slurry near the farm gate. His horse, its saddle off since the girth had burst, poked at him concernedly with its muzzle.

Hoots of laughter rose as Derek, wavering and squelching on short, thick legs, gasped through his blackened face for air. Helen Bawden (Watson) with great presence of mind struggled towards him and without dismounting, thrust a brandy flask into the only visible pink aperture of his face.

A surge of hilarity weakened the field's attention while the whipper-in galloped away to head off a group of hounds pursuing a right-handed course. Derek, unhurt, led his horse to the farm, sinking to his knees at every step.

"The caves," resumed Bart, pulling himself weakly together again, "*that's* how I see it. The paintings. With the men always exaggeratedly smaller than the animals they're hunting."

"I'd never really noticed that."

"*They* knew whom the odds—the gods—favoured," he declared, "now, look what that old fox has done . . . Got on to another fox's line and branched sharply off. I thought we had a cunning one." He urged his horse into a canter. "Come on, he must be swinging home the other way. We'll be lucky to reach him before he crosses the main road."

Olivia's course was closely watched by more than one pair of eyes. "Amy! Get on Cygnet as fast as you can and tell them they're coming this way."

There was a moment of hesitation, then Amy put the bowl of eggs she was carrying down on the wall and flew on long, uncoordinated legs towards the paddock, calling as she went.

Through withering gaps in the hedge she could see the horsebox parked below. It was impossible, especially riding bareback, to go too fast down the stony track, but gripping desperately, clinging to the pony's mane, she pushed on.

Between the lean twigs of elder she glimpsed Barber leading Rosie and her foal through a gap in the outbuildings.

From the bowl of sky at her back, she heard the faint music of hounds rise.

"Daddy! *Daddy!*" she screamed, her voice cracking. But she was too far away to be heard.

"We'll be over your land soon if we're not careful!" shouted Peter Doggart pounding beside Olivia, "I hope to God there are no cattle out . . . Can't say I expected to be going this way today!" And his voice was lost as his horse, leaning hard upon the bit, carried him away from her.

The fox, younger than the one who'd so shamelessly used him to make his own escape, slipped through the stream that ran along the valley overlooked by Sheep Cottages. He was weary, but not yet outwitted.

He was a long way from home, but knew, from previous visits to vixen in this territory last winter, of places where he could safely hole up awhile.

Leo almost wept with frustration.

As if she sensed both distress and betrayal in the air, Rosie, normally so kind, so willing to please, ran back from the ramp of the box dragging Barber with her. Her eye showed white. She whinnied to her foal to flee.

"Get behind her!" Bill Adams took charge. He crouched behind the mare, arms outstretched. He whooped at her and signalled Andrew to do the same.

Rosie swung round, head up and whinnied again.

This time she called to Cygnet whose hooves clattered and skidded through the yard.

Blowing and sweating, the horses were reined in around the birch copse that bordered one side of the lane above Clouds.

Olivia could see Mince barking in the walled garden behind the house but the orgiastic howl of hounds drowned his small domestic effort. Under the force of their search, the slender trees crashed and bent, a few remaining flakes of leaf spinning through the milky sunshine.

Somewhere, amid the badger sets that tunelled deep into this hillside, somewhere, concealed behind mossy roots and softening layers of leaf mould, the fox had slipped knowing his territory, even this rarely visited part, better than any of his pursuers. He also knew their limitations.

And *they* knew he'd got the better of them.

Hounds shrieked, leaping over one another in their desperate attempts to burrow into the opening of a tunnel far too small for them.

The huntsman called them off. No point in hanging about. The fox had taken them well beyond the country they'd stopped up in readiness. Chases like this were surrendered respectfully to the fox. His gift for survival was more cleanly developed, more enduring than their own. And they honoured him for it.

As the sound of the hunt died away, Leo emerged from the feed store where he had hidden, clutching the Greener. He felt absurd and frightened.

When Amy had come with her warning, he had just tried to run. Then, with a miserable attempt to appear cool-headed, had scurried back to take Rosie's head, although Barber was already handling her perfectly competently, crooning and gentling her till she came with him.

It had been Andrew who'd leapt into the horsebox, reversing it and driving it away out of sight.

As usual, he told himself with bitter self-criticism, he'd managed under the cover of activity, to do nothing. Quite suddenly, he was angry with Olivia. Angry that she should have expected him to do this. Why him? What perverse reasoning lay behind that idea? Why, in God's name couldn't the vet do it—impersonally, clinically, at a decent distance from here, with no evidence but a bill to worry about? The vet must think him a perfect fool. And Barber, Adams, Andrew, even . . . none of them had questioned his taking on this ridiculous role of slaughterer, but what had they *thought*? Worse, what did they make of his failure to carry out the role?

He heard the approaching sound of an engine. With much grinding of gears, the horsebox reappeared in the yard. Andrew and Bill drove past him towards the pit. Barber, pushing open the stable door, re-emerged leading Rosie whose coat was dark with sweat.

He looked at them uncertainly. They expected him to carry on. Do what had to be done.

"All right then?" he called out with forced briskness.

"They'll not be back," said Barber, soothing the mare.

Leo began to follow them. Then he saw Amy standing by the pit, looking at him. He tried to read her expression but her face was white, wiped of meaning. He looked at her again, searchingly, as he came closer, hoping for a sign, an encouragement of some kind. Her lips moved.

"Reality," she seemed to be saying. Face reality.

He took it as he understood it. "I think," he said gravely, as if he'd given the matter long and careful consideration. "I think this had all best be put into the proper professional hands."

In the fading light of late afternoon the mares put their heads out over the doors of their boxes and whinnied as Olivia jogged back into the yard. She was tired and happy. Every joint, every muscle ached. Stiffly, she climbed down.

"Good day out, was it?" Barber came through the dusk.

"Wonderful, truly. Did you see us?" And she told him about the unexpected run.

"I'll clean the old fellow down before I go home," he said.

"You should have been home long ago, no, I'll do it. I'll take the mud off later, when it's dry. Don't you worry."

Weary as she was, she would enjoy seeing her horse made comfortable.

Two hours later, after Badger had been cleaned, dried, rugged and bedded down, she went indoors to run a bath for herself. Lovely. She filled the bath with fresh smelling, stinging green salts and dipped a relishing hand in the rising depth of water.

Just as she lowered herself gingerly into the steaming water, the lights went off.

Restraining an involuntary scream, she scrambled out quickly, feeling for a towel in which to wrap herself. There was something very alarming about being naked in a scalding bath in pitch darkness, though it occurred to her that the alarm was foolish since she was no more likely to drown in the dark than she was with the light on.

Nothing was quite where she instinctively felt it should be, not even the light switch. Stupidly she felt for a light switch when she knew perfectly well the light was operated by a cord.

When she found and pulled at the cord, nothing happened. One hand flapped like a stricken butterfly round the door frame, the other gripping the towel, until she discovered the handle. As she tore open the door, blackness fell in on her, huge and empty.

She crossed the bedroom floor, aware that her feet must be making large, sodden imprints on the carpet, but she didn't care.

Clothes. She tried to find clothes, as if they were a form of protection, scrabbling over the bed, under it, along the floor. A dressing gown, a pair of slippers, a pair of pants. Not until she had them did she release the vice on her imagination and let herself wonder what was going on. Not daring to call out for the dog in case her voice betrayed her whereabouts, to some other *thing*, she cautiously crept towards the door.

Of course. It dawned on her.

A power cut, the first of the cuts. She hadn't listened to the warnings.

She cursed herself for not taking the obvious precautions. But neither had Leo, she thought pettily. (Though what she really wanted, was that *he*, rather than a stock of candles and a ready-laid fire should be there.)

Braver now, she opened the bedroom door and called the dog who silently at last appeared, black on black, surprising her with a wet nose on her knee. With him beside her to give her confidence, she felt her way downstairs to the kitchen and there found first matches and then candles. Things improved. Small comforting flares of light, restored serenity revealing things where they had always been.

Clutching a saucer with a lighted candle insecurely stuck to it, she carefully made her way back to the bath and stepped in it a second time, relaxing pleasantly in the now less ferocious temperature. No sooner had she leaned back, than she heard a thunderous knocking at the front door.

Old instinct, dictating that her movement should go undetected, made her blow out the candle without thinking first. When darkness closed down and made her conscious of her own action and its motive, she paused a second, clasping the handle, staring into the unfeatured interior of her house and thought, how quickly we become animals again. How quickly our instincts rush in to the rescue when our minds can't explain . . . And the thought was gone, as swift as a fish-shadow, though her heart beat small and fast.

Two steps. Three. Slippered toes feeling the way like fingers. As she put her saucer down on the landing and felt with both hands for the bannisters, another sensation slipped into the place vacated by the last. A dull knowledge of fear. Not simply that she was afraid. But that she was *always* afraid. That this aloneness she felt now in the great cup of darkness—even the darkness itself—was a constant presence in her that had, by some weird mechanism, been pulled out of the invisible regions of the psyche and been transformed into a real environment. She was native here.

She *knew* the darkness, the aloneness, the apprehension, intimately. It was her natural estate. She had stepped into her own dreams. In waking life this territory was concealed from her by a dense, unnatural cultivation of her own making.

At the head of the stairs, she stopped, then carefully stepped down, each foot descending into space. It never occurred to her not to go down and down again. She had to confront the darkness. The knocking was repeated.

Then, thankfully, she glimpsed a moving beam of light under the doorway. Whoever it was, had a torch and she was drawn more confidently towards it, her step increasing to a stumbling speed.

It was Joe and Peter.

"We thought you might be lonely."

"Or frightened, perhaps . . . we heard the warning on the radio."

She stared at them. Then realised her face, which must be grotesquely lit by the torch, was washed clean of make-up. She stepped back a little into the darkness.

"We came to fetch you for some supper."

"There's a warm fire . . ."

"And plenty of light."

"Yes," she said slowly, "there must be . . ." She looked out from her shadow at them.

"Hang on a second," she begged, "I'll just get changed."

There was a smell of potatoes baking in their jackets.

Once in the softly illumined warmth of the kitchen, she relaxed though a trace of shock, like a faint bruising, lingered at the edge of her relief.

The table was being cleared of an enormous jigsaw puzzle and cooking implements to make room for the supper things. A jug, full of copper beech leaves which Sarah had soaked in glycerine, was left standing in the centre of the table.

"You *haven't* eaten?"

"No, I . . . I don't even know what time it is." She'd taken off her watch to have her bath and not replaced it on her wrist.

"Five to eight," said Joe, looking at his.

"So early? Goodness." She felt as though she'd travelled along a vast curve of time. Or non-time.

Chloe called out to Mab and Andy to come downstairs. Sarah finished washing Biff in the sink and, wrapping him in a towel, gave him to Olivia to hold while she fetched his pyjamas from the stove. He felt very solid and warm.

Seeing her expression, Joe leaned over and took his son from her, finishing off the drying with a tickling session that made Biff bubble with mirth.

Amy sat in the old armchair that was propped up in a corner of the wall with a pile of books under one of its legs, looking furtively at her mother. One eyebrow, she noted had been pencilled in a more astonished arc than the other. Lipstick ran carelessly over her upper lip.

"Can I do anything?" Olivia appealed to Chloe.

"Here you are. Divide this into eight if you can." And she set a hot egg and onion pie down in front of her. It was a good bright yellow and smelled faintly of nutmeg. "Come on everyone, find a chair."

There was a general joggling and scraping while Chloe yelled for the others again, then lowered her voice to gabble a grace. "For what we are about to receive make us . . . Oh, get that cat off the table. . . !" she beseeched.

"What are those two doing?" enquired Olivia, meeting a series of amused or evasive expressions.

"They'll be down soon," said Chloe, putting the potatoes on the table.

Amy came and seated herself at the far end of the table from her mother. Olivia, cutting, hesitated then excised a thinner triangle for her younger daughter, trying not to make the movement obvious.

One hundred and fifty calories, thought Amy automatically, without revolt. It would be all right. It was allowed. She refused a potato, but accepted a glass of milk.

"Did you enjoy yourself today?" she asked in her slow, exhausted voice.

Olivia went on cutting, unable to realise that Amy was addressing her. It was the silence that awoke her. "Oh!" she cried, trying to coat the surprise in her tone, "Darling . . . yes, yes *thank you*."

"Did you kill anything?" The voice sounded as though it had to negotiate each word like a flat stepping stone to the end of the sentence. Chloe sat down, a dangerous eye on her sister.

"No, not a thing. Not one."

"Oh."

It took Amy time to consider this. Tardy impressions of the day filtered through her mind. One fierce part of her had wanted the horses shot. No, had wanted her mother to be there, as witness. Wanted her to see the real shape of things. She picked up the green stained fork and pushed it vaguely towards her food. "Good," she murmured.

The moment was over. It slipped beneath the other babble. Under the table Biff played with his kitten, clumsily tender.

Half-attentively, Olivia listened, her mind more occupied by Amy's attempt to reach out. They were talking about the magazine and their hopes of getting an issue out before Christmas.

"I'll have those woodcuts for the cover finished before the meeting tomorrow," promised Sarah. "At least I will if someone'll amuse Biff for the afternoon?" and she made a face at Chloe who gestured agreement.

"I'm hopeless with babies or I'd . . ." Olivia began.

They looked at her smilingly, acknowledging what they took to be an offer, and passed easily on to questions of type size and lay-out. Joe was saying he expected at least three of the others would get to the meeting, with luck.

From overhead came a profane and smothered sound.

Involuntarily, Olivia looked up. Sarah laughed. "Their supper's getting cold," she remarked.

Burning. Through the copper beech leaves, Olivia looked uneasily at her younger daughter but Amy seemed indifferent to or unaware of what was going on. (Her own face was pierced by small needles of heat. She tried hard not to imagine anything.)

"I've never read anything of yours," Joe was saying, "I'd like to."

The fire still at her neck, she looked at him suspiciously. "I'm a writer of *quantity*," she said a little roughly.

"Not quality?"

"Quantity," she reasserted defensively.

"All the same," he persisted, "*truly* . . ."

She attempted a flattered smile conveying only disbelief.

"I *mean* it!" He was beginning to laugh now at her refusal to yield.

"I tell you," she repeated firmly, "quantity."

"Well, one thing . . ." he pursued a scrap with his fork, "the conifers'll come in handy. Pulp."

Chloe kicked him. "Sorry," he said.

Olivia looked as though she'd been stabbed but recovered quickly. "Absolutely," she said, "I can hardly quarrel with that." And she began to take all the plates that were emptied.

She felt no real animosity towards Joe. He may have been teasing her, maybe not. He was kind. Anyway . . . she thought, scraping leavings into the hen bucket, what does it matter?

But it did matter, that was the stupid thing. She carried a pile of clean plates to the table and realised that she'd come to care what they thought of her. It was a measure of the way her regard for them had changed. Looking round at the young faces, she felt a fondness for them all.

She sat down in their circle, sharing something of their warmth in that she drew on it — though she lacked as yet, the gift of adding to it.

"Let's have a bonfire after the meeting tomorrow," Sarah was saying. "It *is* bonfire night."

"Perhaps somebody *will* blow up the Houses of Parliament," observed Peter.

"Biff would love it."

"Perhaps," said Olivia, struggling, "perhaps, when it's finished, you'd like to read the thing I'm doing now?" And she looked straight at Joe for a second. "I should value your criticisms," she added awkwardly. "I know Chloe thinks highly of your judgement."

Again, she found herself blushing. Then one cause of discomfort seeped into another as Andrew and Mab entered the kitchen looking as rosy and replete as infants. Gratefully, she let the table's attention go from her to them.

Only Chloe, the most luminous of the company, noted the colour of her mother's cheek and understood the nature of the surrenders made that evening.

Part Three

You must yourself believe that good ultimately triumphs over evil, that happiness comes when we try to make others happy, and that Love, or 'sweet charity' as someone has described it, is the greatest power in the world.

Writing the Romantic Novel by Claire Ritchie

When I was a child, I spake as a child, I understood as a child, I thought as a child; but when I became a man, I put away childish things. For now we see through a glass darkly; but then face to face; now I know in part; but then I shall know even as also I am known. And now abideth faith, hope, charity, these three; but the greatest of these is charity.

I CORINTHIANS, 13

16

THE POWER RESTRICTIONS AT LEAST, WERE ORGANISED efficiently, Olivia thought ironically when the lights went off at precisely seven o'clock the following evening.

She too, was efficiently organised. Matches and candles were distributed throughout the house, a log fire burnt cheerfully in the little sitting room and Mrs. Baldwin had managed to get the old Aga going in the kitchen on wood alone. So she even had hot water.

Blowing out a taper, she gazed round the sitting room well pleased with the changes in depth and texture candlelight created. The yellow, white and russet tones, if not the exact shapes, of the shaggy-headed chrysanthemums glowing in their copper bowl, were shadowed in the brown, floral printed paper of this room. The brown, a handsome chocolate colour, was the same as the brown of the velvet upholstery and the curtains which she now went to draw more closely against the sharp night outside.

The whole family retreated to the little sitting room in winter. It was their lair, earth-coloured and snug. She felt a small shudder of pleasure at the comfortable embrace of it all.

Mince gave a single bark and went to the door, wagging his tail. The white cat, stretched out on the armchair looked at him through reproachful slits, and made a waspish movement with his tail. He did not wish to be disturbed.

Olivia crossed the hall. She hadn't expected them to invite her up to Sheep Cottages this evening and now that her home was cosily prepared, wasn't sure she really wanted to go.

She didn't immediately recognise the young man.

"Oh hello," she said. "You must be . . ."

"Arthur," he said.

"*Arthur!*" she echoed. "Of course . . . you must be looking for the meeting."

"Meeting?" He sounded puzzled. Apart from a pair of gold-rimmed spectacles, there was little to see of him, as his navy duffel coat and a navy woollen hat were pulled as close round his face against the cold as possible.

He was, she recalled, the young man she'd seen using the phone in the hall some time this summer.

"Come inside a moment," she urged. "All the freezing air's coming in."

"What meeting?" he repeated, following her.

"At the cottages. The magazine, isn't it?"

"Oh," he said. "Oh, you had me muddled for a moment." He laughed relievedly, and unbuttoned the top toggle of his coat. "No." And he bent to pat the dog rather boisterously. "No, I came to see you, if that's all right, if that is, you know . . ." He cleared his throat suddenly and fell silent, looking at her.

She turned, as if to lead him through to the little sitting room, her mind making churning efforts to place him more exactly, since he seemed to think she must know him. "Of course, Arthur," she cried gladly, "how can I be of help? Come in and sit by the fire."

They went into the more brightly lit room.

"Well now," she said pleasantly, offering him a chair and standing back to look at him. He put his unlighted torch back in his pocket and finished unbuttoning his coat before he sat down. Olivia felt mildly resentful that he showed signs of staying though she took his coat courteously enough.

"You don't remember me, do you?" He pulled off his woolly hat and she recognised the prematurely balding head, the thin, pale curls. He had a pink face, very fair brows and lashes; a face too immaturely formed for the balding scalp somehow. He could be any age between twenty and forty, she thought. "I've seen you before, of course . . ."

"In the hall? On the phone?" he asked anxiously.

"Yes."

He rubbed his hands fiercely together as feeling clearly came back into them and gave a short, breathless laugh. Then he lifted his clasped hands and blew on them. "That was a dare," he bubbled, "doing that."

She began to feel puzzled. She was sure she had seen him only that once, though it was difficult to be absolutely certain, so many people had come and gone through the summer months.

"A dare?" she repeated. She remained standing, a hand resting on the mantelshelf. The fire scorched one side of her body pleasantly.

"Oh, it's silly really . . ." He picked at the laces of very worn suede boots, "I wanted to speak to you then, but I, well, I was a bit overcome really. So I pretended to be on the phone." He gestured and pulled a face without looking up.

"I'm not sure I understand . . ." She began to wonder whether he had nothing to do with Sheep Cottages at all. The possibility made her uneasy. "Are you," she tried, "*collecting* for something?"

He laughed hard, his oddly babyish face squeezing up behind his glasses.

The light voice, the gestures of his hands . . . they didn't identify him specifically for her, but she had a feeling he was queer . . . In an odd sense, this made her feel more comfortable.

"*Well*. . . !" he gasped, a little girlishly. "That's a funny one!" He detected irritation in her as she moved her position by the fire and his face grew more serious. "You must think I'm awful," he said, "awfully rude. Not explaining anything, just inviting myself like this. But I thought you might remember me. Are you sure you don't?" And he leant forward, pushing his face anxiously into the circle of firelight for inspection.

"Not at all, it's I who am being rude. I must be honest, I'm afraid I *don't* . . ."

"Guess."

"I'm awfully sorry, I . . ."

"Oh go on!"

"No, really, I'm so bad at . . ."

"August the fourteenth?"

"I'm sorry?"

"Nineteen forty-three?" His head waggled expectantly.

She stared at him. She felt the blood empty from her face. Her forehead turned ice cold though her body burnt.

"You *do* know!" he cried, triumphant. And then passed a hand over his face as though overwhelmed.

Olivia's mouth was dry and rough like an old flannel.

He was giggling nervously again. "I wanted to see you," he repeated, a fist stuffed to his mouth. "You're so *famous* . . ." He uttered the word incredulously and stared as if to convince himself she was true. "I didn't expect you to *really* be famous."

Her heart, expanded to twice its size, beat in a slow, lumpy rhythm.

"Would you mind," she began, but her voice sounded parched and broken. She tried again. "Would you mind telling me exactly who you are." But she knew.

"Oh *really*!" he exclaimed petulantly.

"I have to be . . . I'm so *sorry* . . . but you understand my position?" Her tone seemed to mollify him. She tried to cling on, fighting a sense of being suddenly caught in thick, spiralling storms of snow.

". . . Documentation and such like . . ." he was saying, "these days, yes . . ." He scratched his head.

She wanted to interrupt him, apologise but found instead that her lips were pressed together to keep words safely in. There was no knowing what unshapely, self-willed pattern they might take. *He* was speaking. She watched the act of speech, not quite hearing.

An ugly, scorching smell reached her and she realised distantly, the smell was coming from herself. She moved a little back from the fire, her foot knocking against the warm, solid body of the dog who half-leaped out of sleep then slumped back again.

He was speaking of his file (his file?), his *particulars*; the word was confidently said. And then he spoke of a hamper. Hamper. Hamper . . . she could only comprehend the word as meaning to obstruct. The word danced buoyantly before her eyes, curving up and down like an accordion.

"The other presents," he was saying, "were never traceable, but the *hamper* . . ." He winked. "Oyster soup, green figs, crystallised apricots, a jar of quails' eggs, lovely, lovely little things. Speckled. And lark's tongues . . . Things I'd never heard of. And other things, pears in brandy. I was so touched, really . . . so *touched*."

The firelight trembled in his face. He gleamed with emotion. "Ever since my mother died," he went on, with renewed self-control, "three years ago, there's been presents. On my birthday, usually. And I couldn't know, I couldn't be *sure* who'd they come from could I? I mean I *thought* . . . I let myself *believe*. But I might have been wrong, you see. Until the hamper."

She experienced a sensation of not being. She was not here, not in her own home, even. Merely watching from a dark corner of a room and the body she'd abandoned by the fireplace was incapable of any speech, response or understanding without her.

"Let yourself down a bit there," he winked again, then clapped his hand to his mouth as though he'd said something dreadful. "Not meaning to offend . . . Not meaning to suggest . . ." The lips wavered round the uncertainty, but seeing no response of any kind, he boldly went on with his incomprehensible narrative.

The important thing was to hang on. Cling on to what was. The clock. The precision of the clock which continued at this moment as it had continued three hours before — marking event, unmarked by it. The exposed brass works swung steadily.

"I rang them up, said the card had been left out, said I wanted to write a thank you letter. Ever so polite. Well, they said, the name yes, but they weren't authorised to give addresses. Wouldn't budge there. Name of Plumb."

The cat, a sleeping white fur slung over the back of the chair on which he sat. The cat. Crowning his chair, a swag of white just above his left shoulder. The cat.

"So I was none the wiser really. So I thought, at least. So I *thought* . . ."

The wicker basket full of logs. Sweet, lichened pear logs. The basket. Woven in Africa by a woman. The basket.

"It was the newspaper!" (He was getting excited.) "Look, look! I can show you."

And he came at her, breaking the sensation of distance. He came at her hands flying from one pocket to another. A small cutting was held in front of her. It was the simple black print of a tabloid. HIDDEN IDENTITIES it read in upper case letters she could read quite clearly. And beneath, a list of names that knocked against one another in frenzy, except for one, her own, which bloomed in a flush of firelight. It made no sense at all.

"And so you see . . . there it was!"

His face, pink and joyful hung before her. A festive lamp. She smelt sweat and scalp, bodily things, then he retreated back, down to the floor where he sat, arms clasped around his knees, speech still spilling out of him in meaningless eddies.

"I daren't believe it. For weeks, well, from July till August, four weeks, I daren't look in *Who's Who*. But I did. Wickford, it said . . . *Wickford*. Where I was born."

She tried once more to will her being out of her body, but this time it remained obstinately within her, revealing itself as the enemy she'd always known it was.

This, then, was it. The stone whose weight had lain in her for years, mossed over, out of sight, causing her always to tread carefully in case it should be kicked against, turned over, exposing the swarming, fleshy things beneath it.

Her hand, holding the edge of the mantelshelf gripped it as though wilfully preventing her from succumbing to the fainting impulse that flowed up into her head.

"Wickford?" she murmured wonderingly, her lips tacky. "But you weren't born at Wickford."

"I was! I was!"

Numbly, she stared at him, shaking her head. His jubilation sickened her. The whole thing. Not real, hammered her heart ... not true.

"I *was*!" He was swivelled towards her on his haunches, palms spread outwards.

"Who was your mother?" She spoke sharply, suddenly, unaware at the moment of speaking of the question's nonsense.

His arms swung like windmills, expostulating gestures.

"I mean," she corrected herself with a sense of horror, "who brought you up, who looked after you ... who...?"

"Oh...!" (He was crying, she saw, crying with a kind of happiness.) "Mary Harrison. Mary and Ted Harrison, they brought me up. They adopted me. And we lived in Wickford from the day I was born till I was three—or just four—and we moved into town and my Dad went working on the lorries." Emotion overcame him completely. He took off his glasses to rub helplessly at his flushed and shining face and she saw then that there were shadows, shapes, small contours, inclines that appeared within the faces of all her children at certain ages, in certain moods. Here lay the documents. Not an identity card or birth certificate. The skin, the eye, the rueful smile that now broke through his tears. There was no falsifying these testimonies.

"Mary Harrison," she breathed, marvelling at the complexities opening out before her.

"I've found you!" he cried, and she, half-hearing his vocabulary, was repelled by it.

Mary ... Mary Harrison ... The young wife of an old man (or he'd seemed old to her as a child). Sole gossip of her mother's. The two of them, improbably, heads bent, whispering. About men, was it? Asking advice about cutting cloth on the cross or making a deft yoke. Two heads together, voices low. Mary who became the mother of two children—a girl and a boy—only six years younger than herself, marrying because they were motherless and she yearned, yearned to devote herself to other lives. Yearned for a baby, did she?

Olivia looked at him as he sat before the fire, the heel of one hand pressed to an eye, and she suffered again the feeling she'd had—and smothered—the previous night. A sensation of dream become reality, but a reality that because of its nature, could not be dealt with unless traduced.

The dog stirred and gave a whimper as his own dreams hunted him.

"Of course it's a shock," he was saying. "It was a shock for *me*, but not so sudden." He sighed heavily, gazing into the low flame. "All those years not knowing, wondering. Why, *why* . . . They always told me the truth, that I wasn't their own, you see. It's a terrible thing . . ."

. . . Being unwanted, she concluded silently, for him. *Mary Harrison*. So. It had all been arranged. And the gifts? Her mother's hand lay there too, unable quite to let go, thinking of him, as she herself had not. Dared not.

"And then, when I found out about the hamper, all the bad and evil things I'd sometimes thought of you—not always, sometimes you were, oh, a princess, you know!" He half-turned, smiling worshippingly, "*Then* though, I dared to, I thought that you too, I knew that you wondered, wanted. And I thought, she's given me a clue. She wants me to find her. And I thought she's shy, she doesn't know either, whether . . . whether . . . And then, perhaps, she's nearing fifty, must be fifty now, married perhaps. Wouldn't want her husband to know. Maybe." A quality of doubt and pleading was creeping into his voice. "So I thought I'd best wait till you were on your own because I didn't know, I just didn't *know* . . ."

She was beginning to emerge from her numbness. Although many of his sentences were too unconnected, unexplained, her own mechanisms were beginning to work on the senseless gaps, pursuing possible histories in the ragged holes of time.

("I called, I hung about, nearly came, oh, half a dozen times . . . but I didn't know . . .")

But alongside this rescuing process another, more primitive part of her mind was suspiciously alerted. In the confusion of the two responses she could not tell how to react to him. His visible delight at discovering her met no corresponding emotion in her. The feelings uppermost were all of fear. Fear at what it might mean. Fear that all the substantial, handsomely constructed years of her life would be nullified by this . . . this *fact*.

"It was so wonderful for me," he was chattering, "to find out you were *famous*, like a dream come true, an unbelievable dream. I was *someone*. And knowing, that after thirty years, you still watched out, still . . ." And he stared at her in a wonderment that made her shift a little from her burning place at the hearth; he was believing dreams of her own that came up unbidden through the cracks of old burial places.

And rudely, her imagination presented her with a picture of young Harry Eastholme, elegant in his dress uniform. Blue and scarlet and silver he stood, on a carpeting of yellow leaves.

She realised from Arthur's expression that he was waiting for her to speak. Her mouth, dry, unused, opened and gave forth a single harsh sob.

"Well?" he demanded, as though he'd asked a question that had long gone unanswered.

"I'm sorry," she whispered, and turning away, weakly sat down in an armchair away from the fire where shadow dealt more kindly with her.

Mary Harrison and her mother, plotting. Never telling.

"Would you," she said, her voice rusting a little, "would you be very kind and pour both of us a drink, if you can find anything in that cupboard over there?" She pointed to an inlaid rosewood cabinet positioned in a corner of the wall behind him and then drew back her hand resting it against her forehead.

"I was wondering when you'd ask!" Gaily, he jumped up and began fiddling with the key in the cabinet door. His nervousness was leaving him, all his movements were more confident, even his accent—a pale, general urban sound, the kind of speech with a faint whine at the back of it—had more body to it.

"A drink would settle us both nicely, I can see you're a bit knocked out by it all, well, naturally—I should have written I suppose, but I just wanted to see your *face*," he declared and laughed at her breathlessly over his shoulder. "I mean, you could have said *anything* in a letter back couldn't you, you could have said you were ill or away or tried to pretend . . . There's not much here," he remarked disappointedly, as though he felt let down by the paucity of the contents. "Brandy? There's enough for two."

"Thank you, yes."

Planting bulbs, daffodils, crocus, narcissus. Digging up the earth in small square sods, packing the bulbs beneath and pressing it down, walking round and round, pressing with the right heel. Harry Eastholme telling her he would probably be killed in action. Telling her he had watched her growing up. November. Like this. Crisp and sunlit in the woods, birches the colour of neglected silver, larches, the colour of marmalade. The leaf mould folding deep round their ankles. Her heart beating wildly. Then. Now. Long shafts of sunlight through the pale green trunks. Pheasants rising.

She looked at him, as he crossed the carpet cautiously holding their drinks. This was what they called part of her flesh. Her doing. She felt no bond of any kind until both their hands, she saw, encircled the glass and heard him say in a mumbled, embarrassed way "I've been trying to find you so long." And she thought then his search was much the same as hers.

It was just that she'd been trying to secure her own mother in words, nailing down memories with words, as though she were building something the wind could not blow away.

"So long..."

And what a poor construction it had turned out to be. Blown already. Her mother had been full of privacies she'd never guessed at. Full of a forbidden love.

She looked at him and knowing so well the great fear she'd had herself, that by her mother's absence, some part of her own existence was necessarily obliterated, she understood better. Her resistance loosened. Gratefully, she sipped her drink.

"So crazy—you, well known, and me not knowing..." He hadn't surmounted his own disbelief yet.

"I wasn't always successful," she said quietly as he reseated himself cross-legged before the fire. His profile was presented to her. The flames, subsiding to a steadier glow, the logs turning to solid, ruddy ash, the light on his face wavered less, reminded her less of goblins and night-tales.

He sat like a child expecting a story and so she began, hesitantly, telling him those things that came to mind first. The home she'd grown up in... he knew it, he said, knew the very cottage. Had seen it only two years ago, overgrown by the surrounding wood, its brickwork pulled out by ivy.

Yes, but the *kind* of home, she insisted, meaning the lack of things. Lack of indulgences, lack of a man to mend and lift things and laugh in the evenings. She talked, combining apology with history so subtly, she was unconscious herself of the sympathetic blending.

Only after she'd married, she said, had she escaped the confinements of considering all things—whether a light could be lit, whether a mile could be travelled—in terms of its cost. Only then had she discovered there were ambitions beyond wanting to create a respectable appearance "whatever the sacrifices". Society was very swift to penalise if that modest standard was offended, she said with a sighing bitterness.

"But that's even better!" he burst out, interrupting her as though his own thought processes had followed an independent course.

"Better?"

"Yes, don't you see? *Better* than a princess. Don't you see? You've overcome everything." He looked eagerly at her and seeing she didn't grasp what he meant, he began itemising on his fingers. "Everything, poverty, class, a lousy education, being a *woman* for God's sake." He laughed derisively, "*That's* something I didn't have to put up with. A real handicap that'd be!" He made another scornful sound. "I mean, *women*. Just things, just pushed around, aren't they? That's another thing I thought about you. Sometimes." He gave her a quick glance as if to reassure himself. "I bet, I thought, I bet she was conned into it, just made a fool of. A *girl*. Or a tramp, sometimes I thought, just a tramp, easy, you know. But no, I thought, more likely a fool. But there! Look at you!" And he gave a sharp thumbs-up sign as if congratulating her on escaping the dismal boundaries of her sex. Then something conflicting struck him.

"But what about *me*?" he said curiously. "What about me? Why did I get left behind too?" He twisted himself fretfully towards her, taking an awkward swallow from his glass.

This was the question she least wished to answer.

The idea of answering it frightened her far more than anything else he could do or demand of her. A vault had been opened and though the contents were incriminating enough, it was, as she knew from the cold and tightening sensation of her skin, not the contents themselves, but their reasons for being thus concealed that contained the real horror.

She stared at him, thankful for the lowering firelight which barely illumined her now.

"I was very young," she said slowly, her voice sticky with dread. "Not seventeen when you were born. Too young to know what to do." She let the years roll back for her. "You were taken away from me."

He looked at her excitedly as if longing to know the outcome of a story, unaware that he was the outcome.

Her lips were dry. "It was the *shame* . . ." she said. "The shame. Then." She wanted him to understand that to be *poor* was immoral. "You had to be clean, decent. You couldn't let them think it was true. That being poor made you—unclean."

In the silence, the fire spat and a last log crumbled into ashes. In the fading light, she was aware of the tension and expectancy within his hunched shape. How *could* he understand? How could she convince him of the power such narrow attitudes had thirty years ago; before money had eased moral restriction. He was merely the bitter fruit of it, bewildered that he should have been so wantonly wronged.

"Simply to exist was shaming. More so for us, since mother had been left. For her . . . it was terrible. For her . . ." There was a long silence. "I'd let her down, everything she'd done to retrieve . . . I'd let her down.' And her voice broke as the memory, so elaborately entombed, burst open. The voice she'd tried—and failed—tried to raise these past months, rose now. Not scratched and distant like an old recording, but clear and plangent; as if she stood beside her. Instinctively, Olivia cringed.

Her mother's face. Anguish. The thin, sharp angles of betrayal. The words that she emitted in a high grieving wail, so unnecessary. No words needed. The torn line of the mouth, the beseeching slope of the brow, the eyes, wounds . . . these were the terrible transmitters of pain.

She'd let her down. Her fault. Made her reviled in her small, important parish.

"We lost our home."

Olivia spoke in a small tight voice, gazing into the raw remains of the fire. "We were turned out . . . Because of the conchies, they said, but we knew why, really . . . the disgrace, you see. Their son."

When he didn't reply, she realised she was unclear, he hadn't understood. In a dull, defensive monotone, she repeated more plainly, what had happened, and why.

"There was precious little money. Food even, in the winter sometimes, hardly anything, unless one of the men came and wrung a chicken's neck for us. There was that. And wartime as well. There was no way of keeping a baby," she looked blankly at the wall, letting its pattern blur. "It all happened at the wrong time. My mother was depending on me. Banking on my going to work. It was the *wrong time* . . ." It was an inadequate thing to say and she knew it. But he seemed enthralled, as though he were listening to a story about somebody else.

"I went away. I was sent away. To a place for girls—like me. In Yorkshire." She was sitting upright, plucking at the roll collar of her jersey. "It was run by Anglican nuns in brown robes. They made us tie our hair tightly back or threatened to cut it and dressed us in overalls, a different shade of brown to theirs. Like a cowman's overalls. We had to work. It was a kind of penance. Hard to believe, isn't it?" She turned to him, her smile harsh, "But it's true. It happened. We were made ugly, made to feel the thing in us was a sin . . . That was a wicked thing to do."

She paused, thinking, then resumed in the same hard tone. "It made us want to be rid of our babies. Can you understand that? That bump," she shaped an imaginary curve over her own flat stomach, "it was like . . ."

"Yeah," his voice, was pulled out, wonderingly, "I can imagine."

He astonished her. His freedom from recrimination. She knelt down and placed a new log on the fire, stirring at it listlessly for a while with the poker. "The day you were born, that morning, I'd been scrubbing a stone flagged floor. They think those things don't happen. But they do. They did."

"The day I was born?" he echoed, as if suddenly reidentifying himself within the narrative. He raised his glass to celebrate the buried event. "Better days!" he cried.

He drank, looked at her, found her detached and raised his glass again. "To me! To Arthur!"

Very well, she thought, reaching out her own, virtually empty glass.

"Why *Arthur*?" he said.

It had been a simple birth, much easier than any of her subsequent children, as though the eagerness to expel this black flesh was greater than the pain.

The relief. She didn't touch it, didn't hold the baby, didn't even look. Her head was turned to the wall away from the sounds of cleaning and weighing. Then they'd taken it away, that livid thing, and she was glad. It had no name.

"It wasn't the name I chose."

"Oh?"

She had chosen no name. You cannot name a tumour you wish to have cut out of your body.

She did not yearn after the baby as they walked away down the corridor. They'd cauterised all normal womanly responses. As if the masked nuns had removed not a baby from her leaking drain, but all the hormones and chromosomes that identified her as a woman. The footsteps receded down the corridor, each sharp, fading step a stroke of relief.

"Oh, I'm sorry about that," he said, "I had a theory about that." He looked at her as though he expected her to be interested.

"Yes?"

"I always had a theory it was to do with Arthur and the Holy Grail thing. A search and that." He sounded so anxious, she smiled at him and said, "I think that's very perceptive of you."

"And then, when I started reading your books, and that kind of thing, well, it all seemed to be...Well, it all hanged together." His manner now was intensely young. He had the gravity of the adolescent.

"You've read...?"

"Oh, quite a lot."

She was touched and amused by that. How desperate his search had been.

"I've got a theory about that too."

"You have?"

"You know, that all this time, you've been trying to recreate everything you lost." His brow was creased with the effort of making a match between his theory and such books as he'd read. To help his concentration he snatched off his glasses, rubbing the bridge of his nose between thumb and forefinger and again she saw ghosts of her children.

"Well, that's how I see it," he was saying. "Trying to recapture a lost happiness." Awkwardly, ponderously, he forced his way into the cheap, prefabricated chambers of psychology.

The sound of it, so lumpen, drove her back to the truth of that time.

Returning to the mean rooms over the shop in Anstead High Street. Creeping back under the canopy of her mother's hurt.

"Oh *God*, I let her down!" she cried out suddenly, disturbing Arthur's clumsy route march. Swiftly, she tried to control herself, tried again to coat herself with the thick, dull submission that protected her against the bitter saw of her mother's voice.

Arthur remained silent, his face revealing mild, clinical interest.

Slut!

The belief in the rightness of that judgement which had overcome the naïvely confused belief that she had in some way, as she'd always been told she should, been trying to better herself.

Besides, she had not.

Harry Eastholme had not come to the shed in the clearing. He had sent his friend. That was his contempt. It confirmed, corroborated other contempts.

So she had accepted the terrible judgements. And the terrible punishments. Sentenced for life to escape and conceal her true nature because it was unfit. The atonement she accepted was non-acceptance of her womanhood, her poverty, all the things that had made her and the thing they had made. And the ugliest remaining evidence of that, was *him*. The boy who sat here, attendant on an explanation it was quite impossible to give.

Seeing that she was not going to continue with anything else of interest, he resumed, or concluded, his own analysis. "Well, the most important thing of all," he said, "is that they all have happy endings."

She stared at him, her face thickened in texture by the fire.

Without taking her eyes off him, she reached out for his glass and climbed stiffly to her feet. Then she crossed the room to replenish their drinks but found all the brandy was gone.

"I'll have a liqueur," he offered. "People always have liqueurs left over from something."

She shifted bottles around, trying to find something suitable.

(Happy endings? But this was no ending. This was a *beginning* ... a new, and difficult plot. The family. Leo. Everything.)

"Benedictine all right for you?" she enquired steadily, the bottle poised.

"Oh pour away, I'll drink anything."

"But you," she said, returning to the hearth, her nervousness groomed to extinction, "I want to know all about *you*."

Desperately she told herself that the telling of his tale would create a foundation of fact between them that would become a foundation of knowing, liking, belonging. Pleasantly, encouragingly, she smiled at him, hiding the cold knowledge that she wished he did not exist.

But he was a reality of a most unvanishing kind. He breathed and smelled and drank and talked. Oddly, though, he seemed disinclined to talk much of himself. He was full of theories which had been fashioned out of the loneliness of his head for thirty years. Compulsively, almost, he emptied himself of them, as though they had to be evacuated from his system before he could really come to grips with the truth. All the time he talked, he kept his eyes on her as a surveyor might check and recheck the accuracy of his calculations. A little this way, a little that.

And as he talked, he grew more confident. As he grew more certain in his assessments he became, in manner, more boastful, almost, she thought, as though their possession one of the other, increased his self-esteem.

17

THE CARRIAGE CLOCK, GLINTING IN THE FRESHLY LEAPING firelight, struck nine.

"Nice room," he commented, "nice house." And he sucked gingerly at his syrupy drink.

She kept putting off the invitation to stay overnight (overnight? . . . a week, a month, a year?) The lights would come on again in an hour's time and then, somehow, it would be easier.

"When I can work the cooker," she said, "I'll make you some supper."

In fact she could have used the Aga that Mrs. Baldwin had spent all morning trying to light, but she wasn't going to leave this room till the lights came on. In here, it was brown and burnished.

"Nice," he said again. "I'm starving."

"Only an hour to go."

This seemed to activate him. "Well!" he announced, gripping both knees and straightening his elbows, "we'd better get down to details."

Immediately she knew it was no accident he had come here while she was alone and in the dark. All her worst suspicions were confirmed, and being confirmed, she felt much less at a loss. He was going to present her with an administrative situation. She waited tense, but clear-headed.

"The way I see it," he began, untangling himself from his position on the floor and returning to the armchair so that they faced one another in a professional manner, "is this . . . You owe me something, right?"

She nodded automatically.

"I like you," he said, newly master of the situation, his accent acquiring a faint mid-Atlantic drawl. "And that matters to me. I shouldn't have liked it if you'd been unpleasant. It was a risk I took. *Think* of the risk."

She looked uncomprehending and he explained as though it were obvious, "To my sense of identity."

She was growing suspicious of these too-frequent references to personality and psychology. She wondered whether they came from lazily-read paperbacks or whether perhaps . . . but she shunned that possibility. She watched him very intently, concentration driving an ache between her eyes.

"I have to like *myself* you see. Very critical, that . . ." He seemed to lose his thread for a moment and stared at her vacantly before resuming his theme. She had the feeling he had rehearsed this speech many times. His manner had altered so strikingly. "The thing *is* — whatever you've done to me — whatever you *did*, was one thing. Girls are always getting themselves messed up. All right. We won't argue that one. I've got my scars, you've got yours. But the thing *is*, as I see it, is you got out of your mess."

"I was very fortunate." She didn't wish to stress her fortune of whichever kind.

"You were very *fortunate*," he laughed. "Well, what I want to know is, why should you be so much more fortunate than me? Doesn't match up, right? Doesn't stand to reason." He leant forward and jabbed a finger at her, reproving almost. "You could just shut the door on it, eh? All over, all done with. No incriminating evidence, so to speak. You got a guy to bale you out. But not me, not Arthur. I was, what I was. No hiding that." His teeth shone dully in the spasmodic light.

"No."

"Not blaming you, no hard feelings, just talking — one rational person to another. Can't undo what's done. Not altogether, anyway." He went more rapidly through his lines. "But what's become of Arthur, I bet you didn't wonder for well on thirty fucking years. And then what happened. Guilty? Little bit guilty did you feel? Presents? *Poor* Arthur . . . All those cheques going off to the retired budgies' home, what about a little something for Arthur? A little *something*!" he spat out. "You went right over the bloody top, didn't you? A food parcel. Now you didn't have to do that, you didn't have to send such a great big bloody basket. I don't like being treated like a poor relation or a charitable organisation. Why wouldn't a few baked beans or a Swiss roll 've done, eh? Oh no, oh no, it has to be things like quails' eggs that don't come off ration books . . ."

"But I don't, I didn't . . ." She stopped. Her mind jangled. If she denied one of his accusations, she opened herself to another. Of not caring. Of doing nothing at all. She knew what had happened. Her mother had always had free access to the account. It was *her* desperate, distant kindness . . . what if she laid claim to no kindness at all?

"Things I can't even *pronounce*. . . !"

The change in him was beyond her. He went on jeering and talking so rapidly his words and grammar became confused. Spittle appeared at the corners of his lips.

"Wanted to send a thank you letter, I said. Ever so nice and polite. Address? No, no authorisation. Do you have a pencil? P.L. . . ."

The words came at her like waves, visible, racing, then suddenly overwhelming, blinding. He was coming at her, glinting — hair, teeth, glasses, moving angry flecks of gold.

She sat very still. He stopped.

"Now look" he said. "Now look what you've made me do — lose my temper and me, a reasonable person. It's not good to get worked up like that. I don't want you thinking I can't control my temper." He wiped his hand over his mouth. "I just wanted to see you. Come to some arrangement." One thumb reached up a nostril for brief exploratory purposes and he calmed.

She held the soft, velvety arm of the chair lightly. She refused to clench her knuckles. Refused him signals, Just remained as smooth as an egg. In forty minutes the lights would come on.

As if reading her thoughts, he glanced at the clock. Then he glanced at her and smiled, head on one side. "A queen of fiction," he mused. "Nice in there is it? In the fantasy world? Done very nicely from it by all accounts . . . Got its real side all right. The money." He rocked thoughtfully on his heels, his demeanour growing serious. "It's getting a bit tough out there in the real world," he said, "putting an end to dreams. No promised land and all that bullshit. And it's hard you know, leaving us to get by on what there is because there isn't a lot of it." He grinned and stuck his hands in his pockets, stepping back into the shadow to lean against the piano which gave forth a bawling chord. He took no notice. "I've got some friends who nick things, well, they all do. Everybody does, but I don't like it. I know some do it just for a bed and three lousy meals inside, but that's just stupid. Anyway, I've got no need for it, have I? I've got you."

In the darkness his mouth widened delightedly across the pale globe of his face. "It's not *wrong* is it? It's only just. You making money and that out of stories, it's only logic."

He seemed quite anxious to persuade her of his case. His apparent need to give it a faintly bogusly political edge irritated her. His case was perfectly good as it was. He had an indisputable claim on her.

"It's my *share*. Do you know what *I* think?" he asked enthusiastically, and she could feel one of his theories swelling up like a balloon. "I think, if it hadn't been for me, you'd never have written those stories . . ." He waited for her, brows raised, waiting for her to concede his point.

He could be right. She stared down at the dog, still slumbering peacefully on the long-haired cream rug, overlaying the dark gold tones of the Indian carpet beneath. If she agreed he might be pleased, vindicated. He might also be angry. If she agreed he might demand why she'd never done anything for him before. He might leap like a cat either way.

She mumbled something incoherent.

"I'm right then!" Pulling his hands out of his pockets, he half clapped them, with relish almost, but turned the gesture into a finger locking movement that made his knuckles crack like wood being chopped. "One thing I got from you," he claimed. "Brains."

She looked at him under the eaves of her caution, trying to establish what image of herself she might have stamped in those cells and features. There was little she could tell. He had a curious lack of definition, exaggerated by the half-light he occupied. A melting roundness. Edges that disappeared in shadow. He was not fat; few people were *fat* any longer, but he had the soft thickness of a pudding at the wrists and neck. In the folds that ran from nose to lips.

"Brains," he said. "An ability to think things out." And he tried out first one flat note of the piano, then another, while keeping his back to the keys.

She saw their resemblance suddenly. It was the resemblance of shapelessness; mass products of their time. Neither of them possessed a lithe and fundamental sense of themselves. Mere blobs of spawn, pushed out across the surface of the lake, gathering accretions as they went, changing shape with the whorls of water. Worse for him, she thought. Even worse for him. A misshapen bundle of prevailing thoughts, tones, prejudices.

"Well," he demanded. "How shall we fix it?" And without awaiting any suggestion he went on. "I've thought it all out. I thought first, I'd like to come here. To live." He looked round with approval. "Plenty of room. Comfortable. Then I thought, no, boring . . . I'd get bored. Then I thought, I wouldn't get on with any of you anyway. Not my sort. Lah-di-dah, as my mum used to say." He struck a thick B flat.

Relief poured over her. She tried not to let it show.

"So, I thought again. And the best plan seemed to be," he looked at her, keen for her reaction, "a contract, a monthly allowance, something of that nature. But that doesn't take all sorts of things into account. Inflation. Sudden extra expenses and so on. So better than that, I'll invoice you each month, eh?" The pale ridge of his brow raised queryingly, "Sometimes more, sometimes less, depending how things go? . . . Fair enough?"

"It sounds perfectly fair," she said quietly, not quite able to grasp the fact of this conversation, just flowing with it in the hope of reaching some safe place. "As long as I can meet it," She pulled gently at the dog's ears.

"Oh, you'll be able to meet it all right," he laughed, satisfied. "No worries on that score." He paused and expressed his confidence another way. "I'm within the law you see, only taking what's my entitlement. It couldn't be called blackmail."

Privately, that was exactly the name she had tried to avoid giving it. But he was right. There was no escaping the debt. Even explaining everything to Leo, if she dared, wouldn't relieve her of it.

"Blackmail's a nasty business," he said.

There was no alternative. "It's the least I can do," she murmured.

"I mean, your other children have benefited, why not me?"

"True."

"One thing though . . ." He scratched thoughtfully behind one ear as though his glasses pinched him, "is the backlog. A backdated sum, lump sum . . ."

"I see." Her voice remained neutral.

"A nice round figure, a respectable sum. Between you, that shouldn't be too difficult."

"I see," she repeated her voice paling, slightly.

"You make me puke!" he yelled, making the dog leap to its

feet uttering small bewildered yelps. "You make me sick the way you sit there. I see. I see," he mimicked her. "So fucking calm. Haven't you *got* any feelings? Sitting there like a bloody company director or something!" His lips worked, unable to find the requisite words for a moment. Then: "You think you can just *buy* me off!" he exclaimed. "Christ Almighty, you should be scared out of your five bloody wits by me. I could ruin you if I wanted to. *Ruin* you! Show you what it's *really* like. Life. It's not all like this you know!" He kicked at the piano making it boom, dully. "Not all culture and booze!" Clumsily he struck out across the room and lurched towards the drinks cabinet pulling bottle and glasses off the shelves. Instead of smashing, they fell and rolled across the thick carpet with a lack of sound that seemed to enrage him. Tearing towards the fire, knocking the cat from the back of the chair he ran his arm along the mantelshelf in a single powerful sweep sending porcelain figures, the clock and a bowl of filberts crashing into the stone-flagged hearth. "There!" he screamed, his face reddened by fire and exertion.

Mince lept to his feet, retreated against Olivia's legs and barked once, awaiting further instruction from her. For a delayed second, she remained, frozen where she was, one hand on the dog's collar. Even if he were capable of attacking someone, she could not set him on her own son. A deep trembling entered her body and a cold, hard mechanism took over in her head.

He was stumbling across the room towards the bookcases, shouting barbarous abuse. An ashtray skidded off the table and struck the bentwood rocking chair making it tip wildly back and forth.

In a single movement, too swift even for the bewildered dog to follow, she rose, slipped backwards towards the curtains, feeling for the unlocked handle of the french windows and, turning it, slid out between the doors, closing them quietly behind her. Then she ran, her legs flowing as swift and smoothly as a skater's across the crisping grass of the walled garden.

There was no moon, but the mild bloom of frost and starlight was enough to illumine the white dab of the wicket door beneath a hang of evergreen honeysuckle. She sped towards it.

Before she could reach it, she was aware of the french doors being wrestled and flung open behind her. A beam of light caught her in its prism. The door ahead gleamed white. His torch. She'd forgotten his torch.

A shout. A cursing that seemed directed at the dog. Lowering her head, she ran on.

She had to pull at the door. It was impeded by a drift of leaves. The light danced. Then she was beyond it, safely into the arms of night.

Her brain worked sharply. No point in going for the car. The garage doors were probably locked and it might, anyway, be without petrol. No point in remaining near the house. If he'd prowled round it before he might know it too well. He had a torch and possibly, more stamina than she. Her one advantage was a better knowledge of the surrounding countryside.

She raced past the hay barn, her lungs already burning. Cats scuttered and sank into the shadows, disturbed in their ratting. Her thighs working like pistons, she headed for the track to Sheep Cottages.

An angry calling indicated he had reached the wicket door and momentarily lost her direction, but even as she thought this, a spinning beam tore through the hedgerow in front of her and instinctively, she crouched low in the hope of making the darker tunnel of the lane before his light could pinion her escape.

Just as she turned, believing herself now out of sight, she heard a triumphant shout and the thud of running feet. He must have picked out the foolish cream badge of her jumper.

She knew she was in danger. But neither fear nor the fire in her chest reached the cool controls of her head. The flight was uphill. It would tell more against her. Her shoes did not grip. Small stones, escaping underfoot, sounded abominably loud. The mud was deeper at the edge of the lane but she clung to it, smearing her jumper along the earthen bank as she struggled upward.

Out of the lane. She must get out of the lane where he could gain on her, trapping her in his light. Into the open country. Strike across the fields beyond the wood that bordered the lane. Longer but safer.

Here, the badger riddled banks were too high and slippery to climb but some twenty yards ahead, she calculated (guessing from the difference of the incline, from the shape of the wych-elm above), the bank was broken down sufficiently to pull herself up. (It had been weakened yesterday when they'd searched for a place to push the horses through into the woods.) There was a broken pole across it now. A loose loop of barbed wire which she might have time to tauten low down.

The beam turned at the bottom of the lane, shone up it, scything to and fro.

She dropped flat on her stomach into the leaves and mud, waiting, the breath rasping violently beneath her ribs. Her face lying sideways, she caught an emerald dazzle of eyes in the thicket before the beam swung away again. Seizing her chance, half-loping, doubled up, she ran for the broken bank.

It was still higher than she'd imagined; at least four feet and the earth was worked hopelessly loose by a succession of hooves. With one hand, she caught at exposed roots, with the other, she grasped a clump of ivy which held her weight and desperately scrabbled up through the sliding earth. At the top, she rolled over, the barbed wire catching a firm hold of her jumper. Immediately, she peeled it over her head rather than waste time struggling. It would leave a clear trace but it would still save the seconds she'd gained by climbing the bank. He would have more difficulty than her negotiating it.

The light swayed up the lane below her.

She plunged into the wood. A screech owl flew up out of the trees marking her with its cry. But the sound might simply frighten *him*, she thought. Might make him hesitate, the skin cooling on his spine.

The leaves hissed round her legs. Twigs snapped underfoot. The violence of the noise she was creating made it all the more crucial to get beyond the wood fast. Out into the fields. Panic began to curl upwards into her mind as her pace was impeded by hidden roots. Once she fell full length striking her shoulder on a smooth young beech trunk. Up, and staggering for several steps, then on.

A burst of movement betrayed deer. Two. Bounding shapes through the pearl-tipped trees.

Then progress became easier as she crossed the hollows where hounds had already severed lower twigs and strands of ground elder. She could tell then roughly how high up the hill she was. The ground rose irregularly in a series of uneven steps that would soon end in a thinning of trees and furze but the effort of climbing them here, where each step was three or four feet in height, was more draining and difficult than travelling horizontally north-westward. It would face her with a larger expanse of open country to cross, but at least it could be crossed silently. She kept going in the direction she faced.

The darkness of the woodland held her close. Only the

amplified sound of her own crashings and the indrawn whine of breath could be heard. But suddenly, some distance to her right, the trunks were lit like a view from a train window, travelling palisades, as the beam sped over them.

Another floundering joined her own, masked it to some extent, but she reduced her movements all the same. Kept them as small and soundless as possible. Size and lightness favoured her. She slipped through gaps a man would pause over.

There was no shouting. Odd. Only a furious stirring and lapping of leaves like waves on an empty beach. No voice.

The light was not reaching for her. Covered by darkness, she dared to turn and saw the beam directed downwards, small in shape and travelling steadily. Of course. He was following the channel she'd carved through the mould.

Her heart contracted, adding a sharp pain to the diffused rawness. She was hardly aware of the weakness in her limbs, only of her foolishness in thinking she could match the fox in cunning. No. Her instincts were clouded by false pursuits, false scents.

Turning between the narrowing spaces she fled, too frightened now to move carefully, knocking her elbows and ankles against close-growing trees, tripping, her face lashed by saplings and thorn.

He caught her in the bright jaws of his beam. Held her there. Took his time, knowing it was easy.

It didn't take long. They were nearly at the perimeter of the wood when he reached her, and seeing how close he'd been to losing his prey by relishing his own cruel delay, his anger increased.

She fell as though she weighed nothing.

He kicked her again and again. In the small of the back, the ribs, the shoulders. Each time his foot made contact, she jerked among the leaves as limp as a dead rabbit. The torchlight swung crazily up and down, branches rearing up and toppling.

When his legs felt weak with pummelling, he changed his hold on the torch, grasping it more fiercely, and brought it down on the side of her head. Twice.

Then, exhausted, he kicked leaves all over the body and descended into the still and darkly opalescent night.

Some indefinable length of time later, life, still weakly operating its diminished senses, caught the pale and drifting screams of horses as the last of Clouds burnt down.

The cries, like needles, tracing faint, sharp peaks on the night sky, made her stir slightly. But that was all.

18

UNDER THE DARKNESS THAT REACHED OVER HER, WEIGHT-less, yet pressing her down, she tried to move herself.

But it was not the crush of the darkness after all that stopped her. It was the stiffness of her body. It was full of old pain that had fossilised. She seemed trapped inside it, as a beetle on its back is trapped by its own plating. The stern instructions of her brain . . . push . . . lift . . . slide . . . were barely heeded. But she could shout now, yes, surely she could shout at least.

First though, she listened carefully for certain sounds. Small movements that would tell her if the wood had subsided.

As she listened she became aware of discrepancies that confused her senses making them scurry like mice in search of alternative havens. The temperature of the air. Warm and very still, no stroking, like hair, of mingled currents. No smell. Her nose stuffed with blockages; not earth, not leaves. One arm caught in a curious way, the other . . . heavy yes . . . a long slow signal passed down her arm and the fingers stirred, their pads pressing downwards for clues.

Soft. And coarse. A heavy weave; cotton. A regular pattern.

Her head. It ached from being pressed into a trough of frozen earth but it was not earth. It was not hard.

At a great distance, she heard a telephone ring. Then squeaking rubber shoes, soles hard-rippled like certain beaches. Squeak, squeak.

She was safe then.

Tense, she waited in the darkness until the spreading, sucking shoes had come to a halt, it seemed fairly close beside her. She waited.

"Hello?" A whispering. "Hello, dear . . ." It whispered down a thin length of piping. Near but not near.

"Hello." Cautiously, she tried to whisper back. So cautiously, no sound emerged at all.

The footsteps moved away a little, paused and then returned. "Hello, Peggy? Can you hear me, dear?"

Her lips, stiffly hinged, strained.

"It's all right, dear. Don't you worry. You're in bed now. You're all right now."

She was safe. The darkness made more sense, then less sense. Her right arm, which had some movement in it, flew up towards her face like a released but heavy spring.

A hand caught her fingers. "No dear, don't do that. Mustn't disturb the bandages. Got to lie very still."

My eyes? Her voice, strained through a slit, made only a moaning sound. An idiot voice, not hers at all. Anxiously she tried again.

"Shh." The hand crouched firmly over her own. "You must rest now. Don't try to talk. You're all right now."

She seemed to have crept into the trussed body of a wounded pig; no real safety there.

It was Bart's voice she heard next.

She must have drifted back into sleep, for she felt herself rising upwards towards the sound, expecting light and finding none.

"Don't be afraid," he was saying. Again, she found it hard to place the speaker—to her right, left, overhead? He was threaded to her by a mischievous sound wave.

"Your eyes are bandaged," he was saying, "and you probably don't, for the moment, hear very well, but it will improve, you mustn't worry about that." And he explained, as he hopped from one distant, sea-encircled sandbank to the next (like a film, amusingly edited) that she would be in pain for some time (she was scarcely aware of pain yet), that she'd been wired up, patched up, nailed together, she had tubes up her nose, plaster round her ribs and a drip fastened to her right hand. "Poor lamb," he said. "Soon you'll be able to speak to us. It's all over now."

His voice was gentle, drifting, reducing the sharpness of bewilderment. He talked on, but she felt herself ebbing away from him, reluctantly. It would have been nice to cling on, but nothing worked at her bidding. She just let herself be carried backwards, downward, again.

Hands touched her continually. Firm, warm, trustworthy. Touch. She welcomed it now.

She was beginning to establish herself at the centre of these tubes and pulleys and plaster casings. A smear of being wired up to life. But she knew she occupied the centre.

Days? How many? It was impossible to tell, so much of the time was spent sleeping. Sleeping and waking the darkness was identical, except for the images of dream and guesswork.

She listened to the voices of her helpers, detected their wholly attentive movements as they tried to haul her towards a surface light. Sometimes she felt like a potholer being dragged to safety. Then more like a foetus, buffeted towards life.

The days would pass. Time lost its shape.

Sounds still came at her from unexpected places, but the temptation to pull towards them lessened. Lying quite still, she let them come to her in their own, unpredictable way. Leo's voice wavered between surges of ocean as if he were on a transatlantic telephone line. Chloe's hung above her, gliding, like a kestrel. Everything had its image.

They spoke, saying little, except to repeat the common message that she was safe. All right, now.

She knew she was getting better when she could distinguish night from day by the patterns of each phase's movements. There were other signs too which she became aware of in retrospect. The better grasp she had, for example, of the contours of her own body and what ailed each separate part; as though her being were slowly reoccupying the devastated areas, warily exploring them before settling. She grew more aware of pain. Each resettled area presented its own peculiar pain, but that was part of its architecture, a means of definition. She came to accept it as an instrument of understanding the landscape of her body.

Beneath the plaster cast that encased almost the entire length of her spine, she felt an itch. That too, was a sign of healing.

Because they didn't hurt (although they were suspended), and gave little indication of themselves, her legs were the most remote part of her. But they received their own attentions. A physiotherapist came and gently unhitched them to bend her feet up and down, rotating them from the ankle.

The girl's palm was warm and strong against the sole of each foot. She talked about the weather in a young, clear, unaccented voice. It was cold, she said. Everybody was promising it would be a bad winter, the berries had been so profuse on the hedges. And snow had already fallen further north. Not thick, but snow just the same. In November.

November.

She had no desire to explore her face. It was bad, she knew that, Bart had said . . . nailed together, sewn up. She was grateful for the darkness.

When she imagined light, the illusion itself entered her eyes like glass splinters, so she was content to be without it for the moment, but she could understand the natural impulse of plants to reach towards light. Soon, she thought, soon I shall be ready for it.

The tour of her body took her into places which had a less evident, private pain of their own; the discomfort caused by her own regard for them.

Merely being lifted on to the hastily warmed metal was difficult enough. It took two people, burrowing their hands under the bedclothes, stealing back her shift.

"Just relax."

"We're trying not to hurt you."

They *were* trying not to . . . dimly, she acknowledged that. But the pan remained empty. The edges dug deeply into her thighs and the exposed part of her buttocks. Since her head seemed the lowest point of her body and since the thick edge of the plaster formed a new, ill-placed joint below her hips, the position was impossible.

"We know it's tricky," they said, holding her and one of them began to whistle encouragingly. Nothing.

Her bladder, swollen beneath the plaster, pressed against it like an egg about to hatch.

"Don't worry. Think of something else. Think of Christmas," said the older voice, so distant she might have thought it belonged to a third person had she not become accustomed to the slyness of sounds.

She thought she might leak with pain. But she didn't. Fingers began exploring the soft, private cleft, creating an intermittent pressure like hot needles being driven in.

"Nothing," said one.

"Don't *resist*," urged the other, the older one. Faintly Scots.

They began talking to one another about a change in shift duties, their voices blown along high telegraph wires, their fingers seducing her urethra.

When it came, hot and stinging, it seemed it would never stop. On and on the healthy flow foamed. She felt it rise up, rewarming the metal, lap the surface, wet her thighs. And still it flowed.

"Don't try and stop. It's good. It doesn't matter."

And so she let it seep over the metal, her bladder aching with deflation. The sheets dripped moisture.

"Good girl."

"That's better."

And sweetly, they cleaned her up, changed her sheet, tidied her, made her feel that she had pleased them. That she was no trouble.

Leo came.

His mouth lit fearfully on her right cheek. "It's hard talking to you, hard to know how much you can hear." His mouth moved across to her ear, tickling the lobe. His breath was warm, "It must be so hard for you . . . not able to reply." She felt him hesitate.

She wanted silence. And companionship. She knew as much as she needed to know. Where she was, the month, the day. She knew that beyond this neutral temperature, there was a wind full of ice. To absorb more was a labour, but she wanted him there.

Her right hand, free of the drip, crept unrhythmically, like a wary spider, towards the place she thought he was and turned, palm upwards on the coverlet. It was left open in silence.

His fingers crept in amongst hers, slinking amongst them. They communicated failure. The fingers paddled out their messages of shame and forgiveness and then they rested, caught peacefully together in a loose knot.

Advancing in tiny movements from the centre, she began to

press against each perimeter as it became familiar to her. She was intimate now with the map of her body. Like an island she'd been cast upon by accident, she slowly found her way along its creeks and peninsulas, assessing the worth of each part, discovering which were the more dependable, which were weak; finding ways of coping with the damaged areas. She was almost ready to make contact with other islands and other inhabitants, instead of leaving them partially sensed. But until her signals could be heard she had to conduct her voyage across the fringeless waters of memory.

The darkness under which she lay was liberating. It was so personal and impenetrable a climate, she could not be watched. She was free to move among the reed beds undisturbed.

She found, once she dared to face it, that her memory was the least damaged part of all. Whatever else he'd done, this part had been left intact.

Everything of that evening remained plain. Unlike the voices of the visitors and attendants round her, the voices of that evening were distinct, more so almost, than the reality itself, as if refined by recall.

It was only the effort of searching over long periods of time that tired her. That she did slowly. But she found everything there. And when she'd returned to every detail, fixing each most exactly in its place, she wondered at it with an absorption so untrammelled by time or detection, it was close to pleasurable. The total security of this unlit viewing room helped convince her that she was safe in the outer world as well. That he would not come back. Ever. That he would think her dead. And if he discovered otherwise, *couldn't* come back.

He had, she thought, forfeited his immunities – both from the impersonal processes of law and the personal claims he had on her. The severance enacted over thirty years was complete now that the illusory blood binding them was spilt.

The belief cocooned her a long time. As if nature had devised a way of protecting her from questions before she was ready for them. And then, as the mind grew healthy and capable of exercise, her certainty grew correspondingly weak.

Was that right? When did the lease of responsibility run out? Perhaps she would have to meet monthly payments still – committed not by his insistence, but her own.

Blood money. What did it mean, money, given to someone who actually felt robbed of something quite different? And how did one provide *that*. She had not, she recognised with bleak incredulity, had not felt any joy at finding him. Felt no love.

It was a dreadful and difficult confession but she made no private attempt to justify it. It took courage to gaze on the implications . . . that she, known as a generous and giving woman, had not love. Whatever motivated her giving, it was not love.

She embraced this possibility reluctantly but with a tearing sense of truth. That she, a public mouthpiece for love, had none. A sounding brass, a tinkling cymbal.

The horror of knowing what was true was partially recompensed by the equivocal peace of knowing it. What had horrified her most about Arthur's presence, she saw, was not his threats, his cajolery, his violence even, but far, far worse, her terror at discovering the very emptiness in herself that had predicated all these things.

Frantically, she searched her behaviour for signs of love and found evidence only of its lack. (The darkness lent the truth of a confessional.) She thought of Leo. Thought how long . . . thought first that sex is not the same as love, then thought that even if it were not, it would be loving to have offered it.

She thought of Corin who'd become a stranger to her. Of Chloe, who so puzzled her. Of Amy, whom, they'd tried to hint, was being harmed by her. Three healthy, wealthy, well-brought up, well-educated children; none of them possessing the one thing her other son envied and truly sought.

Now she turned—in the dark—and faced the harshest aspect of her lovelessness, the most insidious aspect of all, the one that gave promise of no change . . . her self-hatred, which clung to her like a small, angry blue flame, illumining everything she did and was, driving her to an unconscious orgy of concealment. Her clothes, her perfumes, her heroines and charity. How she crouched behind them to obscure from everyone, and most of all, herself, the depth of loathing the unloving, the unlovable possessed.

The violence he had expressed was no more aggressive and alien than the smashing of his own image in a mirror. She was not the victim of it. She was the reflection and co-conspirator.

Somebody unwrapped flowers. The sticky tearing of cellophane was followed by the crumpling of paper and soft, admiring cries of delight. "So many!" she heard faintly. The Scots voice.

So many flowers?

In the end, she took it calmly, this insight.

No one else knew, or if they guessed, would not remark on it.

It was, she told herself plainly, like a lingering infantile disablement. She would simply go on as before. There was no cure. It was too late to alter. Well, not quite as before, the sole difference would be her own awareness of it. You cannot be more loving if there is no love in you. You can only accommodate yourself to the handicap. Only mimic the patterns of the loving more assiduously.

She didn't know whether a whole part of her being had died or come alive. Her one emotion was a long, grey sadness, like a dull winter's dawn.

A new perimeter was opened up.

"You can start to eat a little now, soft things."

Her lips were parted to let thin slop through, let speech dribble out.

Now that she could answer them, however sluggishly, and it was felt that grief wouldn't be left to fester unexpressed, they told her she had lost the left eye and the other was damaged. Bart told her. There was hope for the right eye, he said, but she must remain very still.

It was only one in a series of cruel intimations.

"What else?" she croaked in her dusty monotone. "Face?"

"Listen, Olivia," he said, and she could imagine him, hands in pockets, gazing down his rumpled trousers to unpardonably chalky shoes. "You wouldn't much care for your poor face just now, it's taken a terrible knocking. Not just from . . . from whoever it was . . . from us. What he did, we've tried to put right and it takes time. You'll see it when it's coming along. And this'll make you smile perhaps. I've put in for a nice glass eye, they make absolute beauties these days!"

He knew her well enough. She managed a ghostly, one-sided smile.

Although illogical, the alteration in her outward self was the harder thing to bear. It undermined the suspect triumph of the dark. How *could* she go on as before, if the inner ugliness was stamped unarguably upon the face? There was no tint or powder for that.

A muddy bitterness began to stir. Against Arthur, first of all.

The Detective Chief Inspector had been warned to avoid certain matters. The fire for instance.

Already, he'd thrown his hands up in despair and threatened to go out on another similar case; there was no shortage of such cases. A man could well nigh pick and choose his incident these days. And apart from the delicate omissions he was supposed to make, he'd been forced to wait over two weeks before she was capable of answering any questions at all. What she might remember . . . well, he thought and bent himself to the matter, hoping to find some indication that a single mind, or single group was behind these apparently motiveless cases.

He looked down at her barely moving lips, stiffly tacked to an arc of stitch marks curving from ear to jaw and upward, beneath the bandages. Poor bitch, he thought. And he strained to catch the words she was fighting for. She had a problem with soft consonants—'s' and 'h' and 'w'. He had to raise his voice and ask her to repeat certain words which he then wrote down in his notebook.

"Perforated ear drum," mouthed the Registrar who accompanied him.

No, she had not seen her assailant clearly. He had worn a stocking pulled over his face. Tall. Heavy build. Dark hair, she thought. A woolly hat had been tugged down over his forehead. Between twenty and forty. No, he didn't seem to be there with any intention to rob. More inclined to destroy the things you might expect him to steal.

Useless, reflected the Detective Chief Inspector. Miles out of his usual area, anyway.

Now that she was better, they told her, she was being moved into the general ward. It would be more company for her. She wouldn't brood so much.

The privacy of her darkness was now shattered by continual

movement—whining wheels, rattling bottles, brooms banging against the bed legs, the laughter and lament of middle-aged women. Her serene black waters became choppy and disturbed; she had to fight harder to maintain equilibrium.

Her mind pecked restlessly over a single question. Had she lied to the policeman out of a desire that Arthur should go free, or out of a desire that his relationship to her should remain undiscovered? She knew it was a question of critical importance. Certainly, she reflected grimly, she hadn't lied out of any desire to save him from punishment. Her bitterness was too fresh and raw for that now.

The damage to her face forced the classic cry of the afflicted. Why me? All the justifications she had solemnly accorded him, went. She had dared to think she had done well to admit responsibility to herself. Wasn't that enough?

Why had he exacted so much more than he needed? Marked her for life. Made quite certain she would never forget?

As she put these angry, silent questions to herself, *even* as she put them, she knew that they were falsely put, that her blame attached to the wrong person. That he was not, much as she wished him to be, the true designer of her disfigurement, that he had merely given it outward form and that she had to search elsewhere in her hot need to lay blame.

Why did the imperfection occur at all? Why had love been excised from the keyboard of her soul? Of all the answers she had to find, this was the hardest of all to face. Facing it demanded conversion to heresy and there was not yet any argument sufficiently plausible to shift her.

Chloe came.

"Your speech is improving."

She liked to have Chloe best of all. She prattled on, never asking a question that was complex—nothing that either yes or no wouldn't happily answer. She didn't, unlike Leo, or the police officer, Bart even, try to elicit detail. She didn't seem to share the need for revenge.

But what made her most welcome was that Chloe alone seemed quite undismayed by her condition. The embarrassment that seeped through the solicitude of Madge and Leo and made her guess how monstrous she looked, never stained Chloe's talk. The others found gaps they had to cross open between their words. They brought flowers she could neither see nor smell and fruit she could not eat. It made her realise how profoundly the desire to end unnecessary suffering, as it was called, was based on the suffering of the beholder. This wry amusement at least, she got out of their tense and fidgeting visits.

Chloe was matter of fact. She made her believe everything did and would go on as usual. She was full of the modest oil of gossip.

"I brought some honey. Mrs. Inchcape promises it puts all to rights, even smashed jaws, would you believe. She's insisting we start two hives — there's a good reason mind. Did you know you get a special sugar allocation if you keep bees? Sounds crazy doesn't it? It's to feed them through the winter! I've persuaded Amy to eat some by the way. Because it doesn't make her swell up she thinks it's all right."

"Amy?" Slur.

"Oh, she *will* come. She's much better . . . Looks much better, but it's a difficult journey. Some of the women go without visitors for days, they were telling me, no buses, no petrol. It's hard for them." And unthinking, she turned her head to look down the ward, making it difficult for her mother to catch the last words.

Olivia had supposed Amy was back at school. Chloe had said no, not yet. Not now all this had happened as well.

Amy had grinned at her. Usually, she said, when there's trouble, I'm packed off. It's meant to save me from something.

Then the smile had gone and she'd grown very morbid because she believed — while knowing her belief was superstition only — that in some way, she was responsible for all this. That by *wishing* it, wishing for hurt and humiliation of a grand and vivid kind, she'd caused it all.

That's why she wouldn't come. Not because she was at school, or that there were no buses. Because she *dared* not come and look.

"Joe killed one of the geese the other day, you should have seen! So much blood! So purple, thick . . . the girls couldn't eat it." (She could imagine Chloe's face, all open movement, she restrained nothing, mouth, eyes, brows) "What d'you suppose they'll do when it comes to eating the runts I've got from Gerald?

For nothing, he gave them to me. Two really nice little pigs, I'm keeping them indoors, by the stove and feeding them."

And what are they doing, all your friends? How does life pass by? (She had a hunger to know.)

No need to ask, Chloe streamed on. "This'll amuse you, Mab's taken over your Meals on Wheels."

But you used to sneer at that.

"On Wednesdays she does all the cooking and on Fridays she delivers. She's responsible for the planning, we provide some of the vegetables—she's collecting now for a special Christmas . . . oh, vegetables, the goats got into Peter's broccoli and ate the lot, he's furious. The kale we grew for them they won't eat, but they loved the broccoli. Peter says they've got it in for him. They have, I think. Whenever he milks them, the big one shits in the bucket. Bull's eye!" She laughed. "It's lovely milking in the cold mornings, when it's dark."

And the dawn comes up on the hill opposite the Cottages, a thin red streak first, burning the scrub, then spreading, mauve and gold, upward, into the dark, lifting the plain clear morning with it. Oh, the *eyes*.

"I was going to bring one of the cheeses, but I'll wait till there're three to spare, then you can share them. Mind you, everyone's getting the benefit of your rations at the moment while you're eating pap. All the same, it would be nicer to share. They're soft enough for you to manage."

She broke off, leaning closer to hear what her mother was trying to say.

"But you can't!" she cried. "You can't do any work yet! Forget the manuscript for now."

There are alterations. Urgent things. You don't understand.

"Forget everything."

You *can't* understand.

Chloe was frowning, rubbing a knuckle against her teeth. How to tell her there were no bills, no papers, no manuscript. Nothing. Only a blackened front façade. You could stand in front of it and see Corford camp, dark blue, visible through the staring windows.

In front of the house, reaching down either side of the drive, a small frail regiment of conifers was now encamped, looking like the pathetic force responsible for the devastation.

"I'll talk to Madge," faltered Chloe, unable to think of any better evasion.

Slowly, her mind began to trespass.

The gifts her mother had sent. She had thought of them as desolate love offerings. Now, timidly, she explored the hidden acres of her mother's thinking.

There seemed no good single reason. Searching for one was perhaps the most purposeless pursuit of all . . . what had Chloe once said? About Amy? It's no good trying to grasp things at a rational level . . . behaviour's nothing more than a metaphor of motive?

But she did persist. She couldn't leave it alone. Over and over the same territory she went, blindly parting the grasses.

The matter (not the matter of gifts, the *entire* matter) had never, never been mentioned again between them. Not from the day she'd returned to Anstead still carrying an odour of pinched, nunlike severity, had it ever been referred to. The bolts were slammed across event.

It lingered, of course, intangibly. It was there in the new life they led . . . in the unaccustomed shuddering of traffic, the need to wash their net curtains twice a week and the smell of things drying on the clothes-horse indoors. They had no access to wind and a line any longer. Cooped up. It was there in the thin film of misery that clung like dust to skin and furniture alike.

And in her lifelong act of appeasement. *Her fault.*

And then the detail which had lain stored in her memory without crying its significance out loud, abruptly moved to the forefront of her scrutiny. As if an impersonal archivist had suddenly placed the document on a desk before her. She found herself again reading the letter of eviction which had given so graceful a command for their going. But it was not the words that lied. It was the date. October the first.

Three months' notice.

That was not quite right. The seasons and their fragrances, the garment and stimulant of recollection, whirled as if on a wheel, back and forth while she checked and rechecked, her heart drying as she worked.

The letter itself she'd read for the first time only four months or so ago . . . but the burden of it had been made known to her in the mild, leafless cold of the weeks approaching Christmas. *December.* The shock had been twofold. The shock of the news itself, but more immediate even than that, the shock of having to leave suddenly. In less than three weeks. Not three months. It had been a sudden decision, of that she was quite sure. She remembered her sorrow at having planted the bulbs only a month beforehand, because she wouldn't be able to see them the following spring. She had wanted to dig them up out of spite. That was December.

Beneath the light warmth of the blankets, her skin was ice cold. The letter was dated October, a month *before* the bulbs had been planted.

The months danced, their seasons surrealistically interlaced. One thing though remained still at the centre of the dance. The lie.

And the lie was not in the letter as she'd been led thirty years ago to believe but in the reporting of it.

It had not been her fault then. She was *not* the reason they'd been asked to go. The cruelty of it took her breath away.

Why? The single syllable kept up its pressure . . . *why* had her mother burdened her with *all* the blame, like the goat the Jews once loaded with sin and despatched into the desert?

("We've got to go. After seventeen years, got to leave. Got to pack our bags and go." The acrimony. The dreadful stillness. The shortage of words.)

She had hated the conchies . . . Once, her talk had been full of contempt for their despicable views, not that she regarded them as *views*, exactly. Cowardice. Traitors, trying to make a virtue of their treachery, that was her attitude. Their labour was spit.

Did the reasoning lie somewhere there maybe? Was it that her own labour, so much more honourable by comparison, made the decision intolerably undeserved? Had she simply refused to face it until the arrival of a greater crime, more fitting to her sense of punishment?

Ah, the impossibility of tracking the perverse movements of the human mind . . . superimposed upon the instinctive animal track, the mad course of a wayward, higher intelligence. She found no good reasons. Only observed that it was a remorseless human instinct to lock cause and effect belligerently together, whether correctly or not. Cause and effect, the grand detection of reason, reduced at its simplest to blind blame.

And she saw that she, ready victim of the irrational rational instinct, the vengeance that passed for reason, had oh so willingly accepted herself as the cause of that long, hurt silence. Had found it more endurable to identify herself as a cause than discover no cause at all — since it hadn't occurred to her to look her accuser straight in the eye.

Now it did. Now, she could see.

The grief that Bart had urged on her was finally met with. It was for herself she grieved.

19

ANOTHER PERIMETER.

They removed the dressing from the right eye. Light poured into the socket as if it were some soft, absorbent wound instead of an instrument for defining light and shape.

There was a piercing ache behind the eye. In front of it, a shifting, ragged assemblage of images that assumed their true contours slowly and even then, were liable to dissolve again. But her moorings became plainer to her.

"There. Can you see where you are?"

How odd. She'd had a sense of being invisible before.

"One . . . two . . ."

"Twelve beds. Twelve people."

"Yes."

Partly, she'd felt invisible because the other women had treated her as if she were. Only now did they call out greetings to her and include her directly or by reference in their exchanges. It hadn't been an unkindness, they'd been forced to think of her less than fully alive.

"Oh, that's better, isn't it?" A face, reflecting her own exhilaration, hung there.

She could tell they felt as though an intimation of death had been cleared out of the ward together with the soiled dressings and sweet papers. They laughed more freely.

"Would you like me to read the newspaper to you?"

How weirdly they confused sight and sound. She smiled.

The nurses, when they came to wash tenderly between her toes and gently towel her legs dry, moved their lips most carefully to show her the outline of what they said. And they felt, illogically, that their language was reprieved; they could frame sentences with more complexity.

It was very welcome. All she feared was the assumption that she could now be put to more searching inquiry. She hadn't decided whether or not to tell Leo the truth.

But it was a quite different concern that occupied Leo.

Staying at the town's once best hotel, depressed by its heating restrictions and small, repetitive meals, he arrived on the evening of the day they removed her bandage knowing that his own expression was now more open to querying scrutiny.

Walking with short, quick strides towards her bed he vowed he wouldn't tell her today. Not today, when they had the sight of one another to celebrate. He began to smile long before she could see him. She wasn't allowed to turn her head to one side.

The flowering pot plant—he'd been unable to find anything more uncommon than a poinsettia—slipped a little from the tense and tweedy clasp of his arm as he hastened his step. The fire, he reminded himself grimly, recapitulating all prohibited areas of conversation, the fire could wait. He prayed she would only quiz him on one thing at a time . . . the fire, the house, he thought he could cope with. (He had, for the moment, successfully closed his own mind to the failure of the insurance company.) As to his ready availability, his accessibility, he hoped she would simply consider that a normal freedom for a man whose wife was ill. His smile grew stiff.

"Darling!"

Her lips slid crookedly with pleasure.

Delicately, he hovered over her pitifully blemished face, moved by the sight of it and kissed a new space on her brow. "Wonderful," he breathed, pulling back a little to look tenderly at the weak but healing eye. "Bruised still, but all right, though. You can see?"

"It's lovely," she said, "to *see* you."

He reached up to switch the light on over her bed, but realising it would be too powerful, paused.

"You've bought a new coat!" she said, delighted with her observation.

He clutched at the tell-tale speckled fabric; all he could get. "Yes, yes," he replied in some confusion, searching about for a chair. Seeing his agitation, one of the visitors belonging to the neighbouring bed, offered a spare seat.

Thanks. An enquiry after the women's health. More thanks. He came back and whispered that the woman in the next bed was reading one of *her* books.

"Oh Lord!" she murmured. "Lean over me, darling, would you, so I can see you; don't go away . . . There." She looked up and smiled. "Comfortable?" He wasn't really. While he fidgeted she sighed dryly, "Well, at least she's not going to recognise me."

"Who?"

"The woman next door. Now, let me look at you properly." She put a hand to his face feeling the sub-skin prickle of beard.

Sitting awkwardly, he let himself be studied. No, she wouldn't be easily recognised. He'd noticed the book because of the photograph on the back cover, it was back cover upwards. There was no similarity. He watched the face that watched him.

The left hand was stiff and inflamed round the angry curve of stitches; its immobility affected one side of her mouth, depressing it slightly, a hindrance more marked when she smiled. The impact of whatever—or whoever—it was on the left hand side of her head had worked the uncomely effect of slamming that half of her face across and into the other. The natural symmetry had gone. It would settle, Bart said, but for now, the two halves matched one another neither in feature or size. The single liberated eye, which travelled slowly and raptly across his own features, was streaked with tiny, broken blood vessels, the skin surrounding it marbled violet and green, most deeply violet in the groove running from the inner corner of the eye to the cheek, there, it lay like a streak of paint. But she could *see*. His gladness rose uppermost.

"I'm sorry?" He bent his ear to her lips.

"Which *one*?" Which one was she reading? she tried to ask.

"Oh, I'm not certain. I'll . . ." And he half rose, not to look or check, but to hide his embarrassment, because she would guess it was the back cover he'd seen. But he was being oversensitive.

He felt her hand on his collar, drawing him back into a blurred focus.

"Seeing you," she was saying, "makes me feel . . . makes me feel I should try. Make an effort. Get my own clothes and things perhaps. A few things." Eagerly she was beginning to renew an interest in her appearance.

But Leo could only think that they were encroaching upon a

forbidden area. Clothes. Wardrobe. Possessions. And urgently, he asked. "Does it hurt? Does it hurt to see?"

She made a slight movement as if shaking her head. The hurt was nothing.

"I know!" he said heartily. "I'll buy you a beautiful new nightdress, the most glamorous thing you've ever seen. Would you like that? Something pretty?" His voice tailed away. Dear God, he needed her.

(He shouldn't have drunk so much before coming out. He cramped his lips together so she shouldn't smell the despondency of toothpaste on his breath.)

"Yes, I should like that."

They fell guardedly silent, each maintaining watch over their own secrets, each hoping the other would volunteer a fragment of talk that might be as effortlessly followed as a dance step.

As if out of sympathy, the volume of chatter around them wavered.

"How about looking at some of your cards?"

He got to his feet and shuffled through the heap of half-opened post on top of the locker.

It had been noticed by the other women in the ward, how much post was received. Even after it had been scrupulously sifted and passed as no more than good wishes for her recovery, there was an unusual volume. They'd noticed, and guessed, despite the white hospital shift, despite the plain and common bed, that there was a difference. This observation too, had kept them self-cordoned. It wasn't *just* the desperate and remote nature of her illness that had kept them away. They felt, *smelt* almost, different. The flowers, costly and out of season that had arrived — they could see them, even if she couldn't, and in the opulent texture of roses they read signs that made them hesitate to offer their friendship. Shyness, not unkindness, made them falter.

"Please," she said.

They had no idea *who* she was. The news was old by the time she'd been brought in here. Anyway, they believed that there were still, somewhere, discreet and private beds for such people.

"I'll hold them up," he offered, "and then you can see them."

They were from people she'd never heard of mostly. Strangers, women who regarded her as their valued companion. Women who spoke of the pleasure and comfort she'd given them over twenty-five long years.

Leo turned them this way and that to read the unfamiliar names.

"Hello."

The voice made Leo spin round, half-rise in his chair then, fall back inside his clothes as if they'd suddenly become too large for him.

"Who is it?" Olivia asked, almost sure.

"It's me!" cried Corin, slipping into her vision.

"Corin," echoed Leo unnecessarily.

The bright pinkness of his face advanced and swelled with an unexpected likeness of feature that caused a tightening of alarm in her throat. Something winked above his brow. A badge, on a cap that was removed.

"*Corin!*" Pleasure spread and dispersed the tight sensation.

"Special leave at *last*," he pronounced with a residual tinge of exasperation at the delay. "You must have been so fed up with me." And he produced a vast pot of poinsettias.

"Of course not!" She reached out her one free arm and lightly holding the back of his neck, accepted his kiss delightedly.

"How *are* you? What a dreadful, ghastly thing . . ." Drawing back, he saw the ruins more clearly and fell quiet for a second.

"Better. Much better," she insisted, wanting him not to stare, but wanting him within sight.

"And Dad? It's all been . . ." But Leo tugged at his arm mouthing incomprehensible warnings.

"What is it?" Olivia could feel a rupture in the greetings.

Corin looked from one to the other. His father's face was rolling and creasing like a madman's.

"I tried and tried," he said to his mother, returning to her pull. "But I just couldn't get away before. For this sort of reason." Vaguely he indicated her condition, as though it were a commonplace. "There's so much trouble and not enough of us to cope." He was hypnotised by the wreckage of his mother's face. Worse than he'd expected.

"Trouble?"

"Up north, yes, in the towns. There's looting even, assault, arson." He felt Leo's grip tighten violently on his arm.

"You mustn't worry," she spoke carefully, determined not to let her words sprawl, "about me. I'm doing fine now. You were right to stay."

"Well, I've got a few days now, I'll stay nearby. In the town . . . Where are *you* putting up?" Turning to Leo.

"We'll fix something. Don't . . ." Don't go on, Leo cried silently. Don't go *on*. He was unaware how powerfully his hand gripped Corin's wrist until he felt the resistance and saw his son's expression of bewilderment turn to anger. And then, as if in combat, his own anger rose, the mingled hurt and fury, all the more venomous for being unexpressed, welled up, making for his tongue. And there, torrential, impatient as it was he had to try and hold it, aware of his wife's still shape beneath the sheets. Again, he shook his son's arm, a minor satisfaction for the humiliation he'd suffered. Friends and colleagues, as he'd thought, faking envious sounds at his early retirement, imagining to themselves, in order to make themselves more plausible, whole days on the golf course, a snooze after lunch . . .

Olivia, her senses infinitely sharpened by days of darkness, again pressed more insistently to know what draught it was disturbing the air around them.

Her eye detected only rapid blurs of yellowish brown and grey swimming against one another then flowing irreconcilably apart. But her ear caught the high, strange sound of Leo sobbing.

Sunlight.

Dawn had stained the ward a wild and warning red but now, cold clear oblongs of early morning light were stamped upon the ceiling.

She noticed that the edges of the imprint were less fuzzy than on the previous day. Twenty-four hours ago the brilliance would have been intolerable. With relish almost, she feasted on the twelve golden blocks of reflected sun.

A plastic tumbler fell on the floor a little further up the ward and rolled interminably as though the flooring had developed a slant, otherwise it was, at this hour, utterly peaceful. The women were washed and refolded, left to read their letters, or simply lie and think what questions they would have liked, but dared not ask, the consultant when he came in an hour's time.

She heard the dull mumble of thick china in the distance and then footsteps, which she noted with a further sense of her own improvement, were directed towards her bedside. The curtain rings rattled.

"I didn't come before," said Bart softly, "I thought you needed the sleep and some time to yourself."

He was not as she'd expected him at all, but wore a white coat, the creases starched into it. It identified him differently for a second, as a doctor rather than her friend. But the images coalesced swiftly. "Well?" he mumbled gently, "How do you feel now?" He spoke so that the others, in their attentive quiet, shouldn't hear.

Slowly and carefully she replied. "It was so kind of them to let Leo stay late last night . . . the Sister gave him something you know, a pill, something . . ."

"And you?"

"Fine."

There was a pause. In the corridor one nurse called to another and laughed delightedly.

"Truly?"

"Truly."

"Sometimes," he said, drawing up a metal chair, "you can astonish me." He settled himself, a little of his weight tipping the bed.

"You've had a lot to bear."

"Yes."

Another small silence. The nurses were giggling in a smothered, vainly unconstrained fashion.

"Do you see any better today?" he asked at length.

"Oh yes." And she told him about the light on the ceiling. He looked up. "That's good," he nodded, and found his hand, where it lay in the bed, impulsively sought by hers.

"Bart?"

"Mm?"

"Let me have a mirror."

"Not yet."

"You think I can't take *that*?" (That, what is *that*, compared to the other things, her voice said.)

"You've had enough for the time being. Besides, you improve every day."

"Coward, Bart. I want it all over at once."

"No."

"It must be very bad."

"Tomorrow it'll be better. And the next day."

The woman who changed the flowers pushed her trolley down the ward crying out a cheerful Good Morning to each bed she passed. The sun bore everybody up.

"Which's the worst thing?"

She thought of each great item last. Her home, her work, her beloved creatures.

"Leo," she replied. "Leo's distress. That."

The pain of his concealment, his beaten self-respect. All that.

His terrible conviction that her injuries were the fault of his neglect and absence. That was the worst thing. That, of all things, was the most unjustly borne of his sorrows. And yet still, she hadn't told him the truth. It had seemed to her as he'd sat, head shamefully bowed and buried against her shoulder last night that the truth would increase, not soften, his misery at this moment. So it had seemed.

"*Leo*, Bart," she repeated.

His heart went out to her. But Leo, he believed would recover. Each would be a support for the other in their new indigence. The other things were irrecoverable. He plucked a yellowing leaf from one of the pot plants and folded it neatly down the central vein. "It's hard," he said, "very hard." Then, after a moment, "I'm sorry . . . About Clouds, about your book, about everything . . ."

"It was a worthless book."

He looked up, startled by the vehemence.

"Worthless," she repeated, "a fiction."

"But I thought . . ." he hesitated, then, faintly, he thought, grasped what she meant.

"Tell me something."

"Yes?"

"Did my mother know she was going to die?"

"Nobody knows that."

"Did she *guess*?"

"She was in her *eighties* . . ."

"But did she ever talk about it? To you."

He looked hard at her profile, his friendship tangling with professional ethics. "I think," he began slowly, "I think she felt it couldn't be long. She once said . . ." And he tried to recall what exactly the old woman had said in her dour, flat manner. "She told me that her world was coming to an end. That's all. It could have meant anything. A number of things."

. . . *The days of man are but as grass* . . .

"Yes, I see."

"Why?" he pressed gently, but she didn't respond.

The feelings came in waves, each one unpredictable. Bitterness. Self-pity. A short and failing sense of retribution, justly, if cruelly demanded of her. Then bitterness again. Hatred. And waste . . . dead, white acres of burnt ash. Loss.

It was better to think of Leo.

Last night, when he'd wept and recounted the damage they'd

suffered, she'd almost told him the truth. Not to try and relieve him of the burden of a responsibility he'd falsely assumed, not at first anyway. Out of a vile and naked longing for revenge. So that the boy would be hunted down and punished. That *she* should be robbed of all she loved she could, at every seventh wave, still feel she imperfectly deserved, but that he, Leo, should have been so violated . . . that unleashed a vengeance that seized her like a scream.

"Sometimes," she said hoarsely, "I wish . . ." What? That she'd never married? Never lived? Never come to possess the things whose loss she mourned most?

Not chairs, tables, carpets, pictures, things an insurance assessor might catalogue, but the things beyond price . . . the things that lovingly memorialised shared moods, moments, mutual effort. These were the things that lost, awoke a rancour in her so vicious, she feared it was beyond her to contain.

"Yes?"

"Oh, nothing." Nothing she even wished to hear herself express out loud. Nothing brave.

"I would kiss you if I could." Bart eased the pressure of his body off the edge of the bed. "But it might be thought scandalous." He rose. Paused. "Ah well." She could hear, from the softening of tone, that he smiled. "What if it is?" And bending, he pressed his dry lips lightly to her unhurt cheek. He stood up, looking down at her for a minute. "Good girl," he said briskly— or he meant to say it briskly, but his throat filled. A shade self-consciously, he cleared it. "My patient's coming along . . . beautifully!" he said.

"Mummy?"

She swam up, out of sleep. "Chloe?" The image expanded, dissolved, then crystallised. "Amy . . . ?" she whispered.

"I *wanted* to come."

"Oh, Amy . . ."

20

CHLOE RAN FROM THE STABLE ACROSS THE COLD DARK yard, Mince padding behind her, and called into the house for someone. Anyone.

Peter came, pulling the cord of his pyjama trousers into an absent-minded bow. "What is it?" he yawned, the words stretched out of recognition.

"She's come into season at last!"

"Well?" He was irritable. He scratched his billowing head and tried to open his eyes very wide. "Hang on," he muttered and went to fill the kettle before taking his parka off the hook and coming outside with her.

The cold brought bone closer to the skin. "Oh God!" he shuddered, "I don't see the hurry."

"You know what Bill said!"

A vivid gold and mulberry incision split open the blackness, dividing land from sky to the east. The few bare trees crouching along the hilltop were silhouetted in the widening crack of light.

In the soiled warmth of the stable, lit by a hurricane lamp, the larger of the two goats bleated and again wagged her tail as though a bee had lodged under it.

"D'you see?"

"Oh yes," remarked Peter with more interest.

Bill had warned that a goat sometimes came into season for only half an hour at a time. "You have to catch 'em quick," he'd said.

Ever since her yield had dropped they'd watched out anxiously for signs. Now one bag had dried out completely and they'd almost given up hope of her coming into season. She'd been a maiden milker, never kidding at all.

"Please," begged Chloe, wrapping her anorak more fervently round her nightdress and lifting the bucket out of the goat's way. The goat's condition seemed to make her restless. "I'm really pushed. You could take her in the cart."

The goat gave a yearning cry.

"O.K."

"I need the time."

"I know, O.K."

"Thanks." She pecked his bristly cheek.

In the valley, azure-splashed, the bell for early communion rang.

Sunday. The second Sunday in Advent.

Everybody had to wear extra clothes even for the morning service at ten. The frost which made the fields shine like glass hadn't melted and the cold found many easy ways of entering the church. When the bundled congregation sang, you could almost see the words ... *God is working his purpose out* ... take a pale, spiralling shape in the air. Everybody sang louder than usual.

Even Henry in his blue Advent robes had settled on a means of stirring the blood ... this, the first season of the Church's year, normally a sweet beginning to the birth of Christ when the puddings stood ready in their cloths and the children rehearsed their parts around the crib, he had ringingly altered. He offered a different anticipation that made them quiver hot *and* cold within their layers of clothing. The Second Coming, he seemed to cry in his great resonant voice ... to judge the quick *and* the dead.

Even the children fell silent, their eyes round. The words sounded terrible and marvellous.

Chloe, her fingers bloodless white at the tips and clumsy, plucked at the huge, gilt-edged page half-appalled by the lesson he had asked her to read, her voice no match for his. "And there shall be signs in the sun, and in the moon, and in the stars; and upon earth distress of nations, with perplexity; the sea and the waves roaring; Men's hearts failing them for fear, and for looking after those things which are coming on the earth ..."

Her voice, small as it was, echoed round the old walls and the faces gazed up at her like flowers open in winter.

There were prayers said for Olivia Mathison that morning and in the little silence that followed the liturgical sentences, Chloe prayed without either shame or difficulty for the means to comfort her mother. For the right things to say to someone who had yesterday clung to Amy as though she were the last possession she had on this earth.

It was at lunch that Joe said he would be leaving.

"Leaving?"

A silence fell over them, so thick, it smothered speech. They waited. It was Peter, who was the most astonished, since Joe had said nothing of it this morning when they'd taken the goat to be served, he who nonetheless spoke first, finding a simple and dismissive reason.

"Just because you got butted rather badly in the balls . . ." he laughed.

His laughter slipped anxiously as Joe made an exasperated, not wholly amused movement with his eyes.

"Leaving, Joe?" Sarah's voice expressed the worry of rejection they all felt in other fashions and degrees.

"It's impossible to run the magazine efficiently from here, that's all."

"You're going back?"

"Ahuh," he confirmed, without raising his head. He was the only one eating.

"Positive or negative?" enquired Chloe wryly.

He looked at her and grinned. "That's for you to decide," he said.

She wound the scarf on a final circuit of her neck and bent to pump up the back tyre. The goat, tethered a good ten yards away, head greedily reaching for the last dead leaves of the hedge, smelt appalling. The smell seemed to cling to everything. Her sister Amaryllis had caught one whiff of it and come into season herself —with a blissful expression, she too, had been loaded into the cart and taken to the billy, Joe declining this time, to accompany them.

It was a ten-mile bike ride to the hospital. Because she would need time, she knew she *must* take time to talk to her mother, she'd rung her father at the Castle Hotel on her way home from church. She'd only had enough small change to shout that she was coming and would he, could he, since it would be dark by four strap her bike to the roof of the car and come back with her for supper. He'd sounded vague, though it was partly the fault of the line which was bad and had forced them to ask one another to repeat themselves once or twice. She'd heard him say, "Cheer her up, would you, try and cheer her up."

She demurred over going past Clouds, what was left of it, but in the end, that was the track she chose down to the main road because she wanted to see if anything survived. Something for her to report. She wanted to tell her the good things, nobody had bothered to do that. They'd all taken terrible news to her, or kept silent, hanging on to their silences nervously as if they were devices timed to go off at some uncertain moment.

The bones of the house, black and brave in the cold sunlight stood up to the small army of saplings. The smell of burning was still there, dense and dark, if you went close enough.

Although they were blackened by soot, the walls of the enclosed garden remained intact. In fact, she thought, picking her way across the strewn grass towards the Glastonbury thorn, the plants would thrive on the rich ash. The land could take incredible injury into itself, nurse it and prosper. Two goldcrests fluttered over the wall as she approached.

She found what she'd hoped for. Small green leaves starting from the thorn, more thickly to the top where a single, small white flower was beginning to open.

And as she left the house, cycling past the pond, a winter jasmine which had grown against the wall, concealed all summer long by other sprawling greenery, put forth its clear cascade of yellow flowers.

These were the things, she thought, as she pedalled away from Clouds along a flattish stretch to the next village of Shipton Caundle. These and . . . she kept her eyes open for other continuities.

The fields were churned to mud by cattle who'd been kept out as long as possible and were only now being fed a little straw. They stood, knee-deep in mud, morosely chewing. A cockerel leapt on to the stone wall of a farmhouse as she passed and crowed mightily, feeling the best warmth of the day's sun nudging his feathers in a pretence of spring.

As her legs turned, her mind turned.

But *how* to express it? How to make the loss seem smaller than it was? How to reduce it so that her mother couldn't feel her arms and heart and memory full of it, unable to let go, keening over this dead burden? With one hand, she pulled her scarf up over her mouth to cut out the cold.

Downhill she flew, the ploughed slopes of the field beside her already blurred green by the sturdy tips of winter wheat pushing through. One farmer, an old one, must be, who believed in the 'first bite' making his wheat grow stronger and sweeter than his neighbour's, had let a few cattle out on to his young crop.

That it *had* to go? That one way or another, *that* kind of life had to come to an end as inexorably as one's own span of life, and for much the same reasons, for a lack of the very things that sustained it?

Not very cheering, she thought pulling a face to herself under the wool, warm and slightly damp with her breath.

What she most longed to say was that the loss mustn't be lamented. That all the energies and hopes must be directed forwards, newly charged, not allowed to die with the structures they'd once invested. Easy for me, she reflected, as she bent to struggle up a fresh rise. But for *her* . . . and she could see how beguiling it had all been.

Not to lament though. Not to brood. Not to carry resentment on like sickness through the coming years.

As she worked harder and slower uphill, her thoughts came in more strained and shorter bursts until finally, the physical effort demanded all her attention. Before reaching the brow of the hill she had to get off and push. Here, three miles or so from home, the valleys were wider, great sweeps of land crested with dark woods. And the stone of the few scattered farms and houses was quite different; a blueish-grey that hosted an ochre lichen. From a series of sheds below her, only their neat, parallel roofs visible, came the squeal of pigs.

It was a folly. (Standing at the top of the hill, she drew breath and started again.) A folly, the pursuit of happiness, pursued to the exclusion of all else anyway. Human health and appetite depended on more mingled, ambiguous things, on the sour and the salt as well . . .

But how could she suggest to her mother that pain and suffering were part of the music of things and *had* to be heard again, *had* to be understood, inexplicable as they were? She herself, only knew it in her bones, she hadn't the language for it. Anyway, what unrevealed language was it that permitted one presumptuous person to tell another (one damaged and in pain) that suffering contained its own purpose?

She passed village and woodland. She passed the great gates of a hidden house, she passed barns and a duckless pond, straight thickets of pine and the flat progression of fields that led to the town, its square, orange houses submissively ranked in the distance. She passed a football field where two teams (at least, she assumed it was two teams, though from the number of different coloured shirts, it could have been anything up to seven) of unfit men with quivering office figures played against one another. They shouted a lot until the ball came near and then they ran as though they'd rather die than admit to being a year over twenty. Their sons watched them. She passed them, and she passed the school and the Methodist Hall, the bare-shelved grocer's shop and the hospital itself because she still couldn't think what to say. She went to the Castle Hotel where her father was finishing a drawn-out lunch, where he kissed her, gave her a piece of cheese and an unbuttered biscuit, where he gave her courage and said he believed in her, utterly.

For the past thirty-six hours she'd been mildly sedated and sleep came easily, refusing to be halted by the anxieties that presented themselves, bayonet-fashion. It would not be prevented from its task of healing. Each time she awoke, she emerged a little stronger than before.

Out of the dreaming, she slipped towards an uncommonly bright light. A sun. A tangled sunflower head, bobbing and dipping, a whiter light piercing the translucent tips of its petals.

Chloe.

"You've slept like a baby. So still."

"Yes?" Drowsily she raised a hand to protect her eyes.

Although she'd been sitting beside the bed waiting for twenty minutes, Chloe's face was still flushed from the cycle ride — from that, and the contrasting wall of warm air which met her coldly burning face as she'd entered the ward. Sunday afternoon and the sun poured, deceptively hot, through the glass, baking visitors in their outdoor clothes.

"So," she said quietly, leaning forward, "you know everything now." She searched her mother's face intent, but calm. "It's better that way."

Still pulling off the caul of sleep, Olivia stirred uncomfortably. "I'm so hot . . ." she murmured.

Reaching for the jug of bubbled water, Chloe poured her

mother a glassful and carefully held it to her lips. "Easy," she said. "Take it slowly."

Although she took tiny sips, Olivia felt a little water dribble on her chin. Swiftly, Chloe dabbed it away with a rather grubby ball of tissue she pulled from the sleeve of her jumper.

"How's Daddy?"

"He'll be all right . . . full of blame still." She dabbed again. "That's the worst thing." She sat back, holding the glass ready, should her mother want more. "Are *you*?" she asked.

"Am I what?"

"Full of blame?" She waited.

"Sometimes, yes."

Chloe thought for a while. "About the man who did it?"

Olivia raised a hand to her lips and wiped at a smear of moisture Chloe had missed.

"What *do* you feel about him?"

"Sometimes I frighten myself." She was still snail-like with sleep. She wasn't sure she wanted to talk about it. "Come round the other side," she urged Chloe. Her good side.

As Chloe disappeared towards the end of the bed, her place was filled by another. One of the walking wounded as they jokingly called themselves. The face peered at her, narrow-chinned, with shiny, reddened cheeks. The nose was long and spatula shaped. The face itself was flicked with small scabs, as though fast wheels had driven through blood which had flown up and dried on her skin. The face nodded, smiled at her and said, "How's your mother coming along then?"

"Oh, much better, thank you." Chloe reappeared on Olivia's right. The face continued to gaze down.

"It wasn't the bomb with her, was it?"

"No, it wasn't the bomb."

"What bomb?" Olivia strained towards her daughter.

"In the arcade," said the face, addressing itself to Chloe.

"In the arcade. A month ago." Chloe interpreted.

"That's what most of us are." The brown dressing gown heaved a little and straightened over the thin body. "I'm glad you're better." And she wandered away, Olivia thought, to the next bed. She was horrified. Glass, then, all those scabs. Flying glass and God knows what else. "I didn't know," she breathed. "All of them?"

"Most."

A silence fell between them.

278

"You'll only keep it alive you know, with hate. It's like a fuel." Cautiously, Chloe resumed her warning. "I can see it in Daddy, stopping him . . . Stopping him act. Trapped by it."

She was through sleep now. Her senses began to crackle. "What *do* you expect of us, Chloe? *Forgiveness?*" The word was difficult for her, full of soft sounds, but said with anger.

Chloe looked away, watching the rooks in the bare elm trees beyond the window. "Not exactly," she murmured slowly. "Acceptance, rather." And she tried to recall the many things she'd thought, seeking something shapely out of the confusion. Hesitantly, without looking at her mother, she ventured: "When something's wrong . . . in us, I mean, we always look for a cause outside. There's always one to be found."

But Olivia broke in, full of incredulity. "You're trying to say it was *my* fault?"

"Not you, specifically, heavens, no." Chloe came back from the general to the particular with a rush of protestation. "Just the way things are. Just like . . ." For a moment she struggled. The war we're fighting, she wanted to say, the war you can't see . . . looking for, naming enemies. *We* are the enemy, each one of us, and what we've got to surrender, willingly, without recrimination, is a way of life. But she swallowed and drifted and finally found her gaze fixed elsewhere. Olivia, following her look, saw that the woman was still there, hanging on the filmy edges of her vision.

"Lost my husband," she said.

Into the silence, the conversation of other visitors tumbled warmly.

"Oh . . ." (breathed), ". . . oh, I'm so *sorry* . . ."

"Yes." Nodding and smiling, she stayed there. "Tea'll be here soon," she said and melted from view.

"She's gone." Chloe read the question on her mother's face.

"Awful . . ."

The atmosphere filled and sank, swaying gently, like a hammock.

"Yes."

The moment extended itself, and then both suddenly spoke at once, Olivia begging Chloe to tell her small gossip, Chloe trying to tell her of the flowering thorn.

"In flower?"

"Yes, and the cats, and us . . . all right. There're lots of good things."

"*Good* things?" Olivia echoed painfully. *Good* things. Other than a grudging, spasmodic edging towards atonement, a reaching as it were for a branch beyond her depth of water, there was nothing. A dull acescence, that was all.

"Oh *yes*," insisted Chloe and went through her determined list. It sounded very small.

"But what am I to *do*?" The cry broke out, unguarded as Olivia, forced by her daughter towards a view of the future, saw a flat grey winter landscape open up, unflowering, literally fruitless.

"Come and live with us."

The reverberation—its beat in Chloe's head rather than outside it, in the ward—the reverberation of her mother's cry came to an abrupt stop. "Oh, Chloe, my love. . ."

She saw her mother's expression, a mixture of refusal and ruefulness. "Why ever not?" she demanded, quietly though, in the public place.

Unable either to turn her head towards her daughter or even to smile fully, Olivia gave a small, sad sound. No more than a released breath.

"The past is over. It's gone. Dead." Chloe leant closer, beseeching and insistent; both.

Olivia's head moved and Chloe read a refusal in it, whether it was her mother's refusal to believe what she was saying, or a refusal of her invitation she couldn't tell. She waited.

"Lost my husband."

The flat refrain was repeated. Olivia straining down the awkward focus that was forced on her again glimpsed the brown dressing gown, a man's dressing gown really, she thought. The hands, almost lost within the sleeves, protruded from the central finger joints and plaited themselves uneasily.

"Still," the woman said, her thin plain face gleaming in the sunshine, "I'm one of the lucky ones."

She seemed to be speaking to herself. They made murmuring noises at her, little soothing accompaniments that didn't intrude but implied they'd heard. She smiled more widely without opening her lips, nodded and disappeared on slow, sliding feet up the middle of the ward.

"Poor thing." Chloe was moved by her. She felt her arm touched and looked down at her mother.

"Thank you," muttered Olivia.

Chloe's eyebrows raised in query.

"For asking me . . . But I couldn't. I . . ." Not your life, she was unable to say. Not for me.

She still thought of it as playing, almost, but to have said so would have been unkind. "The way you think," she tried. "The things you reject. Too extreme, for me." But she attempted a smile. "I'd be dead if it weren't for the things they've been able to do for me here." The miracles.

"Not just the hospital. Not just the drugs and techniques . . ." Chloe shook her head. "The leaves."

"Leaves?" She was puzzled.

"You were covered in leaves when we found you. They kept you warm."

"The leaves," she repeated, wonderingly.

The tea trolley was pushed in, a bland and routine clatter.

"Joe's going," said Chloe flatly.

"Why?"

She gave his reason, such as it was. There'd been no time to talk it over. She didn't believe it. "Ah . . ." she heard her mother sigh, and then the desperate, familiar phrase ". . . *doing* something." She winced. No, it wasn't as simple as that. Joe had given up. Not because the goat had butted him, or because he was expected to wash up in his turn or . . . not any of those things exactly.

"Perhaps he's ready to go," she lied. "Perhaps he's learned the thing he needed to know." (In the end, he didn't fit. He'd felt foreign. He yearned for his treeless streets and the ugly, artificial landscape that had reared him. She was half-frightened by the things he might do now.)

". . . what you *achieve* by absenting yourself?" her mother was saying in her nasal, limping voice, "Why, if you care about it all so much, why don't you get involved, *work* for change?"

"Sabotage?" she asked sardonically. "That's the only way. That's the other side of our coin." Joe. What would he do? He'd been very withdrawn and silent after the fire and the attack.

"Rubbish! Work from *within*."

"That's like telling a conscientious objector the only way to stop the evil he objects to is to go out and fight. Kill it. Kill the enemy. That's what we're like, I suppose, conchies. We believe the enemy isn't the *other* man."

The trolley halted at the foot of Olivia's bed. "Tea?" A little angrily, she got up and went to fetch a feeder.

Olivia's head was in a turmoil. Things she had imagined in a

281

fixed order had been curiously flung about by Chloe's last remark. Her daughter appeared, gingerly testing the tea. Blowing on it.

"Sorry," she grinned, catching her mother's face. "It's a bit hot, leave it a little while."

Now the confusions felt threatening, boiling up in her head in a way that transposed event and character beyond proper recognition. In a way that made her fear for the future differently. Although she softly cried again, "What shall I do. . . ?" she meant not, what's to become of me but what *is* become of me, what am I, this person, me? What shall I be?

But Chloe, ignorant of the changed current, said cheerfully, "There's nothing stopping you writing still."

She caught hold of the commonsense note thankfully, used it to haul herself in. "No," she said dryly. "Nothing but the paper shortage." But the moment of rescue was brief. She felt herself drawn away from the firm, safe level of talk Chloe represented.

"Try it now. It's not too bad." Chloe lowered the spout of the feeder to her lips and there was no choice but to suck a little of the hot, leathery flavoured liquid down. Obediently she did so then signalled with her hand that it was enough. A longing had taken hold of her and it had to be satisfied. She longed to tell the truth.

"Chloe?"

"Yes? More?"

"No," she made an agitated movement with her hand. "Do you imagine," she said slowly, moving into an ironic register, "do you suppose there's such a thing as a *true* romance?"

She heard Chloe laugh. She couldn't at this moment see her, laughter had tipped her backwards out of the ragged circle of vision. "Of course. In a sense." She heard her say, "That's what I've been trying to explain to you. That it *had* to end, it couldn't go on. A way of life founded on a basic non-reality and dedicated to another one, doggedly devoted to the pursuit of happiness." She was gleeful that her mother had provided her with precisely the right phrase. *A romance.* "A way of life that simply hadn't the basic means of sustaining itself, like your books and the paper shortage. A belief that perfection was possible."

"No, no . . ." Olivia tried to stem the flow now so readily loosed. "No, that's not at all what I meant. I meant something else. *Listen!*"

The hissed urgency of the word drew Chloe down and leaning

close to her mother's stiffly moving lips she heard the whole tale. The story of Arthur and the story Arthur had been told.

Everyone in the ward was so busy talking they scarcely noticed the December afternoon draw to a close. They'd forgotten about the lights and the ward subsided into a comfortable twilight.

Chloe sat, head lowered, the feeder almost full of cold tea in her hands still. She was stunned. But still, above all the elaborate new incident stored, if not yet sifted, in her understanding, she felt the need—felt it more powerfully even than before—for her mother to be separated from her obstinate embrace of the past and the passion, bound up with it, to make her resentments more endurable by falsely naming as guilty those things and people she chose to see as its destroyers.

Over one or two beds, the individual lights went on creating tender pools around the visitors. She looked at her mother who lay back exhausted and wondered what she could possibly say or do. And she realised, as her mother had—what other reason had she for finally breaking open the silence of years—that Arthur was for ever. He was not an issue neatly settled.

Now all the overhead lights went on and she looked up to see the new shift come on duty. Four girls full of merriment who went from bed to bed, teasing their favourite patients, the ones who were the most lonely.

"Chloe, do you have your bag there?"

She started, thinking her mother had dozed off.

"Yes, what do you need, some money? Hankie?" She was a fraction over-anxious.

"A mirror, do you have a mirror . . . quickly!"

There was a second in which she hesitated, her face deeply serious. Then without a word, she bent down, picking up her old threadbare woollen bag and thrust around in it until she found the shape of what she wanted. It was a broken fragment of a larger, shaving mirror, the kind that magnifies. In the movement of her hand, there was the beginning of uncertainty, then she gave it to her mother thrustingly.

So. This was it. The price.

She could barely believe it was herself she stared at. There was something—for a second—interestingly weird in facing an image of yourself that was not the one you carried in your mind. There was an interval of unlooked-for objectivity . . . The rearrangement, the carelessness of it. With a sense of reproach almost, she observed that she'd let the tint grow out too far.

And then the focus altered and she felt horror.

But she continued to look, the fragment of mirror in her palm concealed by the sheet which she'd pulled over the back of her hand and held with her thumb. And gazing at the grotesquely unexpected features that calmly regarded her own in the glass, she felt as though the unbearable gap between inner and outer image was somehow lessened.

If the truth were unbeautiful, it contained, notwithstanding, the beauty that is peculiar to truth.

The mirror was snatched from her hand and shuffled away by a scarlet Chloe. A nurse, smiling at each bed in turn, came down the ward carrying a tray of drugs. She nodded pleasantly in their direction and passed by, going to the two end beds first. Her white cap stood up on a thick burst of hair like a dove improbably nesting.

They waited in silence, Chloe trembling at what she'd done . . . When the nurse came and placed two white pills on Olivia's locker, asking her to make sure her mother took them, she remained head down.

"All right?" the nurse departed with a lingering look at a huge card that had upraised satin roses like slivers of flesh on it.

Olivia heard her steps retreat.

There was no blame then.

Meaning—no, nothing quite as precise as meaning, but an odd clarity amassed itself out of many random matters and remarks. Perhaps though it *was* meaning, if meaning resembles the crystalline moment that presents itself, like the shining heart in a pale, cloudy star sapphire, that you see only by turning the stone first this way then that.

There was no blame. Nobody singly and criminally at fault. To think that was to make the mistake all the others had made. The avenging error.

She was merely one in a long chain of distortions, the imperfection increased with each generation, imperfection being the single, consistent human characteristic. The distinguishing mark of the species, perhaps. She wasn't made out of cruelty or poverty or anything so easily identifiable. She was human and thus carried, like every single one of her species, the enthralling and dangerous capacity to conceive that one could be other than one was. And believing, in consequence, that one was infinitely less than one might be. And—here was the critical thing—and of having this dilemma compounded by historic accident, born at a speck in time when the notion of human progress or betterment was seen as tangible, material and within the human grasp. The soul had been forgotten in the excitement of this event. The soul, where betterment had once been sought, was a little thing, a printed word that no surgeon could discover on cutting the body open.

Imperfection. There were other ways of describing it. Original sin was too antique and alarming, but if man was distinguished by his freedom of choice, his moral capability, then clearly, in this luxurious small era, when wealth could multiply choices a thousandfold, more and more false choices lay open to be made. Not that one made them *knowingly* or wickedly.

She'd arrived at a condition no one had willed into existence. Been born into a generation of men whose very genius had concealed from them the absolute nature of its own imperfection and believing in it steadfastly, had led humanity to aspire to all that was false, all that was other and better than themselves, led them to abhor the naked simplicity of their own needs and nature.

This was the pitiful thing, the unwittingness of it. This was the disfigurement.

She felt utterly calm.

She heard the nurse's steady tread to the next patient, as though her perception had lasted the unmoving space of a second. Or as if time had stood still for her.

"Oh, what have I done?"

She heard Chloe's troubled whisper and reaching out with her free hand explored for, found and clasped Chloe's tightly to steady the shaking she felt there.

"I'm all right," she said.

"I shouldn't have done that. I *shouldn't* have done it."

"I'm all right," she repeated, smiling upwards.

"You'd better take your pills." Hurriedly, at a loss, Chloe pulled to her feet, thankful to busy herself with something. "What are they? Pain-killers?" She spoke rapidly, over-solicitous in her guilt.

"I'm one of the lucky ones," said the plaintive voice from the end of the bed. "There's others worse."

"Can I give you some help?" Chloe went towards her and

Olivia heard the thin voice say with utter simplicity, "No, I don't need any help thank you." And she caught the angle of a disappearing cheek, smooth and rounded with a smile.

"Here." Chloe came back. She wished passionately that she could ease pain as straightforwardly as the two small white pills in her palm could. "You must be terribly tired."

"Yes, pleasantly." Submissively, she took her pills.

"Here, try some of this." Chloe picked up a bottle of cologne, wet her finger tips with the cool stuff and smoothed a little on her mother's forehead. Then she hovered anxiously, trying to find small things to do. "Shall I take these away?" (Picking up a bag of hard green apples.) "Have you any washing I can do?"

She paused. She saw her mother was close to sleep. The injured face drooped peacefully. Impulsively she knelt down beside the bed and whispered close to her ear, "It'll get better, I *promise* you. Bart promised."

A faint smile creased the lines that ran outward from the closed, lilac eyelid.

"And then you'll come and live with us . . ." Half statement, half question.

The lips moved, but she had to bring her face so close their skin touched to hear her mother murmur, ". . . not your life, my darling, I couldn't. Not for *always*."

"But you will come? For a *while*, perhaps?"

"Perhaps . . ." The fine lines deepened as affection mingled with amusement. "Perhaps, my love, yes."

DO WITH ME WHAT YOU WILL
JOYCE CAROL OATES

From the beginning Elena Howe's beauty was her identity. It was the type of beauty that made women dream and drove men mad.

Three men in particular wanted Elena, and shaped her life. Her alcoholic, obsessive father. Her husband, a brilliant lawyer many years her senior. And the dynamic young lover who tried to consume her in her infidelity. All in turn helped her find herself through love.

'This immensely talented American novelist writes, like Graham Greene, out of a few central obsessions... This latest novel is beautifully structured'
The Sunday Telegraph

CORONET BOOKS

MORE FICTION FROM CORONET

		JOYCE CAROL OATES	
☐	19939 3	Upon the Sweeping Flood	75p
☐	19940 7	Do With Me What You Will	£1·25
		JENNIFER JOHNSTON	
☐	18815 4	The Gates	35p
☐	19950 4	How Many Miles to Babylon?	40p
		MELVYN BRAGG	
☐	19853 2	A Place in England	50p
☐	19852 4	Josh Lawton	40p
☐	19992 X	The Silken Net	£1·25
☐	19991 1	The Nerve	75p

All these books are available at your local bookshop or newsagent, or can be ordered direct from the publisher. Just tick the titles you want and fill in the form below

Prices and availability subject to change without notice.

CORONET BOOKS, P.O. Box 11, Falmouth, Cornwall.

Please send cheque or postal order, and allow the following for postage and packing:

U.K. – One book 18p plus 8p per copy for each additional book ordered, up to a maximum of 66p.

B.F.P.O. and EIRE – 18p for the first book plus 8p per copy for the next 6 books, thereafter 3p per book.

OTHER OVERSEAS CUSTOMERS – 20p for the first book and 10p per copy for each additional book.

Name ....

Address ....

....